THE
DEAD DAYS
OMNIBUS

Praise for *The Book of Dead Days*

'you're in safe hands with Sedgwick. Here is a macabre melodrama inventively told.'   Philip Ardagh, *Guardian*

'Sedgwick has created a world as dark and compelling as the story he tells.'   *Mail on Sunday*

'an impressively atmospheric novel . . . *The Book of Dead Days* is deliciously gothic in atmosphere and gripping to read.'   *Books for Keeps*

'The finely-drawn characters and enthralling story-telling make this Sedgwick's greatest work to date.'
Joanne Owen, *The Bookseller*

Praise for *The Dark Flight Down*

'the atmosphere is laid on both thick and fast to maximum effect.'   Nicholas Tucker, *Books for Keeps*

'Gothic, with echoes of *Gormenghast*, magical and deeply sinister, Sedgwick's many fans will not be disappointed.'
Publishing News

THE
DEAD DAYS
OMNIBUS

Marcus Sedgwick

Orion
Children's Books

This omnibus edition first published in Great Britain in 2006
by Orion Children's Books
a division of the Orion Publishing Group Ltd
Orion House,
5 Upper St Martin's Lane
London WC2H 9EA

1 3 5 7 9 10 8 6 4 2

Originally published as two separate volumes:
The Book of Dead Days
First published in Great Britain in 2003
by Orion Children's Books
The Dark Flight Down
First published in Great Britain in 2004
by Orion Children's Books

A catalogue record for this book
is available from the British Library

ISBN-10: 1 84255 528 6
ISBN-13: 978 1 84255 528 6

Typeset at The Spartan Press Ltd,
Lymington, Hants

Printed in Great Britain by
Clays Ltd, St Ives plc

The Orion Publishing Group's policy is to use papers that
are natural, renewable and recyclable products and made
from wood grown in sustainable forests. The logging and
manufacturing processes are expected to conform to the
environmental regulations of the country of origin.

www.orionbooks.co.uk

Contents

The Book
of Dead Days

For Julian and Isabel

Author's Note

Have you ever felt the stillness of that strange, quiet time between Christmas and New Year? To me these are Dead Days. Days when the doors between our own world and the unseen one that lies just beneath the surface are opened.

In this time that is no-time, the pagan power of the ancient mid-winter feast is with us. All times become one. That's how it seems to me, but I'm not the first to explore the dead days. I drew on ancient Egyptian and Aztec systems, both of which created myths to explain the addition of the five extra days needed to correct their calendars to the solar year. To the Egyptians these days were a gift from the gods; to the Aztecs, they were days of evil omen. Of course, these days bore no relation to our mid-winter, but it seemed that if days out of time belonged anywhere, it was here.

Then a world began to grow, or rather a city so huge and rambling that it is a world in itself. The City is inspired by magical places, like Paris, with its miles of unseen catacombs, Bologna, with its hidden canal system, and Krakow, with its overcrowded cemeteries and, at Christmas, lots and lots of snow.

I placed it at a time with one foot in the superstitious ancient world and one in the rational modern one, when science was starting to become the rigorous discipline it is now, but when, to the uninitiated, early experiments with electricity and magnetism must have appeared to be magic.

And when perhaps genuine magic was still to be found, especially during the Dead Days which, although they come but once a year, are with us always, just hidden from view, waiting.

I'd like to thank all the wonderful people at Orion, but especially Fiona, whose help in navigating *The Book of Dead Days* has been invaluable.

Horsham, West Sussex
31st December 2002

December 29th

The Day of the
Clever Contributor

✤

Darkness.

Two hours to midnight. Boy sat crouched in the box.

As usual, his legs were going to sleep under him, tucked up in the tiny dark space hidden inside the cabinet. Above him, he could hear Valerian going through his routine. Boy could only hear his voice as if from far-off, and tried to work out where he had got to. It wouldn't do to miss the cue; it wouldn't do at all. But Boy knew he didn't really need to worry. He used to try to count his way to it, but had always got lost somewhere, and anyway, there was no need – the cue was obvious enough.

Boy tried to shift his weight ever so slightly, attempting to get some feeling back in his legs. It was no good. The box had been designed specifically for him, and Valerian had seen to it that there was no more than half an inch to spare in any direction.

Suddenly there was a solid thump on the top of the box: the first cue, which meant 'Get ready, Boy.'

Boy heard a noise from the audience, faintly. He couldn't see them, but he knew what the noise meant. It was a murmur of expectation. Valerian had just stepped on to the cabinet and was even now whipping the crowd into greater

3

excitement as he outlined the extraordinary nature of the sight they were about to see.

Boy even caught some of Valerian's words through the hefty oak panels of the cabinet.

'. . . most miraculous . . . feat of obscure . . .'

Oh-ho! thought Boy. *That means we're nearly there.*

'. . . the Man in Two Halves Illusion . . .'

He readied himself, flexing his toes inside the boots, three sizes too big for him. Thump! Thump!

The cue! Boy went to stamp his legs out through the hinged flap at the end of the box, but was suddenly hit by a powerful cramp. His toes curled painfully under him and he instantly felt sick. If he were to ruin it . . .

Desperately he tried to kick again. Still the cramp ate up his legs like a snake, biting, making him unable to move them.

Thump! Thump!

Valerian was getting cross. Boy shuddered as thoughts of what he might do to him passed through his mind. He made one last effort and shoved again. At last his legs responded and he stuck them out of the end of the box, wearing the huge boots identical to the ones Valerian was wearing.

Now, straightened out, Boy waved his legs a little. He knew this would be safe, because he was supposed to wiggle them at this point, to show they were real. They were supposed to be Valerian's, hence the matching boots.

As Valerian had got into the front half of the box, Boy's legs had not appeared where they should have done and the illusion must have been in danger. But Boy seemed to have got away with it. Now his legs were sticking through the flap, the pain began to ease a bit. He got a little more air and could hear better too.

Valerian shouted.

'Behold!'

Boy felt his box start to move stage left. He heard the audience begin to gasp as they understood (at last) what was happening.

'Look!' he heard someone cry. 'He's gone in half!'

It was true. From where the audience sat, they could see Valerian's head and shoulders projecting from one half of the box, while his legs moved away from him in the other part of the contraption. The single cabinet had become two boxes, running on metal tracks. There was a clear space between the two parts of his body, and the crowd went wild.

'It's true!' shouted a woman's voice, somewhere near the front, Boy thought.

Of course it was not true. It was an illusion. Although Boy knew full well what the audience were thinking as the halves of Valerian's body went in opposite directions across the stage, he knew how it was done. He was, after all, *in* on the trick. Boy felt himself smile as the crowd began to applaud wildly. Then he remembered the fiasco with his legs, and the smile faded. What would Valerian say?

Sober again, Boy prepared to pull himself back in at the right time. He could sense the automatic mechanism of the contraption begin to turn the heavy brass cogs in reverse as the two halves of the box drew back together. He felt the boxes bump gently. His cue. He felt himself panicking. He whipped his legs back inside just as Valerian stepped out of the other half of the device. Boy timed it perfectly and now, cramped back in the box, breathed as deep a breath as he could. He felt the machine being trundled off stage. It was being cleared for the finale while Valerian took the applause of the crowd.

Off-stage, Boy pushed the lid of the cabinet up with his head until there was enough space to lift it with his hands.

'Out you come, then,' said a stage hand.

Boy took his hand gratefully, his legs still not working properly. He climbed out and stood for a moment in the wings, rubbing his sore calves and watching as Valerian began his grand finale.

The Fairyland Vanishing Illusion.

Boy was not needed for this part of the act. He watched Valerian from the side of the stage.

How many times has he done this? Boy wondered. He had forgotten how long he had been working for Valerian, but it was years. Boy could only guess at how many thousand times he had hidden in boxes, pulled levers, set off thunder-flashes and opened trapdoors. He helped Valerian with trick after trick, week after week in the Great Theatre, which was as much of a home as anywhere to Boy. In recent years he had probably spent as much time in the theatre as he had in his room in Valerian's house, known as the Yellow House, back in the Old Quarter.

Boy decided to watch the grand finale from the front of the theatre, but not with the audience. He had a special place, and he wanted to be as far away as he could when Valerian came off stage.

He made his way off the stage, past the painted canvas scenery drops and ropes and wires that cluttered the world just beyond the view of the public, pushing past hands and other performers. Briefly, he glanced at Snake-girl, who sat braiding her hair in a corner, then hurried by the actors who'd finished their rowdy routine immediately before Snake-girl's act, rounded a corner and bumped straight into someone.

It was Willow, the girl who helped Madame Beauchance, a rather fat singer, into her costumes. Willow was just like her name, thin and wan. Madame had joined the theatre

6

about a year ago, and Willow had immediately been made her servant. Boy had only spoken to Willow properly once, though. Madame had been screaming for hot water in her dressing room, and Boy had given her a freshly-boiled jug he was taking to Valerian. Afterwards he didn't know why he'd done it, and he'd got in trouble with Valerian over it, too.

'Can't you look where you're going?' Willow said, then saw who it was.

'Oh, it's you,' she added, and rushed past before Boy could say anything. Fetching something for Madame, no doubt. Her mistress was difficult, though nothing like Valerian was to him. No one was like Valerian.

'Sorry,' said Boy, but she had gone.

Boy moved on. He had other things to worry about. He knew something was going on. Something with his master. Valerian had always been erratic, sour-tempered and unpredictable. Violent.

Now he was these things. But something else as well that Boy had never seen before. He couldn't quite put it into words, but if he had really thought about it he might have realised that Valerian was preoccupied. Worried. Maybe even scared. But it would never have occurred to Boy that Valerian could be scared. It was Boy who did the being scared and the worrying – always waiting to get a hiding for any slight mistake he made.

He headed for the stairs. A group of musicians blocked the way.

'You all done for tonight, Boy?' asked the violinist, an oldish man with a bent nose.

Boy didn't answer, but forced a smile and squeezed past.

'Poor monkey,' he heard another of them say as he made his way to the secret gallery in the 'gods' above the highest row of boxes. A tiny staircase led almost up to the roof space

7

and opened on to a tiny corridor. He wasn't really allowed in the box. No one was. It was a secret that only Korp, the director of the Great Theatre, was supposed to know about, though in fact everyone did.

The door was locked, but Boy took a piece of metal from his pocket and flicked the three tumblers of the lock in no time at all. He had learned one or two things from Valerian in their time together. In fact, apart from what he'd picked up living on the streets, most of what Boy knew about anything had been taught him by Valerian.

He dropped down the couple of feet into the box. There was the little stool covered in red velvet and the small hollow table inside which Boy knew was a bottle of the director's favourite schnapps. In the front of the box was a small window. Boy carefully lifted the blind that covered the glassless hole, and peered forward. The glow from the footlights sparkled in his eyes.

Boy knew a lot about Valerian's tricks. He helped perform many of them and helped assemble others. But the grand finale was something very different. So spectacular was this illusion that Valerian was known throughout the whole City for it. It was probably for this trick alone that the Great Theatre was still in business.

The theatre lay in the heart of what had once been the most glamorous part of the City, the Arts Quarter, now fallen into decadence and ruin. The other acts that performed there were by and large terrible. The crowds would eat and drink and talk and laugh throughout the evening, paying little or no attention to what passed on stage. They had come for one thing. Many came night after night to see the Fairyland Vanishing Illusion. Others, new arrivals in town, travellers from distant parts maybe, were about to see it for the first time.

Boy knew nothing of the workings of this trick. He had seen it a thousand times, maybe more, and still marvelled every time. He supposed that it was too valuable, too extraordinary or too complicated for Valerian to tell anyone how it worked.

By the time Boy got up to the box, Valerian was already well into the piece. Boy craned his neck so that his nose was projecting a little through the view-hole.

The Illusion featured a short play about a drunkard who stumbles across a gathering of pixies dancing on the mountainside. They disappear back to fairyland, but the man overhears their secret words and follows them. He captures one of the little people and brings him back to the human world, determined to make his fortune with the fairy.

Valerian was reaching the climax of the show. He moved to the mouth of a cabinet built into a tree-trunk, stage right. Stage left was an identical affair. He was acting without joy or passion. He knew he didn't even have to try to inject any excitement into the audience. They were already beside themselves with anticipation.

Boy watched him carefully. Something was wrong – Valerian seemed even more uninterested than usual. He seemed impatient, in a rush to get it done with. A note had been delivered to Valerian just before the show, and Boy wondered if his strange mood had anything to do with that. He had grown sombre as he'd read.

On stage, Valerian spoke the lines as he had many times before.

'What did those little people say?' he asked, staring at the ceiling, addressing no one in particular.

'Aha! I have it!'

Valerian stepped into the tree-trunk cabinet.

'Ho! And away to fairyland!'

And he vanished. No more than half a second later there was a wisp of smoke from the second tree-trunk and he reappeared, holding a tiny human-like figure in his hands. The thing was tiny, cupped in his hands, and seemed, at least, to be alive. It wriggled in his hands and you would swear you could hear a little voice coming from it. It appeared to be dressed in leaves and flowers. It could have been male or female, but it was certainly a fairy.

Then, just as Valerian, playing the drunkard, appeared to have achieved his goal, there was a double flash of lightning, the fairy seemed to grow for a split second to the size of a man, and then both it and Valerian vanished again, back to fairyland.

The crowd, knowing this to be the pinnacle of the performance, erupted into huge cheers and shouts of delight.

Boy sat back on the red velvet stool and felt something dig into his back. He looked round and jumped out of his skin. Valerian sat behind him, glowering.

'You, Boy,' he said, 'have let me down.'

2

'Name the five principles of Cavallo,' Valerian snapped.

They hurried through the dark streets of the City – the vast, ancient City that sprawled away into the darkness around them in all its rotting magnificence, a tangled mess of grand streets and vulgar alleys, spent and decrepit. Fat houses squatted on either side of them like wild animals lurking in the gloom.

The City. Once it had been the capital of a powerful empire, which now only existed in the peculiar mind of Frederick, the octogenarian Emperor, shut away somewhere behind the high walls of the Palace.

The Emperor's warped memories were utterly unknown to Boy. *His* world began and ended with Valerian. As the two of them made their way along a particularly horrid street called Cat's End, the midnight bells began to strike. The 27th of December had begun.

Valerian strode a pace ahead of Boy, but held his coat tails to pull Boy half-running, half stumbling along behind. He was testing Boy in mind as well as body.

'Well?' he barked.

'Mystery,' Boy panted as they sped along. 'Mystery and preparation and . . . sorry.'

He stumbled on a cobblestone. Valerian dragged him

11

practically in the air around a corner and into a side street. A short-cut home.

'What?' yelled Valerian. 'Mystery and preparation and *what?*'

'Direction?'

'*Mis*-direction, you goat!'

'Mis-direction,' said Boy, and then before Valerian had a chance to shout again, 'and practice and skill. Natural skill,' he added hurriedly.

Valerian grunted in satisfaction, but didn't slow the pace. Boy stumbled after him, having trouble moving his legs properly as he was pulled sideways by the tails of his coat.

After the show, Valerian had glared at Boy for a good long while, so there was no doubt that Boy was in a great deal of trouble. Then he had dragged him out of the box, along the tiny passageway, down the stairs and out into the night without even bothering to collect the money for the performance. Boy had hardly had time to think, but there was something bothering him badly. It had taken him at least three minutes to get from the side of the stage to the box. It had taken Valerian no more than a couple of seconds. At least that was how it seemed, but Boy knew from experience not to trust anything he saw Valerian do. You could never be sure, not really.

They moved on through the City, Valerian clutching Boy's coat tails, looking, from a distance, like some strange beast. They were in Gutter Street. Although there were no street signs in this part of the City (it was much too down-at-heel for refinements like that), nevertheless Boy knew where he was. They passed the Green Bird Inn. Boy had been hoping they might stop for Valerian to have a drink or two. Or more. Then he might have forgotten about Boy's slip-up.

But he strode by without even a glance at the tavern. Boy gulped and staggered on.

'All right then,' said Valerian. 'And if you don't observe the Five Principles you may as well just rely on luck, which is what you made us do tonight. Anyone half sober or with half a mind would have seen–'

'I'm sorry,' said Boy.

Valerian stopped suddenly and Boy ran into the back of him. He looked down into Boy's eyes.

'Well,' he said, and his voice was suddenly quiet, 'well, it's not important. Really.'

He dropped Boy's coat tails and began to head for home, still walking fast.

Boy had been thrashed by Valerian before for much less than this. More confused than ever, he watched him go for a moment. Valerian's tall figure, his longish greying hair flowing behind him, was about to disappear round another corner. Although Boy knew the area, he grew alarmed.

Unpleasant things had been happening in the City recently. Even in the better areas, horror was not unknown. There had been a spate of murders, and the inns, taverns, salons and courts had been full of talk of these crimes. The murders were remarkable for their particularly gory nature, with the bodies sometimes drained of blood. Rumours had spread of the ghastly apparition responsible – 'The Phantom'. There had also been a series of grave-robbings in some of the many cemeteries around the huge City. Many people thought the two were linked.

'Hey!' Boy cried. 'Wait for me!'

It was deep into the night, and they were now in one of the worst parts of the City. Nearly home.

3

Korp, the director of the theatre, began closing up. Half an hour ago he had finally managed to throw the last drunken idiot out, and before he'd even hit the mud of the alley had slammed the door after him. He didn't have to worry about being too nice to his customers. They would come night after night, as long as Valerian kept doing that thing about fairies.

Director Korp sat for a while in his office, staring into space. He felt old and tired and fat, because he was. He daydreamed, remembering days when he had travelled the continent with the greatest show ever assembled. The show had included a giant, five midgets, a two-headed calf, a snake-woman, a disappearing lady, a levitating man, twin wild boys, and many, many more. It was all far behind him, and though he missed the excitement of his youth, he had a theatre to run now, and he would run it as best he could till the day he died.

On the walls around him hung portraits of some of the stars who had appeared in his theatre. There were paintings of Cavallo the Great, a legendary magician. There was Grolsch, a famous escapologist whose career had come to an untimely end one night when he had failed to escape, and Bertrand Black, a bear-tamer who had had a similarly rapid demise on stage. But all the faces were from days long gone, when things had been different, more lucrative.

Korp scratched his bald head for a minute or so, then without looking down, put his hand into a drawer in the ornate desk at which he was sitting. He fumbled around, still without looking. He put his hand on his pistol, and shoved it aside. It wasn't what he wanted.

'Yeush!' he said, with a frown. 'Where's it gone?'

Then he remembered the bottle he'd left in his 'secret' box. Wearily he got to his feet and made his way down the darkened corridors back-stage. As he passed one of the dressing rooms he noticed a light.

'Who's there?' he called.

'Oh, Director,' said a voice from inside. 'It is Madame.'

He stuck his head around the door.

'Ah!' he said. 'Madame! Madame Beauchance! May I say how exquisitely you sang tonight!' He smiled a wide smile.

Madame Beauchance appeared to ignore this compliment.

'It will have to change,' she said.

'Madame?'

Now Korp noticed the girl, Beauchance's assistant, kneeling at the singer's feet and rubbing her ankles. The girl glanced up at him.

'Madame means . . . ?' he began again.

'I mean', said Madame, not even looking at Korp, 'that I will not continue to appear in an *inferior* position. To that prestidigitator.'

Korp blinked.

He felt tired. He wanted to be in bed with Lily curled up around his feet. Lily was his dog.

'The magician,' whispered the girl, almost unheard.

'Exactly!' cried Madame Beauchance.
'Ah!' said Korp. 'Oh!'
Valerian.

4

Midnight.

Boy had caught up with Valerian at the top of the next alley – a little gutter of a lane called Blind Man's Stick, where the roof-tiles of the buildings either side were close enough to touch in places. Here and there it was possible to catch a glimpse of the night sky between them, but Boy was not interested in the stars. Not yet.

He clung tightly to Valerian as they made their way quickly along the foul-smelling culvert. A minute later they emerged into a relatively wide street. An open drain ran down its middle. Valerian stepped across it in a single stride. Boy, small for his years, leapt the gap, slipping as he landed.

He sat dazed in the stream then, realising where he was, leapt to his feet.

'Oh!' he said. 'Ugh!'

Boy looked himself up and down. His bottom half was covered in unnameable filth.

'Ugh! Oh!'

Valerian did not even glance back.

Boy limped after him. They turned a corner and crossed a final street.

Valerian stopped for a moment at a wrought iron gate let

into a high stone wall. He rattled one of the big keys from his pocket in the lock, and shoved the gate open. Only now did he look back long enough to be sure Boy had got through the gate with him, then swung it shut and rattled its lock one more time.

They were home.

Boy stood dripping, trying not to smell himself as he waited in the small walled courtyard that lay between the iron gate and the front door.

Valerian opened the door with another key from the huge bunch and went inside.

The house seemed to tense as Valerian shut the door behind them both. He said nothing but stood absolutely still, as if waiting. Then he turned and looked at Boy.

'What is that vile stench?' he barked.

Boy shrugged.

'I fell over . . .'

'For God's sake go and get clean! Then come to the tower.'

'Yes, sir,' said Boy.

He shuffled down one of the corridors that led off the hall.

'And be quick. You have work to do!'

5

Boy ran along two corridors and then up three flights of rickety wooden stairs to his room. 'Room' was perhaps something of an exaggeration. Room, or space, was one thing the place he slept in did not have. There was a mattress, which was actually quite comfortable though it was a shame, thought Boy, that he did not get to spend more time on it. The smallest of openings ('window' would have been too grand a word for it) let in some light. This was in the sloping roof that made up one wall of his room. His bed lay against the single vertical wall, the entrance lurked in one of the triangular ends to the space, and in the opposite one was a tiny door behind which was an even tinier cupboard. Inside the cupboard were all Boy's possessions. A spoon he'd found in the street and particularly liked. A pair of old boots that were too small and worn out to wear any more. A silk scarf he'd stolen from a rich lady, but which was too nice to wear. Some small empty tins that nested inside each other and some pencils which Valerian had given him to practise his writing.

This was his room.

The day Valerian had put him in it, Boy had come straight back down and eventually found Valerian sipping port in the library.

'But I can't stand up in it,' Boy had complained.

'Then kneel down, Boy,' Valerian had said, and cuffed him round the ear.

Boy was used to clambering about in small spaces. He seemed to spend his life doing it: on stage in coffin-like cabinets and off-stage in the theatre too, slithering along to Korp's supposedly secret box. At home, the last part of his journey meant climbing up a small ladder from the third-floor landing and hunching up to travel down a tiny, low-ceilinged corridor tucked into the roof space that led to his room.

Small, cramped, dark spaces had filled Boy's life. He had even been hiding in one the day he was found by Valerian in an old church, St Colette's. Boy had crammed his narrow frame into a space at the top of a pillar in the nave. It was a long time ago – he had little idea when. Since he had been working for Valerian he had not seen much daylight, never mind been allowed access to such private information as what time it was, or what day or month, for that matter. It was, in fact, March the 6th when Valerian had found Boy, but Boy didn't know that. Only Valerian knew about dates and times, places and names and the like. Boy worked for him, and that was the end of the story. When he wasn't working Boy would climb up to his room and collapse on the tiny mattress, exhausted.

And the beginning of the story, when Valerian had found Boy? He had been in a tiny dark hole then, too. That was probably why Valerian had chosen him, taken him on – because of his expertise in squeezing into ridiculously small spaces. Boy had forgotten much of the detail now; it was long long ago, and unimportant compared to the business of every day. Every day, trying to avoid trouble, trying to avoid upsetting him or getting something wrong and . . .

He could remember one thing about it all though. From the stupidly small gap made where the arch fluted away from the pillar, he had seen Valerian for the first time. He was deep in discussion with someone Boy now knew to be Korp, from the theatre.

Even then Valerian looked haggard and pale. His nose, long and fine, twitched in the dusty atmosphere of the old church. His skin was grey, so was his hair. He looked like a dead man walking. His blue eyes, however, were full of life, and his gaze roamed the dark spaces around him.

Then Boy had heard his midnight rumble of a voice, so deep the stone he was clinging to shivered with it.

'The doctor,' intoned Valerian, 'pronounced me either dangerously sick or dead.'

It was while trying to understand the strangeness of those words that Boy had lost his grip and plummeted to the flag floor of the church, where he lay looking up at Valerian, scratching his nose nervously, his short, cropped black hair stuck up at interesting angles the way it always did.

'O-ho!' Valerian had said. 'What have we here?'

And so they had met.

Boy pulled off his reeking clothes and stood naked in his dark space. He wondered what to do. The pile of clothes at his feet stank up at him. There was no water in his room. The only room with a bath was on the first floor. He had no other clothes, just a long winter overcoat. But if he put that on now he would get it covered in the same filth that was still slimed over his legs.

21

He sighed, picked up the pile of dirty clothes and the coat and crept back along the tube to the ladder.

He dropped the clothes down to the third-floor landing, and followed them, shivering as he went.

6

Boy sat, scratching his nose. He was nervous because Valerian was pacing up and down the Tower room, criss-crossing the floor a dozen times, then pausing, staring into space for a short while before resuming his compulsive journey from the tall, narrow window in one of the sloping walls to the top of the spiral staircase, which was the only means of access by foot to the Tower. Large or heavy items had to be winched into the Tower through a trapdoor in the floor. Despite his nerves Boy noticed that, as usual, Valerian was perfectly happy to stride over the trapdoor. Boy knew the hatch was strong enough, but he would never walk over it, just in case. The trapdoor opened above the landing on the second floor; it was quite a drop.

The rest of the Tower room was filled with clutter, par-aphernalia, ephemera, equipment, things and mechanisms of all descriptions. Astrolabes, hourglasses, armillary spheres, sextants, alembics, retorts, reduction dishes, mortars with pestles, crystals, locks with and without keys, knives, dag-gers, wands of brass and wands of wood, pots, bottles and jars were just some of the odds and ends that lay scattered around the Tower.

Boy knew what some of them were – things they used on stage. As for those he didn't understand, Boy often wondered what they might be. Maybe they were more, and as yet untried, pieces of magical equipment for the act, though Boy had his doubts.

There was the great leather armchair in which Valerian would sit, often in pensive mood, brooding over Boy knew not what, and there were books. Piles and piles and piles of books of all shapes and sizes, leaning at precarious angles against walls and chairs, and, Boy assumed, about all sorts of things.

Right in the middle of the Tower stood the machine. Boy always had trouble remembering what it was called. As he sat, waiting for Valerian to say or do something, he tried to remember its name. It had been designed and built by a man called Kepler, who was the closest thing Valerian had to a friend.

Boy had never seen the machine working, but since it had been installed Valerian had spent even more time in the Tower. It had a strange Latin name, and now Boy remembered that it translated as 'dark room'.

'Do you have no grasp of Latin at all?' Valerian had barked at him. Boy had shaken his head.

Valerian had cursed.

'Idiot boy! If you knew some Latin you would know what it meant! Dark. Room. Camera – room. Obscura – dark. See?'

Boy had smiled nervously, pretending he understood.

'Oh, why do I try to teach you anything!' Valerian had snapped, and sat back in his leather armchair.

'Camera obscura' – that was it!

Now Boy had remembered he felt pleased with himself, and sat, wondering what on earth it was that the thing did.

Valerian kept on walking. Boy sat in just his overcoat, scratching his nose harder.

Then Valerian stopped.

'Boy,' he said, 'I have a job for you.'

I was afraid you'd say that, thought Boy.

'Yes,' said Boy. 'Whatever I can do–'

'You can be quiet!' Valerian snapped. 'Just listen, then do. All right?'

Oh, fine, thought Boy.

He didn't say anything, but nodded.

'I . . .' Valerian began, not looking at Boy but out of the window and across the nightscape of the City. 'We . . . I . . . have a problem. Things are not what they were. Things . . .' he continued, 'are . . . different now. Different. They have changed.'

He stopped and looked at Boy.

'Clear?' he said.

Boy nodded furiously.

'Things have not happened as I had intended and now – and now time is not on our side. Far from it. We must act.'

Boy nodded some more.

'Things have not gone . . . according to plan. So I have a job for you. Tonight.'

'Tonight?' asked Boy, then shut his mouth quickly.

'Yes. Tonight. The Trumpet. You know it?'

Boy grimaced. The Trumpet was an inn about three miles away, near the river-docks. He had been there before, and on leaving had prayed that would be his first and last visit.

'You must go and get something for me. Some information. Tonight. Good. Then go. Look for an ugly man. His name's Green.'

Boy nodded.

25

'Say I sent you and tell him to give you the information. Then come back here. Do nothing else. Talk to no one else.'

Boy hesitated. He wondered whether he dared risk a question.

May as well, he thought.

'Valerian,' he said carefully, 'what is the information? How will I know what he tells me is right?'

'You won't!' snapped Valerian. 'Just go! And do not get it wrong!'

Boy nodded at him.

'And be quick,' said Valerian coldly.

Boy waited, questions playing across his face.

'So what are you waiting for?' Valerian yelled.

Boy jumped to his feet and fled down the stairs.

7

By the time Korp got the fat singer out of his theatre, and the girl too, it was late. There was no way he could move Valerian down the running order, but he had been pleased enough to get Madame from her previous permanent en-gagement in a foreign city many, many miles away. He sighed as he made his way up to his little loft. This was no mean feat due to his considerable proportions and the narrowness of the passage.

He made it to the door, and noticed immediately that it was not locked. Not only that, but the little door swung open on its concealed hinges.

He cursed everyone in the Company, then collapsed into the box. Flicking the lid of the table with one foot, he sank his teeth into the cork of the bottle, removed it and then he drank, long and deep.

He sighed.

Suddenly he heard a noise. It sounded like footsteps, coming from the stage. He leant forward, peering out through the view-hole.

Nothing. At least, it was too dark to see anything. He held his breath.

Still nothing. Just as he had decided he was imagining it, he heard the sound again.

He peered down into the gloom of the auditorium.

His eyes grew wide in their sockets.

8

Boy wasted half an hour while he wondered whether to risk asking Valerian what he should do about the fact that he had no dry clothes. Then, deciding it was best not to bother him, Boy had set out for the Trumpet dressed in his winter overcoat, with a piece of sacking for leggings, and his boots, which he had wiped as clean as he could.

He left, slamming the door behind him. Boy was allowed no keys to the house, but Valerian had designed a special lock that operated automatically when the door was pulled shut. You needed no key to lock the door, just one to open it again. And this was not a lock that Boy could unpick. He knew because he had tried. Shortly after Valerian had shown him how to pick simple locks with a twist of metal, Boy had found himself locked out.

He had gone sneaking out one evening after the show, searching for an extra bite to eat. Food was never plentiful in the house – it didn't interest Valerian greatly and Boy was always trying to find more. Sometimes he could persuade one of the musicians from the theatre to buy him a meal. This particular evening he'd dined thanks to the kindness of the old violinist. Hunger having driven him to the rendez-vous, it was only upon his return that he realised he would not be able to get back into the house.

Aha! Boy said to himself. *Let's see if I've got this right.*

He hunted round in his pockets for his lock-picking metal. It had once served as the artificial tendon in a metal hand that Valerian had dismantled. When he had grown bored with it, Boy had found it just right for the job of lock-picking.

He leant closer to the lock. It was almost completely dark in the street and he peered hard at the hole. He reached forward with his makeshift key, but no sooner had he touched the metal innards of the lock with the metal tendon than he was thrown backwards across the street, landing in a heap in the gutter. His hand, in fact his whole arm, felt as though it had been bitten by a dragon.

Boy rubbed his bad arm with his other hand, cursing his luck.

Some magic device, no doubt, put by Valerian on the door to keep thieves away.

He had been in deep trouble when Valerian had found him the following morning, huddled on the doorstep, having spent a wretched freezing night outside.

Inventing was just one of Valerian's many areas of knowledge. Years ago, when more involved in the life of the Great Theatre, he had invented a system of footlights for the stage – another reason why Korp was deeply indebted to him. The lights worked on some system of chemical fire that only Valerian understood and that only he could control. They gave off a faint, yet pungent smell, but were another reason why Korp's theatre had a reputation as the best in the City.

Boy had learnt much from him because Valerian was, for all his faults, a remarkable man. But despite their years together, Boy actually knew very little about him. He would try and fit bits and pieces together, and over the years had picked up enough scraps of information to put together some of his life story.

Boy knew Valerian had attended the Academy, where Kepler, the man who had recently made the camera obscura, was one of his fellow students. He knew that Valerian had studied Natural Philosophy. He had been considered a more than able scholar, with the potential to become a great one. Something had happened, Boy did not know what, but it was enough to make him fall from grace. Boy once heard Valerian say something that implied it was because of particular studies he was making. Boy gathered that he had been conducting peculiar experiments, explorations into secret or forgotten learning. Boy never found out exactly what, but it was enough to know it was something dark and forbidden.

Around this time Boy knew that Kepler and Valerian had fallen out, or at least lost touch. They had not seen each other until only a few years back. In fact, Boy could remember when Valerian started visiting Kepler in his tall and narrow house across the City, and after a while Boy would occasionally go too.

Boy also knew that Valerian had once been very wealthy, which was when he had bought the house – a huge and rambling edifice that was now a decayed shadow of its former self. It had been purchased from the family of a judge who had died. It was still an opulent building then, a worthy residence for one of the City's highest officials. But Valerian seemed to be rich no more, and over the years the house had gone to seed and the neighbourhood around it had too.

Boy did not know how he had lost his money, but Valerian was no longer rich and seemed not to care very much for anything, except the hours he spent shut away in the Tower, doing heaven knows what with his infernal contraptions and reading books from the teetering piles that lay around the room.

Boy loved the house despite the large number of empty rooms and shamefully dirty corridors, if only because it was the only place he had ever called home. If he kept out of Valerian's way, or at least did nothing to upset him, Boy found a little peace inside its walls. And there was the small paved garden outside the kitchen door, where on hot days Boy would cool himself among ferns and vines that sprouted from the high, damp stone walls, making the garden a secret space. There was a small well in the centre of the paving, from which sometimes Boy fancied that he could hear rushing water, like a river far beneath him, though he knew it was just his fancy. The river was a sluggish, smelly beast, miles away from the house, and the well seemed to be just a dry, bottomless hole.

Boy put his hand against the flat panels of the door, willing it to open, but he would have to go on now. It was a cold night and he was naked under his coat except for the sack-cloth leggings. Boy hoped Valerian would still be awake when he got back, but there was every chance of that. He kept strange hours – working through the night, sometimes resting fitfully during the day and then getting up in the early evening to perform at the theatre. Boy glanced up at the Tower high above the street, but he saw no light coming from within. This was odd. It would be unlike Valerian to sleep at night! For a moment, Boy wondered if Valerian had gone out again himself. The house was so large that from his room he would not have heard the front door close.

There was nothing he could do about it now. The lock had dropped firmly behind him and he was out in the City, alone.

It was about one in the morning and the Quarter was reaching its peak of activity. It only truly seemed to come alive late at night, with street traders still about and the taverns heaving with beer and laughter. People worked long hours and for some of them this was their only chance to pretend they had a life that was something other than total drudgery.

Boy tried, as a rule, to make himself unseen, and most of the time did a good job of avoiding trouble in this way. He was neither short nor tall, but he was very thin, and by emptying his mind and avoiding people's eyes with his own, he made a fair stab at invisibility as he passed through the City at night.

The City was looking its best. Some of its unpleasantness was obscured during the festivities and holidays. As was the custom, evergreen branches had been used to decorate houses, shops and other buildings. It was also traditional to burn candles at this time, and windows everywhere twinkled with pretty lights which, once lit in the evening, burnt long into the night.

Night. It was all he seemed to see, especially during these winter days. Valerian kept Boy busy with this and that all through the small hours, until finally, just as dawn was creeping over the City, he would let him stagger off to his cot to slumber the day away. Then, shouting through all the floors of the house, Valerian would rouse Boy for another evening's performance in the theatre.

'I am a vampire,' Boy said grimly as he stole down Dead Duck Lane. 'That's it. He's a stinking vampire and now I am too!'

Realising he was talking aloud, he looked rapidly around him, but he had gone unnoticed.

Boy thought again about what had happened to Valerian.

It was only a recent thing, maybe just a few weeks or months ago. Valerian had definitely become more irritable than usual. His moods had always swung rapidly from one extreme to another, but now they seemed firmly fixed in one extreme. Surly and preoccupied, he was less violent, less vitriolic. He spent hours on end in the Tower, only emerging to get Boy to run an errand. Boy had delivered a lot of letters for him recently, and collected many in reply.

Letters, thought Boy. *Letters?*

It reminded him – there was one evening, one evening in particular, when he had delivered a letter to Kepler. Kepler lived a good way across the City, in the University Quarter.

Boy didn't like Kepler much. He wasn't sure why exactly. Maybe it was because Valerian listened intently to what Kepler had to say, but showed little or no interest in any opinions Boy might have. There was something about him Boy just didn't warm to.

Kepler was thin like Valerian, but shorter and with none of Valerian's strength. He was always muttering to himself, and tended to scurry about like a rat, Boy thought. But if it was true that Boy didn't like Kepler, it was also true that he was fascinated by him, for he was as much of a hoarder of strange devices and peculiar mechanisms as Valerian.

As well as being a Doctor of Medicine of the Human Animal, Kepler made specialised studies into the field of The Heavens. He had all sorts of equipment with which he looked up at the stars. He recorded his observations in huge leather-bound books, having noted the motions of planets, stars and moons through his metal and glass devices. Kepler had told Boy that he could then make all sorts of predictions about people and their behaviour, just by knowing when they had been born. Increasingly Boy had gone with

34

Valerian on his visits to Kepler's house. He would sit quietly in the corner of Kepler's room and marvel at the astounding discussions they would hold, hearing a lot, and learning a little.

Boy wished someone could tell him about *his* life, predict what would happen to *him*, just by setting his date of birth against the position of the stars. He knew, though, that even Kepler could not do that, because Boy did not know when he had been born.

Once Boy had been worried about this. He had even been bold enough to speak to Valerian about it.

'Who do you think my parents were?' he had asked. 'How could I find out?'

But Valerian had only scoffed at him.

'You will never know, nor does it matter one jot. Nor', he added, 'do you need to know. You are Boy, *my* Boy, and that is enough.'

Boy always tried to do what Valerian told him to – things were safer that way. So Boy tried not to think about the matter any more, but it was not always easy.

On this particular evening, however, when Boy had delivered the letter to Kepler, the Doctor had asked him to wait. Kepler had written a reply to Valerian. Boy had watched him as he scratched away with a sophisticated silver-nibbed fountain pen on a sheet of paper, pausing momentarily to consider his words. Kepler had sprinkled the letter with sand, then folded up the paper and started to melt some sealing wax. As he dripped blood-red wax on to the letter, and pressed his ring into it, he spoke to Boy.

'Take this to him,' he said, without looking up from what he was doing, 'and may God protect his own.'

There was something odd in his manner which Boy remembered. It was when he had taken the letter back that

Valerian's mood had really sunk. That was when it had really started.

At about two o'clock Boy stopped at the top of Pigeon Pie Alley. At the far end of the street stood The Trumpet. All hell was breaking loose inside.

Oh, just perfect! thought Boy.

9

Korp stared at the stage, watching the ghost.

At first he thought it must be the Dark Duke. An old theatre legend told how the ghost of the Dark Duke would stalk across the stage as a portent of disaster. History related how, years ago, the theatre had relied on the Duke for financial backing. If he didn't like the work the theatre was producing, he would storm across the stage during rehearsal, sometimes even during a performance. One day he had tried to stop a rehearsal and was stabbed by the lead actor, a touchy man at the best of times, whose brother had written the play in question. Since then the Dark Duke appeared at times of impending crisis, though he had not been seen in many, many years.

The theatre was in trouble. Korp had seen so many strange things in his life that he was superstitious enough to believe that. There could be no mistake about it. The only question was when.

In fact Korp was mistaken. He had only been watching the ghost for a few moments when it disappeared, leaving behind a slight cloud of dust that hung in the air, glowing.

A second later, Korp heard something behind him.

The thing slashed at Korp's body, and he fell forward, one arm and his head across the edge of the box, dying.

10

Boy hovered in the street, trying to decide what to do. He knew he didn't really have any choice. If Valerian wanted him to go into The Trumpet and meet a big, ugly man called Green, then he would have to do it. It was just that he didn't want to.

There was obviously a fight going on inside – Boy could tell that from where he stood, at the end of Pigeon Pie Alley. He waited, hoping things would settle down, but after a little while he changed his mind. Perhaps everyone would be too busy in the tavern to notice him; he could slip in and take a look around without being seen. Besides, he was freezing in his makeshift clothes. At least inside he'd be warm for a while, and get away from the smell of the river just a street or two away.

As he approached The Trumpet the sound of tables breaking and bottles being smashed grew louder. The inn was really rough. There was no longer a sign with its name outside – its reputation spoke for it. There was grimy glass in some of the windows, though not all by any means. The way in to The Trumpet was in a claustrophobic alley that lay in the gloom between the buildings. Boy glanced in through a window as he headed down the alley. Things were getting lively, to say the least. He took one last gulp of the foul river air, and went inside.

The noise immediately seemed ten times louder, and if the stink was bad in the street, it was worse still inside. The whole place was a lurid riot of colour, sound and smell compared to the darkness of the City's winter streets outside. The effect was overwhelming and for a minute Boy thought he might be sick. His head swam with the confusion of it all. He looked for a place to lurk.

Surprisingly, considering the noise they were making, the fight seemed only to be between two men. The bulk of the din came from the people watching, who were cheering, shouting and fighting amongst themselves.

Boy picked his way to a small table half-hidden in the space under the staircase that led upstairs.

'Beer, love?'

He looked up to see a barmaid staring at him expectantly. She held a tray of empty beer jugs in one hand and was piling short, stubby glasses up with the other.

'Well?'

Damn! thought Boy. *Money. I didn't think of that. Neither did Valerian, but that won't stop me getting a thrashing if I get this wrong.*

'I don't have any money,' he said, looking up sadly at the barmaid.

She scowled briefly, then her face softened and she smiled.

'Did you know you've got nothing on under there?' she asked, smirking.

Boy looked down and hurriedly pulled his coat shut over his legs. He thought for a moment.

'It's cold outside,' he ventured, trying to sound as miserable as he could. 'You know, on the streets . . .'

'All right,' she said, 'but just half an hour, mind, then out you go. Here, take this.'

She put one of the glasses she had collected back down in front of him, and then emptied the dregs of five beer jugs into it. She nodded at the glass now containing a couple of fingers of beer slops and smiled again.

'Better make it last, Gorgeous,' she said, and went off collecting more glasses while they were still unbroken.

Boy took one look at the beer and pushed it away.

The fight was just about over. The victor, a giant of a man, sat on the chest of the vanquished, a fat brute, raining a few last punches down on his face for good measure. But it was all for show now. Finally someone came to pull him off the fat man.

'That's enough, now. Well done.'

The giant got up and for the first time Boy saw his face. He was as ugly as a dead cat.

He seemed not to appreciate being pulled off the fat man, because he swung a fist at his would-be helper and sent him sprawling across a table.

Everyone cheered except Boy, who had a sinking feeling in his stomach. He pulled the sleeve of a toothless old man with a stick who was sitting nearby.

'Who's that?' Boy asked, but he knew the answer already.

'Eh?' said the man. 'Don't you know Jacob Green, The Green Giant?'

The man laughed, spat on the floor and waved his stick in the air for a drink.

Meanwhile Green swaggered around, taking drinks from all and sundry and downing them in a single draught. Boy looked at the giant, ugly, violent man.

Green.

The man he'd come to meet.

Boy looked at his beer.

Green sat talking loudly now to a group in a corner, playing with something tiny in his giant hands, like a child with a toy. It was a small wooden box. He was spinning it between thumb and forefinger. Then he stopped and wound a little handle coming from its side. A small tinkle of musical notes floated through the hubbub of the tavern. A music box.

Around him, two serving girls picked up bits of shattered bottles and broken chairs. It crossed Boy's mind that he did not have a clue what was going on. This was a feeling he often had working for Valerian, but things were definitely getting more peculiar. The business in Korp's box, when Valerian had materialised behind him no more than a few seconds after he'd left the stage, had unnerved him. But Boy had barely had time to puzzle over that before he'd been bundled out in the street to meet Green. Boy wondered what on earth Valerian could need from him. There was only one way to find out.

Boy looked at his beer. Picking up the glass he swigged the cloudy brown liquid straight down, wiped his mouth and took a deep breath. He stood up and made his way across the room.

11

Boy was not the only servant abroad at that moment. Back
in the Quarter of the Arts, Willow ventured out into the
cold night, moaning to herself, wrapping her shawl around
shoulders and over her head. Her mouse-brown hair was
thick and long, keeping her warm. She had been working
for Madame Beauchance for a year now, ever since she had
come to the Great Theatre. It was a year too long in her
opinion.

The woman was large and unattractive, she was vain and
arrogant, she was lazy and spiteful, and miserly too. There
was, though, one thing which redeemed her, and that was
her voice. It was the voice of nothing less than an angel. It
was a voice that could murmur soft and low and soothe a
bawling child, that could rise shrill and clear and shatter a
mirror and that could slide so sweetly over a melody that a
killer might sit down and weep. With her voice she had
made a good career, and a small fortune that she kept to
herself.

Willow had ended up working for her by chance. She had
been employed as tail-carrier in her previous job, working for
the Fellowship of Master Liverymen. Willow didn't know
what the Fellowship actually did, but she knew what she
was supposed to do, and that was enough. And besides,

anything was better than life in the orphanage. The Livery-men wore fancy clothes on official occasions, including long-tailed coats. It was her job to follow behind her master, carrying the tails of his coat so they did not trail in the dirt. There were eleven other girls and boys employed likewise, one for each of the Fellowship. That was the full extent of their duties, but since there were at least two official occasions every day, they were kept busy enough carrying coat tails and brushing off mud where necessary. After three years, she had been told to take a coat to the Great Theatre where they required the costume of a Liveryman.

Willow had immediately fallen for the excitement of the place. It was thrilling. She had begged Korp for a job and had begun scrubbing floors that afternoon. She never went back to the Liverymen and they did not come looking for her – there were plenty more urchins to be had. After a week of odd jobs, Madame B had arrived and immediately demand-ed a personal assistant. Her last one, a man with a weak heart, had collapsed carrying her cases of costumes on the journey to the City.

Willow was not fond of her mistress, especially this even-ing, when she'd blamed Willow for not bringing her hair-brush. She had told Willow to go back to the theatre and get Korp to open up. None of the other hundreds of brushes she had at her lodgings was good enough, apparently, so Willow had set off back to the theatre.

That was how she found the side door to the theatre flap-ping open in the chilly night air, and how she walked cauti-ously into the auditorium, already sensing something was wrong, and how she stood halfway back in the stalls, looking at the stage, when she felt it raining on her head.

She noticed that the footlights were faintly glowing. That

43

too was odd – they were very expensive to run. Then she remembered she was inside and that it couldn't be raining.

She put her hand to her hair and felt the wetness. It was warm. From the dim light coming from the stage she looked at her hand and screamed.

It was covered in blood.

She looked up to see the head and shoulders of Korp's corpse sticking out of the box's window.

She screamed again.

12

Green gave Boy's throat another gentle squeeze. He had one of his huge spade-like fists wrapped around it, though not tightly.

Not yet, thought Boy.

Despite the fact that they were still in the front room of The Trumpet, and in full view of everyone in the tavern, Boy had no doubt that Green would snap his neck like a dry reed if he wanted to. This was not the sort of place where the men of the City Watch ever came. It had its own laws, and one murder or another was probably neither here nor there to these people.

Boy stood in front of Green, who sat with one arm outstretched, his fingers raising Boy on to his tiptoes. Even like this, Green was taller than him. Boy was quite glad because it meant he was not looking straight at Green's foul face. He had a wide nose, with nostrils that had obviously been split at some point or other in his colourful past. The whites of his eyes were yellow and watery, his lips were like two slugs sitting on each other. His hair was thinning and his scalp was diseased. Boy tried not to look, and anyway, he had other things to concentrate on. He had been standing precariously on tiptoe ever since he had had the nerve to approach the giant.

45

'What do you want?' Green had bawled.

'I . . . I . . .' stammered Boy.

'*What?*' Green yelled.

'I've been sent to–'

'Ah!' said Green. '*He* sent you, did he? Too scared to come himself! Perhaps I should just give you what I was going to give him!'

Boy nodded, and next thing he knew he was balancing on the ends of his toes.

'He sent you?'

'U-hurrrr,' squeaked Boy.

'What?' shouted Green, letting Boy drop a little on to his feet.

'Mmm.'

Green scowled, then grabbed Boy tightly again, and picking him off his feet, shook him briskly. He put him down again.

'So I see,' scoffed Green. 'Well, tell him to come himself. I only deal with him.'

'I have to find out–' began Boy, but Green grabbed him by the throat and began to squeeze. 'Tell him he's to come himself. Now get lost!'

He dropped Boy, who fell to his knees choking. Hearing the tinny notes of the music box again he looked up. Green was spinning the handle, laughing to himself, captivated by the simple tune.

Boy caught only a glimpse of it before it was hidden in Green's massive hand, but it was strange and beautiful.

Boy sat in the dirt of the floor, rubbing his sore neck.

Green lurched to his feet and sloped away from Boy across the room, pushing past people as he went.

'I need a leak!' he announced as he staggered through a door in the back.

Boy picked himself up, wondering what to do.

He waited for a few moments, then a few more, and then followed Green to the door that led outside to the latrine.

What followed next was too fast for Boy to see.

As he stepped through the door there was a flash of light and a noise like a cork popping. Then everywhere was shrouded in purple smoke.

He heard a thump and then the sound of feet clambering against the wooden wall of the crap-house.

The smoke cleared and as Boy's eyes grew used to the darkness in the yard, he saw a shape at his feet. He knelt down and put his hand out.

It was Green, and he was dead. Boy could tell that immediately from the peculiar angle of his neck.

Boy was about to run, and then saw something glinting in the dark. His old magpie habits from his days on the street tugged at him. He prised the huge fist fully open and there, unharmed, was the music box.

He grabbed it and stuck it in his pocket. Then he heard the door to The Trumpet open behind him.

He jumped to his feet and sped away up the side alley that led to the street.

'Hey!' shouted a voice behind him. 'Hey!'

'The Phantom!' cried the voice as Boy disappeared. 'The Phantom has got Green!'

Boy did not stop. He simply ran, but as he ran it occurred to him that it was true. Green must have been struck by the Phantom, just as Boy was following him. It was a lucky escape. Any sooner and *he* might be dead too. Boy sped on, trying to ignore the fact that he had not got the information Valerian was after, and that now the source of that information was dead.

Boy ran madly, until finally he turned a corner and ran

slap into someone else. They fell together, flying into the mud of the street. Boy looked at the other runner, who lay sprawled across him.

It was Willow.

'Boy!' she screamed. 'Oh, Boy!'

She was in a state, Boy could see. She was gabbling, trying to find the right words to say.

'I saw – in his box–'

But she did not finish, because a figure suddenly rose up in front of them.

'In a hurry?' it asked.

They looked up to see a shadowy figure staring down at them. From his black cape, and extravagant red-plumed hat, they knew who the man was. This was the garb of a City Watchman.

Boy and Willow had different feelings on seeing the Watchman. Boy had spent much of his homeless years, the years before Valerian, trying to avoid the City Watchmen. In his opinion they spent far too long trying to capture hungry boys who had stolen food, and not enough stopping people killing each other in tavern brawls.

Willow, however, had just seen the body of her former employer hanging from the window of his private box.

'I'm so glad to see you!' she exclaimed.

'Yes,' said the Watchman sarcastically, 'I'm sure you are. Now, would you like to tell me whose blood that is?'

Boy looked at Willow and saw blood in her hair and across her shoulders. Then he noticed the Watchman was staring at *him*.

Boy looked at his legs, and noticed that he was covered in blood too.

Things were getting messy.

'I think you'd better come with me, don't you?'

Before either of them could answer he grabbed them both by the neck and dragged them away down the street.

Some way behind a tall figure followed, slipping in and out of the darknesses of the street.

13

Dawn had risen on the morning of December the 27th, and a pale light had stolen into the cell where Willow and Boy lay. The room was about six feet square, with solid stone walls and a single window with no glass but a closely spaced grid of iron bars instead. This let the cold in and stopped the prisoners from getting out, which was just what the Watch-men wanted. Cold prisoners were less trouble. They often died of exposure before anybody had to decide what to do with them, which saved a lot of trouble all round.

Willow and Boy lay on some sparse and dirty straw, trying to keep away from a hulk of a man who lay snoring next to one of the walls. He was huge. Once or twice he had rolled over and they had shivered on seeing his aggressive, scarred face. Fortunately he had so far shown no sign of waking up.

'Why don't they hurry up?' Willow asked again.

'We've got to get out,' said Boy again.

The window was high up, but by standing on Boy's shoulders Willow was able to peer out across the City below.

'I think it's going to snow today,' she said. For some reason it reminded her of when she was small, just a child, when she hadn't had to work to survive. On a day like that there had been a lovely, thick fall of snow, and she had played in it, carefree.

The sunrise was casting a pinkish light across the whole City. Mile after murderous mile of it stretched away as far as she could see. From high in the dungeon inside the Citadel of the City Watchmen the sprawl of buildings was laid out before her like a carpet. Even this early in the morning the City hummed and bustled with the noise of tradesmen up before the sun. In the gentle pink light, and from this height, the City looked almost beautiful to Willow. Almost. In recent years she had spent too long ducking and weaving her way through its narrow lanes and dark alleys to think of the place as beautiful. From where she teetered on Boy's back she could see a very long way. Could she even see the edge of the City, or was she just imagining it? Remembering it, maybe. A trip to the country when she was a little girl, with her parents. She told herself she was imagining it. She'd been too little when her parents had died to remember them.

'Have you ever been out of the City?' she asked Boy suddenly.

'Are you going to get down?' Boy asked back.

'Oh, sorry, yes.'

She slithered off his back and landed nimbly beside him.

'Thank you,' he said. 'Well?'

'I think it's going to snow.'

'The *window*, Willow?' he said.

'Oh, there's no way we're going anywhere. The bars are solid and besides, there's a drop that'd squash you flat. We're stuck.'

Boy slid back down into the straw.

'Then I'm as good as dead.'

'Korp *is* dead,' said Willow, and shivered again.

They were both silent.

'I don't even know your name,' said Willow after a while.

'Yes you do,' said Boy.

'What? Boy? That's just what he calls you, isn't it?'

She meant Valerian. Boy said nothing.

'That's your real name? Boy? That's not a name. You must have a real name.'

Boy looked at her.

'That's my *only* name. Before Valerian found me no one called me anything at all.'

Willow stared at Boy.

'So where did you come from?'

'I don't know.'

'You don't know?'

'No,' said Boy, beginning to wish he'd been arrested on his own.

'How can you not know? Where did you live before Valerian found you?'

'In the City.'

'Where?'

'Anywhere.'

'Always?'

'Yes,' said Boy. 'Is that so strange? Have you ever lived anywhere else?'

'No,' admitted Willow, 'but I know my name and I know I was born in the City, though I can't remember where.'

'And so do I,' said Boy angrily. 'My name's Boy and I was born in the City too! All right?'

Willow was quiet for a time, flicking her feet with a piece of straw.

'Sorry,' she said.

Boy mumbled something.

'Why are they taking so long?' she asked again.

'We've got to get out,' said Boy again.

There was a rattling of keys in the huge iron lock and the door swung back on its heavy hinges.

The Watchman who had locked them up several hours before ducked his head as he came back into the cell. He seemed surprised to see them. He glanced at the sleeping figure by the wall.

'Lucky for you he drank so much,' he said.

'Did you go and look?' asked Willow.

'Oh yes,' said the Watchman. His hat had a pink plume in it. This meant he was more important than the red-plumed one who'd arrested them. Willow thought this was a good sign, and would mean he could let them go. She'd told them about finding Korp and explained about the blood. She'd told them to go and see for themselves so they knew she was telling the truth. And Boy had just let them imagine that the blood on his clothes was the same blood that was on Willow.

'So you see that what we told you is true?' Willow asked.

'Oh yes. Very much so. And you will both be detained on suspicion of the murder of Director Korp of the Great Theatre.'

14

Valerian lurked in the shadows across the road from the Citadel of the City Watchmen. It was an old building, one of the very oldest in this very old city, and was a crazy mixture of styles and materials. Black-timbered box windows lurched unnecessarily far out of rough stone walls, doors halfway up walls led only to empty space, and ornate towers and spires twisted high into the early morning air above Valerian.

He hated being here, he disliked even being in this part of the City, which was a much richer and altogether *nicer* area than he was used to – than what he had *become* used to. The longest side of the Citadel overlooked the river and the stink coming from it was worse than ever. As if all that were not enough, it was daylight. Valerian could not remember the last time he had been outside during the day. It disturbed him.

It had all gone wrong, and time was running out. Had he really expected the boy to get the information he'd sent him for? And now he'd have to get Boy out of the Citadel, to know for sure that he hadn't. Valerian cursed under his breath. He didn't have time to be messing around like this.

Once, things had been so different for him, but as the last

few years had turned under his feet, the spectre of his past had risen to meet him like the dawn of a terrible day.

Well, there would be worse to come yet, that much Valerian knew for sure.

15

'This is not going well,' said Willow.

'I know,' said Boy, 'but what do you suggest?'

The figure in the straw stirred again. Very soon he might wake up, and with a significant hangover.

'Why did you tell them about Korp?' Boy asked Willow.

'I couldn't not, could I? I was covered in blood. I still am.'

She tried not to look at her clothes. It was bad enough that the stuff had now dried in her hair and matted together in places. She wanted a bath very much. Boy looked no better. For some reason he was wearing only sack-cloth leggings under his overcoat and from the knees down his legs were stained red-brown. Although Red-plume and Pink-plume thought this was Korp's blood too, Willow knew it was not.

'So tell me again how you've got blood on your legs. And where your clothes are. And what you were doing out at three in the morning.'

Boy sighed. Why did she always have to ask so many questions? He changed the subject.

'I can't believe Korp's dead,' he said.

'No,' Willow agreed.

'But that means . . .'

'What?'

'Well, the theatre. What will happen? There's no one to take it over and that means it will close and that means I'm out of a job.'

'Me too,' said Willow, 'but we don't know for sure it's going to close. Someone will take it over.'

'Who?' asked Boy.

'Well . . .' said Willow, thinking hard, 'Valerian?'

Boy was about to laugh, but then thought about it for a moment. Valerian was just about the only reason the Great Theatre was still going anyway. Why shouldn't he take it over? In fact . . . A terrible thought crossed his mind, but he pushed it away. There were other things to think about first. Besides, Valerian was utterly bored with the Theatre these days, only keeping the act going as a steady source of income.

'What will they do to us?' he asked Willow, but he knew the answer.

'Hang us, I expect.'

'Or drown us, maybe.'

They both fell silent again, contemplating a miserable end. The sun climbed higher over the City and shed a little light directly into their cell. Boy and Willow wasted no time in sitting in the patch of sunlight and at last they began to feel warm.

Boy shoved his hands deep into his pockets and his left struck something solid. He pulled out the music box. He turned it over. The only other time he'd seen one was in Kepler's house. He collected clockwork mechanisms of all kinds, and had once shown some to Boy.

Boy daydreamed, remembering the time a year or so ago when Kepler had come to stay in their house for a week while he installed the camera obscura. Even though he brought all the parts with him it had taken Kepler the whole week to fit it into the Tower room. There was a lot of banging and sawing and swearing during those seven days, but at the end Kepler had thrown open the door to the room.

'Behold!' he cried dramatically, and Valerian, who had not been allowed into his own chamber during the building, had entered. Boy had watched the door close behind them, and many months later was still none the wiser about what the machine actually did. As the door had closed, however, he had heard Valerian exclaim that Kepler was the Greatest Doctor of Natural Philosophies that had ever lived.

'What's that?' asked Willow.

Boy waved the music box at her and wound its handle a couple of times before putting it back in his pocket.

'I . . . found it,' he said. 'At The Trumpet. Listen to the music, because it may be the last we hear!'

'Oh, Boy, don't give up. It could be worse.'

'How could it be worse?' Boy asked, but Willow didn't answer, because the figure lying in the straw suddenly rolled over and vomited across the floor.

'Please get me out of here,' wailed Boy to no one in particular, and his prayer was answered.

The door rattled and opened for a third time, and Boy was amazed to see Valerian enter the room.

Before Boy could open his mouth, Valerian put his finger to his lips. Boy understood and said nothing and Valerian came into the cell, followed by Pink-plume.

'Two minutes,' he barked at Valerian, and then saw the mess on the floor. 'Or less, if you prefer.' He pulled a face and locked them in again.

Boy was pleased to see Valerian.

'How did–?'

'How did I know you were here? You don't think I'd trust you to get it right by yourself, do you? Something this important?'

Boy wished Valerian wouldn't talk like that, especially in front of Willow, but he was too relieved to care.

'Well?' said Valerian.

Boy said nothing.

'He wouldn't tell me anything. I–'

Valerian lurched forwards towards Boy, who flinched backwards, but did not hit him as he had expected.

'He's dead,' added Boy. 'Someone murdered him. Some thing. The Phantom.'

'What?' roared Valerian, then seemed to remember where they were and made an effort to calm himself.

'He's dead. He–'

'Not that! Did he tell you anything? What did he say before . . . ?'

'He wouldn't tell me anything,' Boy stammered. 'He–'

'Be quiet!' yelled Valerian, then quietened himself again. 'So he told you nothing before he died? Kepler sent him with information for me – the name of a grave. You're sure?'

Boy nodded, and Valerian flung his arms out wide, failing to find words bad enough to yell at Boy.

'I do have something,' Boy said. He fished in his pocket and pulled out the music box.

'That's it?' Valerian asked. 'Are you trying to be funny? I need a name, not trinkets!'

He stopped.

'Valerian?' asked Willow.

Only now did Valerian seem to notice her presence in the cell.

'Hmm?' he said, still staring at the music box.

'He said two minutes. Are you going to get us out of here?'

Boy cringed. This was not a good way to go about getting anything from his master. There was, in fact, no good way to get anything from him, but Willow didn't know that.

Valerian dragged his eyes away from the tiny mechanical object and shoved it in his pocket.

'I may as well leave you here,' he snarled. 'You are no use to me.'

'Please, Valerian,' Boy begged. 'It wasn't my fault he wouldn't talk to me.'

Valerian considered them both.

'All right then,' he said. 'I suppose so.'

He looked at Boy.

'Well, Boy, it's time you learnt the secret of the Fairyland Vanishing Illusion.'

'But that's just a trick,' said Boy.

'Ah!' said Valerian. 'No. In fact, the secret of the Fairyland Vanishing Illusion is that it is not an illusion at all.'

Boy stared at him. Willow stared at Boy.

'Boy . . .' she began, as keys rattled in the lock again.

'Quick!' commanded Valerian. 'Hold close to me.'

He grabbed them both and pressed them to his side.

Boy heard him muttering in some unknown language, and saw him pull something from one of his many pockets.

The door opened and Pink-plume stood in the doorway.

Valerian's arm swung through the air, throwing something.

'Ho!' he cried. 'Ho! And away to Fairyland!'

There was a huge rush of smoke and Boy lost all sense of where he was. He felt himself lurch upwards for a moment, as if flying.

Then the smoke began to clear.

'Run!' hissed Valerian.

Boy ran, and felt himself being pulled along by a hand he knew well. Valerian's.

They were in a stone corridor, somewhere in the Citadel. Willow was being pulled by Valerian too, and fast. He seemed to know exactly where he was going, and in a few more seconds they burst out on to a roof, high above the City.

'Come on!' Valerian shouted, and hurtled to the edge, pulling them both off after him.

'No!' screamed Boy.

They fell for what seemed like ages, but was measured by only a heartbeat and a half.

They hit the foul and freezing water of the river and, after another couple of heartbeats, surfaced spluttering and coughing quite near the bank.

'Come on!' urged Valerian, as he clambered out of the water by a small wooden jetty to which ferry boats were moored.

'Time we were gone,' he said. 'Besides,' he added, 'I hate daylight.'

Rolling them both into a ferry he climbed after them and pulled a dirty piece of canvas across them all. He set them adrift and they floated away downstream in the brisk current, heading for home.

'Are they following us?' Willow finally managed to splutter.

'No! They won't even know we're gone until the fool with the pink feather wakes up.'

Boy shook his head. He was used to not knowing what was going on, but this was worse than usual.

'Valerian,' he asked. 'Valerian, was that really magic?'

Boy had never believed that Valerian could actually do magic. Real magic. He was not sure he had changed his mind.

'Well, I got you out of the Citadel, didn't I? It must take real magic to do a thing like that, mustn't it?'

Boy lay shivering under the canvas. If it was magic, couldn't Valerian have got them straight home without having to swim in the freezing river? He was cold again, and wet this time too. He was soaked with stinking river water. At least he was back in a nice small dark space. He could cope with that. He decided to let the subject of magic drop. Let Valerian play his games. Boy had other things on his mind, like smoke. As they'd burst from the cell, there had been an awful lot of smoke. Purple smoke. Again. it was the second time in a few hours that Boy had seen purple smoke, and the first time had left Green with his throat cut and his neck broken.

What had Valerian said?

You don't think I'd trust you to get it right by yourself, do you?

Had Valerian been there all along, at The Trumpet? And Green – had Valerian seen to him too? No, he had wanted the precious information from Green. He wouldn't have killed him.

And Korp? Korp must have been killed about the same time that Green was, but the Phantom couldn't have been responsible for both. Boy tried to let the thoughts make sense so he could forget them, but they didn't. He worried.

The boat drifted downriver, back towards the Old Quarter where Valerian and Boy lived in their magnificent crumbling mansion.

16

By the time they made it back to the Yellow House, it was nearly midday.

Valerian slammed the door behind them.

Immediately he took the music box out of his pocket and glared at it.

'Kepler, where are you?' he said to himself. 'Where are you when I need you?'

Then he looked at Boy and Willow.

'Go and get cleaned up, Boy,' he said. 'I seem to say that a lot at the moment, don't I?'

'What are you doing here, girl?' he asked Willow. 'You can get cleaned up too and then leave.'

Valerian turned and made for the stairs to his own rooms.

'I think I had better get changed myself,' he said as he went.

Boy looked at Willow, then after Valerian.

'But where can she go? The theatre will probably have to shut. Korp's dead.'

'I know,' Valerian called back from halfway up the first flight of stairs, 'but this is not a doss-house.'

And he disappeared out of sight.

By the time Boy had found his smelly clothes from the night

before, and washed them and Willow's, and scrubbed his coat and boots again, it was getting dark.

Boy made a fire in the kitchen to dry all their wet things. They sat in front of it wrapped in blankets from Boy's bed, and shivered.

They had been listening to Valerian's curses and threats come floating down through the house all afternoon.

'You live here?' asked Willow, looking around her in wonder. The kitchen alone was vast, with unused implements and pots and pans hanging everywhere. The house must once have fed at least a dozen people every single day. 'Just you and him in this huge house?'

Boy nodded.

'But what are you? His slave?'

'No!' said Boy fiercely.

'Then he pays you?' asked Willow.

Boy hesitated before answering.

'No, but–'

'So you *are* his slave!'

'I am his famulus,' Boy cried.

Willow stopped.

'His what?' she asked.

'Famulus,' said Boy. 'His famulus. It means I attend him in his studies and investigations.'

'Is that what he told you?' Willow asked.

Boy said nothing.

'Isn't there anyone else?' Willow pressed. 'Who does the cooking? The cleaning?'

'I cook when he tells me to. No one does any cleaning.'

'But who taught you to wash clothes? To make fires? Someone must have shown you.'

'I don't know. He teaches me things, but not everyday things. I worked those out for myself.'

'And before you came here? Who are your parents?'

'I don't have any.'

'Neither do I, any more.'

'What happened to them?' Boy asked, wondering as he did so why he was bothering.

'They were killed,' Willow said. 'I was four.'

Boy was about to ask how they were killed, but Willow carried on before he could.

'My aunt put me in the orphanage,' she said.

'That was nice of her,' said Boy.

'She wasn't really my aunt. She was some old relative. I'm not sure what, exactly. But she couldn't look after me. Anyway, she died not long after that. I lived in an orphanage near the Palace walls until I got a job with the Liverymen. I was eleven then, four years ago. How old are you?'

'I don't know,' Boy said.

Girl looked at him, expecting some kind of explanation. Getting none, she carried on with her own story.

'Then I came to the theatre, but you know that,' she said. She looked hard at Boy. 'What about you?'

'What do you mean?' Boy asked.

'Your parents,' Willow said, sounding impatient.

'I said, I haven't got any.'

'I know that,' Willow said, 'but I mean, who *were* they?'

Boy shrugged. He knew she was only interested, but really, he wished she'd shut up.

'Look, I don't know. Since I can remember I just lived in the streets, freezing and starving in the winter, all right more or less in the summer. That's all there's ever been. Then he found me.'

Willow could see she was getting nowhere. She changed tack.

'He treats you like rubbish,' she said.

65

'At least I have a room and food and something to do.'

'That's not a room,' said Willow, remembering the box-like space at the end of the tunnel Boy had fetched the blankets from. She seemed stumped for anything to ask for a moment, then turned to Boy again.

'So who taught you to speak, then?' she asked.

Boy felt the clothes.

'They're dry, more or less,' he said, and Willow gave up.

They turned their backs to each other and dressed quickly. The clothes were warm from the fire and Boy began to feel better than he had for what seemed like a very long time.

'I'm hungry,' said Willow, 'Starving.'

'Let's see if there's some food here,' Boy said, but not very hopefully.

He was right to be pessimistic. He found some dried biscuits, and they ate them slowly.

'Boy,' said Willow suddenly, 'what about me?'

'You'll have to go back to the singer,' he said. 'You're not short of food there, at least.'

'But I can't!' Willow cried. 'I'm a wanted criminal! So are you, come to that.'

Boy hesitated.

'I know,' he said, 'I know. Look, I'll try and talk to Valerian again, see if you can stay. Then maybe you'll be safe from the Watch.'

'Would you?' asked Willow. 'Would you really?'

Boy looked at the hope in her face and felt himself shiver. He wasn't sure it was a good idea, for lots of reasons. And wasn't it like admitting she was guilty if she ran away? But something in him wanted her to stay.

He could *ask*, but the chances of Valerian agreeing were not good.

'Look,' he said, 'I'll try. That's all.'

'Why do you care?' said Willow.

Boy hesitated again. He didn't know that he did.

'I don't know,' he said.

They sat and watched the fire for a while, warming themselves while it lasted. Boy felt exhausted, as much by Willow's constant questions as anything. For the first time in years all sorts of thoughts crowded into his head. He pushed them away. He didn't need to know who his parents were. It wasn't important, no matter what Willow thought. Boy's thoughts became hazier.

Before they knew it, they had fallen asleep on each other's shoulders, and for a short time their weary bodies rested.

17

Darkness had fallen.

Boy and Willow woke up within moments of each other. They both got to their feet, avoiding each other's eyes.

'Well,' said Boy, looking at the floor.

'Yes,' said Willow. 'What do you think? Have you changed your mind?'

'No,' said Boy, looking up, and into Willow's eyes. 'Let's get it over with.'

They made their way up to the Tower room. After hours of hearing Valerian's rage and curses earlier in the day, it was quiet. It seemed as good a time as any to dare to ask him for favours.

Boy knocked on the door. That in itself was strange. Normally he waited to be summoned.

'What is it?' came the voice from within.

'Valerian,' called Boy, 'can we come in?'

There was a pause.

'We? Oh, very well.'

Inside Boy looked at Valerian, but not directly into his eyes. That was usually too much to take. Willow just stared and stared open-mouthed at all the stuff in the room – the vials, the jars, the machines, the devices, the equipment, the drawings, the books, the glass things, the brass things, the wooden things. The camera obscura.

'Why is she still here?' Valerian asked.

'Please, Valerian, can she stay? The Watchmen will be after her.'

And me too, he thought.

Valerian said nothing.

'And she can't go back to Madame, because the theatre will be shut and – oh!'

Boy stopped. The theatre.

'Yes,' said Valerian. 'I expect it will.'

'But that means we'll be out of work and–'

'I could not, at this moment, possibly care less,' said Valerian. 'And the girl cannot stay here. We have too much to do. That is an end to it.'

This stopped Boy in his tracks.

'But Korp is dead,' Willow protested. 'You'll have no-where for your act!'

Valerian stood up, and Boy and Willow cowered where they stood. He seemed to tower above them, taller than ever.

'Listen to me. I do not care about the theatre or the act. The only thing that concerns me at the moment is time. Do you see?'

They both shook their heads, which seemed only to anger Valerian. Boy knew his moods well and shrank back against the wall of the Tower room.

'Listen to me! I am in trouble. Bigger trouble than failing theatres or dead directors. I now have four days left to save my life, and the only way I can do it is hidden from me! Green,' he waved the music box Boy had stolen from Green's dead hand, 'was supposed to give me a name – a name that could just possibly save my wretched cursed skin, and yet I have been tricked! All I have is this worthless gimmick! How can this fairground rubbish give me a name?'

He threw it to the floor.

Willow stepped forward and picked it up. She held it to the light of the single lamp in the room and smiled. She turned the little metal crank and notes of music, tinny and small, rang out across the room.

'I know it does that,' snapped Valerian.

Willow ignored him. She had realised something about the music, which played again and again.

She listened to the tune. It was very simple, with only eight notes. A haunting refrain, and if Valerian had been more astute, he might have heard in it the chords of hope. Willow played it a few times, then a few more.

'Valerian,' she said, 'this is a name. This tune is a name, and the name you have been searching for is Gad Beebe.'

December 28th

The Day of
Worst Fortune

�֍

1

After Willow had explained for the fourth time how she knew what the name was, Valerian began to believe it himself, and as he did so his mood suddenly improved.

'Music!' he exclaimed. 'Hidden in the music! Before my very ears!'

He laughed.

'Kepler knew what he was doing after all – he must have sent this thing for me. Green decided to play difficult and then . . .' He laughed again.

This worried Boy. He had never heard Valerian laugh before. It worried him a lot.

'And you learned this from Madame?' Valerian asked Willow.

She nodded. Yes, she had learned musical notation from Madame Beauchance. And more than that, the older woman had grudgingly told Willow that she had 'perfect pitch'. She could identify any note in isolation of any other note which might be used as a reference point – an ability it seemed Madame herself did not possess.

'And these notes – each one is a letter?'

Willow nodded again.

'G – A – D – B – E – E – B – E.'

'By chance the name uses only letters from the first seven

of the alphabet,' said Valerian. 'Whoever made this thing, or had it made, was not only musical, but had spotted this curious fact about Mr Beebe.'

Willow nodded again, Valerian laughed and Boy worried.

'Beebe,' wondered Valerian aloud. 'Beebe. I'm sure I know the name.'

'So,' ventured Willow, 'about me staying . . . just for a while.'

'Hmm?' said Valerian, his mind elsewhere. 'Hmm? Yes, that's – you might even be useful, unlike Boy.'

He held the music box mechanism in his hand, turning the handle, listening to the vital tune over and over again.

Then, at long last, the many clocks in the house began to strike midnight.

It was December the 28th.

As the last chime died away, Valerian's mood grew sombre again.

'Come,' he said gruffly. 'We have much to do and time is running out.'

Boy relaxed a little. He knew where he was with this Valerian.

2

The three figures stole through the unusually silent city streets. They had entered a Quarter where not many people came. It had not snowed, as Willow had thought it might. It was cold, however, and Boy was glad he had all his clothes on. Yet again he was out traipsing after Valerian. The only difference was that the girl, Willow, was with him this time.

'Put your boots back on,' Valerian had said.

'Again?' said Boy, but Valerian had ignored him.

Willow and Boy lagged behind the tall man as he strode rapidly down dark paths. The City was quiet. Partly it was the sudden cold snap that had sent people to their beds early, but mostly because Valerian was heading into one of the few pockets of the City that was somewhat deserted. This was the Black Quarter, where the last outbreaks of plague had broken out. As its inhabitants had fled the Quarter it had been sealed off by a ring of burning buildings until everyone left inside had survived or died. Although that was many years ago, people had been slow to move back into the Black Quarter, and as a result it was sparsely populated by only the very poorest citizens. The streets were much like any other, but even more dereliction was evident.

The buildings were dark, convoluted, tangled mazes thrown together over the years – crooked houses with slanted windows and warped frames. Between them ran the usual gutter-like streets, reeking and heaving with piles of filth. The three hurried on.

'What are we doing?' Willow panted to Boy, struggling to keep up.

'It's always like this,' Boy said. 'I never know anything. You'd better get used to it.'

But it wasn't always like this, Boy realised as soon as he said it. He was too out of breath to explain to Willow, but Valerian was different. Worse.

Boy was used to his moods, used to getting beaten, used to being ignored – but Valerian had definitely changed. Over the last few months he had become distracted. And now Boy knew why.

Four days to live.

Why?

What it was that was haunting Valerian remained obscured to Boy, but his master had been clear enough. Boy wondered if Valerian was deluding himself. How could he know he had only four days to live? Maybe Valerian had gone a little crazy and was convinced by some make-believe of his own invention.

But no. That would not be like Valerian.

Four days . . . That would take him to New Year's Eve, Boy realised. What could happen that Valerian could be so possessed by?

He had become obsessed. The stage act had become unimportant to Valerian – he had merely been going through the motions for a long time. That was why Boy had not been surprised when his meeting with Green turned out not to be anything to do with the act. Instead Valerian had been expecting a name – a name that he had been searching for.

It was still the first hour of December the 28th.

'Childermass,' Valerian had said quietly as he dropped the automatic latch on the door to the Yellow House.

'Sorry?' Boy had said.

Valerian glowered at them both.

'Childermass,' Valerian said, and began to walk. He called over his shoulder without looking back, 'Today is Childermass. The unluckiest day of the year.'

'Oh,' said Boy, looking at Willow, who opened her mouth to speak but said nothing.

They had trotted after Valerian, who was twenty long paces away already.

'Where do you think we are going?' Willow asked. Boy did not reply, but began to scratch his nose. Willow did not give up.

'Valerian!' she called.

Boy looked at her in alarm, for she still did not understand how to speak to Valerian, how to wait until he spoke to you.

'Valerian, where are we going?'

He did not turn round.

'Valerian!' she called, louder this time. 'Where are–'

And now Valerian was with them. Somehow he covered the paces from where he had been, and loomed over them in the deserted street. His eyes burnt through the darkness at Willow, and she began to shake. It was as if she was standing naked in a snowstorm – she felt cold and small and fragile. Valerian held her gaze until she finally pulled her eyes away and stared at the ground.

'Be quiet, Girl,' he hissed, 'or I'll leave you to rot here.'

He turned and strode off again.

'I told you,' said Boy. 'I told you. Don't upset him.'

He looked at Willow, then saw Valerian about to disappear down yet another shabby alleyway. He looked back at Willow. Her face was drawn and pale.

Boy put his hand on her shoulder.

'Come on.'

'How does he do that?' she asked.

Valerian had vanished around the corner.

Boy tugged at her arm anxiously.

'Come on,' he said. 'We're better off with him.'

Willow still didn't move.

'I know,' he said, 'I know what it's like. But really, it's best if we keep going. Stay with him.'

Willow nodded her head slowly.

'Where's he gone now?' he moaned. 'Come on, Willow. Please?'

At last she began to walk. Boy pulled her sleeve and she sped up slightly, but Boy knew that Valerian would be getting further ahead with every stride.

Valerian had gone down a small alley on the left, but now they were closer, Boy could see there were three of them leading off into even deeper darknesses, and he had no idea which one his master had taken. He scratched his nose.

The thought of being alone in the City at night worried him. It brought back memories of things he had half-forgotten, of all the years he had lived alone on the streets.

Boy hesitated, and the longer he hesitated, the further away Valerian would be getting.

Grabbing Willow by the hand he ran down the nearest alleyway, his boots plucking at the mud and filth underfoot.

'Valerian,' he called, but quietly. 'Valerian!'

It was so dark in the passage that he could barely see.

'Where is he?' Willow asked, still sounding shaken.

Boy kept running.

Suddenly they came out into a torchlit square. It was vast and empty. Beautiful old buildings leant inwards on all four sides, as if trying to get closer to each other across the cobbles that lay between them. Boy took in the square. Compared to the darkness of the alley, the light from the torches was amazingly bright.

There!

There was Valerian, unmistakable, about to disappear down a street that led off the far corner of the square.

Without a word Boy and Willow raced across the open space, feeling vulnerable and watched as they went. The City was quiet, and there still seemed to be no one else around. The sound of their boots on the cobbles of the square rang out like pistol shots.

They made it across and turned into the street Valerian had taken. Boy noticed the name of the street: The Dead-way. Another bad omen.

Valerian was waiting.

'You two make more noise than I care to hear,' he said as they arrived, panting heavily, but he waited for them to get their breath back without further comment.

'Right,' he said. 'Nearly there. Then our work begins.'

The look on his face was deadly serious. There was no anger or intimidation this time, none of his tricks of scaring the hearts out of them.

Just . . . thought Boy. *Just . . . fear?*

Could Valerian be scared? It seemed unlikely.

Valerian set off.

Boy looked at Willow.

'Are you all right now?' he asked as they followed.

She nodded, forcing a smile.

'I know,' Boy whispered. 'He's . . . difficult. But better the devil you know.'

Though Boy said this quietly, Valerian heard.

'What did you say, Boy?' he asked, though not angrily. 'A fair quote from you for once. But do not mention his name here.'

They had come to the end of The Deadway, and stopped.

Before them stood a huge pair of ornate bronze gates set into a long, high stone wall. The gates were covered in iron pictures of confusing and frightening design. Human figures, mostly naked, writhed and hung in peculiar postures and agonising angles from the bars of the gates. Here and there Boy and Willow could see less-than-human figures, but they were not in pain. They grinned demonically and held long sticks or poles or spears, with which they were pricking and piercing the bodies.

'What is this place?' Willow whispered, but Boy had understood.

'Look,' he said.

His voice was deathly. He pointed through the bars of the gates to where, beyond the walls, stretched row after row of cold, grey gravestones.

Above the gates was an arch, upon which were carved some strange words.

'What does that say?' Boy asked Valerian quietly.

'Is your reading still so bad?' Valerian sniped, but merely from habit. There was no life in his voice.

'But it's strange,' Boy protested.

'It's Latin,' Valerian said, 'and it's high time you learnt

some. *Mille habet mors portas quibus exeat vita. Unam inveniam.* It means, more or less, "Death has a thousand doors to let out life. I shall find one." '

3

It was bitterly cold. Boy and Willow were shivering, but not just from the temperature. Row after row of lifeless stones faded away around them into the darkness of the cemetery. They had crept inside through the massive iron gates, which were not locked. They could just make out shapes from the moonlight which slanted low over the wall of the cemetery. The land sloped slightly from where they stood, so that even in the darkness they could see the stones rising away from them. There were thousands, some small and plain, some big, some carved with complex designs. Some were not stones at all but impressive tombs made of huge blocks of stone, surrounded by spiked railings. They were designed to keep people out, though Boy thought how strange they looked, like cages, as if they were actually meant to keep people *in*.

'What are we doing here?' Willow whispered.

Boy shook his head.

'I don't know. He's just got a habit of finding unpleasant places to be.'

'Boy,' said Willow, 'If you don't ask him, I will.'

Boy looked at her, wondering if she'd learnt nothing from her recent experience of Valerian's moods.

'I mean it,' Willow said.

'All right!' he said. 'All right.'

Valerian stood a few paces away, trying to get his bearings in the endless death-field.

Boy approached slowly. Gingerly he tugged at the tall man's sleeve.

'Valerian,' he said.

'Ah! Boy!' Valerian said. 'Good. Now, take these.'

He pulled two candles from his pocket and a couple of large matches.

'There's not too much wind – we won't need lamps. I can almost smell it now! This *must* be the one.'

'Valerian,' Boy was firmer this time.

Valerian looked down at him distractedly.

'Yes, Boy, what is it?'

'What are we doing here?'

A shadow swept across Valerian's face, a flicker of rage.

'I don't have time to debate it, Boy! Don't you understand? Time is running out. Today is the twenty-eighth.'

'No, I don't understand,' shouted Boy, 'because you never tell me anything!'

Valerian clapped a hand across Boy's mouth and held it there.

Willow ran over, then stopped, seeing that Boy was not actually being harmed. She hesitated.

'How many times do I–' Valerian hissed. Willow stared at him. She saw the anger slip from his face.

'No,' he said quietly, and took his hand from Boy's mouth. Willow stepped to Boy's side and held his arm.

'No,' said Valerian again. 'You are right, Boy. I should tell you.'

Boy looked at him intently, waiting.

'I will tell you, but not now. There's no time now. First we must find it.'

'But what?' asked Boy.

'The grave. The grave of Gad Beebe. Isn't that obvious?'

No, it isn't, Boy thought, but he nodded. He smiled.

'That was what the music box told us?' asked Willow. 'To come here?'

'Yes,' said Valerian. 'Well, no, not exactly. I was looking for a grave, and now I have a name. We are looking for the grave of Gad Beebe, and this is the biggest cemetery in the City. We have to start somewhere!'

'And what then? When we find it? Why is it so important?'

'Later. We are running out of time. We'll find the grave first and then – damn!'

'What?' asked Boy.

'A spade. I forgot to bring a spade.'

Valerian stamped his foot and swore at the sky.

'Why do we need a spade?' asked Willow, but she and Boy had a terrible feeling they knew why.

'To dig his grave, of course. Never mind, there must be a sexton's hut here somewhere. The first thing is to find it. Now, let's get these candles alight . . .'

A succession of thoughts swept through Boy's mind, all of them ghastly. The news that was rife in the City about the Phantom and grave-robbers sprang to his mind. He looked at Valerian. Was it possible that he was the one who had been breaking into people's graves? Could Valerian be capable of such a thing?

Of course he could.

'No,' Boy said, 'I won't do it!'

Willow looked at Boy, surprised. Valerian too.

'What now?' he asked. 'Can't you see we must get on?'

'You can get on without me,' said Boy. 'I won't do it. I've done a lot of terrible things for you, but I won't do this.'

'Do what?' asked Valerian, the beginnings of a smile on his face.

'I won't steal people's bodies. People's . . . dead bodies.'

Valerian laughed. A short bark of a laugh. Then he shot a glance around him, and was silent.

'But Boy,' he smiled, 'we're not looking for a body! We're looking for a book.'

4

'Right. To save time, we'll split up. Here, take a candle each of you. Now, Boy, you go along this wall and work inwards, row by row. Work systematically and do not miss one out. Not one. You, Girl–'

'My name's Willow,' she said, then remembered that terrible look he had given her, 'sir.'

But Valerian was too busy thinking to care.

'Willow, go along the other wall. Do the same as Boy. Do not miss one out. I will go up this central avenue and work outwards. It's nearly the third hour after midnight. Meet back here in an hour. And remember – Gad Beebe. Inside his grave we will find the book, and then . . .'

His voice tailed off. He pulled a third candle from his pocket, and as much to amuse himself as to impress Boy and Willow, he pulled it out already alight.

'Can you teach me to do that?' asked Willow, but Valerian did not bother to reply.

Valerian went up the stony path that led into the dark heart of the cemetery, his small candle flickering in his hand, casting weak but unnerving shadows on the stones around him.

Boy and Willow looked at each other. They looked down the separate routes they were supposed to take, leading off into the pitch-black night.

'Book?' asked Willow. 'What's so important about a book?'

Boy shrugged.

'He's always going on about books, how important they are and why I have to learn to read better.'

'Maybe, but that's not enough of a reason to dig them up from graves, is it?'

'I don't know,' he said, 'but then I never do. I just do what Valerian tells me. Life's easier that way.'

Willow looked at him sadly, then she glanced down the rows of elaborate, ornamented graves, and shivered.

'Supposing', said Boy, 'we do half an hour my way and then half an hour your way? That would be about the same thing, wouldn't it?'

No, thought Willow, *it wouldn't*.

'Near enough,' she said, trying to sound bright. 'Anyway, if one of us holds the candles and the other does the reading, we'll be faster.'

'Yes,' said Boy, 'especially if you do the reading,' he added, shuffling slightly where he stood.

Willow smiled.

'Which way first?' she said.

Boy looked at the options.

'This way,' he said.

'Why?'

'No idea. Willow?'

'What?'

'How will we know when an hour has passed?'

'I have no idea. It's about as long as one of Madame's performances and one of Valerian's put together, but you know how time moves differently when you're doing . . . different things.'

'Yes,' agreed Boy.

He had a feeling this was going to be a very long hour.

Elsewhere in the cemetery, Valerian was thinking about time too. In his eyes, time was speeding up, every day, every hour. It seemed to him that every second lasted half the time of the one before, as if time was accelerating towards the end of the year. The end of the year, and the end . . .

He pushed the thought from his mind as he bent down to peer at the seventy-third gravestone he had looked at.

Trying to stay calm, he noted the name. Gad Beebe? No.

Gad Beebe? What kind of name was that? An important one. For Valerian it was a very important one.

What was today?

The twenty-eighth. Just three days left after today. Three days to find an answer, and so much depended on Kepler. Once, many years ago, he had trusted him completely, but things had changed. But he had always respected his learning, and now the stakes were high he needed all the help he could get.

Seventy-fourth. No.

Kepler. The camera obscura worked like a dream. It had cost everything Valerian had earned from the theatre for the last year, but it was worth it. Kepler had laughed at him when he'd first asked him to make it. What is the use? he'd scoffed. It will be of no use to you, at the end. It will not save you to see Fate approaching!

Seventy-fifth. No.

But then, when Valerian had persisted, he had changed his mind. Very well, he had said. Very well, I will waste your money. It will be expensive, he had said. I only make the best pieces of optical equipment.

Seventy-sixth. No.

And so they had agreed, and Valerian had slogged away at that stupid act for another year until the camera was built. Kepler had called him paranoid. Paranoid! He'd be paranoid himself, thought Valerian, if *his* time was running out. If something was coming for *him* he'd damn well be paranoid too!

Seventy-seventh. No.

Valerian straightened and moved on to the next stone, beginning to doubt he was going about this the right way. He knew there had to be a better answer, but just as an idea came into his head, his attention was caught by something up ahead.

A light.

There was a weak light flickering in the darkness ahead of him.

'That boy can't get anything right!' he cursed under his breath. 'I told him to stick to the wall.'

Valerian plucked another candle from his pocket and lit it from the one he was holding. No tricks this time. Pushing the candle into the earth of number seventy-eight to mark his place, he strode off to see what his boy was up to.

Approaching the source of the light, his eyes widened with surprise.

'Well! Hello, Valerian,' said a high, cracked voice.

Valerian turned to run, but a blow to the back of his head had him out cold before he even hit the ground.

5

'What?' whispered Boy.

'What?' replied Willow.

'What did you say?' Boy asked.

'I didn't say anything,' she said.

They were hunched over a grave. Yet another grave. They had been searching stone after stone, until the carved names had become a blur. Nowhere had there been a trace of anyone with a name even vaguely resembling that of Gad Beebe.

'What was that noise?'

'You're imagining things,' said Willow, as much to convince herself as anything.

'Isn't that an hour yet?' asked Boy.

'Yes,' she said. 'Yes, it must be. Come on, let's go back.'

'You are sure it's an hour?' Boy asked. 'I mean, we don't want to—'

At that moment there was another noise, the click of metal on metal, and although it came from a distance, they both heard it.

They froze.

'The candle!' Willow warned.

Boy blew the candle out. Utter blackness surrounded them. After a few moments they began to see a little as their eyes widened to catch as much light as possible. In the vague-grey shadow world, they suddenly both saw the same thing – a flicker of yellow light away to their left, in the heart of the cemetery.

'It must be Valerian,' said Willow.

'Why?'

'Well, who else would be out here?'

Boy didn't want to even think about the answer to that question.

'Yes,' he said, 'it must be. Come on. We may as well meet him there.'

They set off in the darkness and immediately Boy walked into a gravestone. The moonlight had vanished behind a bank of cloud and with no light to guide them the grey stones were as good as invisible. He picked himself up, silently cursing Valerian.

'Boy!' hissed Willow. 'Here's the path. Come on. When you get your feet on it you can follow the stones.'

She was right. By the feel and the sound of the grit underfoot they made their way more quickly towards the light. Boy found that by looking straight ahead rather than at his feet, he could see the faint grey ghost of the path better.

As they got near, something started to worry Boy.

'Willow?' he said quietly.

She ignored him. Either that or she hadn't heard him.

'Willow?' he said, stopping in his tracks.

She turned.

'Come on,' she complained. 'What is it now? I just want to go home.'

'Willow, I don't think that's Valerian.'

'Don't be difficult,' she said. 'Who else could it be?'

Her voice tailed off as she realised the double meaning of her words.

'And,' said Boy, 'Valerian went that way.'

Willow couldn't see the arm he waved in the darkness, but she understood.

For a long time they paused, uncertain what to do. The light was no more than a hundred feet away now and they could hear vague sounds coming to them across the stones.

'What if it *is* him?' Boy said.

'We'll have to go and see,' Willow said.

Boy pulled a face in the darkness.

'All right,' he said, 'but let's be careful. Please.'

Getting down on their hands and knees, they crawled the remaining distance between them and the light, leaving the path and cutting across the rows of small stones and larger memorials.

Boy could feel the damp of the scraggy grass begin to soak through to his knees. His hands pushed into patches of mud, cold but not yet frozen as it soon would as the winter hardened.

After a few minutes he could no longer feel his fingers; a little further and his hands had gone numb.

Still they pressed on, and as they neared the light and sound they saw they were right to have been cautious. It was obvious even from a distance that they were not the only ones working in the cemetery that night.

They came to a large tomb, with mourning angels surmounting the heavy stone cap, and decided to hide behind it. Peeping around the side of the grave, they had a clear view of an unholy scene.

Three men were hard at work in a grave. Around them lay various tools. Beside them a mound of earth spoil was piled on to a large sheet of canvas. A small glass lantern propped against a neighbouring gravestone illuminated the scene. The shadows it cast were long and grim. There was a spare shovel and an iron bar with a hooked end. And there was a large canvas bag with a lump inside it – a large, disturbing lump.

'Grave robbers!' hissed Willow in alarm.

Boy nodded.

There was no sign of Valerian.

'Come on,' said Boy.

Willow ignored him, trying to work out what was wrong with the scene.

The figures in front of them were shovelling earth back into the grave. It was obvious what was in the large sack next to them on the grass.

'Wait,' said Willow. 'Look. They're going. Let's wait.'

'Let's just find Valerian and get out of here.'

'In a minute. Look, they're going.'

It was true. The men worked fast and as soon as they had finished it took them no more than a second or two to gather their things, including the hideous bag, and leave. They swung away into the night, straight down the centre path of the cemetery, as bold as could be.

'He could never keep his nose out,' said one of the men. Boy and Willow started at the sound of his voice. It was high and wavered like that of a dying man.

Boy thought he heard another of them laugh, but maybe he was just imagining it.

Willow meanwhile had abandoned their hiding place and was scampering over to the grave.

Horrified, Boy hesitated by the tomb, unsure if it was more dangerous to follow or to stay where he was. Another glance behind at the yawning rows of death in the darkness persuaded him to move.

When he caught up with Willow she was crouching on the grass by the grave.

'Willow,' pleaded Boy, 'come on. Please. Let's just–'

'Look,' she said. 'You would hardly notice they'd been here. A bit of loose soil, but otherwise . . . just the grave, but then if it was a new one it would look like that anyway.'

She nodded at the fresh soil of the grave.

'Boy,' she said, 'what was wrong with what you just saw?'

Boy frowned at her, but it was wasted in the darkness.

'Apart from the fact they just stole some . . . body?' he asked, sarcastically.

'Exactly!' she said. 'They stole somebody. Well?'

Boy shook his head and looked around, expecting the grave robbers to return at any moment. He noticed a sickly light in the sky. It was still a fair time until dawn, but they could at least see more easily now.

'Look,' Willow said, 'I'm not an expert on the ways of resurrection men, but why would they fill the grave back up once they'd taken the . . . you know.'

'I don't know,' he said. 'All right, so it's strange, but could we find Valerian and discuss it at home?'

'Surely they'd just run – unless they needed to cover their tracks.'

'Or cover something up,' said Boy, despite himself.

'Or some . . . No, that's too horrible.'

They were silent as they stared at the freshly-turned soil at their feet. The daylight was coming stronger and faster now, casting weak light across the vast sprawling area of decay around them.

'Did you hear . . . ?' asked Willow suddenly.

Boy nodded, clenching his mouth tight shut and trying not to scream.

From the grave, just by their feet, they could hear a faint ticking sound. Faint but definite. It grew louder, became a knocking, regular and strong, then stopped.

94

Boy and Willow clutched each other. The noise started again.

Suddenly they understood, and both fell scratching and scrabbling madly at the loose pile of earth in front of them. The soil was not tightly packed but had already started to freeze in the cold morning air, and their hands were still numb and sore from their crawl across the cemetery.

They dug with claw-like hands until they were just paws of mud, scraping up fist after fist of grave-earth, until finally, gasping and straining, they reached the lid of the box.

It was broken. Of course it was broken, for it had already been broached earlier that night to release its horrible but valuable contents.

Were it not for this, they would not have saved him. In the time it would have taken them to find a pick or a chisel and smash their way clumsily into the coffin, he would have been dead.

As it was, it was a near thing. Their weak, failing hands barely managed to prise the broken portion of coffin lid out of the ground to reveal the choking, injured and terrified figure lying there.

Without a word, Boy and Willow fought the remaining soil to give up its prize. Boy began to pull at one of his arms, but as he did so a howl of pain ripped through the air. They put all their weight into pulling him up by his shoulders and then, at last, it was done.

Valerian lay coughing and spluttering on the mess of grass and earth beside the grave, half-dead, his right arm broken and hanging at a disgusting angle.

Next to him Boy and Willow crouched on all fours, panting like dogs, trying to breathe.

6

The journey back to the Yellow House was difficult and slow. Dawn had broken blue and bright before they were halfway back. It was hard going.

Boy was used to running and trotting after Valerian as he strode around the City, but now their roles were reversed. Boy and Willow had to lead him cautiously back through the twisting streets. He stopped frequently, the pain from his broken arm coming in surges, overwhelming him. They had tied the end of his right sleeve to the collar of his coat, in an attempt to fashion a sling to stop him from doing his arm more damage, but it was far from perfect. Willow had nearly been sick as they had moved Valerian's arm back into something like the right position, and he had screamed with pain more than once.

Boy's mind raced. Who had done this to Valerian? Someone had buried him alive – the man with the cracked voice and the others. Was it just because he had disturbed them at their grave-robbing? Nothing made sense.

Boy feared for the future. Valerian was difficult, unpleasant, violent and sour, but at least he kept Boy safe, more or less. Now here Boy was leading *him* back home.

'Nearly there, are we, Boy?' he would ask. 'Nearly there?'

Boy shuddered. They were nowhere near home yet. Why didn't Valerian know that?

But at last they were leaning Valerian against the posts of the outer doors of the Yellow House.

'Pocket,' mumbled Valerian, unable to say any more.

Boy fumbled in Valerian's right-hand pocket until he found his big bunch of heavy keys.

It took Boy a while to find the right one – a sudden clumsiness overtook him as he listened to Willow trying to soothe Valerian.

'Just a minute more, Valerian,' she was saying, 'and we'll get you into bed. You need to rest.'

Finally Boy turned the tumblers of the lock and they half-dragged Valerian inside.

It seemed to take the last of Valerian's strength to get upstairs to the first floor, where his bedrooms were. Even then Boy and Willow had to do their best to lift him up each of the ancient wooden stairs and then along the corridor.

They sat him on the bed and pulled his boots off. When they stood up, the huge man had passed out on the covers. They could not move him any more.

'What about this?' asked Willow, holding up a blanket she had found in a box at the foot of the bed.

Boy nodded.

They covered him up with the deep red quilted blanket and stood back.

'What are we going to do?' asked Willow quietly.

Boy said nothing.

'A doctor,' Willow went on. 'We must fetch a doctor.'

Boy hesitated.

'I don't know,' he said, 'He hates anyone coming here. He hates doctors. He hates interference.'

'But he's in trouble. And we can't do anything.'

'There's only Kepler. I don't even know if he's a real doctor, but–'

'You must go and get him,' said Willow firmly. 'You must get him to come and mend Valerian's arm.'

'Now?'

'Yes.'

'But it's early still. Willow, it's early and I haven't had any sleep. I can't go now. Look at me! Look at us.'

They were still covered in grime and mud from the cemetery.

'Please, Willow,' said Boy, 'I'm so tired . . .'

At the mention of this word, Willow felt her energy slip away.

'Well, he's safe enough for now, I suppose,' she said, looking down at where Valerian lay sprawled across the bed.

She went and sat by him, and then put out a hand to gently touch his forehead. He didn't react, but he was breathing.

'I'll go,' said Boy, sitting down on the bed too. 'Just let me have a little sleep first.'

He looked at his master and felt a rush of panic clear his tiredness for a moment.

'Valerian! Valerian!' he whispered, but there was no response.

Glancing away he saw that Willow had dropped off to sleep beside him.

Boy put his head on the covers next to hers and they slept deep, but troubled, sleep.

98

7

Boy woke screaming, waving his arms out in front of him, pushing at a coffin lid he thought was closing him away from the light for ever.

With his hands still covered in the soil from the grave it was all too easy to dream that it was he and not Valerian who had nearly been buried alive. What a way to kill someone! Boy thought.

He gazed around.

Valerian's room. He remembered bits of the night before. He felt like crying, but tears would not come.

Willow lay snoring softly, tucked in against Valerian's side like a kitten with its mother.

Valerian had not moved from where he lay on his back, more unconscious than asleep, Boy guessed.

And then Valerian spoke.

'Coming!' he said. 'It's coming . . .'

Boy jerked upright. He had never heard anyone talk in their sleep before. He stared at Valerian.

'It's coming!' Valerian mumbled again, barely opening his mouth. The words were slurred and unclear, but they did not stop.

'Time! What's the time? Boy, where are you?'

'Here!' Boy said urgently. 'Valerian, I'm here!'

But Valerian was not listening, only talking.

'Time . . . running out now . . . when? What's the day, today . . . Boy . . . time . . . it's coming.'

Boy tried again to reach Valerian.

'What's coming, Valerian?' he asked.

'Time,' said Valerian.

Was that an answer?

'What's coming? What's the matter?'

'Time is coming. The time is coming,' said Valerian.

'What's the matter, Valerian? What's happening to you?' Boy persisted, desperate now.

'The time . . . time coming . . . the book! Must . . . the book! Oh please . . . the book . . . The Eve of the Year . . .'

The book again! Boy knelt over Valerian, trying to catch every word, but as he did so a knocking from the front door made him jump. No one ever came to the house – no one unexpected. No one called to see Valerian without having been summoned by Boy. Even then Boy could only remember Kepler visiting.

For a moment he thought he might have imagined the sound, but it came again, louder this time. Someone was definitely there.

'Open up!' came a shout from the street.

Boy left the bedroom and ran lightly down the corridor to a small leaded window that looked over the front of the house and down on to the street.

He could just see a red feather.

His heart began to race.

The knocking on the door resumed, louder than ever.

He ran on tiptoe back to the bedroom and found Willow awake and blinking in the strong light of late morning.

'What is it?' she asked. 'What's that noise?'

'Watchmen outside!' hissed Boy, his eyes wide.

100

She nodded.

'Go and hide in my room,' said Boy. 'I'll get rid of them.'

'How? Don't be stupid! We must run!'

'We can't!' Boy said, pointing at Valerian.

'We'll just have to wait until they've gone away.'

'*If* they go away,' said Boy.

They cowered on the bed, not knowing whether to hide or run. They listened to the knocking on the door getting louder and louder, just as their hearts were thumping harder and harder in their chests.

'Open up! We demand you open up!'

'They know we're here,' hissed Willow.

'Maybe,' Boy whispered back, 'maybe not. Just don't move.'

'Open up! Persons in this house are wanted on suspicion of murder!'

Boy put out his hand to stop Willow from speaking.

'I don't think they know that we're here. Just wait.'

The banging on the door went on for another few minutes, and then stopped.

Willow made to get up from the bed, but Boy waved her to sit down.

'Wait,' he mouthed.

Sure enough, a moment later there was another banging on the door. They waited for it to stop, and finally it did. Boy made Willow sit still for nearly five more minutes before he got up and crept to the window.

'They've gone, I think,' he said. 'We've got to leave before they come back.'

'But supposing they've left someone watching the house?' Willow cried.

'What is all this noise?'

Boy and Willow turned and stared.

Valerian stood by the bed.

He looked like death. His clothes were covered in grave-soil, his hair stuck up at stupid angles, and his right arm hung limply by his side, having loosed itself from the make-shift sling.

'Valerian!' cried Boy.

'Boy, be quiet! I can't stand you shouting and wailing all the time! I want quiet!'

Valerian swung his good arm in front of him wildly. He fumbled in his inside pocket and pulled something out, which he raised to his lips. He tipped his head back and drank, then threw the object to the floor.

It was a small glass bottle, not much larger than a phial. Valerian wiped the back of his left hand across his lips and looked at the pair of them. He saw them looking at the bottle on the floor.

'For the pain,' he explained. 'One of Kepler's more useful concoctions.'

'But your arm!' Boy said.

'Is broken. Yes,' said Valerian. 'But there are more important things to deal with.'

'Who was that,' Boy asked, 'in the cemetery? Who did that to you?'

Valerian ignored him.

'We have much to do, and time is running short.'

'I don't believe you!' shouted Willow, breaking her silence. 'I don't believe you! You have us crawling around that death-field all night, hunting for some stupid book. You're practically buried alive and we dig you out with our bare hands and drag you home! And you won't even tell us what it's about! I hate you!'

Boy turned in horror to Willow, and when she had finished, he shook her by the arm.

'She doesn't meant it, Valerian,' Boy said. 'She's just tired and we don't need to—'

But Valerian held up his hand, his only good hand.

'No,' he said, 'the girl is right. It is time to tell you, but we must act fast. I was a fool last night. I thought once I had the name it would be a simple thing to find the grave where the book . . . and then . . . And then I was a fool to risk the cemetery. Those were old acquaintances of mine. I owe them money – quite a lot of money for some things they obtained for me once upon a time. Never mind that now, I must be brief. They seemed to think that putting me in the earth was an appropriate way of settling our differences.'

'But—'

'Listen. I am alive. I want to stay that way. And on the Eve of New Year I will face something much worse than a few grubby resurrection men, unless I can find a way out.'

They nodded.

'I need your help,' said Valerian and then, looking at his broken arm, 'more than ever now.'

8

'What's her name?' Valerian asked Boy.

'Her name is Willow,' she said crossly.

'Willow,' said Valerian. 'Willow, would you go to the Tower and get as many of those as you can find?'

He pointed with his foot at the empty bottle on the wooden floor.

'They're in a cupboard by the narrow window. Boy, where are my keys? Quickly! We have no time to lose.'

Boy found the keys on the floor of Valerian's bedroom where he had dropped them.

'Here,' said Valerian, giving the key to the Tower to Willow.

Boy stared. Valerian was actually giving one of his keys to someone else. To a girl he barely knew! Boy had never had possession of any of his keys before early that morning when he'd plucked them from Valerian's deep pocket.

Willow ran off to the Tower.

'Now, Boy, I need you to do something for me. I wasted time by hunting round the cemetery at random. Why?'

'Because it was too big', ventured Boy, 'and too dark?'

'Partly,' said Valerian, 'but something else too. Do you suppose that's the only cemetery in the City?'

Boy understood.

'You don't even know which cemetery he's buried in? Beebe?'

'Exactly. We were in the largest one, but there are others. And what else?'

Boy thought hard. There were cemeteries and then there were . . . churches!

'Church graveyards!'

'Good!' cried Valerian. 'And have you any idea how many churches and how many churchyards there are in the City?'

Boy thought.

'A dozen?' he asked.

'A hundred and seven. And how long is it going to take us to look through them all?'

Boy thought hard again.

'A very long time?'

'No,' said Valerian, 'it's not going to take us any time at all, because we're not going to look. We're going to find out exactly where Gad Beebe is buried first. I need you to visit someone – the Master of City Burials. I should have done this before, only . . . he's an awkward man.'

'Is he a friend of yours?' asked Boy.

Valerian frowned.

'I know him. At least I used to, in my days at the Academy. He is the only source of cadavers for dissection in the City. Well, the only official source.'

Valerian saw the question on Boy's lips.

'Work it out, Boy! Would it be clearer if I said "bodies to cut up"? To study the nature of the human organism. So I had a few dealings with him until I . . . left . . . academia. There's a building in The Reach that's his official residence. Go there and tell him Valerian sent you. Tell him I need to know the whereabouts of a grave.'

Boy knew The Reach. It was a rich part of town. Before

Valerian had found him, he had often spent summer days there, begging and, when no one was being generous, picking pockets.

'You must go there and get the location of Beebe's burial. All burials that occur in the City are recorded there. All official ones, that is.'

Valerian brushed at the dirt on his coat.

Boy thought about it for a moment.

'What will you do?' he asked.

A look of irritation crossed Valerian's face, but it passed.

'The girl – Willow and I will go to Kepler. I need him to mend my arm. I need someone to help me. I also need someone to go to the Master of Burials, and that will be you. You know the way there and Willow does not. Meet us back here this evening. Only enter the house after dark, light no lights and answer the door to no one. The place is safe enough.'

'How will I get in if I get back first?'

Boy thought about the shock he'd had the time he'd tried to pick the lock.

Valerian smiled.

'It's time you had your own key.'

He pulled a key from the bunch and handed it to Boy.

'The only spare. Don't lose it. Now, back here after dark with the name of the cemetery. Understand?'

Boy nodded, as usual.

'Then go! And do not fail!'

Boy turned to go.

'Valerian.'

'What is it?'

'You said he was awkward. The Master of Burials. What do you mean?'

'He is cantankerous. Prone to strange moods. And difficult to work with, too. When I last knew him he had become involved in some studies of his own. I never found out what. It made it impossible to get what we needed from him any more, and we had to use . . . alternative sources. That's all.'

Boy hesitated still.

'You have nothing to fear! Now, go!' Valerian said, and pushed Boy towards the door.

Boy fled from the house, clutching his key, without even telling Willow where he was going. And this time Valerian would not be there to get him out of trouble.

9

It was long past noon. Boy trotted along the streets, out of habit keeping to the shadows and smaller alleys. He had never liked being on his own, and with the thought of those feather-brained, feather-hatted Watchmen on the lookout for him too, he felt more timid than usual.

It was December the 28th. The sky was clear and ice-blue. Columns of grey smoke twisted feebly up to meet it from chimneys and other funnels on the rooftops. It was still cold, if anything colder than it had yet been all winter, but there was still no sign of the snow that Willow had sensed.

It was a busy day, with people going about their business in the street and behind doors.

Boy had not even had time to clean his hands, and as he made his way along the streets he picked at the soil stuck to his fingers. It gave him the creeps.

He had entered a dream-world. Two days ago everything had been normal, or as normal as life ever was with Valerian.

But everything had changed. Although Boy knew that things had started to change for Valerian months ago, it seemed to be coming to a head now, in these last days of the year.

The festivities and celebrations were over, for the time being, until another burst of frenetic fun at New Year. The

City had been a riot of noise and rare winter colour up to the 25th. Despite the poverty that most people struggled against, they somehow saved and hoarded all the little luxuries they could for the mid-winter feast. Maybe some rare dried fruit, some decent wine or strong beer was all it took to warm their hearts for a few days, reminding them that winter could not last for ever, that spring would return eventually, bursting green and golden. For those very few of the City who were rich, it was a time of greater indulgence and the giving and receiving of gifts, but the purpose of the festivities was just the same, creating a candle-bright haven in the depths of winter.

Now, in the few days before the New Year arrived, there was a lull. It was an unusual time, Boy thought, and he knew he had always felt this. Even in the days before Valerian, the days on his own, when he had lived like a mouse in the hidden nooks and crannies of the City, he had always felt these few days before the New Year to be different from the rest. This interlude was a strange and quiet time, a time somehow outside the rest of the year, outside time itself. It was as if the rest of the year were alive, but these days were dead.

Boy was not surprised that if he *had* entered a dream-world, it had happened during the dead days.

He had had barely any sleep – perhaps that was adding to his sense of the unreal. But it was true that he had been in a prison cell, under suspicion of involvement in the murder of his – and Valerian's – former employer. Korp had been spread all over the box where Boy had spent whatever free time he could. Willow and Boy had been incarcerated in the Watchmen's Citadel, and Valerian had effected a daring escape. They had spent a night crawling around a cemetery looking not for a body, but for a book. Surely a library was the place to look for a book? And he and Willow had then pulled his master half-alive from a freshly-robbed grave.

This was not normal, even for life with Valerian. And Valerian had told them there was worse to come. Nothing Boy knew, or had ever known about Valerian made him doubt it.

Boy trotted along through the City, grim resolution on his face.

10

'Where did you find him?' asked Willow.

'Do you always ask so many questions?' said Valerian, irritated.

'Only when I want to know something,' she said. 'So where did you find him?'

Valerian and Willow were slowly making their way to see Kepler. Willow kept forgetting the reason for their visit, kept forgetting that Valerian's arm was broken. The drug – whatever it was he had taken in the house – was doing a remarkable job of shielding him from the pain. Willow had retied his arm in something much more like a proper sling, and tucked the loose sleeve of his long dark coat into its pocket.

'You wouldn't even know there was anything wrong,' she had said, 'unless you looked hard.'

'I can tell you there's something wrong,' said Valerian, and took a small swig from one of the bottles Willow had found in the cupboard.

'Well?' Willow pressed, but gently. 'Where did you find him?'

Valerian looked down sideways at her, narrowing his eyes, but he was too sleepy from the drug to be really annoyed. He began to talk.

'Boy fell from the sky,' he said, 'sort of. In a church. I was

111

in a church – not something I make a habit of, but it was raining hard and it was somewhere dry, if not warm. And he was in one of his hiding places. I think he had lots of them. He's good at getting into small spaces – that's why I thought he'd be good for the act. Anyway, I was talking to . . . well, Korp, as it happens. Our dear departed Director. We had arranged to meet to discuss the act. And the next moment Boy fell on top of me, more or less. Here, we need to take that street over there.'

Valerian nodded and Willow steered them on their way.

'That can't be all, Valerian,' she said. 'Why does he live with you? What did he do before?'

'I don't know what he did before. He lived on the streets. He says he can't remember a time before that. He could speak, though, so he must have grown up with people somewhere or other.'

Willow nodded thoughtfully.

'And I taught him to read, though he is a terribly lazy scholar . . .'

Did she imagine it, or was there a slight softness in Valerian's voice?

'It must have been hard for him,' said Willow, trying to get Valerian to tell her more.

'What?' he snapped.

'Living by himself. In the City. That must have been hard.'

Valerian snorted.

'Maybe so, but he'd do better if he paid me more attention. It doesn't matter. The point is, he came to live with me. I had started to work at the theatre, being short of money, but although I had created an act, I needed help. I needed someone to be mine – someone who would do exactly what I told them without questioning why. Someone

112

I could trust. Boy's arrival was like a foretold event. It was meant to be, you see.'

'Not really,' said Willow.

'Well, there I was talking to Korp about my state of health, and the act, and the fact that I was nearly ready but just had to find the right assistant, and then . . . there he was. At my feet.'

'I see,' said Willow.

'And do you know, in a strange way I knew straight away he was the one. It was as though we had always been together. It works.'

'So why are you so hard on him?' asked Willow.

'I am not hard on him,' said Valerian. 'He needs a firm, guiding hand. He is prone to laziness and stupidity.'

Willow thought about defending Boy, but sensed Valerian's mood. She changed the subject.

'So why did he fall from his hiding place, then?'

'He said it was what I was saying.'

'What was that?'

'As I recall, I was explaining to Korp why I needed – why I had decided to create the act for the theatre. I was running short of . . . money. As a result of which, a . . . few problems had left me in a state of some ill health. A doctor was called. The doctor pronounced me either dead or dangerously sick. I understand it was those words that surprised Boy into relinquishing his grip on the stones.'

Willow frowned.

' "Dead or dangerously sick"?' she asked. 'What does that mean?'

'Well, I think Boy was as confused as you. This is, however, where I get my mistrust of doctors in general. The man was a charlatan, and nothing he did had the slightest to do with my survival and recovery.'

113

'And Kepler?' asked Willow, thinking of the doctor they were about to meet.

'Kepler is no ordinary doctor. In fact, Kepler is no ordinary man, and will do the best that can be done for my arm.'

11

A mile or two across the City Boy was nearing his destination – the wide and relatively clean street known as The Reach. Halfway along it lay the official residence of the Master of City Burials. Like many of the organisations that ran various aspects of City life, that of City Burials was a little strange. Like the others it operated from the official house of its Master. Each one was a small governance in its own right, with its own set of laws and rules and those in charge giving orders to those who obeyed, with the Master himself at the top.

Each was housed in a grand building, a reminder of the City's ancient and proud past. Some were now more than a little the worse for wear, according to the prosperity of the Chamber or Society that operated from them.

Of course, all these organisations were ultimately ruled by the Emperor, but in practice no one knew much about this. Emperor Frederick was a strange and remote figure, hidden away in the Palace. Something of a city within the City itself, the Palace occupied a vast area atop a low hill near the banks of the river. It was composed of a huge variety of buildings of various ages and styles clambering over one another for supremacy, and all surrounded by a high, crenellated wall. The title Emperor was something of a joke

– a pathetic hangover from the days when the City had been ruled by a leader of awesome power, when there had actually been an Empire to rule, of which the City was its magnificent capital. Not any more. Gone was the Empire, gone was the power and the magnificence of the City, and all that was left was Frederick, the last of his line, with no offspring to rule after him.

It was more than ten years since anyone outside the Palace had seen Frederick, and only then by accident. Life in the City functioned largely without him.

The building which housed City Burials was splendid and wealthy. Death was always good business, and since the Master's men co-ordinated all aspects of a person's life after death, from mortuary services to undertaking to burial and funerary rites, he was very wealthy indeed.

Boy stood on the other side of The Reach in a doorway opposite the ornate building. It stood imposingly, its front doors up a flight of at least a dozen stone steps, each door three times Boy's height, heavy and solid. On them hung huge polished door knockers, shaped like lions' heads.

There was an inscription in the stone above the doors.

'Latin, I suppose, Valerian,' Boy said to himself, and smiled. Then the smile drifted from his face. Valerian was in trouble. It was more than just a broken arm and it was up to Boy to find the solution.

He swallowed, looked up and down the street, and crossed. He skipped nimbly up the stone steps and, reaching up on tiptoe, swung one of the lions against its base.

The loud metal clunk seemed to echo the length of the street, but as Boy looked around nervously he was relieved to see that no one was paying him any attention. Nor, unfortunately, did anyone inside the building seem to have heard.

He swung the lion harder and waited.

'Side entrance,' said a voice beside him.

Startled, Boy looked to his right and noticed a small hatch set in the soaring pillars between which the doors remained implacably shut. Inside the pillar was a tiny room in which sat an incredibly small old woman, with a wrinkled face and an expression to match.

'Come about a death, have you? Round the side.'

'Yes – no – not exactly.'

The woman was unimpressed.

'Death? Round the side. Side door, see? That's where you register.'

Boy was puzzled.

'Then what do *you* do?' he asked.

'Well,' she said, 'I tell people about the side door.'

'That's it?' Boy asked. 'That's all you do?'

'It's important. Someone's got to tell people about the side door. For deaths. Important,' she added.

'And I wonder', he said, 'who tells me where to go if I haven't got a death to register.'

The woman looked blankly at him. She blinked.

'Well,' she said, peering anxiously around before answering, 'well, I could, probably, tell you.'

'Oh good,' said Boy. 'So where do I go to speak to the Master of City Burials?'

'Well, then you'd want to knock on the front door there and . . . *what*?' She spluttered to a stop. 'What do you mean? Don't waste my time!'

'No,' said Boy earnestly. 'No, I really need to see him. My master sent me – his name's Valerian. He said to say he sent me. We have to find out where someone is buried.'

'You can't see him. You think proles like you just wander in off the street for a chat?'

'But look,' he said, 'the thing is, Valerian, he's a friend of the Master. And he needs to find out something, about where a grave is–'

'Listen to me,' she said. 'Listen. No one gets to see him.'

'But I have to see him!' cried Boy.

'No!' snapped the woman. 'He's very busy working on his animals in the Dome. He won't think about anything else. No one talks to him.'

'What's he doing with animals? Doesn't he have lots of work to do for the cemeteries and so on?'

'Well, I don't know, of course, but he's been working in the Dome with his animals for years and it must be very important because he is the Master and it must have lots to do with burying people or he wouldn't be doing it.'

Boy was puzzled, but he nodded anyway.

'What is he doing with them?' he asked. 'What are the animals for?'

'Well, nothing much. They're dead, you see.'

A creeping little curiosity inside Boy told him he was going to have to find out what the Master of City Burials was doing before he went back to Valerian.

12

This was something Boy was good at.

Creeping and climbing around the dark spaces of buildings that no one even knew existed was something he had always done. Even Valerian had to admit that Boy was very good at not being seen.

Standing back in the street he had immediately spotted what he assumed must be the Dome the woman had spoken of. It was a huge glass roof made of hundreds, probably thousands, of individual panes of glass. They arched in a single beautiful sweep from some part of the building out of sight from where Boy looked. He'd spent a long time stalking the area, and now dusk was coming. In the half-light, the dome shone with the light of a thousand torches – or so it seemed to Boy. It was a glowing, shining, crystalline bubble that gleamed out of the filth of the City like a diamond in a dungheap.

Boy had scouted around the streets that joined The Reach, and found a small alley running into the centre of the block. There was a narrow but sturdy iron gate across the entrance to the alley, but Boy was over it before he had even wondered what he was doing. If he had stopped to think, he might have noticed that he was actually enjoying himself. This was like home to him. It was familiar ground –

running, climbing, hiding in the dark, with a mission to perform for Valerian. It was almost like normal.

He skipped down the alley as lightly as a rat, realising as he went that the alley was some kind of rubbish heap for all the buildings that ran behind it. Walls rose up high on either side of him, but just as he expected, there were little gates into the back courtyards of each building.

Accurately, he guessed where the gate for the Burials building would be.

There beyond lay the Dome, and for the first time he could see the stone building that it rose from. In a way he was disappointed that the shining glass roof rested on anything at all – it was so magical it ought to have floated in the air.

He looked to the gate. No way to climb over this one – it was set into the solid stone wall, but he had his bent metal pin out of his pocket and into the lock in a moment.

The gate swung and then he ran, quickly but cautiously, to the base of the Dome.

Some elaborate block work made climbing the building as easy as walking up stairs, and soon he was crouching against the glowing glass of the Dome itself.

He looked down at what lay within, and his jaw dropped. He had listened intently to what the old woman in the pillar had said about the Master of Burials and his animals, but nothing could have prepared him for what he saw now.

13

Dusk was settling over the winter cityscape as Valerian and Willow got to Kepler's house. On the way Valerian chatted almost casually to Willow, mostly about Kepler, about how he had been born of a noble family, but had turned his back on his aristocratic lineage for the pursuit of knowledge. Valerian looked up at the darkening sky.

'The end of the 28th,' said Valerian mournfully. 'Three days . . .'

Valerian rang the bell. Kepler's house was by no means as large as Valerian's, but was in a far better state of repair. This was a much cosier neighbourhood, of terraced houses for the well-to-do if not the rich. Kepler's house was a narrow, but tall affair.

'No light within,' said Valerian, frowning.

'Shall I knock?' asked Willow, but Valerian put out his good hand to stop her.

'He must be out,' said Valerian, but there was no certainty in his voice, 'but . . . he goes out no more than I do. Try the bell again.'

As Willow stepped forward, she noticed something else.

'Valerian!' she whispered. 'The door is open!'

'Careful, child,' said Valerian, but he did not stop her.

Valerian shoved the door further open with his boot, and they listened hard for a minute or so. The street behind them was empty and quiet. They took two steps into the hall and then pushed the door shut behind them.

'Kepler!' hissed Valerian in a stage whisper. 'Kepler, are you there?'

There seemed to be no one in the house.

'I think we can risk a little light.'

Willow started to hunt in her pockets for a match but was puzzled to see Valerian step over to the wall.

He found what he was after, and turned a small metal knob set into the wall itself.

Immediately a dim, flickering light sprang up in a chandelier above their heads.

Willow let out a small shriek.

'Valerian! Your magic *is* real!' she cried.

'No, Willow, no,' said Valerian. 'This is not my magic, but Kepler's genius. He has greater knowledge than anyone in the world of electrical phenomena. He has installed an automatic system of electrical light in his home. He says one day all houses in the City will have the same. He's mad, of course, but you have to admire his invention. My simple chemical lights at the theatre are child's toys compared to this.'

Valerian walked into a room leading off the back of the hall and turned another knob, throwing light across what was clearly Kepler's study.

Willow followed, open-mouthed.

'There's a large array of electrical cells in the cellar,' explained Valerian, but this was lost on Willow. She marvelled at the lights on the walls.

'There's no flame!' she said with disbelief.

'No,' said Valerian, 'but please concentrate.'

'Where is he?' asked Willow, dragging her gaze away from the magical lights.

'We must search the house. Something is wrong.'

Valerian winced as he spoke.

'Damn this arm!' he moaned. He rummaged in his deep left-hand pocket and pulled out another of the small bottles. It was at least his third, and pulling the cork with his teeth, he finished it off.

'Disgusting!' he spat, setting the bottle down on Kepler's desk. 'You start at the top and work down, room by room. If you see any more of those,' he glanced towards the bottle, 'bring them with you.'

Valerian looked at Willow, but she did not move.

'Valerian?' she asked.

'What is it?'

'Do I have to go upstairs by myself?'

'Yes. You'll be quicker than me. Don't tell me you're getting scared like Boy? Go. I'll be down here.'

He turned to the desk and began to open drawers and flip through books. She saw him look with interest at a piece of paper covered in writing and diagrams, which he folded roughly with one hand and put in his pocket. Then he went on rummaging.

Willow didn't understand how that would help find Kepler, and wondered who was really the more scared of what lay upstairs. But she turned and, with her heart in her mouth, set off for the first floor.

14

Willow thought about using the electrical light system, but it was frightening and probably dangerous. Seeing that Valerian was poring intently over papers at Kepler's desk, she lit the stub of the candle from the cemetery expedition with a match she found beside the fireplace.

She reached out a shaking hand to the handle of the first door she came to. Taking a deep breath, she turned the knob and pushed the door gently, and waited. Nothing. Holding the candle out in front of her she moved slowly into the room. There was no one there, nothing strange.

As she went through room after room and found nothing extraordinary in any of them, she began to calm down. Every one was as ordinary as could be imagined. This was just a normal house, the home of an educated man, with normal things in every room. Only the strange electrical switches on the wall showed that it was anything other than totally commonplace. She noted that the bed was made in what she assumed was the main bedroom, with clothes in neat piles on boxes, and everyday things sitting just where they should be.

There was no sign of violence, or robbery, or even untidiness anywhere.

Mystified, she went back to the study to find Valerian.

He was not there.

She swung around as if she were about to be attacked from behind at any moment.

When no one did, she risked calling out.

'Valerian! Valerian, where are you?'

She noticed a small door standing open in the far wall of the study. It was a secret door; she could see that it was made to look like part of the wooden panelling of the walls when it was shut.

Had it been open when they first came in? She crept across the room, trying not to make a sound.

Valerian, she thought angrily, *where are you?*

She made it to the small doorway and was not surprised to see a tiny flight of steps that turned immediately and led down, she presumed, to the cellar.

'Valerian!' she called.

Curse you, Valerian, she thought bitterly.

Still holding her lighted candle, she put her foot on the first step and began to descend. Two more steps and she noticed there was light coming from the cellar – more of that strange yellow electrical illumination.

She blew out her candle and went down.

At the bottom she stopped abruptly.

Valerian stood with his back to her, perfectly still, staring at the floor.

Around the walls were ranks of clay troughs, piled one on top of the other, so that there was almost no wall space left uncovered. In the top of each Willow could see metal plates, and from these came copper wires, which trailed crazily all around the stuff. There was a strong smell of some chemical. Willow supposed this was the source of the weird lighting in the house.

But Valerian was staring instead at the floor space in the centre of the cellar.

He turned and saw Willow.

'No?' he asked.

'There's no one,' said Willow, coming forward.

'Look at this,' said Valerian, nodding at the floor.

Willow stood by Valerian. It took her a moment to work out what she was looking at.

The floor of the cellar was made of packed earth, rammed as solid as brick. In its dusty surface someone, presumably Kepler, had dug a crazy pattern of trenches, each a few fingers wide and maybe a few deep. They criss-crossed and joined and snaked along and turned corners and struck out at odd angles, seemingly at random.

And they were filled with water. At least, Willow assumed it was water – it was hard to tell in the dim light. Whatever it was, it was liquid, a little murky from the packed soil channels through which it ran. For it was not still; somehow, it was moving.

Willow turned to ask Valerian something, but he anticipated her question.

'There's a small device at the far end, pushing it around. It is powered by the cells, just like the lights.'

But that posed another question.

'What . . . is it?' was the best way she could put it.

Valerian could not answer.

'I don't know. I haven't the slightest idea. I rather fear it means my friend has gone mad.'

Willow saw one more thing.

On the far wall, across the other side of the watery maze, was a blank space, not hidden by electrical paraphernalia.

Some words had been painted hastily on it with a thick brush. Willow recognised them as more Latin.

'What does that say?' she asked.

'The ramblings of a madman,' said Valerian sadly. ' "The miller sees not all the water that goes by his mill".'

Valerian stood staring at the nonsense on the floor and on the wall in front of them, and would say no more.

Willow sat down and put her head in her hands. She felt overwhelmed by despair. She had been carried into something she did not understand. It was easy to be swept along by Valerian when he was strong, but now he was weak and broken. He needed Willow, but she had no strength left. It was she who needed someone to guide her, and her only friend was running about the City miles away, on another crazy errand for his master.

They sat in the gloom of the cellar for a long time, until finally the clocks in the house began to chime midnight.

As the chimes died away one by one, Willow looked up at Valerian, who shook his head slowly.

'December the 28th is done,' he said.

December 29th

The Day of
Unnatural Developments

❧

They sat in the Tower, drinking tea and brandy and chewing on stale bread. All three were lost in their own thoughts, and the mood was grim.

It had been about two o'clock in the morning when Valerian and Willow got home. Boy, who had been back for hours, practically throttled Willow when he saw her. Hugging her hard, he hadn't let go of her until she made a small squeaking sound.

'How touching!' Valerian had said.

He looked terrible, and as far as Boy could tell, nothing had been done to his arm.

'Wasn't Kepler there?' Boy had asked.

Neither Willow nor Valerian replied, and that was answer enough.

'Did you succeed, Boy?' Valerian replied.

Boy's face fell. He stared at the floor.

'I'm sorry,' he said quietly.

'What?' spluttered Valerian.

'I couldn't even get past the door,' Boy protested.

'And you told them my name?' Valerian thundered.

'I said, I couldn't even get past the woman on the door.'

'Damnation!' shouted Valerian, and strode away across

the room, kicking over a pile of books, heedless of his damaged arm. He stood with his back to them, his shoulders rising and falling, staring at the floor. Finally he turned round, but he was no longer angry.

'Well, it was Childermas,' he said.

They looked at him blankly.

'The unluckiest day of the year.'

They thought about the graveyard, and the burial, and Valerian's arm and their fruitless trips across the City, and despite themselves, they all smiled.

'Fetch us food and drink,' Valerian had said, and Boy had found what he could, and taken it up to the other two in the Tower room.

When he got there he found Valerian and Willow standing by the table, above which was suspended the camera obscura.

Now, finally, Boy saw what it could do.

'Come and look at this,' whispered Willow.

Valerian turned to him.

'Haven't you seen this before?' he asked.

'No,' he said. 'You've never shown me what it does.'

Valerian shrugged.

'Come and see,' he said.

There were two parts to it. On the floor of the room stood a round table with a clear white circle set in its surface. Above it hung some large pieces of equipment, made up of wooden boxes and tubes of brass. So much Boy had seen before. But now he saw what it did. On the white surface of the table was an image of the City immediately outside the house. It was as if viewed from the very summit of the Tower, but slightly distorted; lines that should have been straight, like the sides of buildings, were gently curved, warped by the seeing-eye of the camera. But nevertheless it was an extraordinary image of the world outside, viewed from within.

And it was a moving image.

Boy watched, his mouth open, as they saw lights flickering in windows along the street, and smoke whispering out of chimneys and up into the night sky.

There was a long wooden lever that seemed to control the camera, and as Valerian moved it, the picture swung so that a different view from the roof of the house was shown on the table-top. They watched tiny figures scurry across it like ants.

'It's so . . .' said Boy.

'Isn't it,' said Valerian, nearly smiling. 'Unfortunately, despite its beauty, it illustrates the precarious nature of my current predicament.'

'What?' asked Boy, not really listening. He gazed at the moving picture in front of him, trying hard to tell himself it was real, that it truly was what was happening that very moment down in the streets beneath the Tower. Strangely, as Boy watched the ant-people hurry along, it gave him a sense of power.

'I had it built to see danger,' Valerian said. 'I keep watch here, night after night.'

Boy looked up. He could feel Valerian's fear. It was there between them, almost tangible.

'What for?' asked Boy. 'What are you watching *for*?'

Valerian spoke, and his voice was clear and calm and full of the promise of death.

'The end,' he said. 'Him. It. Whatever. Kepler said I was stupid to have this built. That it would do me no good even if I *did* see something coming for me. Maybe he was right, but at least this way I might get a little warning.'

Willow and Boy moved closer together and stared at Valerian, who turned his gaze back to the table. He moved the handle this way and that with his good arm, until he had scanned right around the Yellow House, checking all the streets and alleys.

Finally he pulled his eyes away.

'Did you find some food, Boy?' he asked.

They sat down to eat and the camera kept playing its dim but very real image of the outside world into the inner space of the Tower.

Valerian ate just a few mouthfuls and then fell silent, brooding in his great leather chair.

Boy looked at his master.

'You must eat,' said Willow, following Boy's gaze.

So should we, thought Boy. Valerian said nothing.

'How's your arm?' asked Boy. Then, getting no answer, 'You didn't tell me. What happened? Where's Dr Kepler?'

When Valerian still showed no sign of talking, Boy looked at Willow.

'Willow,' he said, 'where is he?'

'I – he–' began Willow, glancing at Valerian. 'It seems–'

'It seems!' cried Valerian. 'It appears! No! It *is* the case that Kepler has disappeared, and from the peculiar rantings in his cellar I think he has probably gone mad. My arm grows more painful, and I am running out of these.'

He waved a nearly empty phial at them.

'And then?' he barked, leaping to his feet. 'And then? Who knows! By the new year I shall be pieces of flesh strewn around this room!'

He stopped, aware that he was shouting. Boy and Willow stared at him, clinging to each other.

Boy felt panic slip up his back and squeeze his throat, making him want to be sick.

But Valerian had regained his composure and sat back down, as if resolved to his fate.

From his pocket he pulled another bottle of the drug. As he did so, both Boy and Willow saw a piece of paper fall from his pocket to the floor. It was the paper that Willow had seen Valerian take from Kepler's study.

Boy looked at Willow, her eyes wide with curiosity. Valerian took a long swig of his drug, then rinsed it down with a few mouthfuls of brandy. It was the weird hours of early morning, and as he slumped back in his seat he immediately fell fast asleep, snoring like an old, old man.

2

At dawn the camera played them a beautiful vision of the waking winter city, but they were all asleep, and the vision went unseen. Across the roofs and towers flooded a soft pink light that presaged snow, without doubt. Yet still it would not come and the City froze in its filth.

The Tower room had grown cold, and Willow lifted her head from the cushion on the floor. Her movement woke Boy. It was very early still, but they were soon wide awake. Boy felt awful. His arms were like wires, his legs like metal trunks, his neck like an iron bar. All he did was live, it seemed – live like one of Valerian's machines, with a heart-machine that pushed acid round his veins until they screamed in fear of what might be.

Boy had not slept well. Nightmares had ridden through his mind while he lay huddled on the floor. Unwanted thoughts returned to him again; those questions that Willow had been asking nagged at him. Who were his parents? Maybe it *was* important to know. Did he need to know, to know who he himself was? He was no longer sure.

He got up and walked around the room, stretching his legs. He found himself standing by the camera obscura table, staring at the moving image of the City waking up, coming to life.

Seeing that Valerian was still asleep, he dared to touch the handle that rotated the image. Willow came to stand by him and watched as Boy moved the lens around to view different scenes.

As he did so, a patch of light moved from the table and fell on the floor, illuminating the paper that Valerian had unknowingly dropped.

Boy looked at Willow, who picked up the paper. Her face creased.

'What is it?' asked Boy.

Willow shook her head.

'I don't know. Look.'

She held it for him to see.

Boy was not very good at reading, and the paper was covered in many symbols and signs that he knew were not words or letters at all.

But there was one word at the top of the paper that he could easily read.

BOY.

He shook his head, unable to understand what he was seeing, and then at last Valerian began to stir. Hurriedly Boy dropped the paper on to the table.

'We cannot stay here long,' Valerian said, rubbing his eyes with his good hand. That same hand began to search impatiently for another of the little bottles that took away his pain. 'The Watchmen will be looking for you. I have no doubt. Perhaps we should move to Kepler's house – it may be a little safer there . . .'

'But there was something,' said Boy.

'What?' said Willow.

'Why I couldn't get to see the Master of Burials.'

'Oh, spare us!' snorted Valerian. He crossed the room and began to fiddle with some bits of the camera, cursing occasionally when he couldn't manage with only one hand.

'I thought you might be interested,' Boy said to Valerian's back. 'What you said about him doing some strange studying and so on.'

Valerian ignored him.

'Tell me,' said Willow to Boy. 'What was it?'

'Well, I got talking to this woman at the gate. It seems he's obsessed with some animals he owns. It's all he spends his time doing. He's got this collection of animals, but they're all strange – he's got bird-headed snakes and dogs with cats' heads. There's cats with wings, and Willow, he's got dragons! They're tiny, but I saw them all!'

Willow stared at him in wonder.

'You're sure?' she said.

'I saw them with my own eyes. Snakes with birds' heads. Fish with a head at each end. And the dragons! But the thing is, they're all dead. I think he wants to make them live. I don't think he's doing his real job at all – he just spends all his time in this huge room under the glass dome, working on them.'

Willow shook her head.

'Dragons? Real dragons?'

'Yes,' said Boy. 'They're small, but–'

'Poppycock!' said Valerian. Neither of them had noticed that he had been listening. 'There are no such things.'

'But Valerian, I saw them!'

'Tell me,' Valerian said. 'What exactly did you see?'

Boy looked at Valerian and suddenly he hated him. Why did he have to treat him so badly all the time? Boy did his best, he always did what he was told, he worked hard, and yet all Valerian ever did was snipe and bark and criticise.

Valerian looked at him now, and Boy expected his face to be full of scorn, but as he held Valerian's gaze, he saw that Valerian was earnest, even interested. He was listening.

'What did you see?' asked Willow in a reassuring voice.

'Animals,' said Boy. 'And there were lots of them. And they were all weird. None of them looked like anything I've ever seen, or seen pictures of, or even heard of. They were all lying on his great table. On marble slabs.'

Boy paused. He pulled a face.

'Oh! There was so much blood.'

'Blood?' asked Valerian, with real interest.

Heartened, Boy went on.

'Yes, blood, and . . . things, from taking them apart.'

'The animals?' Valerian asked.

Boy nodded and scratched his nose.

'So he is dissecting them?' Valerian said.

'He's taking them apart,' said Boy. 'To see why they won't live, I suppose.'

'These animals,' said Valerian, 'all of them are strange, perverse things? Like nothing you have seen before?'

Boy nodded.

'And you think he's trying to make them live?'

Boy nodded.

'And he's taking them apart to see why they don't?'

Boy nodded.

Valerian shook his head.

'No,' he said gently, 'he's not taking them apart, he's trying to put them together.'

Boy thought. He thought for a long time, trying to remember exactly what he had seen.

'Could it be that?' Valerian asked.

Boy nodded.

'I think,' said Valerian, 'I think we should pay another

visit to the Master of Burials. We'll get the name of the cemetery where Gad Beebe is buried yet!'

He began to rummage all around the Tower room, pulling out various peculiar devices and equipment.

'But Valerian,' said Willow. 'Valerian!'

He kept on rummaging.

'Valerian!' she nearly shouted.

He paused.

'What is it?' he shouted back. 'We don't have the time! No time!'

'You were going to tell us. About what's happening to you.'

'Yes,' he snapped, 'but not now. I'll tell you on the way. Here, Boy, take this. It's delicate. Be careful! And Willow, this bag, if you please. Very good.'

Having checked around the outside of the building using the camera, they hurried from the Yellow House. As they went, Boy saw the paper with his name on it on the table and snatched it up, unseen. If Valerian didn't want it, then *he* did. It had his name on it after all – and Boy reasoned therefore that it belonged to him.

3

But Valerian did not tell them on the way. He did not tell them about the approaching horror, about the road which Fate was leading him down.

Instead he instructed them as they walked in the use of the pieces of apparatus they were carrying, repeating himself until they understood as much as they were able.

So now they stood inside the residence of the Master of City Burials. It was not easy to gain access to the Master of Burials, but Valerian had done it. He could be very persuasive.

Valerian had stared at the woman in the pillar, gazing deep into her eyes without saying anything for a long time. Finally he spoke, in a low and soft voice.

'You will go and tell the Master that Valerian is here to see him. Tell him I can make his animals live,' he said, and Boy and Willow watched amazed as without a word the old woman shuffled off her stool and went to do as she was bid. It was just as if Valerian had cast a spell on her.

Five minutes later a small door within the main door opened, and they hurried inside.

They stood facing each other in the grand entrance hall, sizing each other up. The Master was a short man, only a little taller than Boy. He was not quite as ugly as Green, but it still made Boy uncomfortable to look at him. His nose was pushed back, his eyes were small and overshadowed by huge hairy eyebrows. His hair was thin and greasy. He smelt terrible, his clothes were stained and despite their original quality were now little better than rags.

'Valerian! How strange to see you again.'

'A pleasure to renew your acquaintance. How long has it been?'

'Never mind that,' the Master snapped, his eyes, his brow creasing. 'How do you know of my work?'

'All the City knows of your work,' lied Valerian smoothly.

Good start, thought Boy, but the Master said nothing.

'I myself have admired your noble and valuable . . . investigations into this . . . subject,' Valerian went on.

He's losing it, Boy thought. *He doesn't really know what to say.*

'And I believe', Valerian concluded, 'that I may be able to help you.'

'Do what?' said the Master of Burials.

Valerian opened his mouth as if to speak, then shut it again.

'You said you could make them live,' said the Master of Burials.

This was the promise Valerian had made at the door. He shifted a little where he stood.

'Yes,' Valerian said. 'Yes, I believe I can.'

'Believe?' shouted the Master of Burials, furiously striding right up to Valerian. Though Valerian towered a foot or so above his head, Boy was amazed to see that the Master of Burials seemed to intimidate him. Boy had never seen anyone do this.

Fascinated yet nervous, Boy watched the struggle between them.

'Believe?' cried the Master again. 'I thought you said you *could* do it! If you can't you can get out of here and stop wasting my time. This is important work. Important! I have history to think of! How will my name be written across the pages of history if I cannot achieve this . . . masterpiece?'

The Master of Burials stared up at Valerian's face, then turned and spat on the floor.

'Get out of here!' he cried. 'Be away from here!'

Valerian stepped forward.

'No!' he cried. 'No, I can do it. With my two assistants here, I shall do it. Show me your animals. In return all I want is a little of your knowledge.'

The Master of Burials spun back to Valerian and held his gaze steadily for a long time.

'You had better be serious', he growled, 'or you will visit one of my cemeteries very much sooner than you had planned.'

He beckoned them forward, opening the door to the Dome.

'I already have,' said Valerian under his breath, and looked at Boy and Willow. 'Pray we get this right.'

4

Boy looked up to the roof of the Dome, where a few hours before he had clung to the frosty glass like a human fly.

Boy and Willow, who had spent all of their fragile lives in the City, were used to disgusting sights and noxious smells, but nothing could have prepared them for this. Even Valerian put his hand to his mouth and nose.

The inside of the Dome was the most ornate, the richest, most extravagantly decorated slaughterhouse. Under the glass dome above their heads the whole room was one vast experiment. Solid wooden workbenches of elaborate design formed a semi-circle. The top of each was finished with a thick marble surface. There the horror began.

Animals, normal ones, lay dead all over the room. Larger beasts rotted in boxes on the floor, while the smaller specimens hung from hooks or lay in trays on the worktops. From the darkest corners whimpers and howls came from various unknown creatures.

Bits of bodies were lined up on other workbenches. A pair of dogs' legs, a row of crows' wings and four cats' heads were just some of the foul sights they took in with their hasty glances.

The Master was at the far side of the room, at the workbench where Boy had observed him through the glass late the previous evening.

'Come on then,' he snarled. 'Come and see my beautiful creations!'

He waved them forward.

Boy and Willow stared at each other as they walked behind Valerian to the Master. They tried not to look at the pieces of animals around them, but they were fascinated and repelled in equal measure by what they saw. They were used to seeing carcasses and hunks of animals hanging in butchers' shops, but this minute and precise dissection of dogs, sheep, cats, birds – all still furred and feathered – was something else. Seeing this display of muscle, brain and bone made Boy wonder why things lived and then died, and what the difference was.

Then it got worse.

Boy and Willow caught up with Valerian, where he stood inspecting the Master's life's work.

'This is what I saw!' Boy whispered to Willow, but Willow had covered her mouth with her hand, whether to stifle a cry or to stop herself vomiting Boy couldn't tell.

On the ranks of marble slabs in front of them lay the animals. In a glass tray lay a creature the size of a cat. Its body seemed to be that of a weasel, but it had a long cat's tail and its head had once belonged to a large bird. There was no sign of any joins; the Master had evidently become a good craftsman in his time.

Next to the bird-weasel, in a tank of some foul chemical, a large fish with the head of a dog floated obscenely on its side. Further along the workbench Boy saw some of the dogs with cats' heads he had seen from outside, and the bird-headed cats.

And then there were the dragons. At first sight there seemed nothing else they could be but dragons – baby dragons. The largest was perhaps a foot long. It had a body of some greenish-grey lizard and seemed to have its own tail, and possibly even head, but then there were the wings: large, powerful, beautiful wings with feathers the colour of a golden sunrise adorned the creature's back.

As they looked closer they could just see a hint of some fine gut thread hanging down across the dragon's belly from where the wings were attached.

Valerian was hard at work now, letting his charm loose on the Master's ego. Valerian reasoned that anyone with an obsession like this had not only to be a little mad, but very self-centred too. He praised the Master's genius, his insight and his skill.

'And I curse the evil luck that has dogged you,' he went on.

'You are right!' cried the Master, his eyes glowing. 'It is bad luck. What else can have prevented every single one of my fine creations from living?'

'Indeed,' said Valerian.

'I do not merely throw these bodies together,' the Master went on. 'Oh no! Look!'

He took them to another table where he had some work in progress.

He lifted the skin over the haunches of a small deer and showed where he was attaching an eagle's legs.

'See? I attach every muscle to its partner, I link all tendons and tissues and fibres just as they should be. Every organ and vein and artery is thought of! I put back all the blood they lose. Why should they not live?'

'Why indeed?' echoed Valerian.

Boy and Willow looked at each other.

'None of them are sick', the Master rambled on, 'before they come here. They are all well. No disease nor even injury. I only allow the healthiest animals to go under my knife. Why then should they not live?'

'Indeed,' Valerian went on. 'Unless . . .'

He paused for effect, and the Master took the bait.

'What?' he cried breathlessly.

'Unless . . . I have some small knowledge in Natural Philosophies. It may be the case – it may be that there is some small but vital spark that is required to set life in motion.'

'And what is this vital spark?'

Valerian's on stage again, Boy thought. Acting a role, performing his magical skills, as he had done on the stage of the Great Theatre every night for years.

And now the Master was snared. Valerian turned to Boy and Willow with a flourish.

'The apparatus!' he declared, and Boy and Willow set their canvas sacks on the floor, carefully lifting out the things Valerian had given them to carry.

The Master stared at what he saw. He was a near wreck now, a mixture of excitement, worry and ignorance. Under Valerian's direction Boy and Willow set up the equipment.

From inside a wooden case Boy pulled a long glass tube, about two fingers thick and an arm's length. It had a metal cap at each of its ends and a small screw point for attaching a copper wire.

Willow lifted out her piece. It was a wooden and metal cased object, the size of a bucket. It was round, like a small barrel, with a handle on one of its flat sides. On its top was another screw point, to which Valerian quickly attached a length of copper wire. The other end was soon fixed to Boy's glass tube.

'Now,' said Valerian, 'which specimen do you want to live first?'

The Master was nearly beside himself with anticipation, hopping from one foot to the other.

'Now?' he cried. 'You can do it now? Just like that?'

'I can,' stated Valerian in a booming voice, 'on one condition.'

The Master didn't even break step.

'Yes! Anything! Anything! Just make my animals live!'

'We require information. On a burial in the City. You will promise us this if – when I make your beasts come alive?'

'Yes,' said the Master, now almost weeping with excitement. 'I promise! You have my word!'

'Very well. Show us your latest creation. Is there anything you have recently finished?'

'The dragon! The dragon!' shouted the Master, hopping and pointing frantically.

Boy nearly blew it.

They lifted the equipment closer to the dragon, so that it was within touching distance.

What if we really do bring it to life? thought Boy. *What if we don't?*

But then Valerian was speaking.

'Now!' he said. 'Like I told you.'

Suddenly he winced in pain. He took another swig from his small bottle, and after a few seconds lowered his head. He nodded for them to start.

Willow knelt down by the barrel-thing, and began to wind the handle. No one spoke. The tension in the room was truly electric. The barrel hissed and crackled and fizzed.

Then Boy, who was holding the glass tube, made a mistake.

Hold it by the glass only, Valerian had warned, but Boy forgot. Losing his grip on the tube and fearful of dropping it, he touched one of its metal ends.

Instantly he shrieked. His hair stuck up in the air and his feet smoked slightly. He dropped the tube.

By a miracle it did not break.

'What is this nonsense?' screamed the Master. 'Are you trying to ridicule me?'

Valerian hurried forward.

'No, my friend! No! This is just a demonstration of the immense power we will instil in your creation!'

He picked up the tube and shoved it back in Boy's hands.

'Get it right, idiot!' whispered Valerian in his ear. 'Or I'll cut you up like one of these brutes!'

Dumbly Boy held the tube again. To be honest, he had little idea of anything for a moment or two. He felt as if his brain had been fried. His hair still stuck up vertically; he looked like a brush on legs. It felt like – it felt like the time he'd tried to pick the lock on the Yellow House and had been blown backwards across the street.

Boy realised that Valerian was using the same power now – something shown to him by Kepler, no doubt.

'Again!' cried Valerian. 'Willow. If you please.'

Willow wound again, and this time Boy held the tube only by the glass.

After a minute Valerian cried, 'Enough!'

He took the tube from Boy.

'Boy! The wires!' he cried.

Boy undid the wire from the tube, being very careful only to touch its leather sheath, avoiding the metal clips.

Valerian took one last look at the Master and approached the dragon.

'Behold!' he said melodramatically, and he touched the metal tip of the tube to the legs of the creature.

Immediately they began to twitch and flex.

Next Valerian touched the wings, and they too sprang into life, opening and then relaxing.

'It lives!' cried the Master. 'It lives! You have done it!'

He began to jump up and down on the spot, hitting his hands against the side of his head.

'I have done it at last! I am a genius!'

He approached Valerian, arms open wide. Valerian took a step backwards and held up his hand.

'Your promise,' he said.

The Master smiled.

'Anything you want! Just name it!'

'I need to know where someone is buried.'

'You have a name?' asked the Master, scuttling to the side of the room. There he pulled on a purple rope that hung from the ceiling. A distant bell tinkled and one of the Master's servants appeared. He looked a little surprised to have been called at all, and even more surprised to see that his master had guests.

'Sir?' enquired the servant.

'Get this man whatever he asks. You will need the alphabetical register of burials. Now leave me! I have many more animals to bring to life!'

Valerian looked nervously at Boy and Willow, who were looking at the dragon.

'Yes,' he said to the Master, 'I am sure you have much to do. We will leave you. All you have to do is turn the handle to charge the wand, then touch it to your animals. You may keep the equipment,' he added graciously.

Boy looked at the dragon. It had stopped twitching and now lay totally lifeless on the marble slab, but the Master of City Burials had not noticed. He was too busy winding the handle of the charger, talking to himself, trying to decide which of his bizarre beasts he would bring to life next.

Valerian looked at the servant.

'Would you mind?' he asked, and the servant led them away into a library stuffed with books full of the names of dead people.

Within two minutes the answer was in their grasp, but it was not one Valerian had expected.

There, in the register of dead people whose last names began with B, was a simple and clear entry.

Beebe, Gad. The Churchyard of Our Lady of Sorrows, Linden.

'Linden?' Valerian asked the servant. 'I've never heard of that part of the City.'

'That's because it's not in the City,' he said. 'It's a village.'

'Outside?' said Valerian. 'Outside the City?'

'Outside?' Boy echoed, unable to understand. 'We have to go outside?'

5

It was still only ten o'clock in the morning, even though they had already brought fantastical dead beasts to life, and found the key to Gad Beebe's whereabouts, and felt they had done more than a lifetime's work.

But they had hardly begun the struggles they would face before December 29th was over.

It was a fiercely cold morning. They stood outside the residence of the Master of City Burials, shivering in their boots. People hurried by, wrapped up against the biting cold in furs and capes.

'What do we do?' asked Boy.

'First', said Valerian, 'we get away from here. It won't be long before that madman realises his beasts will only twitch for a bit, and then we'll be in trouble. As if it weren't enough to have the Watch after us already.'

Willow and Boy had nearly forgotten about that. Nearly, but not quite.

'You mean you didn't really bring them to life?' asked Willow.

Valerian snorted.

'Of course not! No one could do that. It's just a trick that one of Kepler's teachers discovered some years ago.

Amusing but pointless. However, as I planned, it fooled him long enough to get what we were after.'

That was a pretty big gamble, thought Boy, but he said nothing.

'And now', Valerian went on, 'we have to get to the village of Linden. And quickly. We must find a coaching inn.'

'I know one!' said Willow. 'I was sent to meet Madame at the Black Four when she arrived in the City. We can find a coach there.'

'Good,' said Valerian. 'Lead on. I need the book.'

6

The Black Four was a handsome place, one of the best-looking inns that Boy had ever seen. He wished he'd known about it in his days on the streets, because it was filled with rich travellers coming and going, forgetting where they'd left their bags and valuables. It would have made easy pickings.

To the side of the tavern was a huge pair of double gates that swung open whenever a coach came or went. Just as they arrived, a vast black coach pulled by four black horses swung down the road and into the courtyard behind the inn.

'Look!' said Willow to Boy, tugging his sleeve. 'Just like the sign!'

She pointed at the sign of the Black Four, with a picture of a coach and horses just like the one that had arrived.

'Do you know anyone here?' Valerian asked Willow.

'I spoke to the landlord while Madame rested. She was tired after her journey.'

'Poor thing,' said Valerian unpleasantly. 'Well, what's his name?'

'Budge. Or Bridge, or something like that,' Willow said.

Valerian muttered impatiently and strode in through the doors of the inn, his long black coat swirling behind him. He made an even more alarming sight than usual. Tall, dressed in black, with his grey-white hair straggling around his shoulders, he was usually quite imposing. Now, with his arm broken, hitched up and hidden under his soiled and muddied coat, and with eyes that burned despite having not slept properly for many nights, he looked like a minor demon.

Silence fell as he walked into the saloon bar of the inn. The room was filled with guests and servants. All eyes fell on Valerian and the two urchins who shuffled nervously behind him.

Valerian stopped in the centre of the room.

'The landlord?' he asked, fixing the serving girl nearest to him with his best glare.

Speechless, she nodded at the frosted glass door in the corner, too intimidated even to speak.

Valerian walked over to the door.

'Wait here,' he said to Boy and Willow, then strode in, unannounced.

Boy and Willow stood and waited. Gradually the people in the bar stopped staring at them and went back to their own business.

'What do you think this book is?' asked Willow.

'What?' asked Boy stupidly. Why did she always have to ask questions? By now all he wanted to do was sleep. They had been chasing around for almost three days, with little in the way of food and sleep. He just wanted to collapse in some small dark space and be left alone.

'The book,' said Willow impatiently. 'How is it going to save him?'

'Oh,' said Boy. 'I have no idea. But if Valerian thinks it will work, it probably will.'

'What's going to happen to him anyway on New Year's Eve?'

Boy shrugged.

'Ask him,' he said.

'I will. I just thought you might have some idea.'

'I'm hungry,' said Boy, changing the subject. 'Let's see if we can get Valerian to buy us something to eat.'

Willow agreed, and they pushed timidly through the door they had seen Valerian enter.

They found Valerian and the landlord shaking hands.

'Ah, children,' Valerian said, as if he was some kindly uncle. 'It is time to go. I have agreed a price for some transport to take us to Linden immediately.'

The landlord was smiling from ear to ear.

'Perhaps not my best coach, but since you are in a hurry you will not mind . . . ?'

Valerian nodded.

'Valerian,' said Boy, 'can we get something to eat?'

'Indeed,' said Valerian. 'Mr Birch here has packed a luncheon aboard our vehicle. Now we must be going. There is no time to waste. You have your money, do you not?' he added, turning to the landlord.

'Yes indeed, a very fair price,' he said. 'Well, this way then.'

Birch took them through a back door from his office and into the courtyard. The large sumptuous black coach they had seen arriving earlier was being made ready to depart.

'Our coach?' enquired Valerian amiably.

The landlord hesitated.

'Er . . . no,' he said. 'Yours lies just beyond.'

Without another word he hurried away. The large black coach pulled forward slightly, revealing their own transport. It was a joke. It was little better than a hay-wagon, a small cart that would have been better taking carrots from the fields to the markets. It was open to the skies and there was barely room in the back for the three of them.

The cart was hitched to a solitary and very old-looking horse, with a grey coat and a saddle-bag. Inside, their luncheon was a loaf and a bag of carrots, most probably for the horse. Holding the reins was an equally decrepit coachman.

He stared at them, sucking his gums.

'The crook!' cried Valerian. 'This will not do! Where's he gone?'

'What's the use?' said the cart-driver. 'I'll get you there. You won't find anyone else to go out into the country today. It's going to snow.'

Valerian drew in his breath as if he might explode.

'Come on,' he said to Willow and Boy grimly.

They clambered aboard.

'Drive on!' Valerian shouted to the coachman, who jolted the beast into life.

They trotted, at a fair speed, out of the gates and on to the street. As they did so, the grand coach they had seen pulled out of the yard behind them. Valerian leant forward, with some difficulty because of his arm, to speak to the driver.

'That was where you met Madame?' Boy asked, nodding at the Inn.

Willow turned to Boy, smiling.

'That's funny. I was just thinking about her too.'

'You could still go back to her,' said Boy quietly to Willow. 'All you have to do is jump off. Go back to the theatre. She'd take you back.'

Willow turned to look at Boy.

'No,' she said sadly. 'I hated her. She hated me. I'm sick of it. And anyway, she'd probably turn me over to the Watch for Korp's murder.'

'I can't believe you think working for Valerian is any better,' said Boy.

'I don't. I mean, I'm not working for Valerian.'

'Then what are you doing here?' asked Boy.

'Don't you know?' She said no more.

'What, Willow?' asked Boy. 'I don't understand.'

'I thought you could have guessed. You should know. You were alone for so long. All those years on the street, that you can't even properly remember now. And then you found Valerian, or rather he found you.'

She glanced up to check that Valerian was still busy in discussion with the coachman about their route.

'And he's awful,' she whispered. 'He beats you, he ignores you, he's unpleasant and ungrateful and foul. And yet you stay with him. Why?'

'Because I . . .' said Boy. 'Because I want to be with someone.'

'Exactly,' said Willow, and looked over the side of the cart at the buildings going by. 'I want to be with you,' she said, but not loud enough for Boy to hear.

They rode towards the City wall.

Valerian struggled to sit back down, having got little joy from the driver over their journey and its destination. Boy lent a hand to Valerian and helped him sit back down.

Valerian grunted with pain.

'Gods! It's cold this morning,' he muttered.

'Look, here are some blankets,' said Willow, rummaging under the side benches that were supposed to provide seating. She pulled out two large, moth-eaten blankets, and they were grateful for them.

Willow spread one over Valerian and tucked it under him.

'Thank you, Willow,' he said, and shut his eyes as they bounced on through the City.

Willow and Boy spread the other blanket around them as best they could. They chewed slowly on the bread and carrots, grateful at least for some food, but Boy's mind was on other things. The cart was too exposed. Anyone could look at them, and at any moment he expected to see a gang of red- or pink-plumed Watchmen come charging down the street after them. But none did. They were just another small cart with some human cargo winding its way through the City, a scene that was occurring a thousand times in every corner of the vast metropolis. No one paid them the slightest attention. No one could tell that the three figures in the back of this particular cart were engaged in a most unusual and deadly history.

7

It took the rest of the morning for the cart to get to the City gates. It was painfully cold now, and as they huddled in the back of the cart under the blankets and passed under the massive arch of the South Gate, the first few feeble flakes of snow fell, just as the driver had predicted.

The South Gate was a vast stone construction. Its entire surface was covered with bizarre stone carvings, designed by the City Architects to impart improving lessons to the populace. It seemed that much of the populace was even now gathered in and around the South Gate, a busy market place. No one paid the instructional carvings any attention as they called and shouted to each other in the process of trading. Around them the City walls were still decorated with fir tree branches and other greenery from the festivities of a few days before.

A *few days*, thought Boy, *but it feels like months*. The dead days had a knack of stretching themselves. When the days are out of the normal flow of time, time can stand very still indeed. All time, and no time. The dead time of the dead days.

Their cart approached the gates, for a heartbeat they were under the flying stone arch, and then they were outside.

'Have you ever been out of the City, Valerian?' asked Boy.

'Oh yes,' he said. 'Many times, though not for many years. The last time – I suppose the last time was fifteen years ago.'

'And you've never been outside since?' asked Willow.

Valerian didn't answer, lost in his memory. Then he seemed to hear Willow and shook his head.

'That was enough for a lifetime,' he said grimly. 'For a lifetime.'

'What's it like?' asked Boy.

'You'll see,' said Valerian, indicating the changing landscape around them.

Boy and Willow had never believed there could be so little of everything. So much empty space.

The last few miles through the City had been much like any other, but there had been a subtle change. The outermost parts were the poorest and the houses the most dilapidated. The coachman had picked up the pace a bit as they wound through some particularly unpleasant areas, even though it was midday.

Now there was nothing. Around them lay mile upon mile of empty fields. Away in the distance were forests and beyond them some hills. Boy and Willow were scared by it, feeling exposed and vulnerable.

The snow was falling thickly. For days it had threatened but had held off. It was as if the promise of all that snow had been stored up for this moment, for very soon the world had disappeared under a blanket of pure whiteness.

Into Willow's mind once more came a picture of herself, as a little girl, playing in the snow somewhere in the countryside. It seemed more real this time. She was with her parents, and she had the feeling they had been going to see someone. But no more would come, and the vision evaporated.

*

'Where is this place?' asked Boy. 'Linden?'

'You are becoming too much like the girl,' said Valerian irritably. 'Too many questions.' He took a swig from his bottle.

But when Willow asked the same question, he relented.

'It may take some hours to get there.'

'Have you been there before?'

'No.'

'Valerian.'

Valerian stowed the bottle back in his coat pocket with some difficult, and looked up at Willow.

'What is it, girl?'

'What's happening to you? What's going to happen?'

Valerian stared out at the whitening world around them.

'You said you were going to tell us.'

The cart trundled on. Its driver did not look back once. The snow fell ever harder as they made their way to a minor track which plunged them into dense forests of silver birch. The trees were stripped of their leaves and had a ghastly air of desolation about them. The wheels of the cart slipped against the mud of the track, frozen hard into great ruts. All around them was the absolute silence of the dormant forest.

And as the old nag led them ever closer to the grave of Gad Beebe in the remote village of Linden, Valerian spoke.

'You remember I said that I had last ventured out of the City fifteen years ago. I will tell you about that excursion.

'Then I was still a young man. Perhaps. But I could feel time was passing for me. Passing too quickly. I had left the Academy. I was not well-liked at that time. In fact I was disgraced. In my defence I can only say that I was doing what

162

my timid colleagues were too scared to do! If you under-stand.'

Boy shook his head but said nothing to disturb Valerian. He had waited years to hear this story, and he wanted nothing to distract Valerian from its telling.

'How can I explain? I was a Natural Philosopher too, then. I studied every aspect of Natural Philosophy – what some younger men are now calling "Science". I studied hard. Like Kepler still . . . like Kepler. I studied all branches of investigation into our world. So did we all. Myself, Kepler, and those who later denounced me.

'The intense pursuit of any idea that takes complete possession of me is one of the qualities that makes me differ-ent – sometimes for good, sometimes, I dare say, for evil – from other men. It was because I had a greater thirst for knowledge, a greater hunger and desire to know all that could be known, that I became interested in stranger aspects of these studies. Dark, strange knowledge. Hidden know-ledge.

'And I soon learnt that our modern thinking is but half the story. That there is a hidden world of a precious and powerful nature that has been known for as long as man has been thinking and doing.

'In my stupidity, in my pride, I rushed to share this with my colleagues, but I was a fool, for they shunned me. The things I did were dark and powerful, yes, and they were afraid of me. They threw me out! They turned their backs on me! And I was disgraced.

'In my anger, their treatment of me only served to make me delve even deeper into these unknown forces. I worked long and hard and began to create things I should not have done. I began to conjure powers that should not be known. I summoned them. Small spirits at first, then greater and

163

greater life-forms, with the power to change the world if they so desired.

'I thought I could control them. And indeed I could. I summoned these things from their hidden places and they did my bidding. Small matters like money were no problem. That was easy in those days. They did whatever I wished. Now I would not dare . . .'

He paused for a moment.

There were so many questions Boy longed to ask, but still he did not want to break the spell. Willow, however, had the habit of asking questions, and so she did. It was a simple one.

'Why?' she said.

'There is something else,' said Valerian. 'Something else I have not told you – someone else, I should say. A woman.

'She was fair, like the clear moon that shone down on my labours night after night. She was beautiful. Her hair was long and blonde like golden corn, but she always wore black. The beauty of this extreme drove me to distraction.

'Yes, she was beautiful. But more than that. Light danced behind her eyes, such eyes as I have never seen before nor since. Her voice sparkled like a glittering stream, and her mind was both sharp and playful.

'She was rich. Her father was a great and powerful noble-man. She was unattainable. She would not even have noticed a nobody like me, thrown out even from my college. And so I resolved to make something of myself. To make myself powerful and rich and strong. Then she could be mine.

'And so, having learnt of a most powerful conjuration, I summoned a thing – a thing I should not have done. I thought it would help me, grant me my wishes. And so it did. But I was oblivious to the price for all the power and wealth I was granted.'

Valerian stopped again, wincing at a twinge of pain from his arm.

'Look at me now!' he said bitterly as he fished in his pocket for the bottle. It was nearly empty and he drained the last few drops and threw the bottle over the side of the cart to land unheard in the thick snow. 'A wreck! This cart may as well be taking my coffin to the ground as taking us to God-knows-where in this forsaken land.'

'Don't say that!' cried Boy.

'No?' asked Valerian bitterly. 'I have now a little over two days to live unless there's a way out of this mess. I have not yet told you of the price I was set. I was granted power and wealth and I got them. And there was her. I was granted the power to have her.

'In return, I gave my life. I did not realise it at first, but the conditions were spelt out. I was given fifteen years. Fifteen years to use my power and money and make what I could with it, and at the end of which I will belong to the thing I summoned. My life is his. My body and soul are his. It is over, then. And it was almost exactly fifteen years ago that I made this pact, this bargain, deep in the forest. On New Year's Eve.

'Do you think it's strange to risk so much?'

Neither Boy nor Willow answered.

'I was blind. Love had made me blind, and I thought a night – even an hour with her would be enough. And I was arrogant, and I knew that in fifteen years I would find a way out of the pact. How clever I was then! How stupid!

'At first I was still foolish enough to think I would find a way out, but as the years passed I grew older and wiser and doubt began to grow. I had spent all my money, and never again will I summon those powers to help me get more.'

165

Willow was about to ask Valerian the woman's name, but Boy asked a different question first.

'And Kepler's been helping you find a way out?'

Valerian nodded.

'So why didn't you ask him for help sooner? Why wait until the last few years to get his help?'

Valerian spoke to Boy, but his gaze went right through him.

'Kepler and I had fallen out at the time of my making the pact. We . . . disagreed over something. We did not see each other for maybe ten years. But many things can be forgiven in time, and when I went to see him again he agreed to help me find the book.'

'What did you disagree about?' Boy asked.

A shadow crossed Valerian's face. He chose to ignore this question, but some intuition told Willow it had something to do with the woman.

'My time is up,' he said instead. 'My only chance lies with the book. I had heard of it, and when I told Kepler about it he spent many months finding out about it. His knowledge of ancient libraries is second to none. He gathered references to the book – a mention here, half a line there – until we learnt that if it still existed, it was probably in our very own City. Then we began to believe we might actually find the thing itself.

'It is a book full of such ancient and powerful knowledge that we believe it contains some spell or other way of breaking the contract I am under. Indeed Kepler firmly believes that it contains the answer. From his researches he discovered that it is no normal book. For it is not just pages with writing, information to be learnt, the mundane and the extraordinary. No, it is more than that. Kepler believes that the book is itself a magical device, and each person who looks into it learns something different – something about

166

only themselves, the thing uppermost in their mind, the thing they most want to know . . .

'For five years we have been tracking it down. About a year ago we thought we had it. We were mistaken. Then a few months ago it was promised to us, and again we were tricked. It is a powerful thing, and across the years many people have struggled to claim possession of it.

'I was relying on things happening more quickly than they have, but maybe there is still time. Maybe. Kepler was sure of it, and despite . . . the things that occurred between us, he is my one salvation in all this.'

Valerian broke off, obviously thinking of Kepler.

Willow watched him, her mind wandering to something Valerian had said.

'Valerian?' she asked, brushing more flakes of snow from her hair.

'What?' he asked, almost inaudibly.

'The woman. The woman you did it all for. What happened to her?'

Valerian lifted his head and his cold stare ran straight through Willow.

'She?' he said, 'She . . . rejected me. Despite the enchantment, somehow she still rejected me. I never saw her again.'

There was silence.

Willow still wanted to know her name, but could not bring herself to speak. Boy wondered how someone could risk so much, face such horrors, enter such a pact, all for someone who would cast them away, but Willow, looking at Boy, could feel differently.

To risk everything for someone – that was something she understood.

'Boy,' she said, quietly, 'I'm cold.'

'Come here,' he said, and put his arm around her.

8

Silence fell over them as the cart ploughed on through the snow-bound forest.

Boy felt a mixture of emotions, and none of them good – fear, horror, sadness, hopelessness. Willow felt pity, and a dread of Valerian's situation that she felt she could not begin to cope with.

And Valerian? Who knows what deep and dangerous thoughts ran through his disturbed mind?

Dead to everything around them, they plodded on through mile after mile of snow-laden silver birch forests. Dimly, it seemed to Boy impossible that there could be so many trees and impossible that it could snow for so long. And yet the trees went on for ever and so did the snow.

Willow, though smaller than Boy, kept a firm grip on the blanket spread across them despite the fact that she was virtually insensitive to everything around her. Boy had been lulled by the rhythmic stagger of the cart into a half-sleep, in which the waking world and his troubled imagination fought for control. And then his imagination won. He plunged into a bizarre sequence of mind-pictures in which he was back in his favourite kind of place: a small, confined darkness. Yet there was horror somewhere nearby, something that wanted to be bad to him. He scurried deeper into the cramped black spaces until he felt safer, only to feel the hunting presence coming closer and closer once more. In his perverse dream-world he could feel himself being pulled further away from himself, until at last there was an answer and he *became* the small dark space himself, and in doing so was free.

And Valerian?

There was nothing. He had either passed out or slept as they went on through the paper-white trees, and the soft, deathly snow.

And yet . . . and yet, then there came the end to the trees.

Dusk was only an hour or so away when they emerged from the forest at last. Far off in the distance stood a wretched little village.

The driver spat one word back over his shoulder.

'Linden!'

Then, in a cracked and bleak voice, he began to sing. It was a miserable song and suited all their moods as they were roused from their fitful sleep.

> *In the morning you should think*
> *You might not last unto the night,*
> *In the evening you should think*
> *You might not last unto the morn.*
> *So dance, my dears, dance,*
> *Before you take the dark flight down.*

As he finished his dirge, they pulled into Linden. It was just a handful of houses, an old watermill and the odd barn. For some reason, however, it had an imposing and ancient church that towered in the dusk like a man-made mountain of cut stone.

There, past a rickety fence, lay their goal – the church-yard.

169

The driver pulled the horse to a stop.

'We shouldn't need long,' Valerian said to him.

'I don't care how long you need,' said the driver. 'We can't go back tonight.'

He got down and started to unhitch the horse from the cart.

Valerian turned to argue, but the old man cut him off.

'If you don't get out of there before it's unhitched you'll fall off,' he grunted. 'And by the look of your arm I don't think you'd want that.'

Defeated, Valerian scrambled down, grimacing with pain as he reached the ground.

'Is it getting worse?' asked Willow.

'Do you have any left?' asked Boy, and Valerian pulled a final, somewhat larger bottle of Kepler's magic drug from his pocket.

'That's all,' he said forlornly. He turned to the driver who was leading his horse over to one of the barns.

'Where are we to stay then?'

The driver didn't look back as he called, 'You should have thought of that before you set out.'

He led the horse into the barn and followed him inside. The door closed. There was a time, Boy knew, not too long ago, when Valerian would have fought the driver, compelled him to do his bidding. But now Valerian was a different man from the one Boy had grown up serving. A broken man, he was nearly spent.

They looked around the village. Even in the fading light they could see it all from where they stood.

There were three houses, each standing by itself on a patch of land with a low wooden fence. Each had a variety of little shacks and outhouses clustered behind it, and vegetable gardens that ran down to where the fields proper started.

There was the water mill. It had a large mill pond up-stream, frozen solid and now covered in snow as well. The entire mill race seemed to be frozen, though water must have been moving underneath the icy surface. The wheel was frozen solid, and long fingers of icicles hung down from the blades that in summer would have ducked powerfully into the water.

There were two large barns, into one of which the coach driver had vanished with his horse. The other was a little smaller. And there was the church.

There was no one around, though they could see firelight inside some of the windows and could hear the sounds of a village preparing to rest at the end of a winter's day. A dog barked behind one of the houses. A rickety door slammed. They felt utterly alone.

'I don't like the countryside,' said Willow.

'Hmm,' said Valerian. 'It can be a little . . . quiet.'

'What are we going to do?' asked Boy. 'Where are we going to sleep?'

'We're not,' said Valerian. 'The first thing to do is find what we came here for – the book. Then we'll get a horse and take ourselves back.'

'You mean . . . steal one?' asked Willow.

'If we have to,' said Valerian. 'I'll be damned if I spend the night in this hole.'

He realised the other meaning of his words and fell silent.

9

It did not go well.

They made their way to the churchyard.

'We'll need to find a spade,' said Valerian. 'There'll be something in the mill . . .'

He tripped and fell forward, landing on his knees.

'Damn this arm!' he spat.

Willow and Boy knelt beside him.

'Don't fuss!' he snapped at them, and they jumped back.

He struggled to his feet, but this time when Boy and Willow each put a hand out to help him, he did not argue.

Supporting Valerian between them, they staggered to the churchyard, where they leant him against the wall on a low buttress that ran around the outside.

He shook his head.

'You'll have to do it,' he whispered. He drank the first of his last bottle and pulled a face. 'You two will have to do it.'

Boy and Willow looked at each other.

'Dammit!' cried Valerian. 'I can't move for pain. I can't walk and I certainly won't be able to dig. You'll have to do it.'

They nodded in unison.

'Boy! Go to the mill. They must have some sort of shovel for moving the corn. Girl! Start looking. Remember, Gad Beebe is the–'

'Of course I remember,' said Willow. 'I found the name for you!'

She glared at Valerian, who hung his head. He lifted his hand and waved them feebly away.

'Come on,' said Boy quietly.

The light was failing fast but there was just enough to see the names on the gravestones, though Willow had to scrape the snow off a few of them to be able to read the name of their occupants.

Before Boy returned with the spade, Willow had made a full circuit of all the stones in the small yard. The name Gad Beebe was not among them.

Boy found her standing in a far corner of the graveyard.

'Which one is it?' he asked, clutching a long-handled wooden spade.

She shook her head.

'He's got it wrong,' she said. 'It's none of them.'

Boy stared at her.

'I'm too afraid to tell him.'

'You must be wrong. Let's have another look.'

'Boy–'

'We can't tell him that,' said Boy. He looked over to the far side of the churchyard where Valerian leant slumped against the wall of the church. 'Let's have another look.'

So they did. Boy felt a strange sense come over him as they searched the stones. A sense of being outside himself, of not needing to be there in the snowy village deep in the countryside. Yes, he was cold and hungry and miserable, but it was something more than that. It felt as if he was in the wrong place, going the wrong way.

Maybe he was right, because though they searched the

graveyard carefully until the light was nearly gone, Gad Beebe's last resting place was not to be found.

When they got back to Valerian he looked like death. The snow had stopped but it was very, very cold. He looked old and on the point of freezing.

He lifted his head as they approached. His eyes read their faces and they were spared the job of having to tell him.

'He's not there, is he,' Valerian said, but it was not a question.

His head dropped.

Boy, still clutching the spade, opened his mouth.

'Don't say "What are we going to do?"' Valerian said without looking up, 'because I don't know.'

'We need to get inside somewhere,' said Willow.

Boy nodded.

'Valerian?' he said. 'Let get inside somewhere. Yes?'

Valerian didn't reply.

'What about here?' suggested Willow. She meant the church.

'Very well,' said Valerian hoarsely. 'Help me up.'

Gratefully, Boy and Willow pulled and levered Valerian into a standing position. It seemed that his legs had practically frozen solid where he leant against the church. Boy put the spade under his arm for him to use as a crutch, and they crept slowly forward.

Once again they staggered through the graveyard, taking the path to the church door. It was not locked and they pulled Valerian out of the bitter, biting wind.

The heavy oak door swung behind them, pulled shut by a counterweight. A massive church silence descended.

They settled Valerian on a pew at the side of the aisle. There were candles burning all around the altar and in other alcoves. Having been lit for the festival, they would be kept alight for twelve days. Willow was mightily glad to see them.

'Come on,' she said to Boy, and started to collect them two at a time. They took about two dozen thick and tall goose-white candles back to where Valerian lay on the pew, and placed them on the flagstones in front of him. The effect of the flames from the tallow candles was impressive, like a small fire, and slowly Valerian came back to life.

Using the spade as a prop he pushed himself upright, until he was sitting more or less vertically on the pew.

'Well,' he said, 'let me ask you a question, Boy. Willow. What are we going to do now?'

'Don't joke,' said Willow.

'I'm not,' said Valerian. 'Everything I have tried has failed. I have been foiled at every twist and turn. All my decisions have turned out badly and now we are sitting in a freezing church in the middle of nowhere with no way of getting home and even if we did . . . my prospects are not good. So I think that you may as well decide what we do next?'

What is there to do? thought Boy miserably.

'We ought to find something to eat,' he said. 'We could ask at one of the houses. The driver must be staying in one of them. Maybe he'll help us.'

'Him?' said Valerian. 'That swine!'

'Well,' said Willow, 'we can't just sit here.'

She looked at Valerian, who was staring into space behind her head.

'*Non omnem videt molitor aquam molam praeterfluentem!*' he said.

'Valerian!' Boy cried. 'Stop it! You're scaring me!'

But Valerian rose to his feet and pointed at the wall.

'*Non omnem videt molitor aquam molam praeterfluentem!*' he said again.

175

'Valerian!' Boy shouted. 'Stop it!'

'No! Look! *Non omnem videt molitor aquam molam praeter-fluentem.* "The miller sees not all the water that goes by his mill." Willow and I have seen that before!'

There on the wall behind them was a huge shield, a coat of arms, painted on to the stone. Its central image was a waterwheel, just like the sort frozen solid in the winter's night outside the churchyard. Emblazoned across the top was the motto Valerian had read.

'I don't understand,' said Boy. 'What's so important—'

'Look!' said Willow. 'There!'

She ran over and pointed to the name beneath the crest. William Beebe.

'Beebe! This is his family crest!' said Valerian. 'It must have been a wealthy family. He's not buried outside at all. He's in here somewhere! Look! There's another!'

He pointed.

A little further down was the same coat of arms, with another name. Daniel Hawthorn Beebe.

'Quick!' Valerian cried, his strength miraculously returning. 'Quick!'

But Boy was already scampering down the church.

Joseph and Sophia Beebe.

John Israel Beebe.

And then, there it was.

Gad Beebe.

'Here!' called Boy. 'It's here!'

Willow ran to him, Valerian not far behind.

'I can't believe it!' said Valerian. 'He really exists! Or he did exist, anyway. To see the name, written!'

'But where is he?' asked Boy. 'He can't be in the wall.'

Valerian turned and looked down at Boy, pulling one of his most devilish smiles. Then he raised a finger in front of boy's face and turned it slowly so it pointed straight at where Boy was standing.

'Indeed,' he said. 'He's under your feet.'

Boy shrieked and jumped back. By the light from Willow's candle they could see an inscribed stone in the floor.

'Fetch that spade, will you, Boy?' said Valerian. 'Let's get on with it.'

Boy brought the spade over.

'When was he – you know – put here?' he said.

'I have no idea,' said Valerian. 'Why?'

'Well, I was wondering what sort of – what we might find.'

'Ah! Well, let's have a look at the date.'

Valerian knelt down, wincing as he did so.

'Bring that candle a little closer, will you? Good. Now. There we are. Years ago, so no need to worry. It won't be too foul. Anyway, it's the book I'm after, not the man.'

Still Boy dithered.

'Get on with it,' said Valerian icily.

Boy shoved the tip of the spade along the crack between the stone with Beebe's inscription and its neighbour. He levered it back and pulled. He went flying backwards as the spade splintered on the stone, which had not moved.

Boy picked himself up.

'Are you all right?' Willow asked.

'Never mind him,' said Valerian. 'We'll have to find something else to prise it up. Quick. Someone could come at any time.'

They found a tall, heavy candlestick, its massive spike exposed when Willow removed one of the candles.

Putting the metal spike into the crevice, Boy and Willow both leant on it with all their weight. There wasn't as much leverage as with the spade, but the candlestick was strong and with a sudden lurch the slab lifted an inch or two.

177

'Quick!' said Valerian. 'Get something under there!'

With his foot Boy slid the handle of the spade under the stone flag.

Still cold, and not having eaten all day, everything they did now exhausted them. They rested for a moment, panting after the exertion.

'What are you waiting for?' Valerian growled. 'Get on with it!'

Wearily, they lifted the candlestick and shoved the top end as far as it would go under the small space they'd created.

Again they pushed down and the slab lifted some more.

'Lean to the side,' ordered Valerian, and they did. The slab rolled along the top of the candlestick and away from the hole. Repeating this motion a couple more times freed the stone completely.

'Now dig,' said Valerian, pointing at the patch of earth they had exposed.

Boy picked up the broken spade. Most of its face was still usable and he began to lift out the earth.

It came away surprisingly easily, and before even a few minutes had passed the spade hit the top of something else wooden.

Valerian could hardly contain his frustration. He hovered by the hole, grunting and cursing as Boy and Willow pulled at the dirt with their bare hands.

'Why do we always end up doing this?' muttered Willow as she and Boy once again scraped in grave-soil.

'Shut up and dig,' said Boy.

And then it was done. They had exposed the surface of the coffin.

'Oh no!' said Boy. 'Not again!'

'What is it?' asked Valerian, his voice tense.

Boy shook his head.

'The box is broken.'

He leant down and with one hand was able to pull up the top section of coffin lid. Just like the one in which Valerian had nearly met his end, the top third of the lid had been broken, snapped off to leave a jagged edge of flimsy wood.

Boy threw the wood to one side. He looked back into the hole. Willow gasped. Inside lay a skeleton, mostly clean but only mostly.

Its arms were folded across the tatters and rags of its chest.

And that was all. There was no book.

'It can't be!' cried Valerian. 'Look further in! At the feet!'

Boy didn't move. He looked down at the skeleton and knew he could not make himself get that close to it.

'Do it!' shouted Valerian.

'I . . .' Boy stammered, 'I can't.'

Valerian stopped and then kicked the candlestick hard so it skittered away into some pews.

'I'll do it,' said Willow hurriedly, and before Valerian could say another word, she held up a candle and peered into the depths of the grave.

She stood up.

'Nothing,' she said.

'Tricked!' Valerian said bitterly.

'Then . . . ?' began Boy.

'Yes,' said Valerian. 'Yes. This looks rather like a dead end.'

10

'Can't you just run away somewhere?' asked Boy. 'Hide? Until after New Year?'

'If only it were that simple,' said Valerian, 'I would already be on the other side of the world. The force with which I made my pact . . . is powerful. It transcends time and space. It will come for me wherever I am on New Year's Eve. The day after tomorrow.'

They were sitting in the church, by the candles, trying to keep warm.

'But there is something,' said Valerian suddenly. 'How could I have forgotten . . . the motto? The Beebe family motto! Willow, I said we have we seen it before! Where?'

'At Kepler's house. In the basement. But why?'

Valerian stood up.

'Why?' he said slowly. 'Because Kepler must have known about Gad Beebe. He knew about his family motto. Perhaps he already has the book! Come!'

'What?' cried Boy. 'Where?'

'Back to the City. To find Kepler. We must find him! He knows something. Find him and we may find the book.'

'Do you think he was here?'

'No. No, I don't think so, but he knew about Gad Beebe. Now we just have to work out where he's gone.'

'But how will we get back?' asked Willow.

As she spoke the clock in the tower of the church above them began to strike midnight.

'Willow,' said Valerian, 'it's time to steal a horse.'

December 30th

The Day of
Unfailing Coincidence

❧

But things were not to turn out that way.

'No!' Willow had said for the fourth time, and Boy had worried about what Valerian might do to her.

'No,' she said. 'You can't just take someone else's horse!'

But Valerian did nothing to her. It almost seemed he was soft with Willow. Boy watched, amazed, as she argued in the persistent snowfall outside the villager's stable.

'I have no money left!' shouted Valerian. 'We must get back to the City and there is no other way.'

Finally Boy at least managed to get them to have their argument inside. In the stable they saw why they had found no trace of the driver – his cart had gone and so had the beast.

But they could make out the shapes and smell of two young horses.

'These people have nothing!' cried Willow. 'You can't take their horses from them!'

'And if I don't, I'll be dead,' Valerian said, but it seemed there was less strength in his words than there might have been. Boy wondered if his arm was affecting him. At times he seemed delirious with pain.

'That's not their concern, is it?' Willow said.

'No,' said Valerian, sounding exhausted. 'No, it's mine.'

He stared into Willow's eyes and there was a stand-off. Boy held his breath, and in the silence of the snowstorm they heard an angry cry.

It came from the direction of the church.

Boy stuck his head through the door and just as quickly pulled it back in.

'They've found our mess!' he hissed. 'In the church! There's at least three of them and they're coming this way!'

Valerian looked at Willow.

'When this is all over I'll come back and buy them a dozen horses,' he said. 'I promise!'

Willow said nothing.

Boy ran over to her.

'Willow! Come on!'

It would never even have occurred to Boy that it might be wrong to steal the horses. In the way he'd grown up, first on his own and then with Valerian, he'd learned different lessons. If you needed something, and you could get it without getting caught, you took it. Willow thought differently, and he could tell she was very serious about it.

'Willow!' he cried again.

'All right!' she said at last. 'Do it! But you have to promise! A dozen horses!' she added to Valerian.

'Yes, yes,' he said. 'Come on!'

It was too late.

Boy pulled the stable door open to find a group of four or five villagers.

They were large men, and their burning torches and sharp-edged farming tools looked ghastly in the darkness and the swirling snow.

Boy backed into the barn, trying to think fast but failing.

'Come on!' Valerian called.

He spurred his horse forward, but when the animal came close to its masters it stopped. One of the villagers put his hand up to the horse's cheek and whispered to it. Immediately the horse rose on its back legs and let out a loud whinny. Valerian slipped from the horse's back and fell into the thin straw on the stable floor.

As he hit the ground he howled with pain and then blacked out.

Two men stepped forward, and Boy saw the cart driver behind them. Boy swore at himself, and at Valerian, for having been so stupid as to trust him not to have said anything about their arrival in the village. Another of the villagers lowered an old but sturdy pitchfork at Boy, pointing its three prongs at his throat. The man was not tall, but strong and broad. His face was weather-worn and dirty. He was angry.

'Now,' he said, 'my fine City boy, what have you done to our church?'

'Us?' said Boy.

The villager swung the pitchfork, hitting Boy across the side of the head with the handle. Willow rushed as he fell next to Valerian.

'No so fast!' shouted one, but Willow took no notice. She crouched by Boy. He did not move.

'You've killed him!' she screamed.

The man spat in the straw.

'Not yet,' he said. 'He's breathing yet.'

With relief Willow saw it was true. She looked about her. Boy and Valerian both lay, out cold, in the foul-smelling straw of a barn in a village miles away from the City. Around her stood a gang bent on revenge, and she knew there was nothing she could do.

2

Dawn rose on the morning of December the 30th, but Boy and Willow did not see the day break. Valerian did not see anything.

Boy had come round from the blow to his head quite soon, and immediately been sick in the straw. He put his hand to his head, and felt blood and broken skin. He had a murderous headache.

The villagers had taken Willow and Boy back to the church, and had carried Valerian none too gently with them.

They took them to the hole in the church floor, Gad Beebe's place of interment. Seeing it again, Willow was shocked by what they had done, the violation they had caused.

'You did this?' grunted a man with sunken cheeks.

Boy was too fearful to speak after his last try. Willow couldn't see that there was any point in denying it, but couldn't bring herself to admit to it either.

Then Pitchfork Man spoke.

'What are we going to do with them?'

'Kill them now,' said one.

'We ought to send for the Watch,' said a taller man, who seemed nervous.

'That will take days,' said Pitchfork. 'Let's drown them in the mill race.'

'It's frozen, you fool! It'll take hours to make a hole big enough.'

And so they argued, and eventually decided to lock their prisoners in the crypt while they decided what to do.

The sunken-cheeked man pushed Boy and Willow ahead of him, waving his scythe threateningly. At the far end of the church, in a corner of the nave, was a low archway. Four steps led down from it to a metal grille. Sunken Cheeks, who seemed to have taken charge, had sent a younger man for the keys. When he returned he came back not just with the keys, but with women from the village, eager to see what was happening.

Sunken Cheeks pointed, unlocking the gate to the under-world.

Boy and Willow hesistated, but when he lowered the tip of his scythe at them they slunk into the darkness. Beyond the grille there were at least a dozen more steps that curved around, taking them back under the body of the church itself. At the bottom, they stopped. They had little choice, for they were in complete darkness.

There was a noise like a scuttling animal, then a flash of sparks behind them and they understood what the noise was – a burning torch had been thrown down the stairs so there was light to carry Valerian down.

He was dumped roughly on the floor.

'Heavy, he is,' said one, and they left. The nervous one turned and bent to take the torch back with them.

'Please!' said Willow. 'Please leave us some light!' She tried to make herself sound as pitiful as possible, but that wasn't hard. The man looked at her and was reminded of his own daughter sleeping safely in her bed in the farmhouse.

Without a word he handed her the torch and followed his friend back up the curving steps to the church.

Boy rushed after him, but the gate was already shut and locked.

'Please,' he begged through the metal grille of the crypt entrance, 'please can we have a blanket for Valerian?'

Sunken Cheeks looked at him.

'No,' he said.

Their footsteps disappeared up the four stone steps and they were gone.

3

The crypt was small, a cramped room with a vaulted ceiling low above their heads, which made it feel as if they were sitting inside a treasure chest. In the centre stood a large stone sarcophagus, and along each of the longer walls were three cists capped with headstones commemorating the person whose bones lay inside.

On one of the shorter walls was an iron bracket, and Willow put the torch there so that they could see a little better. Boy returned from the metal grille at the top of the steps.

'It's not good,' he said. 'It's locked tight.'

He shook his head.

'It's not like they need to stop people getting out of here, is it?'

'No,' said Willow. 'It's to stop people getting in. To stop them . . .'

'Stealing bodies,' said Boy, finishing what she was unable to.

'Boy,' cried Willow suddenly, 'what are we doing? What have we got into?'

'You, you mean,' said Boy. 'I was always a part of this. Whatever he does, I do. You had a choice.'

Willow looked at Valerian.

'Let's see what we can do for him.'

They lifted his head and folded the wide collar of his coat out, then rested his head back on it. His arm was worse. There was a distinctly unpleasant smell coming from it. They pulled his coat tight around him.

'Where's that last bottle?' said Willow.

Boy fished in Valerian's pockets and pulled out the last of Kepler's potion.

Lifting Valerian's head again, they tipped a small amount of the thin green liquid into his mouth.

Automatically he swallowed, coughing.

Boy sniffed the liquid before shoving the cork back. He pulled a face. As Willow was busy trying to lower Valerian's head, a burning curiosity came over him. Holding his nose, he took a small swig of the stuff.

He choked but swallowed. Immediately fire spread through his body. The taste was awful, but it was soon replaced by a wonderful feeling – a feeling of strength and power and lightness. He felt better than he had in days, in ages, and he liked it.

His body no longer ached. He felt no hunger, no pain, no fear. He looked at the bottle in his hand and then at Valerian, who already showed signs of stirring.

Willow turned round to Boy.

'What are you doing?' she asked.

'Nothing,' he said. 'Nothing.'

He smiled at Willow. Despite everything he was amazed to feel calm, confident, even *glad*.

'Well,' he said, 'what are we going to do?'

Willow crumpled in front of his eyes.

'What can we do?' she wailed. 'We're locked in a stone hole, underground, under a church, in a god-forsaken village miles from home. Valerian has two days left unless maybe we find the book, and we still have no idea where it is!'

She stopped.

'Don't we?' said a voice behind her.

Valerian looked up at them from the stones. He raised himself on one arm, then lifted himself back to his feet. Willow was amazed by this, but Boy no longer was. He knew the secret that was kept in Kepler's green liquid.

'Boy!' said Valerian, fishing in his pocket. 'Where's my bottle?'

'Here,' said Boy, bringing it to him. 'We just fed you a little of it. We thought it might help.' He couldn't hide the smile on his face as he saw Valerian on his feet again, and as Valerian took the bottle back from him with his good arm, he smiled back.

Boy felt good, strong and happy.

Valerian looked at the bottle. It was half empty.

'You were right,' he said, 'but there is little left. Still, it is time we were about things.'

He put a hand out to Boy's cheek for a moment, then seemed to remember himself and instantly pulled it back. It happened so fast that Boy wondered if he'd imagined it.

'But what can we do?' said Willow.

Valerian turned to her, his bad arm swinging loosely at his side.

'Come now, Willow, it's not like you to be weak! It's usually the boy here.'

Boy laughed. He didn't even mind Valerian making fun of him. He felt good and that was all.

Valerian began to circle the crypt. He prowled, a smile growing on his face.

'There is more to this church than we know,' he said. 'There has to be – it is far too big a place for a tiny hole of a village like Linden.'

He rested his hand on top of the sarcophagus.

'Listen!' he said. 'Listen! Can you hear it?'

Willow stared at him, convinced he had gone mad. Boy, who had spent a few more years with Valerian than Willow, recognised when his master was on to something.

'What?' he asked.

'Listen!' hissed Valerian, wobbling slightly on his feet. 'No! Look!'

He pointed at the wall of the crypt, the short wall opposite the one where Willow had placed the torch.

There again were those mysterious words.

Non omnem videt molitor aquam molam praeterfluentem.

'The miller . . . ?' began Boy.

'. . . sees not all the water that goes by his mill,' finished Willow.

'And outside the churchyard, there stands . . . Boy! What?'

'A mill!' he said confidently.

'Exactly!' declared Valerian.

'I don't understand,' cried Willow. 'What does it mean?'

'It means,' said Valerian, 'it means it is more than a motto! It is a family saying, maybe, but more than that. Listen! Place your ears to the sarcophagus and listen!'

'The – the what?' asked Boy.

'The sarcophagus, Boy! You do know what a sarcophagus is, don't you? From your Greek! Eater-of-bodies. Flesh-eater. Sarco-phagus.'

Boy looked blankly at him.

'The stone coffin, Boy!'

Valerian pointed to where Willow, who had already understood, stood on tiptoe to put her ear flat against the lid of the sarcophagus.

'I thought I heard something as I lay on the floor. It's faint, but you can hear it better through that.'

Boy ran over to Willow. It was true; you didn't even have to put your head close to the stone box to hear the sound of water flowing somewhere underneath.

'Valerian!' Willow said. 'Valerian! Look! Is this . . . ?'

She was staring at a pattern engraved in the lid of the coffin.

'Yes. The pattern that Kepler had dug into his cellar floor, repeated here on the lid of this supposed grave!'

Indeed, the lid of the sarcophagus was deeply cut with a manic pattern of lines crossing, re-crossing, intersecting and splitting. Without remembering exactly, Willow could recognise it.

Boy stared at her.

'What is it?' he asked.

'These marks,' she said. 'It's what the doctor had dug into his floor and filled with water. Water that flowed by the aid of a machine. And above it on the wall were those words.'

She pointed.

Boy understood.

'The mill outside – not all of the water goes past it. Some goes here. So the miller . . .'

'. . . sees not all the water that . . .'

'Exactly!' cried Valerian. He stared at them, a little mad, a little proud, waiting for the moment to deliver his final piece of wisdom.

'See that long line that comes out of the pattern, straight down the length of the sarcophagus lid?'

They nodded.

'What would you say that is, at the end of it? That symbol?'

There was a circle with short lines radiating out from it.

'It's a mill wheel!' said Boy.

'Just so!' said Valerian, and he grew more serious. 'Now, you two, lift the lid and let's be away from here!'

Willow turned to him.

'I am not dealing with any more corpses,' she said firmly. 'Is that clear? I've had enough!'

Valerian smiled at her infuriatingly.

'But there will be no corpse inside here,' he said, tapping the lid. 'There will be no bones, no flesh, no decomposing material of any sort whatsoever. There will be simply a way back to the City.'

'You're mad,' she said. Valerian ignored her.

'I thought Kepler was mad but I was wrong. I should have realised sooner what we were looking at in his cellar. This is a map. It is a map of the ancient canals under the City. And this is our way back.'

'That can't be,' said Boy. 'There are no canals in the City.'

'Not *in* the City, *under* it,' snapped Valerian. 'Under the City is an ancient network of canals. They were once exposed to the sky but were slowly bridged, then built over and re-built over, until only the rumour of them remains. I myself explored a tiny fraction of them one evil day when I was a student. I quickly became lost. It took me a day to find my way out and I never dared go back.

'It is said they feed into the river, or that the river feeds into them. Few know where their entrances lie. And now I believe we have found one, here, in this stinking village. The mill race must run underground and join the canals!'

Valerian fetched the torch from the wall.

'Hurry!' he said. 'There is no time to be lost.'

'But we don't even know if you're right,' protested Willow. 'There may be nothing inside here at all.'

'I am right,' said Valerian. 'And you two must open the lid. I cannot. Hurry!'

Willow looked at Boy, and Boy looked at Valerian, who glared at him so hard that he jumped and started to try to shift the heavy stone lid. It didn't budge.

'Wait!' said Valerian. 'We ought to copy this map.' He tapped the lid once more.

'I have some paper!' said Boy proudly, and pulled out a leaf of folded parchment from his pocket. Delighted at being useful for once, he smiled as Valerian took it from him.

'Boy, you astound me! What is this? Have you been studying at last, or . . . ?'

Valerian stopped.

'Where did you get this?' he said.

'It's mine!' said Boy, wishing he had left it in his pocket.

It was the paper he'd found on the viewing table of the camera obscura in the Tower room, the one with his name at the top and the strange words and symbols underneath.

'It is not yours,' shouted Valerian. 'It is *about* you.'

He turned and looked at Willow.

'Here,' he said. 'I have a stub of charcoal. Use the reverse of the paper to copy the map. Do it well!'

So by the flickering torchlight Willow set about trying to copy the lines on to the back of the paper, using a piece of soft charcoal that kept on breaking.

'I can't see!' she complained, but she kept at it.

'You've missed a bit,' said Boy. 'Look, there! And that line joins that one, not that one.'

'You do it if you're so–'

'Boy will not do it,' said Valerian, holding the torch. 'You will. You'll be quicker and neater.'

But it was hard to concentrate with Valerian glaring at her.

'Hurry!' he said. 'God knows how long those thugs will be away for.'

197

'They're just people,' said Willow. 'We offended them. They're angry. Perhaps if we had just asked to–'

'To what?' interrupted Valerian, 'Asked to smash a hole in the floor of their church and dig up the remains of one of the local gentry? I think you should concentrate on what you're doing.'

'There!' said Willow. 'I've finished.'

'Are you sure?' said Valerian, comparing the engraved lines with the drawing Willow had made.

'Yes,' said Willow, but she was not sure. She was not even convinced there was anything under the lid of the sarcophagus apart from decaying bodies.

'Then come on, put your backs into it. Don't take it right off – we must cover our tracks when we leave.'

But if Willow was not convinced, Boy certainly was. He still felt strong after the slug from the bottle. He had never felt so confident in his life, and had never felt he understood Valerian so well. It was as though some of *his* power was inside him.

'Come on, Willow, I need your help,' he said, putting his back against the lid and beginning to shove.

Reluctantly, Willow started to push too.

'Do it together!' urged Valerian. 'On my mark! Now!'

And they both gave a sudden shove and the stone lid not only moved but slid right off the sarcophagus and smashed to the stone floor of the crypt where it shattered.

The sound echoed around the small vault and they began to panic, casting anxious glances back up the steps. Valerian leant over into the hole they had uncovered and smiled, satisfied. There was a series of iron rungs let into the shaft that dropped down into the darkness. Now they could not only hear the sound of running water, they could smell its dankness.

'So much for covering our tracks,' said Valerian, looking at the broken lid. 'Still, we have a map, and if they follow, they won't have.'

'Why did they put us down here if they knew there was this way out?' asked Boy.

'Well, obviously they *didn't* know,' said Valerian. 'It's my guess this is some secret of the Beebe family. But we don't have time to debate it. They'll come sooner or later and the torch won't last for more than an hour or two. Let's go.'

He took a pull on the phial. As he lowered his head, he saw Boy staring at him.

'What is it, Boy?'

'I – I was just thinking, wondering whether it would be a good idea if Willow and I had . . . a little of that . . . to help us.'

'How dare you! No! What a suggestion! This is for my arm. Anyway, it's not good for you. Too much can . . . That's not your business. Take the torch and get down that hole, Boy, before I decide to leave you here.'

Boy tried to hide his disappointment and did as he was bid.

'You next, Willow.'

And then Valerian swung his long legs up on to the ledge of the shaft and placed his feet on the rungs. The light from the torch had already stopped swinging about beneath him.

Valerian was glad the bottom was not far. He had little idea how he would have managed if he'd had to climb down a ladder with only one hand for more than a few feet. As it was it was difficult enough, but quite soon he had reached the bottom and stepped off to find Boy and Willow waiting for him.

'Look!' said Boy. 'Boats!'

They were in a cavern, standing on a jetty made of iron

and wood which clung to the wall of the chamber. There was the river flowing slowly and steadily past them in the darkness, and tied to the jetty were several boats of a strange sort. They were flat-bottomed and had no oars, but each had a short pole lying in its bottom.

'I wonder when anyone last came this way,' said Willow. 'It feels so forgotten.'

It was true. The whole place seemed to have been untouched for many years. The rust on the iron rungs had been undisturbed. The landing stage was rotting in places, and they had to tread carefully to avoid the weaker parts of the platform, but the boats bobbed gently in the current, as if happy to see someone after years of abandonment in the darkness. They chose the one that seemed to be the sturdiest.

'Let's be gone,' said Valerian.

4

They began well.

The boat, once untied, seemed keen to take them off down the tunnel that led from the chamber, and only leaked a little. Willow sat at the front with the torch, Valerian sat in the middle with the map, giving orders, and Boy crouched in the back, holding the pole and steering them away from the walls when necessary. There was little need to propel them forward – the current was enough to keep them moving at a decent speed. Once or twice Boy gave an extra push, but he rocked the boat so badly it made them feel unsafe.

Soon they would be back in the City.

Time. Who had any idea how time was passing as they sailed along in the long straight tunnel?

Distance. They had no more idea about how far they had travelled than they had about how long they'd been going. What had seemed so easy to start with began to seem a surreal voyage from nowhere to nowhere. The tunnel was apparently endless.

As they went, Valerian's drugs began to wear off and the pain grew again in his arm. With it he began to remember the desperate nature of his situation.

So what if he made it back to the City? He knew what

waited for him on New Year's Eve, wherever he was. For the ten-thousandth time he wondered if there were any way out that he hadn't considered before. Maybe there was something staring him right in the face that he hadn't seen. But fifteen years is a long time to think and he had no more ideas.

They drifted on in the gloom, the torch sputtering, showing signs that it would soon fail.

It was not much warmer in the underground canal than it had been in the crypt, or in the church, or in the snowstorm itself. It was airless too. Despite the flowing water there was a powerful smell of dampness and decay. Once or twice their faces were brushed by dripping fronds and unseen tentacles, maybe the roots of plants hanging from the bricked vault of the low tunnel. The sound of splashes from the prow of the boat fell dead against the claustrophobic walls of the tunnel which, it seemed, would never end.

Valerian's mind was a haze of horror and pain. Boy began to feel his joy slip from him. He could see little but Willow by the light of the torch.

What had he brought her into? This life with the madman who was his master. He was possibly a murderer, whose life was now forfeit over something that had happened fifteen years before. Valerian had thrown it all away for one night with a woman who had rejected him.

Nothing made sense, especially not this stupidly straight tunnel.

'Boy,' said Willow quietly, 'I'm scared.'

'It's all right,' Boy said. 'It's . . .'

And then Willow shrieked and dropped the torch into the canal, where it was extinguished at once with a short hiss of dissent.

'Willow!' called Boy. 'Are you all right?'

'I dropped the torch,' she cried pointlessly. 'Something hit me! I'm sorry – oh, I'm sorry!'

'Are you all right?' Boy asked again.

'Yes, but what will we do now? We can't see where we're going!'

'What does it matter anyway?' said Boy. 'We're only going one way and that's forward. I don't know what else to do.'

'But we could be down here forever,' cried Willow.

The darkness was total, and still they floated on.

Valerian barely seemed to have noticed. Boy now gently eased himself into the bottom of the boat from his perch on the stern, and Willow, a little hysterical, felt her way back towards Valerian and curled up at his feet.

Then she sat up.

'I've still got a bit of a candle,' she called to Boy.

'But we've no way of lighting it,' he said miserably.

They fell silent again, and so they went, knowing little about anything, Boy and Willow half numbed by the cold and half asleep, and Valerian in some strange place where the pain and the last of the drugs had taken him.

5

Had they had any idea how time was passing they might have guessed that it was now well past midday on the day before New Year's Eve.

Had they any idea of how far they had travelled they might have known that they were indeed back in the City or, at least, beneath it.

Valerian was right. Valerian was always right. They were in the maze of underground canals that lay far from sight and far from knowledge, forgotten and corrupt, while the City sprawled above.

They had drifted into the canal system proper, where the current had become more gentle. Had they had any light to see by, they would have been able to make out ruined doorways and steps, landing stages and blocked in windows, where once a thriving business life had been conducted along the waterways of the City. Now the only life came from the water itself, gurgling and slurping its way towards various hidden gutters where it rushed unseen into the pestilent river that bisected the City itself.

Boy was half-awake now. Despite his exhaustion, he had been unable to sleep for long. There was too much fear running through his body to give him much peace. Valerian was unconscious again, Willow whimpering in her sleep like a disturbed dog at his feet. So it was only Boy who knew what happened when the boat suddenly struck something in the dark and came to a halt.

He put both hands out slowly into the darkness. The boat was resting against a low wall on his left. He could hear the sound of wood on wood in front of him. On the other the side of the boat he felt another prow under his fingers. He guessed rightly that the boat had hit another one moored at a landing point.

'Valerian!' he called as loudly as he dared. 'Willow! Wake up!'

He felt around the wall and found a crevice between two of the stones. He dug his fingers in and found it did not take much effort to keep their boat against the side. Keeping careful hold, he called out again.

'Valerian! Wake up! I think we might be able to get out. Willow! We're at some sort of jetty again. We're somewhere at last.'

'What is it?' came Valerian's voice from the darkness. 'Where are we? Why is it dark?'

'The torch went out,' said Boy. There was no need for Valerian to know that Willow had dropped it. 'It went out ages ago.'

'Where are we?' said Willow.

'What difference does it make?' asked Boy. 'It's dark everywhere.'

'No, it isn't,' said Willow. 'Look there!'

'Where?' asked Valerian.

In the dark it was impossible to know where Willow was looking, but then Boy saw.

Away to one side of them was a speck of light in a distant tunnel. It seemed to be very far away.

'Can you get out of the boat?' Valerian said.

'Who are you talking to?' asked Boy.

'Either of you!' Valerian barked, and his voice echoed around them, finally dying away after many beats of the heart. They were at the edge of some vast chamber, from across the far side of which came the faint light.

'I think I can,' said Willow, but Boy was already slithering over the side of the boat on to what turned out to be a quayside, long forgotten in this abandoned subterranean world.

'Find my hand,' said Willow, holding it out in the blackness.

Boy worked along the side of the quay, gripping the low edge of the boat, until his arm bumped into Willow's.

'Take the rope,' she said, passing it to Boy, who, fumbling around, found an iron ring to tie it to.

He pulled Willow up, and then they both helped lift Valerian out.

Once on firm ground, he seemed to recover and take charge again.

'We may as well head for the light. Perhaps it is coming in from the outside.'

And so they walked.

It was like walking on a black night, lit only by a few stars. They could make out their destination clearly enough, but the ground under their feet not at all.

On more than one occasion they caught their boots on rough ground and twice Willow was unlucky enough to walk into low stone bollards and fall over. It was an ancient square, which seemed to slope slightly uphill away from the canal, and with every step they could see more clearly that the light they were heading for was not daylight but artificial.

It was coming from a low archway in the corner of the

square, and beyond it a series of smaller arches that led into tiny tunnels, each half the height of an average man.

Boy and Willow hesitated, but Valerian strode through the entrance arch and then bent down at the opening of the small passage that now seemed to their eyes to be dazzling with light.

He jumped back.

The light wavered and then emerged from the hole. It was followed by a man.

'Valerian!' he gasped.

'Kepler!' spluttered Valerian.

6

Valerian and Kepler stood staring at each other, apparently unable to speak, then Kepler noticed the strange way Valerian was standing.

'What's happened to your arm?' he said.

'Broken,' said Valerian. 'I ran into Meade and his gang.'

'I warned you—'

'You warned me about a lot of things. But how are you here? The book! What about the book?'

'You would have done better to listen to me,' said Kepler, ignoring Valerian's question. 'If you had, you might not be in this mess.'

Kepler was thin, and dwarfed by Valerian. His receding hair lay in black straggles scraped across his head. He wore small glasses of his own design and manufacture. He was dressed in a black frock-coat and worn boots and his two gold teeth shone.

Boy and Willow were amazed by the light he was carrying. It was one of his own devices, without doubt. Slung over his shoulder on a wide canvas strap was a box with a brass handle protruding from it. From this one of his special wires connected to a wooden handle with a glass ball on the end. It was this glass ball that was glowing with a strong yellow light. From time to time the light weakened and Kepler would wind the handle on the box furiously. As he did so the light would return to its full strength.

Kepler walked over to Boy and Willow and inspected them by the light.

'Boy I know. Who is this?'

'A girl. Of some use. She's cleverer than Boy.'

Kepler grunted.

'What are you doing here?' he asked Valerian.

'No! Listen!' replied Valerian. 'Have you found the book?'

He grasped Kepler with his good hand.

Kepler sighed deeply.

'Alas, Valerian,' he sighed, 'I have not.'

'But what were you doing in there?' asked Valerian, pointing at the small tunnel from which Kepler had emerged.

Kepler hesitated just a fraction before answering.

'That was my last attempt,' he said. 'My investigations, on your behalf, led me down here. I was led to believe that the answer lay in these catacombs. It has not been easy. Finding a safe entrance to this world was hard enough. I succeeded, but now I have failed. I am sorry, Valerian. There can be no other way. You will have to face your future and your past tomorrow night.'

'But the motto!' Valerian cried. 'The Beebe motto led you down here?'

'Yes. The motto. That led me close. I learned that the Beebes knew of the catacombs. The family were advisors to the Emperor for many years. They came and went, from Linden to the Palace, through the canals. I thought the book was hidden here. It was not. You will have to face your past and your future tomorrow night.'

Valerian raged, cursing himself, cursing Kepler and Boy, cursing life itself. Again and again he cried, No! It seemed there would be no end to his anguish, but at last his rage spent itself and he fell silent. His head dropped.

'There is no other way,' Kepler said eventually. 'You know that. It is over after all.'

Valerian fell to his knees and did not move.

Boy put his hands to his head. What could he possibly say? Willow looked at Boy, then at Valerian.

'It can't happen!' she suddenly cried. 'You can't give up!'

Valerian remained motionless as she wrapped her arms around his head.

'Come on!' she cried. 'Boy, tell him.'

But Boy knew it was hopelesss and tears poured down his face. Kepler watched, motionless.

All four stayed that way for a long time.

Finally Kepler spoke.

'We should go. Back to the City.'

No one answered.

'There is no point staying down here,' he said.

'Not for you three,' said Valerian. 'You go. Leave me here.'

'We can't leave you,' cried Boy.

'It may as well happen here as anywhere,' said Valerian. 'There is no escaping it now. If I die here, at least no one will have to bury me.'

'No!' cried Boy. 'Don't give up!'

'I am not moving,' Valerian said. 'Give me the last of the medicine, Boy. Kepler, do you have any more of these with you? No? Never mind. I shall not be moving far now.'

He sat against a wall and bowed his head.

'I can't believe he's giving up,' Willow said to Boy, but Boy did not answer.

Kepler came and crouched by Valerian.

'Valerian! Listen! You will do what I say. You will come with me.'

'I will not! The only reason I like you is because you never preach at me, so don't start now. I am too ill and tired to move. I will stay here.'

Kepler got to his feet and gave his light another few cranks of the handle.

'Very well, he said. 'You leave me no alternative. I will not see you die in this way. I am going to mend your arm at least. I will take Boy, for help. The girl can stay with you.'

'But I don't want to go!' cried Boy

'And I don't want to leave Boy!' cried Willow.

'You will both do as I say,' said Kepler, 'for Valerian. I need Boy to help me carry things to mend his arm. Someone must stay with him.'

They argued a while longer, but Kepler would not be dissuaded and eventually Boy and Willow agreed. Valerian watched it all – it seemed to have no effect on him now.

Kepler had brought some torches in case his light device stopped working. He handed one to Boy and set it burning with a chemical match.

Then they left Willow and Valerian with Kepler's special light.

'Just turn the handle if it starts to fade,' Kepler instructed Willow. 'We'll be gone no more than a few hours.'

Then Boy and Kepler left for the boats.

As they went, Willow called after them, 'Don't be long!'

Her voice wavered in the darkness as they disappeared from view.

'Please.'

7

Kepler held the torch over the prow of the boat. He seemed not to need a map. Boy sat in the back of the boat and they followed the natural flow of the canal towards one of the river inlets, but making two difficult turns. Boy was not sure he could find his way back to Willow and Valerian if Kepler were not with him.

'Doesn't really take that long,' said Kepler over his shoulder. 'You just have to know which way to go, or you could be in here forever.'

He laughed. It was not a nice laugh.

Kepler called out more directions and Boy obeyed.

'Did you know the girl well?' said Kepler.

What did he mean, 'Did'? thought Boy.

'Willow's a friend of mine,' he said. There was a note of surprise in his voice, as if he himself were only now realising this. But it felt right saying it. 'A good friend.'

'And bad about Valerian, too,' Kepler went on. 'It can't be helped though. It has to be like this.'

'What are you talking about?' asked Boy, shipping the pole into the boat. They drifted.

'That I found the book. Oh yes, I found it days ago, but when I saw – well, I knew I had to hide it again. I was just hiding it when you and Valerian and the girl arrived. That

212

was your good fortune. If he had found it! Well. Shame they'll have to die. Although I suppose the girl *might* find her way out. That's why I left her the lamp, but otherwise . . .'

Boy felt himself go cold. Then fear and anger rushed through him. He was sitting in a boat with a madman. Kepler seemed to think Valerian was the enemy and that he had to hide the book from him, not find it for him.

Kepler rambled on.

'I have known him a long time, but then he deserves no better after all he's done. We will have to get along without him!'

He laughed again, then peered ahead into the gloom.

'A left coming up, I think. Yes. Boy? A left! A left!'

But Boy had another use for the pole. He took careful aim and swiped Kepler around the head with it. His aim was true and Kepler fell clean over the side into the water.

To Boy's good fortune, the torch dropped inside the boat.

Boy started to push the boat hard against the current. He had to find his way back to Valerian. His life depended on it, and Boy was not going to let him down.

'Valerian!' he called into the darkness. 'I'm coming. I'm coming!'

Behind him, Kepler sunk under the water for a moment then, as the cold revived him, came spluttering to the surface.

'Boy!' he coughed. 'Boy! Come back! Boy! You don't understand! Come back!'

But he could only gasp the words, and Boy was already far away.

8

Boy hurried back to his master. Some strange power entered him, and he remembered without hesitation every turn he had made in the dark. The torch guttered on its side in the bottom of the boat, and the wood where it lay started to smoulder, but Boy fixed his eyes on the tunnels ahead, until he was back at the quayside of the underground square.

He leapt from the boat and ran across the square, holding the torch in front of him.

'Valerian! Willow! Valerian! Valerian!'

Willow lifted her lamp high and scrambled to her feet as he arrived.

'Valerian! I know where the book is! I know!'

Now even Valerian was roused from his stupor.

Boy ran right to the entrance of the low tunnel where Kepler had emerged and pointed.

'The book's in there! Kepler's crazy! He was trying to hide it from us! I wouldn't let him do that. I hit him! Maybe I – I don't know, but I *can't* let you go, Valerian.'

Valerian almost leapt to his feet, despite his arm.

'Kepler . . .' he murmured to himself. 'Kepler! I was wrong to think the past was the past. I, of all people, should know that!'

He looked at Boy.

'You have done well,' he said, his eyes shining with a renewed power. 'I am pleased with you.'

Boy stood, speechless.

'Now!' said Valerian. 'Give me the light, Willow. I'm going inside.'

Valerian got down on his hands and knees, and shoving the lamp ahead of him, he crawled into the tunnel, moving along like a three-legged dog.

Boy turned to Willow.

'I think I've killed Kepler,' he said.

Willow said nothing. Boy did not stop, could not stop. The words tumbled from his mouth.

'He was just leaving you here to die with Valerian. I didn't think. I just did it.'

'What did you do?' Willow asked.

'I hit him with the pole. He went into the water. I–'

'Boy . . .' she stopped, then held her hand out to him. 'Let's hope the book gives Valerian the answer he needs. Then it may have been worth it.'

Boy sat down with Willow to wait. They leant against each other in the dank air and watched the flame of the torch flicker and spark. Its smoke twisted away to the low ceiling of the passage from which the many smaller tunnels led.

'It's going out,' said Boy.

'No, it isn't,' Willow said firmly. 'It can't be.'

But it was. They tried to turn the torch this way and that, to coax the flame back into life, but they only seemed to be making it worse. It went out, and they held each other, trying not to panic.

'He'll be back soon,' said Boy. 'Soon.'

They waited.

Eventually they heard a sound, and saw the light flooding the entrance.

Valerian emerged, triumphant. He backed out of the low tunnel, dragging something behind him. It was a huge book, vastly ancient and tattered beyond belief. There was a strange expression on Valerian's face as he clutched it. A look of joy. Stronger than joy – it was joy and delight and rapture and hope combined. His eyes burned at Boy and Willow, and then at the thick tome grasped in his strong fingers.

'Is that it?' asked Boy, though there was no need.

It was undoubtedly what they had been looking for for so long. At last the weight was too much for Valerian to hold in one hand and he put the book on the ground in front of him.

'Now let us see . . .' he said, his voice quiet and strangely high.

He lifted the book so it balanced on its spine.

'Wind this infernal contraption for me, will you?' he said to Willow. 'Good. Now hold it there.'

Valerian let the book fall open, as if letting it choose which page it would show to him, what secrets it would impart to him.

Boy stared as Valerian flicked backwards and forwards through the book, searching for his answer. None of them moved, save for Valerian occasionally turning a page and Willow winding the light whenever it began to fail.

Valerian's face drew closer to the book as he seemed to find what he was looking for. Or was it that the book was showing him what it wanted to show him?

Willow, holding the lamp, tried to read what she could, but the book was written in many different and strange languages, and she could only understand a few words.

Suddenly Valerian gripped the edges of the book so

tightly Boy thought he might pull it apart. He leant closer, his hands shaking.

With fumbling fingers he delved deep into his coat pocket and pulled out a piece of paper – a piece of paper that Boy immediately recognised as the one Kepler had written about him, on the back of which Willow had copied the map.

Now Valerian began to pore over this paper as well as a certain page of the book, and a frown spread across his face and then vanished just as easily.

He looked up.

'Boy,' he said quietly, 'I have my answer.'

'What – what is it, Valerian?' Boy asked.

'You. You are my answer,' Valerian said, grinning.

Willow, who had been silently trying to read the book over Valerian's shoulder, suddenly gasped. She was not even trying to decipher the peculiar words any more, but somehow there was knowledge in her head – a picture that filled her mind with horror.

'Oh . . . Boy!' she yelled. 'He wants to kill you! Boy! Run!'

The grin slipped from Valerian's face as he swung his arm and punched Willow hard in the face. She dropped to the ground, spilling the light. She did not move.

Valerian turned to Boy.

'There's nothing to be scared of,' said Valerian smoothly, his voice calm. 'Come here. There's nothing wrong. Come closer.'

But Boy did not come closer.

He took a quick, faltering glance at Willow's still body on the stone flags, and then he turned and ran.

December 31st – New Year's Eve

The Day of
Absolute Promotion

❧

Boy ran automatically, without thinking, without realising what he was doing. He ran off into the darkness, and only after some time of running blindly did he realise that he had no light to run by. He stopped. Everything was inky around him, and now he found himself paralysed by the darkness. He felt unable to move without seeing where it was he was moving to.

He was aware of a light behind him.

He had gone perhaps fifty paces into the gloom across the square. He turned, and with alarm saw that Valerian was following, though slowly. He was walking unevenly, almost staggering.

He doesn't know where I am, Boy thought.

Boy could see Valerian clearly enough. He had grabbed Kepler's light device from beside Willow's body and was heading in the direction he thought Boy had gone. But blinded somewhat by his light, he could not see far enough into the gloom to see Boy.

All this passed through Boy's head in a flash.

He could see Valerian because of the light, and it was enough to dimly pick up a little of the shapes of old buildings around him. If he was careful, very careful, Boy guessed he might be able to use Valerian's own light to see his way, and provided he kept as far from Valerian as the faint light would allow, Valerian would have no idea where he was.

He would have to be careful – if he judged it wrong, Valerian would see him.

Nervously, Boy began to edge backwards and tripped over a low stone kerb. He fell with a groan and saw Valerian freeze. Boy watched in horror as Valerian held the lamp higher, away from his face, and looked right at where Boy sat on his backside.

'Boy!' called Valerian. 'Come here, Boy.'

Boy scrambled to his feet and scuttled further into the darkness.

'There you are!' cried Valerian, and started to follow, more quickly this time.

Boy hurried on and as silently as he could began to circle around sideways from his last position.

Crouching low to the pavement, Boy watched as Valerian moved straight on ahead, unaware of where he was. The tall man looked demonic as he passed within a few yards of Boy. His face was illuminated from underneath by the lamp, picking out its shadows and crevices.

'Boy!' called Valerian. 'I know you're there, Boy.'

But it was clear that he did not.

This was better. Boy waited until Valerian had passed him and gone a fair way ahead, and then began to follow him.

Perhaps, eventually, Valerian would lead him to the outside. Or maybe they would pass within sight of a channel of daylight, if indeed it was day outside, and then Boy could find his own way out.

He had no idea what time it was or what day it was, and maybe only Valerian knew, somehow, deep inside, that his last day had arrived.

Indeed, a few stone feet above their heads midnight had

come and gone and the early hours of New Year's Eve were starting to unwind across the length and breadth of the City. Most people were shut up fast in their beds, trying to sleep as deeply as possible to prepare for the manic celebrations that would entwine the City that night to welcome in the new year.

Boy crept along behind Valerian, who called ahead of him into the darkness.

'Boy. Boy! Are you there? Come here, Boy. I won't hurt you.'

Willow woke and began to panic. There was not the slightest suspicion of light anywhere, and the more she strained to see something – anything at all – and failed, the worse she felt. She couldn't believe there could be no difference between having her eyes open and shut and realised what it must be to be blind. She felt like screaming, but remembered that Valerian was out there in the blackness somewhere, his mind set on murder.

Murder? Was that really what she'd seen in his eyes when he'd read the book and found his answer? It was hard, but maybe not impossible to believe. She had been looking over Valerian's shoulder, trying to understand the strange writing and symbols. She had seen the piece of paper about Boy, too, but it was not these things that had told her.

No. That knowledge had simply appeared in her head as she looked at the pages of the book. She had seen what Valerian intended for Boy. The book had *shown* it to her.

If that was not evidence enough, the blow he had struck her was. Why else would he silence her so brutally? She felt her face in the darkness. Her eye hurt. She thought she could feel the stickiness of blood on her fingers.

She heard a sound, and tensed.

A low, grating noise. She tried to place it, to identify its source and direction, but she could not. Everything was disorientating without sight. Again she wanted to scream, and to be sick from the fear, but she fought the impulse.

She tried to breathe more deeply and slowly. She listened again, thinking she had perhaps imagined it. But no, there it was again, coming closer and getting louder.

She tried to decide what to do but found herself struggling to think clearly. She could try and crawl away from the noise but that would be difficult, and where could she go? Maybe it was better to stay where she was – she couldn't see whatever it was that was making the noise so maybe it couldn't see her either. Maybe. If, on the other hand, it was some *thing* from the canal, it would be used to moving in darkness. Perhaps it could even see in the dark and was coming right for her.

She heard a different noise, a small scraping sound, and saw – or maybe she only imagined it – the briefest spark of light. The light, had it been there at all, was gone, and she thought she heard a voice.

She sprang to her feet. Her head throbbed from Valerian's fist and she felt dizzy. Stumbling against some unseen pavement in the blackness, she fell.

She let out a groan as she hit the ground, her wrists taking the fall.

'Boy?' came a voice. 'Willow?'

Willow lay still, her head pounding, her breath coming short and fast. Her face was inches from the stone flags and she could feel their dampness seep into her.

She noticed that the sound had stopped.

'Willow?' came the voice from the darkness. 'It's me. It's Kepler.'

Willow was too surprised to say anything. Kepler, who had left her to die with Valerian, was not who she would have chosen to have found her. Boy had half-killed him, trying to save . . . Valerian, who was lurking somewhere, threatening death in the dark.

There was nothing else to do.

'Kepler!' she called out. 'It's me, Willow!'

'Where are you, child? Is Boy with you? I fear for his safety.'

'What about my safety?' asked Willow bitterly.

There was no reply.

'Well?' said Willow again in the dark.

'You are safe,' Kepler said. 'You are safe from Valerian. It is only Boy who can save him. Only Boy's life is in danger. We would have come back for you—'

Willow cut him short.

'Oh! I don't believe you!'

'I swear,' said Kepler, 'I swear you were safe. The danger lies only to Valerian and to Boy. Once Valerian had . . . gone, I would have returned for you.'

'I don't understand,' said Willow, hesitating. 'I don't understand any of it. I don't know what I'm doing. I don't know where Boy is . . .'

'Yes,' said Kepler, 'we have to find Boy. He's the one in danger.'

'Why?' asked Willow. 'What does Valerian want him for?'

'I will explain,' said Kepler, 'but let me find you first. Where are you?'

'I don't know,' said Willow. 'Where are you?'

'Over here,' said Kepler. 'I have some matches but they are a little damp . . .'

Willow heard the noise she had heard before – the small scraping sound and then a fizz of sparks, which rapidly died away.

'Wet. Where are you?'

226

Willow nearly laughed in spite of herself, in spite of the horror which she found herself in.

The louder noise started again and Willow knew that Kepler was getting closer. She didn't like the idea, but equally she didn't like the thought of being alone in darkness any more.

'That's it,' she said. 'I'm this way. Yes, this way.'

And then Kepler bumped into her foot.

'That's close enough,' she said. 'Now, tell me what is going on.'

3

It was working, after a fashion.

Boy crawled on his hands and knees a handful of paces behind Valerian, who made slow progress. In fact, Valerian was walking more and more slowly all the time. Boy wondered if he was getting tired, or if his arm was giving him more pain, but whatever the reason, Boy found it no trouble at all to keep up with him, even crawling as he was.

Slowly they made their way on through the catacombs. Occasionally they would come across a branch of the canal, gurgling gently, the water an oily black snake that shugged off into the next section of tunnel.

Now they were in a long corridor, a straight path with a low ceiling composed, Boy supposed, of buildings that soared away into the City above their heads, into the long-forgotten daylight.

It was an unsettling world. Far underground, this deserted empire lurked unknown to almost everyone. Boy was now following Valerian down a low tunnel in which sound behaved strangely. There was an echo from the scrape of Valerian's boots, but it was a short, dry sound, cut off almost as soon as it had begun. The ceiling hung with miniature stalactites, at the end of which were small, ice-cool drops of water. When one of these fell on to Boy's neck it was all he could do to stop himself from shrieking and giving himself away. And then there was the smell of the place – musty, damp, full of spores of unseen fungus noiselessly swelling in the lightless passages and caverns.

They passed a gateway – an iron gate, with a massive rusty iron lock. Behind it the darkness stretched away into depths that no one would ever see.

Along each side of the corridor were low doorways, and at each one of these Valerian would stop a few feet short.

As Boy passed them, there was still enough light from Valerian's lamp to see strange numbers over the lintels, carved and then painted. The numbers made no sense to Boy, but some of the doorways bore inscriptions instead. *Sometimes,* said one, *it is better to die than to live.*

Oh good! thought Boy. *Just the sort of thing Valerian will love.*

Then he saw something which bothered him, though he couldn't work out why. Valerian began to scratch his nose in a nervous way. For a long time Boy watched, trying but failing to work out what it was that upset him about this.

Boy scratched his nose.

Valerian peered into the doorways. Suddenly he dropped his pace near to a dead halt and tiptoed the last inches to the doorway, swinging the lantern round in a rush.

'Boy?' he called into each doorway, and something in his voice made Boy's skin creep. He hung back further from Valerian's light, until he was sure he would not be seen by his master.

Valerian moved on.

'Boy!' he called. 'Boy, I know you're there. Come out. Let's talk. There's really nothing to be scared of. I need your help.'

Boy didn't want to listen, but had no choice. He crawled

on after Valerian, all the time hoping that he would see a way out, maybe a patch of light or a breeze of fresh air.

Valerian had stopped. The light from the device was failing and he could not carry it and wind the handle at the same time. He placed the box on the ground and, steadying it with his foot, he leant down and began to wind the handle evenly, looking about as he did. The light from the globe shone strongly again, and Valerian picked it up.

'I don't want to hurt you,' Valerian said, and Boy thought about Willow and wondered if she was dead. If she wasn't, he shouldn't have left her. But what could he do? He had had to run, or Valerian would have had him. Broken arm or not, he would have had him, of that Boy was sure. Valerian always got what he wanted. Always.

'Come out, Boy. I know you're there. Come out, Boy. I need your help. Haven't I helped you all these years?'

Valerian sounded tired. He sounded old and pathetic and sad, and Boy wished he would be quiet.

'I found you. In the streets I found you, grovelling in dark places. I gave you a life, and a place to sleep and food. We've come a long way, Boy, you and I, haven't we?'

Boy thought about just how far he'd come. Here he was, still grovelling around in dark places. Well, at least that was familiar ground. He watched as Valerian slid up to another of the low doorways and repeated his trick of stealing the last inches on tiptoe. Finding nothing, he moved on.

'I've always looked after you, haven't I, Boy? Yes, I have. But now I need you to help me. That's not so much to ask, is it? You know I'm in trouble, Boy, don't you? You know I need help. You are my famulus! I need *your* help, Boy. You're the only one who can help me now.'

Boy listened as Valerian drawled on, his voice full of pain and pitiful to hear.

230

Boy found himself crying in the darkness.

'Please, Boy. Come out. We can go on as we did before. I'm not going to hurt you, Boy. I need you. You don't know how much you mean to me. And besides, there are things I've never told you – things I should tell you. About who you are, where you came from. You'd like to know about who you really are, wouldn't you?'

Now Boy was listening hard. Valerian couldn't know anything about his parents, could he? But supposing he did? What if Valerian died and he never found out?

'Yes, I can tell you who you are, Boy. I can tell you about your father, your mother. So come out and let me talk to you.'

Boy stood up. Valerian could not yet see him, but Boy began to walk slowly, his heart thumping in his chest, towards the light.

'I do need your help. And I can tell you who you are, Boy. Who you are, and where you came from.'

Now Boy stood a few feet behind Valerian.

'Who am I, Valerian?' he asked quietly.

Valerian jerked round and lifted the light high, making sure it was really Boy he was looking at.

'Boy!' he shouted. 'There you are! Come on, there's no time to lose!'

But Boy stood still, and though his blood beat through his veins as if they would burst, he spoke calmly to his master.

'I'm not going anywhere, Valerian, until you tell me who I am.'

Valerian took a step towards Boy, his face blank.

'I give the orders, Boy, you know that. Now come here. I won't hurt you.'

Boy took another step backwards.

'Who am I, Valerian?' he cried. 'You said you'd tell me.'

'Boy,' growled Valerian, coming closer, and for the first time Boy faltered. He could see Valerian's eyes more clearly now, he could feel them eat into his own, finding their way into his mind, making him feel so small, so helpless. He would do anything Valerian told him. He always had, he always would . . .

With an effort, Boy wrenched his eyes away and ran several steps back into the shadows.

'Come here,' said Valerian. 'Come here!'

'No,' said Boy.

'Come here!' Valerian shouted, his face filled with rage and frustration. 'You! Boy! Come here!'

Boy turned and ran into the nearest doorway that led from the corridor.

Valerian's light bobbed after him.

4

'But what can we do?' Willow said.

'We need to find a light', said Kepler, 'or we shall die down here. Let me try another match now. The warmth from my hands may have dried them a little.'

This time there was a stronger flicker of flame that lasted longer but died as it reached the wood of the match.

In that short time Willow saw Kepler had a cut above his right ear, a vivid slash of red across his face. He stared at the failing match intently, his desperation clearly visible.

'What happened to your head?' asked Willow. 'Did you fall?'

'In a way,' he answered. 'Never mind that now. It happened when Boy and I parted company in the canals.'

'But the canals . . . ?'

'Are not deep. No more than waist-high in most places. You need to watch your step occasionally. There's one place a little further along where–'

'But why were you coming down here? To find the book?'

'No,' said Kepler, and he laughed, a snorting noise that Willow hated him for. 'No! I came down here to hide it.'

Now Willow was confused.

'To hide it? To hide it?'

'Yes. You see, Willow, I learnt things. I have been helping

Valerian for a long time. We had not seen each other since . . . for years, until one day he just arrived at my house and told me about the spectre he faced. He turned up as if nothing had ever happened between us! But when he told me about the book, I knew I would put the past behind me. Now is not the time, and certainly not the place to tell you all the trials and troubles we faced, attempting to find the book. Suffice to say that I discovered that an answer would be contained therein.'

'But what is the book? What did you learn?'

'It is an almanack, but much more than that. It holds answers to questions that men ask. It holds information about all manner of dealings, both light and dark. It contains much information on the nature of the . . . agreement into which Valerian placed himself. And it answers questions – questions in the mind of the reader. It could solve Valerian's problem – of that there is no doubt.'

'You mean–'

'Yes, I mean exactly that. Valerian's life ending in a most horrible way.'

Willow thought of something that had been bothering her. Something important.

'Why?' she asked.

'What?' Kepler replied.

'You were supposed to be helping Valerian find the book. And now you're telling me you've been trying to hide it from him. Why?'

'I thought you had realised that. The horoscope. Boy's horoscope. That gave me the answer, really.

'What's a–?'

'Horoscope? It's a method of thinking about people, based on the patterns of the stars and the planets. It explains who people are, and why they are. It has deep scientific basis which few men truly understand, and yet the results of such investigation can be powerful.

'It concerns the heavens. The stars and the planets and their motions around the Sun, which is the centre of the universe, and their relative motions around the Earth.'

'I don't understand,' said Willow, feeling lost and lonely again.

'That doesn't matter. Just understand this. The position of all these things in the sky at the moment of an individual's conception determines the nature, the character, of that individual. Irrevocably.'

Now Willow began to understand.

'The piece of paper Valerian found, with Boy's name on it – is that his horoscope?'

'Sort of,' said Kepler. 'Sort of.'

'But how can you have worked these things out about Boy? You said you have to know where the planets were at the moment someone was born, but you can't have known that for Boy. No one knows when he was born – not even he does!'

'I made a guess. I felt a coincidence. An enormous coincidence, maybe, or Fate working its path through Boy and Valerian's lives. And mine, too. And then I found the book, and the book confirmed it. It *showed* me. I found out the truth of things.'

'But what is this coincidence?' asked Willow.

'That two people have come to be together. In all this sprawling city of tens of thousands, that two people should find each other. No, I think it is not coincidence. I think this is how Fate works.'

'So why were you trying to hide it? I still don't understand . . .'

'Valerian will kill Boy,' said Kepler. 'That is the answer.

That is the only way he can save himself now – for him to give Boy's life in place of his own. The pact can be broken only by a life exactly as long as the term of the bargain. That is what I discovered. I guessed much of this. The book confirmed it to me. I guessed who Boy is, and when he was conceived, and I drew up his horoscope. I found that it described the boy I knew very well. And so then, knowing who Boy is and having looked into the book, I knew what Valerian would do if he found out. And so I began to try to hide the path I had started to clear. I came down here to hide the book.

'In a few hours from now Valerian can offer Boy in place of himself, and he will go free. That is how and why Valerian will kill Boy. That is why we have to find Boy before Valerian does.'

Willow's heart thumped inside its rib-prison.

Boy. Valerian would kill Boy to save himself. Finally she began to understand the insane nature of the journey they had all been making. A dance – a hideous dance with Fate and Death.

Something else occurred to her.

'But why do you care about Boy?' she asked.

'Why do you?' said Kepler.

Before Willow could answer, Kepler spoke again.

'I have my reasons, as I'm sure do you. And I want the book.'

'So where did you find it?' Willow asked, 'Who does it belong to?'

'I heard, after years of searching far and wide, that it had been in the possession of a rich and powerful family. A family who lived in the City itself. A family called Beebe.'

In the darkness, Willow jumped at the name, but Kepler continued unaware.

'A large and powerful family, though corrupt and broken

now. They once owned properties in the City, and a large estate in the countryside. They built a church there, as their private place of worship, and eternal rest. That was where I found the book.'

'Where?'

'In Gad Beebe's grave. I had traced it as far as the Beebes. A sum of money to one of their more degenerate members, and the book's whereabouts became mine . . .'

'But . . .' Willow felt her head swimming, 'But I don't understand.'

'What?' asked Kepler.

'Gad Beebe. We looked in Gad Beebe's grave – there was nothing in there but his bones . . . you must have got there before us.'

Now it was Kepler's turn to be surprised.

'You went to Linden? You went to Beebe's grave? But how? How did you know his name?'

Willow smiled.

'I worked it out, from the music box that Boy got from Green. I don't know where Green had got it from, but the notes of the tune it played spelled his name. Gad Beebe.'

In the darkness Kepler started to laugh, bitterly. Then he stopped abruptly.

'But that is too ridiculous.'

'What?' asked Willow.

'That music box . . . I found it in Beebe's grave. I gave it to Green. Me! I'd brought it back from Linden. It amused me. Then I sent for Green, I needed him to go and meet Valerian. He saw it on my desk, and asked what it was. When I showed him he smiled like a child. He asked for it, along with the money I was paying him. He refused to do the job unless I gave it to him. That thug! But it was nothing to me, so I gave it to him. He must have had it with him when he went out to meet Valerian in The Trumpet.'

'But it held Gad Beebe's name!' cried Willow. 'Without it we'd have never found the grave . . .'

'Fate, once more,' Kepler said, 'Fate steering us all for its own ends . . .'

Willow thought about what he'd said. It did seem extraordinary. That little music box had made its way from Gad Beebe's grave, to Kepler and Green to Boy to Valerian, and only she had known what it held. Without it Valerian would still be struggling for the answer, and Boy would be safe. It was a coincidence too great to be anything other than true. The true path of Fate.

Then something occurred to her.

'But why?' she asked. 'Why did you send Green to meet Boy, in The Trumpet?'

'I sent him to meet Valerian – did he send Boy instead? That may have saved his life.'

'What do you mean?' asked Willow.

'I was supposed to meet Valerian that evening, to report any progress on the book. He knew I was close to finding it. In fact, I already had the book, and had read it. I'd learnt what it would mean for Valerian. For Boy. So I had to send Green instead. I sent a letter to Valerian at the theatre, telling him to meet Green.'

'But what did you tell Green to say to Valerian? He was expecting to get some news from you.'

'I didn't tell him to say anything, I told him to kill him.'

Willow froze.

'Yes, Willow, I told him to kill him. In another few days he'd be dead anyway, and I knew if he found the book that Boy's life would be in danger.'

'But he's your friend! You've known him for years. Worked with him! You couldn't just have him killed!'

'We were friends. Once, a long time ago, maybe. Then we fell out. We became rivals. He . . . hurt someone, someone I cared for. He betrayed me. Around the time he was expelled by the Academy. We didn't see each other for ten years. Then he came to ask for my help, but we were never friends again . . . He told me about the book. And I wanted it. I was never interested in helping Valerian, I wanted the book.'

'I still don't believe it,' Willow said, fiercely.

'Listen, girl,' cried Kepler, growing angry. 'It's him or Boy now. Understand that! Only one of them can live! And I want it to be Boy . . .'

They sat in silence for a long time, until all the questions in Willow's head fought to be answered.

'So, what did you do then? After Linden? Did you use the tunnel to get here?'

'Tunnel?' asked Kepler.

'It's how we got here,' Willow said, 'We found the entrance to a tunnel in the crypt of the church, and an underground river that led all the way here.'

'I thought it was maybe so,' said Kepler. 'During my researches into the book, I found a map of all the catacombs and canals. I made a model of them in my cellar, to try to learn the routes by heart. It is only because I did, that I was able to find my way back here in the dark.'

'In your basement? The canals and the writing?'

Kepler nodded in the darkness.

'But I did not have time to investigate while I was in Linden. To see if I was right about a tunnel all the way out there. It was built by the Beebes, when they were most powerful, as a link to the heart of the City. That tunnel is much newer than the rest of this place.'

'So you came back to the City overland?'

'Yes, I had hired a horse. I had the book. I'd found the book in the grave, and the music box there, too, and brought them both back from Linden, but it took me a long time. When I got back to the City, things had become complicated. Valerian's house is being guarded by the Watch. And there have been deaths, I understand.'

Willow was silent.

'Yes, I know about the deaths,' Kepler said. 'I heard about Green, though we may never know exactly what happened that night. I went to The Trumpet yesterday. And Korp, too.'

'Who told you?' Willow asked.

'Korp's murder is big news,' said Kepler.

'Valerian? Was it Valerian who did it?'

'I have no idea. Even I cannot work out everything that is going on here. I wonder where the book is now. Valerian must have taken it with him.'

'I don't know that he has,' said Willow. 'He can't carry that and the light, can he?

'True.'

'But what about the paper? The horoscope? Valerian found it in your desk.'

'The horoscope. So, I made another mistake! I think I left it there, in my hurry to get to Linden. Well, that was as good as handing Valerian a key, but it would still not have been any use had he not found the book. That was why I had to get him away from here. When you three found me, I was hiding the book. Valerian was terrified of this place. He came down here once as a student. He got lost and nearly died. He vowed never to come here again. I thought this the best place to hide it.'

'You could have burned it. Thrown it in the river!'

'I could no more do that than cut off my own hand!' cried Kepler. 'I want the book when Valerian is . . . I want the book. It is full of all knowledge. It holds enormous power, as the success of the Beebe family demonstrates. But more than that, it shows things to the reader, things only about them and their destiny . . .'

'But if it is so great a thing, so powerful, then why did the Beebes bury it with Gad?'

'Apparently they thought it dangerous. That its power was not always . . . good. That it could corrupt.'

Willow shivered.

'Are you sure it's safe to use it?' she began, but Kepler cut her off.

'Of course!' he said dismissively. 'The Beebes were fools. They used it unwisely and their downfall was the result. So they decided to hide the book. But in the right hands . . . it's nonsense to suggest it could do anything other than impart wisdom.'

They sat without speaking as Kepler's last words drifted away into the darkness around them. Willow began to panic.

'And we still have no light,' she said desperately.

'No,' agreed Kepler, 'we do not.'

'No!' cried Willow suddenly. 'No. I mean, maybe we do.'

She rummaged around in her coat. In her pocket she found the candle stub they had used in the great cemetery, and later in Kepler's house.

'Why didn't I remember before?' Willow wailed, though in truth it would have been no use without a source of flame to light it from.

'What is it?' asked Kepler, unable to see what she was doing.

'I have a bit of a candle,' she explained. 'Maybe you could try one more match and see if we can get it alight.'

241

'Excellent,' he said.

She heard him move and then felt him put out his hands.

'Where's the candle?' he said. 'Hold still, stay close. Right.'

Again the match flared briefly, and before the head could burn away, he held it to the wick of Willow's candle stub. It took, and a small glow grew about them.

The relief was enormous, though the tiny patch of light only seemed to reinforce the oppressive gloom.

Now Kepler saw Willow's face.

'Your face?' he asked.

Willow nodded.

'Yes,' she said. 'Valerian.'

'We must find Boy.'

Then, in the light of the candle, which Kepler had taken from Willow and was shielding with one hand, they saw something else.

'The book!' Willow cried.

'That is good fortune. Our luck is turning. That is often how Fate works. One piece of good fortune begets another. Now come on! To your feet! I can get us out of here, but first we *must* find Boy!'

It had been a mistake to show himself to Valerian, and Boy knew it. How could he trust Valerian any more? How could he? Valerian was probably already a murderer. Korp or Green – or both? No, he couldn't have killed them both.

What was certain was that Boy could not trust himself with Valerian. Just to be held by his eyes for a moment too long was to forget right and wrong, to mistake black and white.

The game of cat and mouse resumed, but now with Valerian pursuing Boy rather than Boy trailing his master. Valerian was unable to travel fast, and the tunnel was low. He walked hunched over the lamp. The tunnel Boy had chosen was small and straight and narrow, and Valerian could clearly see Boy ahead of him, hurrying away.

Sickeningly, Boy knew this, and he scuttled along as fast as he could.

And then, abruptly, the roof lifted away above his head and Boy stood in a vast open space, though still far beneath the City streets. There were small hills in front of him, it seemed – piles of whiteness in the gloom. As he heard Valerian coming closer, nearing the edge of the tunnel, Boy realised that he had stopped at the threshold of this new space.

Valerian approached, and as he did, the light intensified. Boy lurched forward, missed his footing, and stumbled into one of the piles of white stuff. It was hard, but scattered under his weight. He could hear things cracking. Valerian emerged from the tunnel and shone the light straight at Boy.

'So!' he cried. 'I have you at last.'

In the light Boy realised he was sitting in piles of bones. Human bones of all sorts. He knew they were human by the large number of skulls rolling around at his feet.

He screamed.

As Valerian came closer, Boy picked up a skull and threw it. Valerian ducked but was too slow, and the ancient head-bone hit his bad arm. He howled, and wavered where he stood. In that split second Boy scrambled clumsily to his feet, bones skidding away under him, and picking one of many possible routes, he spun away between the piles of skeletons that filled this vast hall.

Boy ran and ran, hurtling into pile after pile of bones, making such a terrible noise that he was sure Valerian must be a moment away from catching him.

Finally it was too dark to see at all. Boy staggered on a few more feet, tripped over yet another skull, and collapsed into one of the heaps, too scared of Valerian to worry about what he was lying on.

He lay still, breathing quietly, and realised there was no sound of pursuit. There was no light anywhere. Valerian was probably out in the bone-field somewhere, but Boy seemed to have lost him for now. Without light he could move no further, but Boy was too upset and tired to care. He had passed over and by countless human remains in the last few days. Thousands of bones that were once people, maybe hundreds of thousands, and all because of one man's struggle to avoid joining them.

Boy lay in the bone-field, where the exhumed remains from over-flowing cemeteries all around the City had been moved hundreds of years before to make space for new arrivals. Exhausted, he put his head on to his outstretched arm and amazingly, sleep came for him and took him away.

He woke screaming. He clamped his hand to his mouth and sobbed violently until he felt the panic subsiding. He got to his feet in the darkness and began to walk.

He tried to pretend that he was not blind, that he could see where he was going, and determined to walk until he hit something. He very soon did. It was a wall, but it felt peculiar. He ran his fingers across its surface and felt small strange knobs, each about the size of his fist. He followed the wall and found a corner. Putting his hand out to the right, he found another wall close by that felt the same as the first. He was in another corridor. He put a hand on either wall and began to walk down the corridor as fast as he dared.

The knobs felt funny – smooth and cold, dry despite the general clammy nature of the catacombs. They were evenly spaced, with small gaps between, in an incredibly neat row from the floor to above his head. The whole wall was made of these things stacked in orderly fashion on top of each other. Just as he was trying to work out what they were, his left hand ran over something else in the wall, and he knew what it was instantly.

A skull. It was set into the wall, which Boy realised was made of bones – thigh bones, stacked on top of each other so the thick knobs at the end overlapped and formed the wall.

The panic welled up inside him again and he ran, blind and shrieking, to nowhere.

He ran out through the end of the passageway. Had there been light to see by, and had he stopped to look, he might have seen another inscription above the doorway from which he had emerged.

Stop! This is the Empire of Death.

At least he was going the right way.

6

Valerian prowled on. He had long ago lost Boy.

His arm hurt so much that his mind was clouded by the pain, and yet he could not stop. He knew that his last day must have dawned, but down in this infernal darkness he had no idea what time it was or how long he had left.

The thought made him shudder, and he wondered what was happening in the City, above this subterranean empire. It was presumably going about its normal business, whether sleeping, or waking, or working, or getting ready for the New Year's Eve festival.

The end of the Dead Days, and the end of Valerian's quest, one way or another.

He had to find Boy and he had to find him fast. That was all he knew. Very soon the gates of horror would open and a force would come to hunt over the Earth until he was found, speared and delivered to hell.

Valerian staggered slowly on, his mind fixed on one thing and one thing alone. Boy.

And then, from his right, he felt a breeze on his face. Its freshness was so distinct against the foetid air of the catacombs that he noticed it immediately, and it gave him hope.

Valerian changed course and headed for the breeze. Quickly he came upon another, larger space, where one of the canals passed by, although here for some reason the water flowed as in a fast river. He looked about, saw a doorway, and then a shaft of light rising straight up above his head, and he began to wonder.

Very soon, he began to smile.

He turned back in to the low room, and waited.

7

Kepler led the way, holding the candle in front of him. Willow clasped the book against her chest. It was so large and heavy that occasionally they would have to stop while she shifted it to her other arm. She wanted nothing to do with the book at all, but Kepler insisted they bring it with them.

'Can't we leave it here?' she said. 'You were going to hide it. Can't we do that and come back for it when we've got a light?'

'Absolutely not!' Kepler said. 'I made that mistake once. Valerian knows it's down here now. I shall hold on to it – or rather you will, until we get out.'

So they had made their way across that open square where Willow, Valerian and Boy had first stepped ashore after docking their boat behind Kepler's.

'If the other boat's still there, then maybe we have a chance,' Kepler said.

There was a noise – a cry, and footsteps, coming at them from the side.

Boy stood in front of them.

'Willow!' he cried, and embraced her. The horrors he had felt drained away and were replaced by hope, as he held Willow tight and felt her clasp his hands to her.

'Boy!' she cried, delighted. 'Boy! Boy!'

Swinging her around, Boy saw Kepler too.

'You!' he said.

Boy did not know what to say, because he did not know what he felt.

'You shouldn't have done that,' was all he could blurt out.

'We would have come back for her,' Kepler replied. 'Willow will tell you herself.'

But Willow said nothing.

'We had to get you away from him,' Kepler tried to explain. 'You're the one who's in danger.'

'Why?' cried Boy. 'What does he want me for?'

'Later. All the time you are down here, with Valerian somewhere around, you are in danger. Let us leave this place. It does not lift my spirits, for it provides shelter from everything except death. When we are back in the air of the City I will tell you.'

'The other boat, Boy,' said Willow. 'Hurry.'

There indeed was the boat, still with its pole.

They climbed aboard and with Kepler in front, Willow sitting in the middle clutching the book and Boy holding the pole in the rear, they set off for the outside world.

Many thoughts passed through Boy's mind, but there was one question above all.

'Why does he want to hurt me?' he asked.

Silence.

'One of you answer me!' shouted Boy. 'Answer me! What does he want me for?'

'Don't!' whispered Willow. 'Someone might hear you!'

'So answer me!' shouted Boy.

'He wants your life,' Kepler said coldly. 'Your life is the only way out for him now.'

Boy shook his head in the darkness.

'No,' he said, choking. 'He can't be trying – I don't believe it!'

'Then tell me, Boy, why were you running?' Kepler asked.

Boy said nothing and they drifted on with the current. Kepler started to mutter to himself, then spoke.

'There's a tunnel we must take!' he called. 'On the right, somewhere soon . . . There it is!'

Boy shoved the pole as hard as he could into the bottom of the canal, but the current was strong. He wrestled with the boat and forced it to make the turn, but the pole suddenly held fast in the mud of the canal bottom.

'Quick!' he called. 'Help me!'

The current pulled the boat on. On the point of being pulled in, Boy let the pole go and the boat slipped away. They were now rudderless.

'It doesn't matter,' called Kepler. 'We just need to get to the side up ahead. That's where we get out!'

The canal narrowed even more and the current turned into a powerful surge.

A few more yards and the canal plunged into a small tunnel, across which lay an ancient grille with gaps no wider than a man's hand. The water hurtled through the grille at high speed, off into even more remote depths. The boat smashed into the grille, tearing a gaping hole in its prow.

Willow nearly fell as the boat was pounded again and again against the grille by the relentless force of the water. At least they were going nowhere for the moment. Then, with horror, Boy saw that the grinding of the boat against the decrepit iron grille was starting to weaken it. If it gave way there would be no stopping them from plunging into an even blacker abyss.

Boy had always been led to believe that hell was a hot and fiery place, but he had changed his mind. If hell existed it

251

was this place, here and now. Cold, and wet, and very, very dark.

They clutched at the bank, and with a struggle Willow scrambled on to the stone quayside, throwing the book ahead of her.

She rolled over on to her back and found herself staring up into Valerian's eyes.

'Help them out,' he said to her.

She lay, frozen with terror.

'Help them out!' Valerian screamed at her, and Willow had no choice. In a few more seconds the weight of the boat would have smashed the grille away and they would be lost for ever.

She stretched her arms and pulled Kepler out, then they both did the same for Boy.

They stood facing Valerian.

The book lay between them on the stone flags.

Valerian held Kepler's light device. It began to weaken, and without taking his eyes off it, Valerian put it on the floor and, once again steadying it with his foot, wound the handle until it shone brightly.

He didn't pick it up again.

'So, Boy,' said Valerian.

'Leave him, Valerian,' said Kepler.

'Silence! You traitor! You were supposed to be my friend!'

'I was once. I was. *You* taught *me* about betrayal long ago. Things are not what they once were. You have to admit defeat. You can't take Boy where you should go instead. It's your doing, not his.'

'But now we know what Boy can do for me,' Valerian said, smiling unpleasantly. 'And in this case, I think it's only fitting that he should go instead of me.'

'No!' cried Willow. 'No! You're evil!'

Valerian laughed at her.

'I am not dead! That's all that matters. Now, Boy, come to me!'

Boy began to back away.

Willow and Kepler closed together in front of Boy, trying to keep Valerian from him, but he just laughed.

With his left hand he pulled a slim black tube from inside his coat. He shook it with a flick of his wrist and a spike, long and sharp, hissed out and locked in place with a click. He pointed it at them.

'All I want is the boy,' he said, coming forward again.

They began to circle, Valerian leading the dance, edging them backwards, closer to the canal.

There were three of them against Valerian, with only one good arm but a pointed knife. They stood near the canal bank, Valerian looking beaten, wounded and old. Seeing him like this, their confidence grew and they approached, united in a common purpose.

Boy felt his heart stirring for his master. His end would come now, one way or another. He watched as in slow motion Valerian stuck his stiletto between his teeth, then reached inside his huge black coat one more time.

'No! Stop him!' Boy began, but it was too late.

Valerian's hand flourished back out from the coat in a way that Boy had seen before.

There was a brilliant flash of light which illuminated the whole underground room, and a moment later the space was filled with purple smoke.

'Ho!'

The voice was dry and full of bitter humour – a voice that Boy knew was only Valerian's.

'Ho! And away to Fairyland!'

They choked on the smoke, could still see the flash of

light even with their eyes closed. The smoke took its time to clear, with little air to blow it away, but eventually it began to dissipate.

At last Willow, who had staggered into Kepler, looked around wildly. There was the lamp device Kepler had made lying on the floor, its glow still strong. But that was all.

'He's gone!'

'Valerian!' coughed Kepler, still trying to clear the smoke from his lungs and eyes.

'Oh no!' cried Willow. 'Oh please, no! He's got Boy. He's taken Boy with him!'

'Quick!' Kepler shouted. 'We must save Boy!'

'But how?' she cried. 'He's vanished with his magic again. We can't follow him.'

'Magic?' Kepler said. 'Magic? Valerian has no such thing as magic these days!'

'But I've seen him vanish! And you saw what he just did!'

'No, we did not see what he did! That is only a trick. He must have discovered a way out. An exit to this tombland. A door.

'Look around, Willow! Look around!'

8

Boy felt himself dragged along by the scruff of his neck. A familiar feeling, and he knew it was Valerian doing the pulling. He shuffled along behind him, choking in the smoke, wondering how he had let himself fall for this trick when he had seen it before. He was dragged up a long twisting flight of steps and lost his footing many times, but Valerian seemed to have regained his incredible strength, and Boy felt as if he practically flew up the stairway.

He knew Valerian had no real magic any more. Those days were past – he was just a theatrical showman. But there was a legacy from his dabblings with real magic that awaited them, that was in fact running to meet them with every passing second.

As the smoke cleared from Boy's eyes, and they stopped watering, he began to look around, and what he saw shocked him more than anything.

They were outside.

Not only that, but they were outside in the garden of the Yellow House.

'How – how did we get here?' coughed Boy.

'Simple enough', said Valerian, 'when you work out where

you are. I knew a little, I guessed the rest. Took me longer than it should have. Now be quiet and do as you're told.'

Boy felt the past tickle his mind, and he remembered days when he had sat in the garden and dreamt he could hear running water. It seemed he had not dreamt it after all.

He turned to break away but froze as he felt the point of Valerian's knife at his neck.

'One more inch,' he hissed. 'One more inch and it's your last. Now get up the stairs.'

Valerian, fumbling with keys while holding the knife, shoved open the back door to the Yellow House, which led into the kitchens. He pushed Boy ahead of him.

'Hurry! There's little time!'

They made their way into the halls as the clocks chimed a quarter to the hour.

But which hour?

'Damnation!' cried Valerian. 'Midnight!'

He urged Boy up the stairs, up, up, up, all the way to the Tower.

Valerian kicked the door open, thrust Boy through, and slammed it shut behind him.

Locking the door, he put the key in his pocket and staggered over to the camera obscura. He began to adjust its controls, swearing loudly when he was clumsy with his only usable hand.

'Valerian,' Boy said, but his master held up his hand.

'Shut your mouth, Boy!' Valerian screamed, whirling round to face him. 'Shut. Your. Mouth. Say nothing. Do nothing.'

'But–'

'I said, be quiet!'

Boy said nothing. Valerian closed his eyes for a moment or two, then fiddled with the focus of the camera again. Satisfied, he began to scan the streets around the House. Boy heard him speaking softly to himself.

> *'The stars still move, time still runs,*
> *the clocks will strike, the devil will come.'*

After a while, finding nothing unusual, he gave it up.

'Perhaps Kepler was right,' Valerian said, turning back to Boy. 'Maybe it was a waste of money, but I'm not beaten yet.'

He moved over to sit in his armchair.

'Now all we have to do is wait. In a few minutes, it will come. The time will come. Then you go instead of me, and I am saved. I hope that's clear.'

It seemed to Boy as if Valerian was asking him a question. 'No,' he said.

'Be quiet!' Valerian shouted. 'It is not for you to ask. You have served me all these years; you are going to do this last thing for me.'

Outside, it was snowing heavily. There was a sudden bang and flash of light outside the window. Valerian jumped from his seat and hurried to the camera's projection.

Then they both saw the twinkle of fireworks scatter across the City sky, and Valerian slunk back to his chair. They heard the sounds of revellers from the New Year's Eve parties winding through the street below.

'People having fun,' he said. 'Something to celebrate. Well, I shall have something to celebrate too, very soon.'

He glanced at one of his clocks on the wall of the Tower room. Boy looked about desperately. The camera obscura, the tricks, the stage props, the experiments, the chemicals. He could see no help from anything.

'How can you do this to me? I've done nothing to hurt you. I've helped you all I can, but I don't want—'

'To die? No, neither do I, Boy. That's why you're going to instead of me.'

'But I don't understand!' shouted Boy. 'Why me, of all people?'

'That is something of a joke. It is precisely you, of all people, and only you, that can save me. We were meant to be together, you and I. When you fell from the ceiling in the church, that was meant to be, too.'

Boy stood staring at his master. He had mistreated him, beaten him, shouted at him. That much was true, but he had also helped him, fed him and clothed him, after a fashion. He couldn't believe that Valerian was really going to send him to his death.

'But why? Why me?'

'You are the solution,' said Valerian evenly. 'That is what the book told me. There you were, right in front of me all the time. I know this now, as Kepler does. *You* are the answer.'

Boy shook his head dumbly.

The clock on the wall ticked on and its long hand slid another minute closer to midnight.

'Fifteen years ago – fifteen years ago I made a bargain. I told you that. With a terrible price to pay at the end. What I didn't tell you is what I couldn't know. When I made the pact, something else was created then, too. *Someone*, I should say. Another soul.'

Boy shook his head again, not wanting to believe what he was hearing. The clock clunked and whirred. One minute to midnight.

'What . . .' he stammered, 'What?'

'Not what, Boy, but who. You. You were conceived on the very evening that I made my bargain, fifteen years ago on New Year's Eve. You are a vessel for me to use. This was what the book told me, and it also told me, as it must have told Kepler, about the only way out. A life the same age, as measured from conception, as the term of the pact. So you go instead of me. Then the bargain will be satisfied and I shall walk free.'

'But I'll die!'

'Yes,' said Valerian, 'but I won't.'

The clock, precise instrument that it was, began to sound midnight. As its twelve chimes died, the thing began to come.

The room was filled with light, and this time they knew it was no firework. The light was as bright as day, brighter even, and behind it came a great wind which lifted up all the loose papers in the room and swirled them madly around.

Boy staggered backwards and fell to the floor. Valerian rose to his feet, struggling against the storm that had entered the room, the tails of his great black coat waving in the vortex of wind.

Boy peered up at the light, which had now developed a black hole in its centre. Small at first, the black hole grew in size until there was a swirling darkness the size and shape of a man hovering just above the floor.

Then came a voice. At least, Boy thought it was a voice, but there was no one to say the words. He simply heard the words in his head and all around him. The voice was small and quiet, but strangely could be clearly heard. It was flat and colourless.

'Valerian, your time has come. Step forward.'

Boy felt a surge of pain, a mental pain that left him rigid with fear.

Valerian stood, swaying slightly in front of the hole.

'No,' he said, his voice wavering, 'No. The boy will go instead of me.'

There was silence.

'Is that not my right?' asked Valerian.

259

'Send the boy forward.'

And Valerian turned to Boy.

'Get up,' he said coldly.

Boy didn't move.

'Get up!'

This time he roared the words, and Boy automatically got to his feet. It was *what he did*, he thought. *What he did* was do what Valerian told him.

'Am I really just an empty vessel?' he asked Valerian quietly.

Valerian nodded.

'You are just a vessel, and you have served your purpose. You were made for me. I am your only family, and your family needs you.'

'No!' cried Boy. 'You're not my family. I must have a mother and father! Everyone does.'

'Not you, Boy. You don't even have a name.'

'You could have given me one. Why didn't you?'

Behind them the blackness swirled angrily, evil colours pouring from within it.

The voice came again.

'It is time! Step forward!'

'You could have given me a name if you'd ever cared about me!' cried Boy. 'But you never did! All you ever did was hurt me and shout at me and tell me I'm stupid, and kick me and threaten me! I've spent my life running around the City, in dark holes, in dangerous places, and you never cared! Not ever!'

'Boy–' said Valerian.

'Don't call me that! I want a real name! I want to know who I am, not this nonsense! I must have a life. I must have. This can't be *all* I am!'

Valerian looked at Boy. He seemed to be about to speak

but said nothing, and turned to look at the rushing nothingness which threatened to engulf the whole room.

And then there was another sound. It was a thump at the Tower door. Valerian did not hear it. His whole attention was fixed on the inky centre of the vortex.

The thump came again, and once more, and Kepler and Willow burst into the room, the door flying wide on its ancient hinges, bits of wood from the splintered lock scattering across the floor. In a glance they saw the horror in the room.

'No!' screamed Kepler. 'No!'

Valerian turned to face him.

'You!' he threw back. 'You! What right have you to tell me to do anything?'

'Valerian! No, no, no! You must not kill Boy! You must not.'

Willow ran to Boy and they clung to each other, cowering in the maelstrom that filled the room. Unheard, other, less precise clocks all around the house chimed midnight.

'You cannot kill him,' Kepler repeated.

'And why not?' sneered Valerian. 'Tell me why not! He is mine, he has always been mine, and I will do with him as I like!'

'Yes, he is yours,' Kepler pleaded, desperation tearing his expression into a sickening gape.

'He is my slave, and–'

'No, Valerian! No! He is your son,' and Kepler took a step towards Valerian.

'Don't be–'

'I said, he is your son!' Kepler shouted, raising a fist towards Valerian.

Valerian stopped, as if physically struck. He said nothing. He seemed to be thinking.

261

'I saw it in the book! It is the truth. Think about his age, Valerian. His age!'

Boy stood, struggling to get to his feet. He turned to Valerian.

Valerian stared deep into his eyes. He felt Valerian coming for him, as so often before, through his eyes, feeling for his soul, but this time it was different. He was not controlling, not manipulating, but feeling, sensing.

Boy felt his master's mind walk through his, as if for the first time really seeing what was there, finally understanding Boy's life. The years on his own, living off his wits on the harsh City streets. Being found by Valerian, hoping for so much but getting so little.

Valerian found that his own pain was nothing compared with Boy's.

He pulled away and stepped back, but still he looked deep into Boy's eyes.

He stepped backwards towards the swirling pit, and backwards once more, and fell into the darkness, already a dead man.

He spoke one more word as he went.

'Boy!'

Boy stood, numb.

The hole, the light, the wind disappeared faster than they had come, and Boy stared into space. All that remained was a faint wisp of yellow smoke that hung in the air, and a pungent smell that vexed their nostrils.

Valerian was gone.

Willow rushed to Boy and held him in her arms while he screamed and screamed.

Eventually his screams subsided and became cries and then the cries became tears, and he sat, staring at Willow.

'He went. He changed his mind. He let me live.'

'Don't talk,' said Willow. 'Not now.'

'But there's so much I don't understand. My father . . . my father?'

He turned to Kepler who stood looking down at him, a strange expression on his face.

'Was he – was he really my father?' Boy said.

Kepler looked hard at Boy. Long seconds passed, in which he said nothing.

'Was he my father? Tell me!' Boy said, more urgently this time.

'Of course he wasn't,' Kepler snapped. 'Don't be ridiculous. I just said that to make you live. I knew it was the only thing I could say that might save you.'

'No!' cried Boy, 'No! You're lying. You're lying now! You said I was his son.'

'There are things you don't know about, Boy,' said Kepler. 'Things that happened long ago. I was simply using those things to save your life.'

He turned to the door.

'No!' cried Boy, 'Wait . . .'

'You're alive, aren't you, Boy? Just be grateful for that.'

Kepler stooped, and picked up the book from the floor where Willow had dropped it.

'I'll see you're all right,' said Kepler. 'Both of you. Now that Valerian's gone.'

He walked out through the shattered doorway.

Boy collapsed into Willow's arms, and began to sob once more. Around them lay the devastation of what had once been the heart of Valerian's world. From the streets below came the noise of happy, drunken people, and from the skies overhead came the rush and bang of fireworks.

A long time passed. Boy's tears flowed freely down his face, Willow holding him all the while. He thought about what he'd heard, what he'd seen, but couldn't begin to understand. He pushed the thoughts away.

There would be time enough to think, later.

And there was something else. Someone else.

As if only now noticing her, Boy felt Willow's arms around him. He lifted his head, and looked up at her face, and at last he saw the love that was waiting for him there.

A new year had dawned, with a new, and different future, one that Boy had not foreseen. He sensed that the path ahead was obscured by many, many questions, but one thing, at least, was clear.

Boy and Willow would walk that path together.

The Dark
Flight Down

For Pippa

Prologue

Midnight at the Imperial Court of Emperor Frederick III. The Court has been emptied for the evening of its usual crowd of sycophants and entertainers, of its alchemists, astrologers, doctors, faith-healers, druggists, noblemen, ne'er-do-wells, priests, actors and occultists.

The Emperor sits on his throne, apparently alone, brooding. He lifts a pale hand, slowly, lazily.

'Maxim!' he calls, in his high, pathetic voice. 'Dammit, Maxim, where are you?'

From the shadows behind the throne a tall, heavy figure emerges, swathed in a dark red robe that trails in the dust on the marble Court floor. Maxim, the Emperor's right hand, his confidant and oracle.

'Sire?' Maxim says. He is tired, but careful to show no sign of this to Frederick. He runs a hand across the top of his shaven head.

'There you are!' Frederick declares, but without emotion. 'There you are.'

'Sire,' Maxim says, ready to do the Emperor's bidding.

'Maxim, how many years have I left to live?'

Maxim hesitates briefly before answering, wondering how many times he has had this conversation with the

Emperor, and then, depressingly, he wonders how many *more* times he will have it.

'Sire, we have established beyond all possible doubt that you will live to a venerable age.'

He bows, to try to emphasise the significance of his words, hoping they will be sufficient to keep Frederick happy.

'Yes, yes,' says Frederick, far from happy. He lifts a long, thin finger and scratches the side of his nose. Flakes of skin float into the gloom of the deserted Court. 'But how long exactly, would you say?'

Maxim sighs inwardly. It is not to be short, then.

'Ah!' he says brightly. 'Well, our finest thinkers are convinced that you will live to be . . . a hundred!'

Frederick is silent for a while. Maxim begins to edge away.

'But what then?' Frederick cries suddenly.

Maxim hurries back to the foot of the throne.

'Well,' he says. 'Well! We have every right, every reason, to suppose that you will live to be a hundred and twenty. There is no reason why not.'

'Ah. I see. One hundred. And twenty.'

'Sire,' says Maxim, wondering if he dare retire from the Emperor's presence.

'But! But what then? What then, Maxim? What. Then?'

Maxim is tired, and would very much like to be upstairs in his chambers, asleep, but he knows there is little chance of that now. Still, he is careful to show no sign of his tiredness, his irritation.

'Sire, Your Excellency may then have the good grace to die.'

That should shut him up, Maxim thinks, bowing his large frame as low as he can manage without falling on to his nose.

'Die?' Frederick whines. 'Die? And what then?'

Maxim jerks his head upright, now irritated beyond reason by the Emperor's voice.

'Well, Sire,' he says slowly, gazing at the ceiling, 'there'll be . . . mourning. A period of great sorrow across the whole City. People will . . . stop to remember the great Frederick, and celebrate. They'll make . . .'

Maxim hesitates, inspiration deserting him. He looks down, and finds the Emperor scowling at him.

'They'll make . . . ?'

'Yes, Sire,' says Maxim. 'They'll make . . . boom boom.'

'Boom boom?' Frederick asks. 'They'll make boom boom? What in heaven's name do you mean? A celebration? Fireworks? Is that it? Is that all I will have to show for my time?'

Maxim lifts his head to the Emperor, opens his hands wide, and for once is at a loss for words.

Frederick rises to his feet. Even standing, his short, skinny frame is dwarfed by his towering throne.

He points at Maxim.

'They will not make "boom boom" because I am not going to die! Not ever. I will reach one hundred, and then another one after that, and then another after that. Do you see, Maxim? Do you? I am the last of the line, Maxim; you know that as well as anyone. I have no kith, Maxim, no kin, no offspring nor progeny. If I die, the chain is broken. The end is reached. The Empire will have no Emperor. There is only one answer. I am not going to die!

You, my loyal servant, will see to it. I am not to die, and you are going to make sure of it.'

Maxim hesitates. The Emperor is a fool. And he is a liar too. Some things cannot be forgotten, cannot be hidden as easily as Frederick would like, but Maxim doesn't dare tell him that.

'But, Sire, I—'

'No, it is no use. I have made up my mind. Either you find a way to make me immortal, or your own end will be swifter than you might expect. Now get out of my sight, and find someone to carry me up to bed. You have no idea how bad it is for me, sitting on this throne all day.'

'No, Sire,' says Maxim, his hand already pulling a bell-rope.

'And don't forget! Find a way to make me live for ever. Or . . .'

And Maxim watches with a familiar prickle of horror as the feeble old Emperor whisks a skinny finger across his own throat.

'Phht!'

The City

The Place of Obscured Memories

❦

1

The City froze hard that Winter, iron-cold and stone-still. When the snows came, they settled in to stay. It had started with snowstorms that seemed as if they were angry with something, as the wind whirled snowflakes down on to the City's filthy streets and crumbling buildings. It had started in the last few days of the year as Boy and Willow had been swept along by the magician Valerian in his ultimately futile quest for survival.

Then, early on New Year's Day, the fury abated, but still for day after day large fluffy flakes of pure whiteness drifted gently down, covering the muck and the mire, hiding the decay of the old City beneath a thick layer of pristine white youth.

The snow obliterated broken slates and chimney stacks, removed all traces of dilapidated walls and rotting windowsills, and laid a clean and soft white carpet along every single alley, street, avenue and parade, that was renewed every night.

It was as if the snow was trying to purify the squalid City, or at least hide its evil under a shroud of forgetting. Each night, the old, horrible and grim was replaced by something new, young and beautiful.

But there was a price for this rebirth. It was cold, bitterly cold, and the City froze deep, and deathly still.

With it, something inside Boy froze too.

Too much had happened too quickly.

Valerian. Boy couldn't even begin to think, to understand, about Valerian. He could barely feel.

He struggled to order, let alone comprehend, the events of the dead days at the end of the year that had just died, taking Valerian with it. And beyond Valerian's death, there was what Kepler had said, right before the end – the thing that had tormented Boy's brain ever since, the truth of which still lay obscured.

That Valerian was Boy's father.

The new year that had just begun had hardly been a few hours old when Boy's one comfort had been taken from him too.

Willow.

2

'Come, Boy. It's time.'

Boy turned for a moment from the window where he had been watching the snow fall. He had been trying to watch every single snowflake's path to earth, without knowing quite why he was doing it. He was almost obsessed. Every flake that fell hid the dark horror of the City a little more. Hid the horror, and dulled the memory. If it went on snowing, perhaps the horror would go too.

His attention drifted back to the snow.

'Boy!' said Kepler again from the door. 'It's time to go.'

Boy turned to his new master.

'Time for what?'

Kepler came into Boy's bedroom. It was a small room, simply furnished with a bed, a chair and a washstand, but after the tiny space he had slept in at Valerian's house, it was luxurious. Boy had not yet got used to it, and woke frequently through the night, feeling exposed and vulnerable, as if death threatened. But maybe that had little to do with his new room.

Kepler joined him by the window and put his skinny hand out to touch Boy's shoulder, but Boy flinched and pulled away. A scowl crossed Kepler's face as he drew back.

'For the funeral,' he snapped. 'You do still want to go to the funeral?'

Dumbly Boy nodded.

'Is it the fifth already?' he asked, but Kepler ignored him.

'I'll meet you in the hall in five minutes,' he said, and left.

Boy was already watching the snow.

The fifth of January. Korp's funeral. Boy couldn't believe five days had already passed since Valerian had died.

There should be a funeral for him too, thought Boy.

But then, there was nothing to bury.

Just twenty more flakes, Boy said to himself, *then I'll get ready*. He watched the intricate dance that each flake made as it fell, trying to guess which way it would go, whether it would miss the top of the garden wall or whether it would change direction at the last moment and make the foot of snow that capped the wall one flake thicker. After a while he began not merely to predict but to try to influence the journey of each flake, pushing out with his mind into the frozen air outside his window, though he knew his imaginings were fanciful.

'Boy! It's time to go.'

Boy dragged his gaze away from the window, grabbed his coat from the back of the chair and ran to the door.

'I'm coming!' he called. He didn't want to miss the funeral. It wasn't so much that he wanted to bury Korp, the director of the theatre where Valerian and Boy had performed. He had been murdered a few days before

276

Valerian's own demise. Boy had liked the fat old director well enough, and felt he should honour him by attending his funeral, but that was not really why he wanted to be there. He had spent enough time in graveyards recently to last a lifetime.

The real reason was Willow. Boy hoped she might be there too.

Five days had passed since he had seen her last, but those days had been a long clouded dream, in which he had struggled to control events and failed, unable to think or act clearly.

Kepler had sent her away.

Just a few hours after Valerian's death, Kepler had returned to them where they were still cowering in the ruined shell of Valerian's Tower room.

'Boy, you will work for me now,' he had said. 'I have made preparations. Go to my house. Wait for me there. Willow, come with me, I need your help.'

But it had been a trick. He did not need Willow for anything other than to leave her somewhere and come back without her.

Boy had shouted at Kepler when he discovered what had happened. So timid and cowering around Valerian, Boy had found no trouble being angry with Kepler, no fear shouting at him.

'Bring her back!' he had screamed at his new master, who stood, slowly shaking his head.

'You can't do this to us! Willow's all I've got now. Bring her back.'

Kepler continued to shake his head.

'Wrong, Boy,' he said. 'You have me now. We will get to

know each other better. I need you, and Valerian has seen that you are not wholly uneducated.'

'Why do you need my help?'

Kepler hesitated. Boy didn't like it.

'I need your help. You'll help me with my plans. In time, we'll come to like each other. That's all you need to know for now.'

'I don't . . .' Boy had said. 'I just want Willow. Why can't she live here too?'

'But don't worry, she is safe enough,' Kepler went on. 'She is working, so she will be able to look after herself. You need not think about her any more.'

'Tell me where she is!' Boy demanded. 'Let me go to her!'

Boy had shouted and screamed, but Kepler withstood it all, and left Boy to his own devices in his new bedroom.

Since that outburst, Boy had spent his time looking out of the window, brooding. Trying to make sense of things that had no sense. That Valerian might have been his father all the while, without him knowing. And Kepler. Why had he wanted to keep Willow from him? Why did he think he needed Boy's help? He was rich enough to employ a dozen assistants, so why was *he* so special?

Answers refused to come, and as the days passed, Boy became hypnotised by the falling snow, which seemed to have no intention of stopping, ever.

Valerian had once told him that each snowflake was different from every other. Each with its own pattern, its own identity, and as they fell from the sky, Boy discovered they each had their own behaviour. No two fell in the same way. Every one was unique – just, thought Boy, like people. And when the snowflake landed in the wrong place, on a warm roof or a pond, it vanished instantly, gone forever. Its unique nature lost. Boy's thoughts turned again to Valerian, to Willow.

With a start he realised he couldn't clearly recall her face, even though they had only been separated for a few days. He had to force a memory of her delicate features and long hair into his mind, and was only satisfied when he could see her clearly again.

Now he ran down the stairs of Kepler's house and met his new master, who was waiting impatiently for him.

They set off into the City snowscape.

'Let's get on with it,' Kepler said irritably. 'It's another freezing day and I don't want to waste it all perishing in some abysmal cemetery.'

Now Boy kept pace with Kepler, dodging the larger drifts caught by corners and crevices but still having to wade knee-deep through it in places. With every footstep Boy crushed the identity from a thousand snowflakes, but he felt no pain for them.

His mind was on one thing, Willow, and why Kepler wanted to keep them apart.

Within hours of Valerian's death Boy was under the control of Valerian's supposed friend, Kepler. In reality Boy had discovered him to be Valerian's mortal enemy, to have contrived his death. It was a bitter history. At least to see Willow would remind him of sanity, of a kindness and care, even if she had no explanation for the madness of his world.

Though living in a haze since New Year, Boy could feel new things starting to emerge in his mind. Like feeling something for Willow, maybe for seeing things as they really were; knowing that one day he might see his life with Valerian in a different light; sensing that the real trouble with life always lay ahead – the future, with all its traps and surprises and uncertainties, waiting to be faced. He supposed it was something to do with getting older.

The funeral was to be held in a small church, St Hilary's, in the Quarter of the Arts, not far from the Old Theatre, which had remained shut since Korp's murder. As Boy and Kepler made their way closer to the Quarter, Boy suddenly realised something he had utterly forgotten. He was still wanted by the City Watch on suspicion of Korp's murder. So was Willow.

'Wait!' he said to Kepler.

'What is it, Boy?' Kepler asked, stopping. 'We're going to be late at this rate. I didn't think the snow was this bad.'

'The Watch. Supposing they come to the funeral – looking for Willow and me?'

'You need not fear,' said Kepler. 'I've been asking around. They've changed their tack. They think it was The Phantom who murdered Korp. When they stopped to think about it, they saw lots of similarities between his murder and those of other victims. The excessive force. The considerable blood loss. Not something you or Willow could have done.'

Boy was only partially reassured. In his experience the Watch were a dim-witted lot, who could easily think anything that came into their heads from one minute to the next. But it was worth the risk of being arrested if it meant seeing Willow.

They were at the end of a narrow lane that opened into

a small square called Well Court, at the far end of which Boy saw the side of St Hilary's. It looked as if the church had been squeezed in among the gaggle of taller buildings that surrounded it, though in fact the church had been there first. They skirted the church wall and came to the small churchyard that lay beyond. People were gathering round a hard-dug hole in the frozen ground. The snow continued to fall. The funeral was about to begin.

3

More people than Boy imagined turned up for Korp's funeral. There were many of his old friends from the theatre, the musicians, the stage hands and costume girls. He gazed around at the faces of all the performers and musicians and actors who had come to pay their respects to the old Director. He tried to guess who they were, and what they were, singers or jugglers. Maybe, like Valerian, there was a magician among them. No, there was no one like Valerian. There could never be a magician like Valerian – Valerian, whose magic was sometimes just stage trickery and sometimes . . . sometimes something more.

Boy saw a small old lady at the front of the crowd with a fluffy dog on a lead. It took him a moment to remember it was Korp's housekeeper. She had brought Korp's faithful dog, Lily, with her. There was Snake-girl, looking quite plain without her snake. Boy realised only now that it was her snake and her costume that made her seem so mysterious and alluring. It was like a new kind of vision, seeing with eyes as keen as scalpel blades that cut away desires and emotions and wishful thinking and left only what was fact. It hurt, sometimes, if you looked upon the wrong thing, and it could burn. Not seeing Willow among the many still arriving for Korp's funeral, he turned his face to the sky and watched the hundreds upon thousands of huge feathery snowflakes fall into the churchyard.

Now Boy noticed something else. People were looking at him, nudging each other and pointing at him with a nod of their heads. As he caught their eye they'd look away, and Boy soon heard enough of a whisper to know what it was. Valerian. Here was Valerian's boy, somehow still alive despite the rumours that both he and Valerian had perished in some awful, occult cataclysm in The Yellow House on New Year's Eve.

'Ignore them,' Kepler said quietly.

News travelled fast, and rumour and gossip even faster. Yes, Valerian was dead, but that was only half the story. Boy had survived, after all. The crowds stared at him, looking thinner than ever, his pale skin ghost-like and grey, but nonetheless alive.

And what would they think, Boy thought bitterly, *if they knew the rest of it? That Valerian was my father?*

Kepler had said so, and then denied it almost as soon as he had uttered the words.

It seemed so unreal to Boy, the Boy who was finally seeing what was truth and what was untruth. Maybe he'd just imagined Kepler had said it. It had been so chaotic, those last few minutes before Valerian had gone – the noise, the light, the wind in the Tower. Maybe he'd just wanted to hear what he thought Kepler had said, and had imagined it.

But no. Kepler had told Valerian that he was Boy's father. Why he had denied it as soon as Valerian himself was dead, Boy had no idea, but he had definitely said it. And there had been a witness, too.

At the thought of her, Boy's eyes lifted from the snow and slush around his feet, and he looked up, to find himself looking into a smiling face he had been longing to see.

Willow.

Willow stood on the far side of the grave, hidden from the waist down by the pile of earth spoil that would soon be covering up Korp's coffin. Boy made to move towards her, but there was Kepler's hand on his shoulder immediately.

'Have some respect, Boy.'

Kepler nodded to where the pall-bearers were making their way through the crowd.

The ceremony began and ended and finally they shovelled some of the earth back into the hole, hiding the coffin like the City was being hidden by snow. Hiding it from sight, as if that could hide it from memory.

Boy knew there was something wrong with what he was watching, but couldn't place what it was. Lily, however, could. As the frozen clods of earth began to drum on to the wood of the coffin lid, the sad little mutt shivered and then let out a pathetic whimper. She knew that simply because something was gone from sight did not mean it was gone from memory, and she missed her master.

The snow fell, and Boy shut his mind to everything but its falling, and waited for it to calm his nerves and dull his pain.

Now he knew what was strange about the funeral. All these people were united by the one thing that wasn't there: the dead. It was the first funeral Boy had ever been to, and it struck him as profoundly strange.

Korp was not the only person missed by the mourners. It seemed strange that Valerian was not there, too. As people started to drift away Boy looked across the gathering, and caught a glimpse of a tall figure in black striding along the street. For a second he thought it was his dead master come back to life, but he saw he was mistaken. It was only a priest hurrying through the snow.

Suddenly the old violinist who had often been kind to Boy clapped his hands.

'Wait! We cannot leave it at that! Will you join me, friends, in celebrating the life of our dear Director?'

People murmured and nodded.

'Quite so!' someone called.

'To The Feather, then?' the violinist said. 'The first drinks are on me!'

Boy had lost sight of Willow, then he saw her through the crowd, beckoning him.

'Can we go?' Boy asked Kepler. 'Can we go to The Feather?'

'No,' said Kepler, 'We've done what we came to do.'

But before they could move the old violinist and a couple of his friends came over to where Boy and Kepler stood. Without a glance at Kepler, they fussed over Boy, walking him away from the grave, along with everyone else heading for the tavern, and Kepler could do nothing but follow, hopping at their heels like an unwanted dog.

Several streets later and at least Boy could feel his feet again, and somewhere in the crowd of people up ahead was Willow. That in itself gave him warmth.

5

'So you're the boy's new master?'

Now Boy and Kepler found themselves sitting squashed around a table in the filthy tavern called The Feather. Talk quickly moved from the uncertain future of the theatre to Valerian, and then to Boy. Boy watched, squirming uneasily while the old violinist, Georg, and the others questioned Kepler. Willow was nearby, picking greedily at a bowl of sweet raisins in the middle of the table. She glanced over at Boy, smiling.

Kepler saw this.

'We must go. Boy and I have work to do,' he said for the fourth time in as many minutes, but no one got up to let him out.

A large man on Kepler's left smiled at Boy.

'Run and fetch the barmaid, will you? More drinks all round.'

'And get her to bring some absinthe, eh? A game of Snapdragon, anyone? Korp would have loved that!'

There was a loud cheer round the table as Boy pushed his way through to find the barmaid, trying to catch Willow's eye as he left.

By the time he got back, they'd already found a bottle of

absinthe from somewhere else. They had dispensed with beer in favour of this devilish green liquor, and had embarked upon a game of Snapdragon.

Boy loved this game, largely because he usually got away without having to play himself, just watching as others fell off their chairs from the drink. He almost felt sorry for Kepler, who had obviously never heard of Snapdragon before, and was about to learn all about it the hard way.

'Right,' Georg was saying to Kepler. 'Now you know how to play, let's do it properly.'

On the table was a small saucer into which a little of the absinthe had been poured. A handful of raisins were added. The game was to pick up a raisin from the saucer and eat it. If you succeeded, the play moved round to the next person at the table. If you dropped the raisin, you had to sink a glass of the drink.

'What do you mean, properly?' Kepler asked Georg.

'Well, that time we were just showing you how it's played. Now we're going to do it properly. Wilfred? Will you?'

And Wilfred, the strong man, took a box of matches from his pocket and set light to the absinthe.

'You can start,' Wilfred said, smiling at Kepler.

'What? But it's burning!'

'Well, it wouldn't be much of a game if it wasn't,' Georg said, nudging Wilfred, who started chuckling.

Kepler stared nervously around him, then at the saucer of burning raisins and schnapps. He darted his hand to the flames. He managed to pick one up, but dropped it on the table with a squeal and sucked his burned fingers.

Everyone roared with laughter, and Wilfred shoved a

glass of absinthe under his nose. Kepler looked at it miserably, then, with the strong man glaring at him, took a sip.

'Not like that!' Wilfred cried, and pulling Kepler's nose back, tipped the whole lot down his open mouth.

Everyone hooted with laughter again, and play moved round to Wilfred, who deftly snatched a raisin and popped it into his mouth in a single motion.

'Doesn't it burn your fingers?' said a voice beside Boy, and there at last was Willow.

Boy smiled and for a moment didn't know what to do or say. He simply stared into her eyes, her face for once not framed by her hair, which she had pulled back into a bunch.

'Or your mouth, come to that,' Willow added, staring as Georg took two at once, and flicked them into his mouth with professional skill.

'Not if you do it quickly,' Boy replied. 'And shut your mouth as soon as it's in. I watched Valerian play this hundreds of times. He always won. It amused him, and he'd win money too, sometimes. There'd be everyone else drinking their heads off, and he'd just sit watching them.'

Willow laughed, and without thinking, Boy laughed too.

'I used to pick their pockets if I thought Valerian wasn't watching!'

'Boy!' said Willow. 'You are bad!'

'It meant I could buy something extra to eat . . .' Boy said defensively, but then saw Willow was only teasing.

The game was getting noisier. Kepler tried to make one more attempt to leave, but Boy could see he was very drunk, and he fell back in his chair without anyone even making him stay this time.

'Valerian could do it slowly, though, too,' Boy said. 'When everyone was really drunk, he'd start to show off. He could pick one up ever so slowly, with his fingertips right in the fire, and slowly put the raisin on his tongue, and let it burn there for a bit, as if it wasn't hurting at all. I don't know how he did that.'

Willow shrugged. 'Maybe he was just good at controlling pain.'

Boy said nothing, lost in memories.

Controlling pain, he thought.

He roused himself and looked at Willow. She looked well enough. It had only been five days, but it felt like months.

'Willow . . . ?'

'I'm all right. He took me to an orphanage. I thought just to live there, but he's got me a job. I didn't like the idea at first, but it's much nicer than the one I grew up in. I'll even get paid! I sneaked out today. I'll probably be in trouble, but it won't be bad. There's a woman who's in charge. She's quite fierce, but I think she's soft enough underneath. She's called Martha.'

Boy stared at Willow, at her long brown hair and wax-white face. He put his hand out to her cheek, and she took it away gently and held it in hers.

'How are you, Boy?' she said softly. 'Is he all right with you?'

Boy wondered who she meant, then realised she was talking about Kepler.

'Yes. He feeds me. And doesn't shout at me, and doesn't beat me, or even get cross with me. It's fine.'

'But what are you doing?'

'Nothing. He says he needs me to help him, but we've done nothing. I just sit in my room. I've been watching the snow, Willow. There's so much of it. So much snow. It's hard to recognise some bits of the City. Have you seen? Just so much snow.'

Willow looked at Boy, a frown on her face. Then she forced a smile.

'Will you stay with him?' she asked.

Boy shrugged.

'I don't know. I suppose so. I don't want to go back to the streets. Even living with Valerian was better than that, and . . .'

He stopped.

'What is it?' Willow asked.

'Willow. What Kepler said. You remember?'

'That Valerian was your father? Yes.'

'Tell me. Tell me honestly. Do you think it's true?'

Willow tried to look down and away, but Boy wouldn't let her.

'I don't know,' she said finally.

Boy said nothing.

'Would it change anything? Would it change how you felt about him if he was? Would it change how you felt about how he treated you? Or that he's dead?'

Boy shrugged and looked away.

'Let him go, Boy,' she said. 'Let him go, and let yourself go too. You've got a new life to start.'

Boy turned back to her.

'Have I? With Kepler?'

'No,' said Willow. 'I thought – I thought with me.'

She spoke quickly, not giving Boy a chance to interrupt.

'I've got a proper job now. Imagine that. I'll have money! We could find somewhere to live. Maybe you could find work too. We could go to another part of the City, where Kepler would never find you. Maybe we could even leave the City itself . . .'

She stopped, biting her lower lip.

'But maybe you don't . . .'

'Yes,' said Boy. 'Yes, Willow, I do.'

Willow flung her arms around him and they both began to cry, while beside them the Snapdragon got louder and louder and more drunken with every round.

Willow and Boy knew nothing of this, as they talked and talked and quietly began to make plans for themselves. It felt strange to both of them – that they could decide what to do with their lives, not have them dictated by other people.

When they finally stopped talking, only Georg and Wilfred were left sitting at the table.

'Where's . . . ?' Boy asked, open-mouthed.

'Your Mr Kepler?' Georg asked. He pointed a finger at the floor.

Leaning over in his chair, Boy looked under the table to see Kepler asleep on the floor.

'I'd better get him home,' Boy said. 'He'll get himself slit if he stays here.'

'Well, there's one thing at least,' Georg said to Boy.

'What's that?'

'Your master will be kinder to you tomorrow.'

'Why?' asked Willow.

'Well,' said Georg, winking at Wilfred, 'everyone knows. Absinthe makes the heart grow fonder!'

And he and Wilfred burst into fits of drunken giggles at what was obviously a joke they'd told many, many times.

Boy frowned.

'Don't fret,' said Wilfred to Boy, still chuckling. 'I'll carry him for you if you show me the way.'

'You can trust him,' said Georg, 'He's my good friend, and there's no way you can carry your master, is there?'

Boy smiled.

'You're right. Thank you,' he said, 'for everything.'

Georg tipped his hat to Boy and Willow, and made to leave himself. Wilfred knelt down beside Kepler and swung his sagging body up on to his shoulder.

'He'll have a head tomorrow,' he said.

Boy looked at Willow.

'So, I'll see you tomorrow evening. By St Valentine's Fountain?'

Willow nodded, smiling. She skipped forward, kissed Boy quickly on the lips, and ran off.

Boy led the way back to Kepler's house. Wilfred was silent and Boy was happy for it to be so, because all he wanted to do was think about Willow.

He thought about what he knew about her. It seemed he knew very little. That she had been born in the countryside but had been orphaned when she was tiny. She had lived in an orphanage, had worked for the City Liverymen, and had then come to the Theatre. That was really all he knew, and he felt it was out of balance with how much they had gone through together in the last few days. It was from those experiences that he really knew who Willow was, what she was. Strong, brave and kind. With a shock, Boy realised that although he knew very little of Willow's life, he still knew more about her history than he did about his own.

As he went he kept himself warm with the memory of the fleeting kiss and the thought that from tomorrow he and Willow would be together for good.

Nothing could have been further from the truth.

6

Boy got to bed at around three in the morning, having first seen that his master was safely asleep.

Wilfred had taken Kepler upstairs and tipped him on to the mattress, then tipped his hat just as easily to Boy, and turned to go.

'Strange dreams for him tonight,' Wilfred had chuckled.

Boy looked at him quizzically.

'The absinthe,' he winked, and went.

Boy considered Kepler for a while, then decided he was too tired to do anything much for him. He pulled Kepler's boots off and drew a coverlet up to his chin.

Boy slept late into the morning, and if Kepler's dreams were strange, then Boy's were every bit as disturbing. When Boy woke finally, it was with no gentle arousal, but with a lurch and a jolt as his dream frightened him awake. He sat up in bed for several slow minutes, breathing hard, trying to calm down. It had been a long time since he had dreamed at all, he realised. As if to make up for that, he had been ridden into the ground by a stampede of nightmares.

Almost automatically Boy thought of snow as he swung his legs over the side of the bed. His dreams had been frozen like mountain snow, and with a sudden warm spell had thawed, sending a deluge of meltwater cascading down on him.

Dreams still lay in his mind like a fog as he staggered over to the washstand and splashed icy water into the bowl from the jug beside it. He had been in a dark space, a small dark space. That was not the frightening part. Not for Boy. Small dark spaces were where he felt safest, as he had grown up on the streets, and later with Valerian too. They had always been good places for him.

Having stolen a purse or a loaf, anywhere he could tuck his narrow bones to hide from the watch was good for Boy; a tiny crevice in a church roof was heaven. Being with Valerian on stage, tucked into magical cabinets and other boxes, was at least one time when his new master could not beat him or curse him. And in the Yellow House Boy's room had been that narrow triangular tunnel, too small even to stand in but a place of safety nonetheless.

So it wasn't the small dark space in his dream that had been scary, but something else. Something lurking nearby. Something that breathed with a low, husky rattle, like a creature being half-throttled. Some sort of fiend.

Boy remembered the dream and cursed it, for it signalled an end to his view of darkness as a benevolent thing. He plunged his face into the cold water in the bowl in front of him, and held it there, opening his eyes so the water washed them, hoping it would wash the black clouds from his brain too.

But it did not. He was starting to fully feel the shock of all that had happened in the dead days. He stood upright again, breathing hard, knowing that the safety of darkness had already long gone. It had not just vanished with last night's dream of some foul monster in the dark. It had died in those vile underground tunnels when he had been hunted by Valerian, his former master. His father?

Boy dressed and stood in front of the window. Outside, the snow was falling as heavily as it ever had over the last week. Boy tried his trick of watching the snow, to hypnotise himself into forgetting, but it failed.

His dreams had unlocked his emotions, the fear jerking him from the stupor of the previous few days. And this flood of emotions had unleashed another dreadful realisation. He knew he had to find out the truth about Valerian, one way or the other. Not knowing had been tormenting him, he saw that clearly now, and he had to put a stop to it.

He knew how to do it. He himself had helped provide the answer to his problem.

The book. The magical book. It contained answers, truths and secrets, and the histories and destinies of any who dared to read its pages. It had enlightened some but had fooled many more, for its answers were not always clear and precise. The book revealed something of its readers' fates, but Boy had already learned that Fortune was a fickle mistress, largely because people saw only what it suited them to see.

Nonetheless, the book itself was all-knowing, as Boy was only too aware. He and Willow had helped Valerian hunt down the book only to find that Kepler already had it and, ensnared by its power, was trying to keep it from Valerian.

If Boy was going to look in the book, now was the time to do it, while Kepler slept off his absinthe-curdled dreams.

The enormity of what he had decided to do dawned on him, and his heart began to pound.

Something else occurred to Boy. The book would also be able to tell him another thing he desperately wanted to know and which no one else would ever be able to tell him.

His real name.

7

The house was quiet. The whole City felt quiet, as if everyone and everything in it were watching off-stage, as Boy crept down the corridor from his room.

Words came into Boy's head from nowhere. They felt familiar, though he couldn't work out why. It was true that the snowfall had been hypnotising him, helping him bury his troubles, but if some parts of his memory were being hidden, at the same time he had become strangely awake to others.

'*Surely you won't run when your boat is ready to sail.*'

He pushed the words to the back of his mind, but they would not disappear.

'*Surely you will stay and face the gentle rain.*'

He couldn't place the words, and tried again to ignore them.

Now he drew level with Kepler's door and paused, on tiptoe. He held his boots in his hands, not daring to risk booted footsteps on the bare wooden boards of the corridor.

Boy held his breath, straining to hear any sound from Kepler, any noise that might show he was stirring. All was quiet.

Boy breathed out and headed for the top of the stairs.

A first doubt rose in his mind. It wasn't conscience, but fear. He had no qualms about looking at the book, which he supposed now belonged to Kepler. He had stolen enough things in his life not to worry about borrowing something without permission. No, that was not the cause of his doubt. The cause was fear.

Sitting on the last stair he pulled his boots on. The floor was carpeted here, and he was no longer scared about Kepler hearing him. What he was scared of lay, he assumed, in front of him, in Kepler's study, where he had last seen Kepler put the book.

Boy crossed the hall, and the rogue words pushed into his head again.

'*Surely you won't run . . . ?*'

Willow had thought the book dangerous. He knew that much from the brief time they had spent together before Valerian's end on New Year's Eve. Why else would the Beebe family have buried it with one of their sons – its last owner, Gad – if it were not dangerous? It had lain undisturbed in his grave in the church at Linden until Kepler had located it and stolen it. Boy hadn't at first understood how a book could be dangerous, but he knew it was powerful, and that was enough to make him nervous. The book was unadulterated knowledge, pure and powerful.

Boy reached the study door and put his finger to the brass knob. The house was cold; he had lit no fires and with no one else to do it, it would remain that way. He shivered, but turned the knob and pushed the door open.

Quickly he stepped inside and gently pushed the door to

behind him, without risking making any noise by closing it properly.

He looked at the desk. Unless Kepler had moved it, the book lay inside the bottom drawer on the right-hand side, waiting.

The thing was just to do it, without thinking, without worrying. Boy thought of snowfall and took seven short strides over to the desk.

He sat down in the leather-covered chair and looked at the drawer. It would be locked, Boy knew that, and Kepler had the only key, but that was no problem for Boy. He rummaged in his pocket and pulled out the bent piece of metal that he used to pick locks. It had belonged to a metal hand that Kepler had once dissected with Valerian, and it had been Valerian who had shown Boy how to pick locks. So, he reasoned, they only had themselves to blame.

He leant down to the lock of the bottom drawer, and twisted the metal around inside, feeling for the tumblers.

Boy usually sprang a lock in a few moments, but he was not surprised that Kepler, a man of invention and mechanism, should have superior devices to secure his property. The lock resisted.

Boy got out of the chair and knelt down at eye-level with the lock, determined not to be beaten.

On the other side of a finger's width of oak lay the book, waiting to tell Boy everything.

He jiggled the metal pin inside the lock once more, still getting nowhere. He began to grow desperate, and struggled with the lock frantically. He could sense the book only inches away, could sense its power, but there was no give in the lock, which defeated all his attempts to open it.

He sat back in the chair, angry now, and kicked the desk.

He looked around, and his eyes rested on the fireplace. There was a heavy iron poker by the grate.

Boy didn't hesitate.

He would smash the stupid desk apart and take the book. He and Willow had agreed to meet by the fountain later that day, and so he would, but with the knowledge of his past and his future revealed. Kepler would be angry, but that wouldn't matter – he would never see him again.

Boy reached the fireplace and grasped the poker by its twisted handle.

As he turned to make for the desk, the door swung open and Kepler walked in.

For a second a hateful vision of violence passed through Boy's mind, as he saw himself bringing the poker down on Kepler's head, spilling his brains on to the red carpet of the study floor.

But it was gone in an instant. If anyone was in the mood for violence, it was Kepler. No doubt as a result of the absinthe, he was in a strange mood. Boy saw the turmoil in his master's eyes, and the sudden craving he had felt for the book disappeared. Boy had seen absinthe do this to people before. Normally calm people might practically murder each other when recovering from the strange hallucinations that the wormwood-ridden drink could induce.

'Boy!' Kepler snapped, 'It's perishing cold. Why aren't the fires lit?'

'I'm just doing them,' Boy said quickly, waving the poker as if that were the truth. 'The house will be warm soon.'

Kepler ignored him and staggered to the desk, where he sat in the chair. He was too hung over to notice either that Boy was poking a fire that had not yet been lit, or that the papers on his desk and the chair were not where he'd left them.

'You are not to see those people again,' said Kepler. He meant Georg and the others from the theatre.

Boy was about to argue, but thought better of it. He would be gone by this evening, and what Kepler thought or said would not matter. He could be angry about it then, could laugh about it then, so for now he just nodded and went on preparing the fire.

'I need you to do something for me,' said Kepler thickly. 'I need you to fetch something for me this morning.'

Boy stood and looked at Kepler, whose head was still in his hands. Now he lifted it, but slowly.

'I need you to fetch something for me from the Yellow House.'

Boy froze. The Yellow House. Valerian's house.

'I—' began Boy, but Kepler was in no mood to argue.

'Just go,' he said, 'I need a lens from the camera. It's the only one of its kind in the City, and cost a fortune. I want it back. I built that thing after all, it belongs to me now Valerian's gone. I want it to project an image . . .'

Boy wondered what he was talking about, but said nothing.

'You must unscrew the bottom section of the brass tube and the lens will drop out. Don't break it! And come straight back.'

Boy was used to being told what to do. It was all he had ever had from Valerian. He would help Kepler with this last thing. It wouldn't take very long, and anyway he would have to wait now for another chance to look at the book. Once he had, he could disappear to be with Willow.

Kepler had saved his life, after all, by sending Valerian to his death, instead of Valerian sending Boy to his. He decided he owed him one favour at least, but there was something else too. He wanted to go to the Yellow House one more time, see what had become of where he had lived with Valerian all those years. Maybe, in some way, say goodbye.

He put on his coat and made for the door, leaving Kepler clutching his head.

The Yellow House

The Place of Broken Futures

❧

1

The New Year was not quite a week old. Life in the City was not yet in full swing; it was a quiet time of year anyway, but people seemed to be using the excessive snow as an excuse for doing as little as possible.

Boy turned into a squalid and narrow street called Three Horse Run to find it empty of its usual loiterers and layabouts, and as he made his way along it, his were the first footsteps that broke the snow's perfection.

Everywhere was the same; he saw barely half a dozen souls as he headed for the place he knew so well, The Yellow House. Despite Kepler's insistence that the men of the Watch were no longer after him, he retained his instinct to go unnoticed wherever possible, and was glad of the emptiness of the streets.

Finally, as he made his way down Salted Frog Alley, he did hear voices approaching. He looked up and saw three costermongers wheeling a barrow of vegetables slowly through the snow. Relieved that they were not Watchmen, Boy nonetheless still had no desire to see anyone, let alone talk to anyone, and pressed himself into a deep doorway at the side of the alley.

He waited as they passed. They were deep in conversation and didn't notice Boy, but even if they had been looking for him they would probably have missed him, he was so good at hiding.

Boy heard snatches of their conversation.

'. . . all over the street . . .'

'. . . couldn't even tell who it was. Poor blighter!'

'They said the snow was turned red for two hundred yards. This great long trail. Then it stopped at a gutter by the river.'

'I heard the blood was sprayed everywhere, like a firework.'

Boy shuddered. He knew what they were talking about.

'Bits of the body were missing, that's for sure. The same as the others.'

'Nonsense!' said one of the others. 'It's the blood it's after. The Phantom can't be seen or killed. It won't be stopped.'

'You're both exaggerating. It's just some lunatic on the loose.'

His friend spat in the snow as they passed near Boy.

'Maybe. But whatever it is, it's still killing for fun, isn't it? The Watch have no idea what to do.'

Boy shrunk back in the doorway. The Phantom had killed again.

It was around one in the afternoon when Boy turned the corner of Blind Man's Stick, and there was The Yellow House, looking the same as it always did apart from the snow covering its roofs: tall and imposing, but faded and in need of repair.

Boy couldn't help lifting his eyes to the very top of the

house, to the Tower, where it had all ended for Valerian. It was a bizarre addition to the top of the rambling house, showing no sign of the horrors that had unfolded there on New Year's Eve. Inside it lay the camera, and the lens that Kepler wanted. Boy would have to face his memories.

He still had the key to the house that Valerian had given him only a few days before, on Childermas, the unluckiest day of the year. Well, the key was one piece of good luck, Boy thought, as he rattled it in the lock of the outer gates.

He had to force the heavy iron gates away from him through the deep snow. With some effort he managed to make them move, and he squeezed through. Now he opened the door to the house itself.

Boy stepped into the hall and closed the door behind him, having first checked, from force of habit, that no one had seen him enter.

It had only been six days since anyone had been there, but The Yellow House had already acquired that strange eerie silence that houses gather about themselves when left alone for any length of time.

'Hello?' Boy said quietly into the air around him, then felt faintly stupid for doing so. Of course there was no one there. There had been no one there since the early hours of the new year when Kepler had come back for him and Willow.

He made his way upstairs to the third-floor landing. From there he could have gone along to where the ladder led up to his little room, but he didn't want to see it.

Only six days, but it felt like an eternity had passed since Boy was last here. He couldn't believe the house was so still, so empty, so big, and wondered if it had always been like that, and whether he just hadn't noticed when Valerian had been there issuing orders and threats in equal measure.

He turned his back on the corridor and headed for the foot of the spiral staircase that led to the Tower. As he made his way up he could already see the remains of the shattered door where Kepler and Willow had burst in to save him from Valerian. Just the sight of the fractured wood made Boy panic, as a rush of memories rose unbidden in his mind.

He tried to concentrate on what he had come to do, but as he stepped over the threshold into the room itself, the events of New Year's Eve overwhelmed him and he sank to the floor, weak and shaking.

He shook his head, trying to clear it.

'The lens,' he said aloud, as if the sound of his voice could dispel the demons lurking in the room. 'Just get the lens and go.'

He looked up.

The room was a mess. They had left it exactly as it was after the awful cataclysm, the wind, the apparition. The hundreds upon hundreds of Valerian's books lay in chaotic heaps across the floor, various papers and parchments strewn over them. Even the trapdoor in the middle of the room was covered in books and papers. Valerian's great leather armchair lay on its side. Broken glass and tangled metal from his experimental equipment lay in confusion across the table tops. The only thing that seemed unharmed was the camera obscura itself. The shutters were drawn and in the half-darkness of the room, Boy saw that the camera was still working. Kepler had warned Valerian that it would be of no use in saving his skin, but he had built a good machine and it worked still, projecting a curved but clear image of the streets outside on to the circular white tabletop beneath it.

Boy scrambled over to it, passing the upturned armchair as he did. He paused, and then pulled Valerian's favourite chair back on to its feet.

'That's better,' he said, and smiled as he remembered Valerian sitting in it.

He turned to the camera. At the base that overhung the table was a wide brass cylinder. From this the image poured on to the table. He supposed this was what Kepler had been talking about, so he climbed on to the table top and lay looking up at the apparatus.

He pushed and pulled the thing, and could see no way of loosening it, but then remembered what Kepler had said about unscrewing it, and he began to twist. Immediately it turned, opening a join that was so finely wrought it had been invisible before the thread began to unwind.

Boy twisted some more, and the bottom half of the cylinder came away from the top. As it did, he suddenly recalled what Kepler had warned about breaking the glass lens, and slid underneath the projection device. The image of the City outside was now played out on Boy's face and chest, and had there been anyone there to see, and had they looked closely, they would have seen snow falling across him. It fell across his eyes and face, but unlike the snow falling outside, which gathered in piles, the flake after flake after flake that crossed Boy's face kept on falling, but hid no horror.

He nearly had it apart now, and chewed his lip as he lowered the bottom half of brass away from the top.

'Hold hard there, you brat!' said a voice from the door, and Boy jerked upright, hitting his head on the camera. He clutched the lens as he swung down to the floor.

'I said hold!'

At first Boy thought he was being faced by men of the City Watch. Three figures stood in the doorway, but now he noticed their uniforms were not the black of the Watch, but the dark grey garb of the Imperial Guard. If there was any doubt over this, the white feathers on their helmets confirmed it: Watchmen wore either red or pink, only the Imperial Guard wore white.

'Looting? That your game, boy?'

The leader stepped forward.

'Give that to me,' he said, indicating the lens in Boy's hand.

For a moment Boy was too stunned to say anything, then he remembered where he was.

'No,' said Boy. 'I'm not stealing. I live here.'

This seemed to throw the guard.

'What do you mean you live here? This is the house of Valerian, the magician. Now deceased, we understand. No one else lives here.'

'That's not true!' Boy cried. 'I do. I've lived here for years. I'm Valerian's boy.'

'His son? He has no son! Don't make a fool of me, boy.'

'No, not his son. That is, I'm not sure . . .'

At this all three of the guards laughed and began to move towards Boy.

'You're not sure!' said the leader. 'You lived here for years and you don't really know if you're his son or not? I'll tell you what, you rascal! You are a thief. Now get out of here. We have serious business to attend to.'

'No!' shouted Boy, 'You get out of here. This is Valerian's house, and yes, he's dead. But I live here and this place belongs to me if it belongs to anyone! I was his boy!'

Now the leader of the guards looked at his two men, then back at Boy.

'You say you were his?'

Boy nodded.

'I lived here and worked for him. I was his assistant.'

'Right, then you're coming with us. We have orders to remove all articles belonging to Valerian and if you were his boy then that includes you.'

Boy laughed nervously.

'You don't really mean that, do you?'

'Don't give us trouble now. You can't get away. It will be easier for all of us if you just come along with us to the Palace.'

'The Palace?' Boy spluttered. 'You can't!'

'I've had enough of this,' the guard said to his men, 'Get him out of my sight.'

And with that the two other Imperial Guards made for Boy.

'No!' cried Boy. He glanced at the guards, then leapt to the wall where the release for the trapdoor lay. He pulled the lever and the floor opened up between the guards and himself, shedding books and papers that tumbled down into the air.

The guards, surprised for a moment, smiled when they looked down through the trapdoor and saw the perilous drop, not to the third but the second-floor landing – a leg-breaking fall.

'That's not going to help you!'

'We'll see,' said Boy, and shoving the lens into his coat pocket launched himself for the gap, catching hold of the winch rope that was used to hoist things up to the Tower.

He had gambled that it would unwind slowly enough to break his fall somewhat, and because of his slight frame, it worked. He landed on the second floor with a thump, but nothing bad enough to stop him.

'Get him!' cried a voice from above.

Boy scrambled to his feet, briefly glancing up. The guards peered down at him, seeing if he was hurt or not. The end of the hoist rope had freed itself from the pulley and fell around Boy's legs.

'Don't just gawp at him! After him! The stairs!'

Boy wasted no more time.

He leapt, with all the speed he could muster, for the stairs, taking them three at a time. As he made the ground floor he felt safe. He could hear the guards lumbering along the second-floor landing. He sprinted across the hall for the door, and then something tangled his legs and he went sprawling along the stone floor, jarring his wrist as he fell. He looked to see what had caught him, and glimpsed one of the guards leaning over the banister. He had thrown the winch rope in a bundle, which had snagged Boy's calves as he ran.

Hearing footsteps thudding closer, Boy struggled to his feet and started to pull at the front door.

He flung it open and ran straight into a fourth guard, waiting there for such an event. The guard was surprised and took a second to react. Boy tried to side-step him, but it was too late.

First one, then two pairs of hands pulled him back and wrestled him to the ground.

'Right, you little swine!' said the guard. 'You're coming to the Palace.'

They brought the rope and tied his arms behind him and then his legs, leaving him trussed up like a slaughtered deer.

None of them saw the lens fall from Boy's pocket and roll a little way away into the snow.

Outside in the street was a cart attached to a sturdy-looking horse. Boy was the first of Valerian's possessions to be thrown into it, and while one of the guards waited with him, the other three spent the afternoon loading anything from the Tower room that wasn't bolted down alongside him.

Darkness had fallen as the cart finally set off at walking pace. Boy lay uncomfortably on his side, half-covered by Valerian's books and other possessions. His arms and legs had gone numb hours before, and it was all he could do to keep one eye on where they were going. After a while he gave up, and tried to ask the guards what they were going to do with him.

They did not reply.

'Please,' pleaded Boy, 'at least tell me where we're going.'

One of them turned round and grunted.

'We told you. The Palace. You belong to the Emperor now.'

3

Willow waited by St Valentine's fountain, but Boy did not come. As the night deepened, the temperature fell from freezing to well below that. For a while she stood and chatted to an old woman huddled over a brazier of roasting chestnuts, until finally the cold was too much. Though Willow had said nothing, the old woman glanced back at her.

'He ain't coming, you know,' she said, and before Willow could reply, shuffled away.

Willow started to worry. They were supposed to have met as the church bells rang seven, but it was long after nine by now. Willow had studied every inch of the frozen fountain, whose long icicles hung from its spout like tusks, where in the summer the water gushed.

Something must have happened to Boy. She thought about what the old woman had said, and worried some more. Something must have happened to him, because there could be no mistaking the plans they had made.

Unless . . . what if she had misread him? She had been doing most of the talking. Maybe she had just heard what she wanted to hear – that Boy wanted to come with her.

She stamped around on the snowy ground by the fountain, getting colder all the time.

It had all seemed so easy sitting in The Feather the night before, but out in the freezing streets it was different. How would they find somewhere to live? She wasn't earning enough to feed them both, let alone rent a room. Perhaps Boy had thought it over, perhaps he'd realised how stupid it was, and maybe he didn't even want her the way she wanted him. He was living in splendour now, relatively. Kepler had given him clothes and a proper room with a real bed in a well-to-do house. It even had that amazing system of electrical lighting Kepler had created. Why on earth would Boy want to leave all that to come and live on the streets again?

She hadn't even known Boy that well at the theatre. It was only in those last five days of the year, when she and Boy had become entwined in Valerian's terrible adventure, that she had realised that she felt something for him.

Willow brushed some snow off the edge of the fountain's basin and sat down. She put her head in her hands and cried.

The bell of St Valentine's chimed ten.

Now Willow was angry. If Boy had decided not to be with her, the least he could have done was tell her to her face, rather than leave her freezing by the fountain. Her anger grew as she began to feel shamed by being so foolish as to believe Boy cared about her, and she decided to let him know how angry she was.

She set off for Kepler's house. She had been there twice briefly, but she knew she could find the way. It would be a long walk, but at least she would be moving and might feel a little warmer.

She was in a fury, and as she walked as fast as she was able along the snow-bound alleys of the City, her mood did not improve.

But as she turned into the Square of Adam and Sophia, something softened in her. Though her route did not take her that way, she knew she was only a street or two away from The Reach, where she and Boy had been together just over a week ago. It was enough to trigger a flood of memories of the fraught time they had spent together trying to save Valerian's life, only to have him try to take Boy's in return. Maybe they had been wrong about Valerian, but she couldn't be wrong about Boy, there was no way to fake what had passed between them, and she began to worry again, knowing that something must have happened to him.

When she got to Kepler's front door, it flew open almost the moment she pulled the bell handle.

'Oh, it's you. Where is he?'

Kepler seemed distracted, even a little angry, but Willow could see that he too was worried more than anything.

'Where is he?' Kepler asked again.

'Can I come in?' Willow said. 'Please. I'm freezing.'

Kepler blinked.

'Yes . . .' he said, standing aside. 'Yes.'

He pushed the door behind her and ushered her into the study.

'Well?' Kepler asked, as Willow moved to stand in front of the fire. 'Have you seen him?'

Willow shook her head. She suddenly felt incredibly numb. Her teeth chattered and she started to shake.

Kepler pulled a chair up by the fireplace for her, muttering as he did so. He fished around in his desk, and pulled out a small bottle that Willow recognised.

She shook her head, afraid of what the drug Valerian had taken so much of in the days before he died might do to her, but Kepler ignored her protests.

He poured a capful of the green liquid into her mouth, and waited. Warmth and strength began to wash over Willow in such a delightful way that she immediately felt herself begin to recover. She felt light-headed, even felt like laughing.

Kepler pulled another chair up by the fire and sat down.

'Well, Willow?' he asked again.

Willow shook her head.

'I came here to find him. We were supposed to meet . . .'

She stopped, realising she shouldn't have told Kepler that, but he seemed too preoccupied to notice or to care, staring down into the fire.

'I sent him out earlier, he was supposed to come straight back . . .'

'Where?' asked Willow.

Kepler looked up at her.

'What?'

'Where did you send him?'

'To Valerian's.'

'You sent him there!' cried Willow. 'You shouldn't have sent him there. Anything might have . . .'

'What?' Kepler snapped. 'What might have happened to

him? It's an empty house. There's nothing dangerous there. Not now. Not now Valerian's gone.'

'You still shouldn't have made him go there. It's a bad place for him.'

Kepler shrugged.

'I don't want him hurt any more than you do.'

'Really?' said Willow sharply. 'Why is that?'

'I assure you I want the best for him. You could not understand.'

'Well, if you did you wouldn't have sent him there.'

Kepler opened his mouth to bite back at Willow, but then shut it again. He thought briefly, frowning.

'What matters is this: where is he? There's nowhere else for him to go except back on the streets, and this is the coldest winter in memory.'

Willow nodded.

'You're right. I'm sorry. I'm just worried that . . .'

'The Yellow House. That's the only place to look. You can stay here and get warm, I'll be—'

'No,' Willow said firmly, getting to her feet. 'I'm coming too.'

'Nonsense,' said Kepler. 'You aren't fit to go anywhere. I look after the boy now. You can stay here until—'

'No!' shouted Willow. 'I'm coming with you. You have no right to tell me what to do. If you care anything for how I feel then you'll give me another drink of that stuff and help me find Boy!'

With that Kepler thrust the bottle at Willow and went off to find a coat.

Willow smiled as he went, took another sip of the drug, and put the bottle in her pocket. She found Kepler in the hall, wrestling with a long winter coat. By his feet was a canvas shoulder pack, which he picked up and swung on to his back.

'Well?' he said.

'Let's go, Mr Kepler,' Willow said brightly, and led the way to the door and out into the snow-swirling night.

The Dungeon

The Place of Deceitful Histories

❉

1

Boy's first view of the Imperial Palace of Emperor Frederick was not welcoming.

The cart trundled wearily uphill towards the Palace walls for ages, but when almost at the gates, turned on to a path that wound back down around the outskirts of the mound on which the walls were built. This path reached an end at a solid iron gate right at the base of the Palace hill. Behind it a long, low tunnel led deep into the earth under the Palace buildings.

Boy looked up at the mouldy ceiling of the tunnel as the cart was manhandled along it by torchlight, being too small for the horse to make it down. The tunnel was pitted every now and again by defensive openings, through which arrows or crossbow bolts could be fired should anyone try to attack the Palace by this particular route.

Far above Boy's head, through the bedrock of the Palace hill, perched the magnificent, sprawling splendour of the Palace itself, but Boy saw nothing of this. Up in the dark night sky the Palace burned like a precious jewel, torches and lights flaring from every ornate window, picking out a gleam here and there from the gilded dome of the Palace chapel or the spire of the bell tower. The Palace was a place of wonder, made to impress the onlooker with the greatness of the Imperial line and to dwarf the ordinary mortal. It had been built over many years, each Emperor adding something new, trying to find a way of outdoing his predecessor with a more elaborate spire or a more preposterous tower. The result was a vast, heaven-reaching concoction of architectural hallucination, all teetering on a low hill south of the river. The Palace faced in on itself; the wonder was not, after all, for the rabble in the City to admire. They were impressed enough by the high walls and battlements that marked its perimeter. The true splendour of the place was only visible from inside, from the Great Court or the Emperor's Green or the Royal Gardens. Then one could stop and stand and stare open-mouthed at the acres of gilded rooftops, copper-topped cupolas and sculpted marble embellishments.

Much of its finery was presently hidden under several feet of snow, but Boy saw none of it anyway. He was shuffled down the tunnel into a wider, higher space deep underground, where the cart was upended and he, along with all Valerian's other possessions, fell out on to the cold, unforgiving flagstones.

He heard the squeak of a door or gates, and then the sound of a heavy lock being secured. Footsteps led away, and then all was quiet.

Boy tried to wriggle on to his backside, and having achieved this, managed to sit up and lean against the wall.

All around was blackness. His wrist still hurt from the fall in the house, and he was cold and tired.

Straining to see anything at all, he suddenly became aware of something.

A noise.

It was faint at first, then got a little louder, coming nearer towards him. The sound was a shuffling scraping, soft but heavy, and with it there seemed to be a low, rasping breathing, like a creature half-throttled. But almost as soon as Boy was convinced it was not mere imagination, the sound receded and then disappeared entirely, leaving something else behind. A smell.

The smell of fresh blood.

Willow and Kepler stood on the doorstep of The Yellow House, and knew something was wrong. Neither of them had a key to the house, but they didn't need one. The snow on the porch and outside the house was a confused mess of footsteps and the tracks of cartwheels. The door was ajar.

'Thieves?' whispered Kepler.

'They could still be in there,' Willow said, her voice wavering.

'Then we'd better tread quietly.'

Kepler took a step forwards and as he did, his foot kicked something lying in the snow. He looked down and picked it up. With surprise he saw it was the lens.

'What is it?' Willow asked.

'It's the very thing I sent Boy here to collect.'

They both fell silent, and looked again at the open doorway of The Yellow House.

It was dark in the house and they had brought no light.

As they made their way gingerly inside, Willow and Kepler waited for their eyes to grow accustomed to the gloom. Only the faintest shimmer of light made its way into the house from the torchlit street, showing feebly through the grimy windows high up in the hall.

They listened keenly, but though no sound could be heard, they didn't relax. The house seemed predatory, like a vicious animal waiting to pounce.

They moved upstairs and found themselves drawn inexorably to the spiral staircase that led to the Tower.

There was a little more light drifting down through the high glass skylight above the third-floor landing, and they were able to pick their way up to the Tower more easily, but still they went cautiously.

Instinctively, they had found their way to the wounded heart of the house. Kepler led the way, and they immediately saw that the Tower room had had its guts ripped out. The room was stripped of almost everything valuable. All the books were gone, all the scientific apparatus and magical paraphernalia that had given it its identity. All that was left was anything that was too big to move or was broken, the projection table of the camera obscura and the old leather armchair.

Kepler shook his head.

'What in God's name has happened here?' he said.

Willow said nothing.

'Dare we risk some light?' she asked. 'He kept a packet of matches on the window sill . . .'

Willow fumbled in the gloom, but soon she found the matches where she had seen them last.

Kepler turned to her and nodded.

'Very well,' he said. 'The villains are long gone.'

Willow struck a match and held it up above her head, letting its feeble light cast a glow around the room.

'Look out!' she shouted suddenly, but at the same moment Kepler had seen that the trapdoor lay wide open, the hatch a gaping black mouth in the floor just inches from where he stood.

He stepped back a pace.

'So they stole everything they could . . .'

'Who?'

Kepler shrugged.

'I don't know.'

'But where's Boy?' Willow asked.

Kepler looked around the mess.

Willow squealed and dropped the match, which had burned to her fingertips.

'Quick!' Kepler said, 'Light another one! I saw something.'

Willow struck another match and once more a little patch of light spread around them.

'There!' said Kepler, 'Over there!'

'What is it?' Willow asked and followed Kepler carefully to the edge of the hole left by the trapdoor, where something on the floor had caught his eye.

He picked it up.

It was a white feather.

'What?' asked Willow, desperately. 'What does it mean?'

'It means that our crooks were rather powerful people. And I think it means I know where Boy is. The Imperial Palace.'

'How do you know?' Willow asked.

'The feather. The feather is from the uniform of an Imperial Guardsman. That's where he is.'

Willow dropped the match again, and they were left in darkness.

'I will get him out,' Kepler said, but not really to Willow. 'I'll help. I'll come too.'

'Not this time, girl!' Kepler declared. 'I've had enough of you tailing around. Boy is mine, and I don't need your help with anything. Not least Boy. You go back to the orphanage and be grateful I found you a job!'

Willow said nothing.

She knew what she was going to do, whether Kepler liked it or not, and there was no point in arguing about it. Without another word she left the Tower, and the house, behind her.

Kepler stood in the ruins of the Tower, brooding.

'Boy!' he said to the thick dark air. 'This wasn't supposed to happen. Not yet. But your fate is mine now. You will be mine.'

He pulled the lens from his pocket and held it tight in his fist.

'And I have this, at least . . .'

3

For a long, long time Boy saw nothing, heard nothing. It was as if he had become deaf and blind, and panic began to well up inside him. Finally he could stand no more, and as much to prove he had not gone deaf, he shouted into the darkness.

'Hello! Hello?'

His voice fell dead around him, with a short, curtailed echo. It reminded him of those dank underground tunnels where he had been pursued by Valerian, and he didn't like the memory one bit.

'Please! Please don't leave me here!'

The heavy silence covered him the moment his voice was killed by the close stone walls and low damp ceiling. He was about to cry out for a third time, when he caught a whiff of the smell he had sensed before. His heart beat faster, but he heard nothing. Maybe it wasn't such a good idea to be calling out into the nothingness.

He put his head back on the cold stone floor and, still trussed up like a slaughtered beast, he lay still for a while.

He must have slept.

He was woken up being pulled roughly by his ankles from where he lay.

Hands seemed to be everywhere, grabbing at him, but he still could not see anything, being dazzled by the light from several oil lamps.

'What . . . ?' he tried to say, but was winded as he was thrown over someone's shoulder.

'Get on with it,' said a voice. 'He's in a foul mood. And he wants it all now.'

'As usual,' said another voice.

In an instant Boy was swung away down a low, gloomy tunnel, but he felt that they were rising this time, heading up to the real world. He was glad of that, at least. Maybe there would be someone he could talk to, explain things and get himself set free. It all had to be a silly mistake. He couldn't *really* belong to the Emperor. Like most people in the City, Boy knew little of the Emperor, just vague stories about him – that he was very old and maybe a little crazy. No one knew anything for sure.

As his eyes grew used to the lights bobbing ahead of him, he saw that he was being carried by one of a long line of men, each with some burden or other. He was hanging upside down, and it was hard to be sure, but as the file of carriers made its way into a larger and this time torchlit tunnel, he saw what it was they were carrying. Valerian's things. All of them.

Before he had time to wonder what was going on, Boy sensed something else. That smell again. He twisted around to see its source, and in the dim light could just make out a small, rough-cut entrance to a flight of stairs leading down from the corridor they were in. It was barred by an iron grille, with a padlocked chain holding it shut.

Beyond the grille, Boy could see that the stairs were

narrow and hideously steep. It made him feel sick merely looking at them. Then they plunged down into darkness and there was no sign that they ever ended.

'Stop wriggling, you monkey,' snarled the man carrying Boy. He let himself hang loosely again and they moved past the entrance to the dark flight down.

They were still trudging upwards, and now turned and climbed three stone steps. Then there was a doorway, and suddenly the light was brilliant all around them.

They were in a long, beautiful, ornate corridor, with a polished wooden floor. Bright morning daylight spilled in through high leaded windows. Along the walls hung huge, elaborately framed portraits of people in royal attire.

The corridor seemed to stretch for ever, and when they finally left it, they turned and the long file of men made their way down another identical gallery.

As they went, taking a flight of stairs here and entering and leaving countless golden-glimmering rooms and passages, Boy finally understood that he really was in the Imperial Palace.

He heard voices ahead, and saw from his upside-down point of view that they were in a chamber large enough to be a ballroom. Huge windows took up much of one wall, flooding the room with more light than Boy's eyes could bear for the time being. He squinted as he was dumped on to a table top, blinking and trying to get the right way up.

'Stay there, you little brat!' snapped his porter, and cuffed him round the head. Boy lay, blinking.

As he got used to the light he gradually opened his eyes a little more, and dared to look around. Men were standing in groups, others were still filing in from where Boy had come, all bearing more and more of Valerian's things. Boy lost count of how many came in carrying a stack of a dozen or so thick leather-bound books, depositing them on long polished oak tables, just like the one he was lying on.

Occasionally someone would glance at him, but when he tried to get their attention they ignored him, merely regarding him as if he was an animal or some curiosity in a market-place.

Suddenly there was a commotion, and the porters hurried frantically along the tables and made their way out. A trumpet blast sounded at the far end of the hall, and the groups broke up to form an orderly line. They all bowed, ridiculously low.

A nervous voice cried out: 'His Imperial Majesty, his Royal Greatness, Emperor Frederick!'

Boy twisted round where he lay and regarded the far end of the room.

A tall, imposing figure in flowing blood-red robes swept into the room. The silence was total.

Boy, like many people in the City itself, had often doubted that there was an Emperor at all behind the high walls of the Palace. No one had seen him in years. Life in the City seemed to go on perfectly well by itself, and some people even believed him to be nothing more than a legend.

Now, right before his eyes, Boy saw an impressive, powerful man with a shaven head striding down the length of the ballroom, and knew the rumours were false. Another figure trailed after the first. A small old man, richly dressed but shrunken, hobbled in after the Emperor, who stood waiting with his hand resting on a high-backed chair so sumptuous it could have been a throne.

Boy watched, puzzled. The line of men still bowed with their noses near their knees, while the old man scurried along, taking short hopping steps. He reached the throne, and sat down in it, then put his head back, his eyes closed.

Finally he opened them again, and turned to look at the tall man beside him.

'This had better be worth it, Maxim,' he whined. 'I haven't been down to the Eastern State rooms since . . . well, I can't remember, but there's far too many flights of stairs on the way. You should have had a chair sent for me.'

'My apologies, Emperor,' said Maxim.

And now Boy understood. The decrepit little man was the Emperor, not the tall figure in red.

Emperor Frederick. The last of his line, at least eighty years old, with no kin to succeed him.

'I do indeed believe,' Maxim went on, 'that you should see everything we recovered from the magician's house. And I recall that you did yourself say that the Eastern ballroom would be the only place large enough—'

'Nonsense!' snapped Frederick. 'I said no such thing. I never change my mind, you know that! What's wrong with the Court? That's twice the size, and several floors closer to my chambers! Dare you contradict me, Maxim?'

'Indeed no,' said Maxim flatly. 'I do not question you, Sire. But some of the items were . . . a trifle awkward to carry that far. Shall we?'

Maxim gestured for Frederick to join him, but the Emperor shut his eyes and shook his head.

340

'I can see from here. You may begin.'

Maxim clicked his fingers. The line of bowing courtiers jerked upright, some a little faster than others. One or two older ones straightened very slowly, hands clasped to the smalls of their backs. They made their way over to join Maxim, who was walking along the line of tables, inspecting the things lying there.

Unable to move himself upright, Boy had a rather sideways view of what was going on. Nonetheless, he could sense there was something familiar about Maxim. It was in the way he moved, the way he looked at the Emperor, and the way he seemed to be restraining his voice whenever he spoke. There was something restless about him, something hungry, though Boy did not know what it was exactly.

'Magical apparatus, Sire!' Maxim announced from across the room.

Frederick yawned, opened his eyes for a second, then shut them again.

'Why did we have to do this so early in the day?' he sniped at Maxim. 'You know my stomach hurts if I have to rise early.'

'It's nearly noon,' Maxim said calmly, 'and I thought the matter too urgent to wait. This magical equipment could hold the secret to occult powers that may aid us in our quest.'

Boy looked at the things Maxim had indicated and frowned. He didn't see that a box that chickens disappeared inside, and a device for making smoke-screens for Valerian's stage act were going to be of much use for anything the Emperor could be interested in.

Maxim and the other members of court moved on, then stopped at the next group of tables.

'Books, Sire,' Maxim announced to Frederick, who remained with his eyes shut and waved a hand dismissively.

'What of it? We have lots of books.'

Maxim bit his tongue.

'Yes, Sire, but the magician was known to have certain books of considerable power. Certain. Books.'

He paused, thinking Frederick would respond to this, but the Emperor was barely listening. Maxim sighed and went on.

'It may be that some answer to our search lies within one of these tomes. I will bend my researches in their direction, scour every page for the slightest clue.'

He flourished a hand at the hundreds of books stacked in crazy piles on the tables.

And that should keep him off my back for a while, he thought, but said nothing. Instead he spread a large and very fake smile across his face and continued.

'In fact,' Maxim continued, 'I am convinced our solution lies in that direction. The magician . . .'

But Maxim stopped mid-sentence. He had seen something that surprised him. Curled up on one of the tables, with hands and legs tied behind him, was a thin youth with spiky hair.

For a moment he was thrown. He glanced at one of the porters, who rapidly whispered in his ear.

'The magician's famulus!' he declared.

Frederick coughed and opened his eyes. He followed Maxim's hand pointing to where Boy lay.

'His what?' he spluttered.

'His assistant,' Maxim replied. 'His apprentice. His . . . boy. We found him in the ruins of the house. He belonged to the magician. We believe he may be of considerable use in explaining many of the practices and skills of the magician himself.'

Boy frowned, wishing he could scratch an itch that had started on his nose.

There was silence. The Emperor stared, his little eyes blinking slowly.

'Maxim, I have had enough,' he said.

'But Sire, this is a great development in our search. We are getting closer—'

'Shut up!' Frederick whined. 'Shut up! You are not getting closer to anything. I am getting closer to lunch-time, and I haven't even had my breakfast yet.'

'Sire—'

'And you, Maxim, are getting closer to the executioner's block.'

'Sire, I—'

'Understand me, Maxim. I mean you to succeed in this quest. That is vital. But how you do it is of no interest to me whatsoever. Understand? So get me a chair to take me to breakfast, and make sure that damn chef does the eggs properly. You know they make me ill if they're too runny. I swear he's trying to kill me.'

'Yes, Sire, I—' Maxim tried again, but the Emperor was not listening.

'I'm running out of patience, really I am. You'd better find an answer soon. Where's that blasted chair? I can't wait all day, you know. I won't have time for breakfast before lunch, and you know that I get a headache if I don't get enough rest between meals. You're trying to kill me too! Well, I won't have it.'

The Emperor got to his feet.

'Come, Maxim! We shall walk back, though you know how my feet ache. If I faint on the way you'll have to carry me.'

He scurried away down the hall, and Maxim followed.

'Keep up, Maxim! Keep up!' Frederick was saying. 'Oh, and one more thing. Have that brat thrown into the river. He's dirty and probably spreading disease. You have no thought for my welfare! None at all! He's only some street brat on the make, you know. Honestly! There's thousands of them just like him out there! This whole city is like a scabrous beggar holding out its hands for a penny. Well, I won't have it. Throw him in the river and then get me my breakfast. Maxim!'

He had reached the end of the hall and disappeared round a corner.

'Sire,' Maxim called, hurrying after him. 'Coming, Sire.'

Boy had jolted upright. He tried to sit up some more and in doing so fell off his table.

Guards hurried over to where he lay writhing on the floor.

'Right,' said one of the courtiers. 'You heard His Majesty. Into the river with him.'

With that, several hands clutched at Boy's clothes. Once again he was thrown over someone's shoulder.

'No!' he cried, 'No!'

As he made to scream again, a rolled-up handkerchief

was shoved into his mouth, stopping him from making any more noise.

'Get on with it,' someone said. 'We've got enough to do today as it is.'

4

Boy struggled, but it was no use. Four pairs of hands held him firmly, so firmly that there was no chance of escape.

He spat the handkerchief from his mouth.

'You can't do this!' he yelled as he tried to kick out at the men carrying him. 'I've done nothing! You can't do this!'

The men did not reply, but one of them struck Boy across the back of his head with an open hand.

'Little brat!' he said to his companions.

They were hurrying down a narrow dark passage, the rough-cut stone floor sloping away before them.

'Would be easier just to chuck him down there,' one of them muttered.

'Where?'

'You know where I mean.'

'And save some other poor soul,' said another voice.

'You heard what he said,' said the second voice. 'Put him in the river and get back to work.'

There was no more talk after that.

The men renewed their pace. Boy doubled his efforts to break free and was cuffed around the head again, and punched in the ribs this time too. Now he could hear the sound of running water rushing past somewhere nearby.

'Right then, let's be done with it.'

Boy knew they were standing by an underground quay. He could hear and smell the water, and knew he was once more at the edge of the subterranean maze of canals and catacombs through which he had been relentlessly pursued by Valerian in the dead days before the end of the year and the end of Valerian. So there was at least one connection from the Palace to that cold, damp hidden world beneath the City itself.

'Right!' shouted one of the men. 'On three . . .'

Boy had given up trying to plead, but tried to wriggle and kick harder than ever. He was helpless, and he knew as soon as he hit the water he would sink like a stone.

'One!' the man shouted.

'Two!'

Then there was another shout from behind them.

'Hold!'

Boy already recognised that commanding voice. It belonged to Maxim.

Two of the men hesitated. The third had already begun to swing Boy's knees out, and lost his grip. Boy's bottom half sank under the water. The two holding him by the shoulders nearly overbalanced and followed them all into the water.

Maxim ran over to the men and with his help, Boy was easily retrieved from the under-river and saved.

The men stood back from where Boy now lay on the quayside.

'Sire?' one of them said, looking up at Maxim.

Boy could sense the relationship between the men and Maxim, based on something he knew well from life with Valerian. Fear.

Valerian. Boy now knew who Maxim had reminded him of when he had first seen him in the ballroom. They shared the same strange mix of desperation and frightening power.

Maxim surveyed the scene before him. He wrung the sleeve of his robe, which had dipped into the water.

'The Emperor may not think he needs the boy,' he said, 'but I do. Leave him with me.'

The men shuffled away a step or two, heading back for the steps to the Palace.

'Very good, Sire,' said one of them.

Boy rolled over and managed to get to his knees. He looked up at Maxim.

'Oh,' Maxim said, as they went. 'One more thing. Forget what happened here. If anyone asks, you threw the boy in the river as you were told. I'll see to him from now on.'

Boy, soaked from the waist down, dripped on to the stone flags and shivered, finding no comfort at all in Maxim's words.

5

Boy's body lay asleep one hundred and fifty feet below the shiny bright marble floor of the Court, but his mind was elsewhere. In feverish dreaming he made his way along a stone corridor, crumbling and night-black. He thought he would stop at the top of the flight of stone steps he had been expecting, but with alarm found that he had already begun to go down them, step by steep step.

Unable to stop, his feet moved by themselves, drawing him deeper down towards the thing waiting for him. For he knew without question that something lived at the foot of the dark flight of stairs, something that could take his life from him.

The stairs were narrow, their treads not even wide enough for him to get the whole of his foot on each one, and they were so sickeningly steep as to make his head reel.

He looked round and could no longer see the entrance at the top of the stairs. Panicking, he turned and missed his footing. He slipped forward, tipping headlong down the awful staircase, plummeting towards the thing.

He screamed.

He woke.

6

Boy had no idea how long he'd been in the cell.

After Maxim had saved him from being drowned in the under-river, he'd been dragged by his neck down unfathomable passages to a high-vaulted chamber somewhere deep beneath the Palace. Around its walls were a series of cells, constructed from iron bars on three sides, and whose backs were the stone wall of the dungeon itself. The bars ran right up to the roof, so there was no way to climb over them.

Boy could see at least three cells on either side of him, and a similar row on the far side of the chamber, which was lit by a smoky oil-lamp hanging on a long chain that dangled from the centre of the ceiling.

Maxim had swung the door of his cell shut and clanked a key in its lock.

'I'll be back,' was all he had said, and left.

But Boy had no idea how long ago that had been.

Whether by oversight or ignorance, Boy had not been searched by any of his captors at any point, and still had his lock-pick in his pocket.

Having waited a good while after Maxim had left, Boy looked about him. As far as he could see in the half-light, there was no one in any of the other cells, but once or twice he wondered if he had heard something away on the other side of the room.

He rummaged around in the lock and soon flicked the tumblers into their right positions. The lock turned and Boy once more paused and looked about. Still nothing. He tiptoed out of his cell and moved to the centre of the chamber, underneath the oil lamp.

In the darkness, Boy could not see all of the dungeon at once. He could just make out groups of cells against the walls, and in the space in the middle a simple fireplace with a stand for a pot or cauldron to be hung above it. There were some other things in the middle of the room: a table of sorts, and a chair more like a wooden throne. Boy went closer. The table and chair reminded him for a moment of some of the bits of equipment Valerian had used in their stage act, but then he realised what they were: a chair with locks on the arms, a table with a ratchet at the end.

Boy decided not to wait any longer.

The floor of the dungeon sloped slightly up at one side, and in the wall on the highest side was the door through which Maxim had left.

Boy made for the door quickly, and tried the handle. It was locked, of course, but there was no keyhole on the inside.

Boy's heart began to pound, and he shook the handle violently. It was no use. He sat down on the floor with his back to the door, trying to decide what to do.

He sat still, thinking about how he might escape at first, but as he failed to find any solution other thoughts came to mind. He thought of Willow, of where she was and what she was doing. He wondered what she might be thinking after he had not turned up by the fountain.

His brooding was interrupted by the sound of footsteps. He got up and as quickly as he could skipped back to his cell, locking the door behind him. If he was going to be stuck, then he reasoned it was a good idea not to let his captors know he could pick locks, and that he could at least get out of the inner cell. Just as Boy hid the lock-pick in his pocket once more, the far door banged open.

Boy was surprised and also somewhat relieved to see that it was not Maxim who entered the room, but a small crooked man, bald, in shabby clothes. That at least meant that one other person knew where Boy was, that his life was not solely dependent on Maxim's interest in him.

The man carried a tray on which were two bowls. He came over to Boy's cell, and put the tray on the floor. Only now could Boy see that the man was blind. His eyes were open but stared blankly, focussing on nothing. Boy wondered how he was able to move across the chamber to the one cell where Boy was without hesitating, and guessed it must mean he had done it many, many times before.

The blind jailer picked one of the bowls up and slid it between the bars.

'There you go,' he said. 'Make it last.'

Boy looked in the wooden bowl and saw a slop of grey sludge. There was no spoon.

The man got to his feet and picked up the tray once more, taking the other bowl with it.

'Wait!' Boy cried. 'Don't go! Tell me what's going on! What are they going to do with me?'

The man didn't stop.

'I've no idea,' he said as he went. 'I just bring the food.'

'Wait! Please come back!' Boy called, but the jailer was already away on the far side of the chamber, and paid Boy no more attention.

He got up and paced around the cell, trying not to think about anything other than how to get out of the foul hole in which he found himself.

After a while he stopped, having failed to come up with anything, though it occurred to him that there was something significant he had learnt.

He had learnt that there was someone else in one of the other cells – the second bowl of food must have been for another prisoner.

Boy looked at his own food.

He determined to eat it, then go to find out who else was locked up in the dungeon, but he had taken no more than a mouthful before the oil-lamp began to flicker and die.

Very soon it gave up the ghost entirely, and Boy finished his food in darkness. Unable to see, he dared not venture out, and lay down.

Some time later he heard, or at least thought he heard, a sound – the sound of someone singing. It was so faint that he couldn't be sure he wasn't imagining it, and very soon he could hear nothing more at all, though he strained hard to.

Since then he had heard nothing else, nor seen anything else. With no stimulus to his senses, all that lay before his eyes was a ghost image – the image of a stone staircase dropping down to the dark unknown.

7

For two days Willow had hung around near the Palace walls, trying to find some way into the vast complex of buildings. Despite its size the Palace had relatively few entrances, to make its defence easier. In actual fact, the Palace had never been attacked by any invading force or local uprising. Long ago, when the power of the empire still existed, its strength had been so great that no army would ever have dared to invade. These days, the empire long gone, the Palace was a strange curiosity to most people, and though it still governed the City in name, most decisions were taken by various guilds, leagues and organisations, and the City and the Palace largely ignored each other.

Still, due to the paranoia and vanity of a succession of peculiar emperors, each more dotty than the last, the Palace retained notions that it was a castle, and as a result, ingress to and egress from it were strictly controlled. Despite its current state of decline, the reputation of the Palace as a seat of influence, wealth and great learning remained alluring to travellers across the entire continent.

Willow had run away from the orphanage without even collecting her week's pay. For the first time in her life she was out on the streets, and had already started to learn what it must have been like for Boy all those years. Hunger had taken the edge off her sharp sense of right and wrong, and she had stolen some bread from a street merchant. As soon as she had eaten it, however, she had felt guilty, and vowed she would pay the man back three times over when she could.

Now she sat on a stone bollard across the street from one of the main entrances to the Palace, the East Gate. Like its only other main entrance, the North Gate, this way into the Palace was heavily guarded and fortified. Willow had watched for hours to see if there was some chink in the armour that might offer her a chance to get inside, but she had seen none. Every trader or visitor had to present themselves at a grilled window and explain the purpose of their visit. Many of them seemed to wave a paper document or similar at the guard inside before the heavy iron spiked portcullis was raised to allow them in.

There was no way in through the East Gate unless you had official business to attend to. It was exactly the same at the North Gate, Willow knew, because she had spent several hours there the day before, doing just the same thing.

She sat disconsolately on her bollard, getting colder by the minute. It was late afternoon and the snow fell incessantly. It had been days since anyone had seen the sun, and the City was grinding to a halt. Willow had heard two merchants muttering that there would be food shortages soon if the snow went on. They seemed solemn for a moment, then laughed about putting their prices up as supplies became scarcer.

Willow got up and began to walk around the Palace again. There was a cobbled street that ran right around its base. It was called the Planting, because on either side the street was lined with lime trees. In the summer they provided beautiful rustling shade from the sun, in the winter they were bare, stripped things that pointed fingers rudely at the sky.

Willow had walked nearly a mile and was close to the North Gate once more. As she gazed at its impenetrable face yet again, she noticed something.

Keeping herself alert to all the comings and goings, she watched one particular man. He was carrying a large bag on his shoulders, and after a lengthy conversation with two of the guards, was let in through the outer gates.

Willow ran forward, and was in time to see the man being escorted by another guard up the sloping road that led to the inner gates.

Suddenly she heard footsteps close in behind her, and before she could turn felt her arms grabbed from behind.

She wrenched herself free and spun around.

'You!' she cried.

In front of her stood Kepler, scowling.

'Willow!' he said. 'Why am I not surprised to see you here?'

8

On the third day Maxim paid Boy a visit.

He stood outside the cell in which Boy had been
mouldering, by turns sleeping and waking, ravaged by
hunger.

'You, boy,' he said. 'What's your name?'

Boy wondered what he meant. Maxim stared at him,
fixing him to the spot. Boy looked back at him. He was
tall, perhaps as tall as Valerian, but he was bigger, heavier.
His face was somewhat round, giving way to the passing
years maybe, but it was nevertheless a striking face, with
strong eyes and nose. He had no hair, which made his
large ears even more pronounced. He had the devil's own
deep voice.

'Answer me, you insolent boy!' he barked suddenly at
Boy. 'What is your name?'

Now Boy understood. Of course, the man in front of
him didn't know he was called Boy.

'Boy,' Boy said.

'Don't try to be clever with me,' Maxim threatened, 'or
my patience may run out quicker than you would like.'

'I'm not,' said Boy. 'Boy's my name.'

Maxim paused.

'You—'

'I don't have a name,' Boy said helpfully.

'You must have a name,' Maxim said. 'What do people call you?'

'Boy. They call me Boy. That's what I'm trying to tell you. I grew up on the streets. No one knows who my parents are.'

'How touching,' said Maxim unkindly. 'Very well. I shall call you Boy too. Listen to me, Boy. You are going to help me. I need information and you're going to give it to me. If you tell me what I need to know, I will reward you by letting you go free from here, back to the streets. If you fail me, you'll die down here.'

Boy took a step back, despite the bars between them.

'What . . .' he said, 'what do you want me to do? I don't know anything.'

'Yes, you do. Yes,' Maxim said. 'You were until recently the famulus of the magician, Valerian. Correct?'

Boy did not answer.

'Correct?' Maxim shouted.

'Yes,' said Boy. 'Yes, I was.'

'Then you must have been privy to his dealings. I know you assisted him in his work, both on and off stage. Don't look surprised. You think I don't have men out in the City? I have spies everywhere and I know much about Valerian. For example, I know he was more than just a stage conjuror. Correct?'

Boy nodded.

'Yes, but I never really knew—'

'Be quiet, Boy,' Maxim said harshly. 'Wait until I ask you to think. Now, I know you know about his magical

359

skills, and I also know he was looking for something shortly before his death. A book. You know about that?'

Boy went cold.

'No,' he said. 'I don't know about any book.'

Maxim stepped right up to the bars of the cell.

'You're lying. Don't lie to me, Boy, or I will get someone down here to hurt you. Tell me about the book.'

Just to hear mention of the book was enough to put a chill in Boy's heart. He knew it was danger, he had seen what it had done to Valerian and Kepler, he knew of its deceitful power. And yet he himself wanted it too.

'I don't know what you mean,' said Boy, backing away across the cell. His heels suddenly hit the back wall and he jumped.

'I mean,' he said, 'I know a little about his tricks, and I know he had lots of books, but I don't know anything about them. I can't read very well, you see.'

'Be quiet!' Maxim said. 'Don't play games with me! I know you know about one particular book, one very special book. Where is it? Did Valerian find it before he died? Tell me!'

Boy shook his head, and hoped his voice wasn't shaking too badly.

'I don't know,' he cried, 'I really don't. I know about his tricks and some of the equipment, but I don't know about a special book.'

Maxim turned away, scowling. Boy held his breath, wondering if he'd been convincing enough. His mind was racing, as he frantically tried to work out if Maxim could know about the book, and if so, from whom. And, more crucially, what he wanted it for.

Maxim turned back to him.

'That's enough for now,' he said. He gave no sign betraying whether he believed Boy's story or not. 'I'll be back soon. And you had better be more forthcoming next time. I promise you that. I have plenty of need for blood down here, Boy, so think about what you do, and don't, know. Think very carefully.'

He moved off, still glowering at Boy and then turned on his heel and spun away through the door.

9

Maxim chewed his lip. He waited, at the right hand of Frederick's throne, while the Emperor considered the situation before him.

The Court was full. The usual crowd was present.

The doctors. A feckless assortment with less knowledge of medicine than Maxim, but they served their purpose. Frederick was never well. There was always something wrong with him – at least, in his mind there was always something wrong with him. The doctors were very useful to Maxim. He could, and did, blame them for the Emperor's poor state of health, deflecting any complaints Frederick made from himself. And if, as rarely happened, Frederick chanced to say he felt a bit better than usual one morning, Maxim would take the praise, pretending he had told the doctors to improve their efforts.

There were the stargazers, the astrologists. Maxim had less control of this group. Not that they were any less spineless than the doctors, but they were altogether unpredictable. They wore the badges of their office – pointed caps emblazoned with stars – and carried charts and diagrams with them always. Frederick set great store by astrological computations, and never did anything if

Saturn was in retrograde motion. Maxim did his best to use the information the astrologers imparted to further his own position, but they were apt to come out with the most unexpected bit of news at any time, with little or no warning, and Frederick would be sent into fits of panic. When this happened he was likely to start accusing Maxim of disloyalty, or even treason, and at the very least criticise Maxim's lack of care for his Emperor, his health and general well-being.

There were alchemists, necromancers, and other magical practitioners that Frederick had seen fit to assemble around him. Many of them were entirely laughable and ineffectual, but some were devious and clever enough to give Maxim cause for concern. Frederick seemed to think the answer to his problems lay with men of this sort. He never welcomed Maxim's suggestions that there were perhaps too many of them and that they might do better with a dozen fewer.

Then there was the Court itself, with its entourages and hangers-on – the noblemen and ladies of the Court, all from rich and powerful families, dukes and duchesses, lords and ladies, but not one with a direct claim to the throne. In the event of Frederick's death, this was the group Maxim feared the most. They were a conniving and greedy bunch out for nothing but their own gain. Maxim recognised these motives well, since they were his own, and to be feared in others.

Then there were the staff, though most of them existed almost unseen.

It was Maxim's lot to rule this exotic collection, to see things in the Palace ran smoothly, to make sure Frederick was attended to in the smallest detail, every minute of every day.

Now Maxim stood by Frederick's throne as the Emperor considered the application of another occultist.

The influence of Frederick's Court was not what it had once been, but stories of its very real wealth still spread far and wide, and it was commonplace for several new applicants to arrive at the Palace gates each week, all hoping to gain the special favour of the Emperor and earn a fortune in the process.

This latest candidate was a youngish man with thin hair and roaming eyes. Maxim, however, was fretting not about him, but about the boy in the dungeon. Maxim was convinced that Boy had to know about the book. His spies had told him that it had been rediscovered, and Maxim knew that Valerian had been looking for it. If he *had* found it, then it stood to reason that his boy had to know the truth about its current whereabouts.

Maxim quite rightly believed the book would be the only way to find a solution to his predicament. There had to be some way out of the dilemma Frederick had placed him in, yet it managed to elude him despite his best efforts.

The Emperor wanted immortality, and nothing would stop his relentless search for it. Any day the neurotic decrepit ruler might decide he'd had enough of his current right-hand man.

As things stood, their relationship suited Maxim. He commanded respect, or at least fear, throughout the Palace, and had luxurious chambers in which to live. But things could not stay that way for ever, and Maxim's schemes were going slightly awry.

For the moment, it worked well enough to help Frederick on his mad quest until such time as Maxim had his plans in place, to keep his position and power whether the Emperor were alive or not. But he was not ready for that yet, not by a long way. He saw that maybe the book was the answer to his problems, one way or another.

'You say you can divine the future?' Frederick asked.

He didn't do it directly, but spoke through Maxim.

Maxim repeated the Emperor's question, and the man eagerly nodded.

'Oh yes,' he said. 'Oh yes!'

'Very well,' said Frederick to Maxim. 'See what he can do.'

'The Emperor wishes to see an example of your skill,' Maxim said.

'Very well. Of course!' the man said, looking a little nervous. He began to rummage in his bag and pulled out a tray and some cups.

'I will ask one of you,' he said, speaking very quickly, 'to hide this ball beneath one of the cups and—'

'Enough,' said the Emperor quietly.

Maxim stepped forward.

'Stop!' he said to the man. 'We have enough prestidigitators already. We are seeking genuine clairvoyant ability. You will have to do better than this. Let me show you.'

Maxim called to the back of the Court.

'Wolfram! Come here!'

A murmur spread through the room as the crowds parted to let a rather strange-looking man walk forward to the dais where Frederick sat. He was dressed very plainly, and wore a cap with brown feathers poking out of it. He mumbled to himself as he walked. He was one of the seers of the court, whose occupation was to scry the future for Frederick. This particular seer must have been reasonably good, for he had been in Court for several years. The less accurate tended to vanish quickly.

'Sire?' he said, without emotion.

Frederick nodded at Maxim.

Maxim turned back to the man.

'You say you can foretell the future. So tell us. What is going to happen to you in the next five minutes?'

The man dropped his bag and wiped his forehead.

'I . . . I don't . . .' he began, then steadied himself. 'I mean, I think I will be happy to accept your generous offer of a position in your command.'

He forced a wide smile.

Maxim turned to the seer.

'Seer?' he asked.

For the first time a glimmer of emotion showed on Wolfram's face. He shut his eyes and a frown developed. He opened his eyes, now moist, but it was a flat, almost disembodied, voice that spoke to Maxim.

'He will die.'

That was all. He turned and shambled back into the crowd.

'Ha!' said Frederick. 'Correct! He is correct!'

The man began to protest.

'You can't do that. He can't . . . It's set-up! You can't just kill me . . .'

He stepped forward and suddenly from inside his tunic

pulled a knife. Instantly, and without fuss, two guards closed in on him and slew him where he stood.

'Silly man,' said Frederick. 'Oh, do take him away! Don't just stand there! He's bleeding on my carpets.'

Maxim sighed. It was a scene he had seen too often to find amusing any more.

His thoughts turned to the strange boy in the dungeon.

As soon as the blind jailer left, Boy wasted no time.

He'd come back with more slop, and more oil for the lamp, having finally smelt that it had gone out.

He was in no particular hurry as he lowered the lamp on its long chain from the centre of the ceiling, and poured more oil into its base.

Boy saw a scratch of sparks away in the centre of the dungeon and the lamp was lit.

The jailer hoisted it back to the ceiling, brought Boy his food, and once more took a second bowl over to some-where else.

As soon as he was gone, Boy took out his lock-pick and set himself free again. He headed straight in the direction the jailer had taken to the dungeon's far wall.

When Boy was a little less than halfway across, having averted his eyes from the hideous machines in the centre of the room, he heard the sound of singing again. It was still faint but now, with the weak light from the lamp, Boy knew he was awake and not only imagining it.

He passed the centre of the chamber and the oil lamp, and once he had, the blackness began to grow again. He waited to see if his eyes would get used to the deepening gloom, and after a moment, went on.

The singing grew louder. It was a man's voice but it was high and wavering.

'Hello?' he called.

Nothing except the singing. Now he could make out some of the words, and without consciously realising it, they felt familiar to him.

> *Surely you won't run?*
> *When your boat is ready to sail.*
> *Surely you will stand*
> *And face the gentle rain?*

Then he saw something – a small pinprick of light, so tiny that at first he couldn't be sure it wasn't only his eyes playing a trick on him. As he stepped towards it, however, the light grew in size. It was still small, but bright, and shone like a jewel through the deepness of the dark in the dungeon.

He moved closer and came to a row of cells that he had not seen before. They were like his own, set into the wall in a row of four or five.

Beyond them lay the light, and now Boy saw it was a window cut through the solid rock, very small, just wider than a couple of hands. It was divided in four by a sturdy iron cross, so not even Boy would have been able to get more than a few fingers through its gaps.

He went closer, and still the singing continued.

> *In the morning you should think*
> *You might not last unto the night,*

In the evening you should think
You might not last unto the morn.
So dance, my dears, dance,
Before you take the dark flight down

'Hello?' Boy said. He knew this had to be where the jailer was bringing the other bowl of food.

'Hello?' he tried again.

Still nothing. He had to go closer.

He realised he was breathing light and fast, taking short uneven gulps of air. To compensate, his heart began to beat faster too, trying to get enough air into his body. He was an arm's length from the window now. It was slightly above his head height, and as he approached, he put out a trembling hand to the grille. He stood up on tiptoe to peer inside, a warm orange light like fire spilled across his face. He had been holding his breath, but what he saw on the other side of the window took that breath clean away.

It was a room, of decent proportions but not vast by any means. It had a low ceiling, unlike the high domed one of the dungeon, and was obviously some antechamber that had been carved from the rock. It was clearly still part of the dungeon, but there any similarity to that foul grimy place ended.

The room was beautiful. Light came from two oil lamps, one on a small table, the other hanging from the ceiling. Thick rugs lay on the floor, hiding the bare rock beneath. It was exquisitely furnished. There was a writing desk with an upholstered chair, a small but ornate bed covered in sumptuous sheets and plump pillows, red and gold. There were two wardrobes and a chest of drawers, again all of the finest quality. A small mirror with an enormously intricate gold frame hung on one wall, above a washstand with a fine porcelain bowl and jug to match. There was even a small fireplace, with a chimney that must have been bored right through the bedrock all the way up to the Palace and eventually away to the cold City air, for the room was completely free of smoke and the fire was drawing well.

Boy's eyes widened in wonder, and then he saw him – the man who had been singing.

He was sitting in a low armchair by the fire. Boy tried to speak again, and the words caught in his mouth.

But he had been seen.

'Don't ask me for food. I ate it all. You can't have mine.'

Boy was still too stunned to speak.

The man went back to his singing. Boy struggled to think what to say, what to ask, but he was distracted by the song. He knew it. He knew it, but could still not remember where from.

'Who are you?'

It was a simple question, but the man seemed confused.

He looked up at Boy, then into the fire. He did not reply.

'I'm Boy,' said Boy. 'My name . . . is Boy. Who are you?'

The man looked back at Boy. He was old, quite tall, and had probably even been strong once upon a time. He wore a short grey pointed beard, and his features were fine, though his eyes seemed dead.

'Me?' he asked. 'Me? I . . . can't remember.'

He stopped and looked around again.

Boy stuttered another question.

'What are you doing down here?'

371

As soon as it was uttered, he realised his question was foolish, and asked another.

'Are you in charge here? Do you look after the prisoners?'

The man started to laugh, softly at first, and then louder and louder.

'Prisoners?' he said. 'What prisoners? I am the only one down here now.'

Boy shook himself. His feet were aching from standing on tiptoe at the small window. He looked around to see if there was a door that led into the chamber, but could see nothing. He tried to pull himself up with his fingers again to make it easier.

'How long?' asked Boy. 'When did they put you down here?'

The man blinked at Boy.

'I don't know what you mean.'

Boy felt a shuddering fear take hold of him. The man couldn't remember his own name, and Boy couldn't understand how you could forget your name if you were lucky enough to have one. Unless it had been a long time since anyone had used it. Boy's question about time had thrown him too. Just how long had he been mouldering in the dungeon?

But something didn't make sense. If this man was a prisoner, why was he living in luxury? Why the fine clothes and furnishings? If it was a prison, it was a strange, gilded cage.

'Why are you down here?' Boy asked.

'Too long ago,' said the man, obliquely.

Now he asked Boy a question.

'What did you say your name was?'

'I'm called Boy and I've got to get out of here.'

'I haven't seen anyone else here in a long time,' he said, apparently disregarding Boy. 'They don't keep prisoners any more. They have other uses for them . . .'

'What do you mean?' Boy asked.

'It's been a long time since they've had anyone here. They don't usually bother waiting, just take them straight to it. I expect they'll be taking you down soon, though.'

'What do you mean? What is it?'

'You don't know?' asked the man. 'You don't know?'

He stopped and in the silence Boy could hear himself struggling to breathe.

'You don't know?' the man repeated. 'Then I fear for you. But maybe it's best you don't know what's going to happen.'

'What is it?' asked Boy, urgently. 'Tell me!'

Boy pressed his face against the iron cross in the little window.

'Please!' he begged. 'What is it? What is it? An animal?'

'No!' said the man. 'Not an animal. It's a thing. A living thing, but they call it The Phantom.'

And Boy now knew it was the thing from his nightmares, the thing lurking at the foot of the dark flight down. The Phantom.

'He's coming to take the bowl away,' the man said casually. 'He'd better not find you here!'

Confused, Boy said nothing.

'The jailer's coming. For the bowl.'

He nodded at the table where the empty bowl lay.

'Get away from the window!' he whispered.

As he did so, Boy saw a door on the far wall of the chamber open.

He ducked down out of sight, and realised that if the jailer had come for the empty bowl he would be coming for Boy's next.

He crouched low and sprinted as quietly as he could back to his own cell, determined to visit the man again as soon as he could.

Boy was alone again. Thoughts whirled through his mind – thoughts of the days he'd spent with Valerian, dark days before the end, of the trip to The Trumpet where a man had been slain, and of Willow finding Korp's body in the secret room in the Theatre. A victim of The Phantom.

The Phantom which had been terrorising the City for years.

The Phantom in whose domain Boy now found himself trapped.

11

Far up above the dark catacomb in which Boy lay, the snow still fell on the City, a flake here and there sparkling in the flickering torchlight that spilled over the Palace walls.

Down in the dungeons Boy waited, and as soon as the jailer had gone, he stole once again towards the shining window.

The old man had not moved but remained in his armchair, staring into the fire.

Boy felt awkward, as if he was spying, but he had already been noticed.

'You again? You're still here? I thought he might have taken you away.'

Boy tried to ignore the implication of his words.

'What you said about The Phantom,' he said. 'How do you know about it? How do you know it's the same thing that's been killing in the City?'

The man looked up.

'I've been thinking,' he said. 'I've been thinking and I've remembered something.'

'What?' Boy asked patiently.

'I've remembered my name.'

'That's good,' said Boy. 'What is it?'

'Bedrich,' the man said. 'At least, I think so.'

Boy sighed.

'Well,' he said, 'perhaps I can call you that anyway.'

The man thought about this for a while.

'Yes,' he agreed. 'Yes, that's a good idea. Or was it Gustav . . . ?'

'Bedrich sounds fine to me,' said Boy quickly, then smiled. 'I'll call you that.'

Bedrich nodded, nearly smiling.

'So tell me. Tell me about The Phantom.'

The half-smile disappeared from Bedrich's face immediately.

'Why do you want to know?' he asked.

'I don't know . . .' Boy said.

This was true, he realised. He hadn't actually stopped to think about it.

'But it killed someone I knew. Someone I worked for, in a way. The Director of the theatre where I worked with . . .'

He stopped again. There was no point telling this poor old man all his stories.

'So how do you know about it?'

'I look after it,' Bedrich said simply.

Boy was too shocked to speak.

'I am the doctor. I am the Palace doctor, you see.'

'That can't be,' said Boy. 'I mean—'

'No,' said Bedrich, holding up one hand. He rose from his chair and came over to the window. He inspected Boy's face closely, as if that would tell him something.

'I am the doctor, Frederick's doctor. Or rather, I was

once. Now I only have one patient: The Phantom. They keep me down here for that alone. I sedate it. I try to stop it from the worst of its excesses. It's been getting harder and harder recently. I try my best, but I am not always successful.

'And when I am not successful, then it needs blood. And that is why I fear for you. Though why you are not dead already, I do not know.'

'But what is it?' Boy asked.

Bedrich stepped back from the window. He looked around furtively, melodramatically, though there was no one to hear him other than Boy in this subterranean prison.

'I cannot tell you.'

'You mean you can't, or you won't?' Boy pressed, but Bedrich would say no more.

He turned and went back to his chair by the fire.

'Please,' said Boy. 'Please tell me some more.'

'I'm tired,' he said. 'Leave me alone.'

The old man snuffled quietly to himself for some time, and then fell asleep.

Boy had no choice but to return to his own cell, where he curled into a ball on the hard floor and closed his eyes.

But sleep would not come. In a way he was glad, for he sensed it would bring no relief from the nightmare he was living.

12

Next time a meal was brought, which from the rumble in his belly Boy believed had to be another whole day, something else came with the food.

'You've got company,' said the jailer as he rattled a key in the cell next to Boy.

Boy was amazed to see Bedrich being led into the cell. The door was shut behind him.

'No point me walking over to two sides of the place to feed you, is there?' said the jailer.

Boy looked at Bedrich. He was grateful for the company, but there was something not quite right with the jailer's explanation of why they had been put together.

For some reason, the jailer stood waiting while they both ate, and when they had finished, he took their bowls from them.

'By the way, you're to go free,' he said, in an offhand manner.

Boy leapt to his feet.

'When?' he cried. 'Please, when?'

The jailer tilted his head to one side.

'Not you,' he said. 'Him.'

Boy put his hands up and lightly touched the bars of his cell. He turned to Bedrich, forcing a smile.

'Did you hear? That's good.'

Bedrich had heard.

A smile washed across his face, but it was quickly followed by a frown.

He looked hard at the jailer, but it was impossible to read that blind expression.

'You mean it?' he croaked. 'This isn't a trick or—'

'Do you want to argue about it?' the jailer said. 'I'm sure we can change their minds if you'd rather stay.'

'No!' cried Bedrich. 'No! Only I just . . .'

He stopped.

Boy looked at the jailer.

'Why? Why are they letting him go? Will you ask about me? Please will you ask when I'm going to be let out?'

'No,' said the jailer bluntly. 'Not my business. Yours. As for him, I don't know. Maybe he's been pardoned for his crimes. Going now.'

With that he went.

Bedrich called after him.

'When? When?'

There was no answer, but it seemed enough for now to know.

'Boy!' he cried. 'Did you hear that, Boy? They're going to let me out!'

Boy watched Bedrich, thinking, waiting, judging. The last time they had spoken Bedrich had been surly, and refused to speak of The Phantom or anything else. Boy needed Bedrich now. He needed him to speak. He needed his help.

379

Watching Bedrich, Boy finally remembered the song that Bedrich had been singing. It was *The Linden Song*, which he and Willow and Valerian had heard the miserable cart driver sing as they hunted for the book in that desolate village in the snow-laden countryside.

Like falling snow, its words floated freely through his head now, as he re-lived the horror of that frozen churchyard, and inside the church itself Gad Beebe's grave, where they believed the book lay. And so it had, once, but someone had beaten them to it. Kepler.

It was no surprise that Boy's thoughts had drifted to the book, no surprise at all. He was sure that his destiny lay entwined with it. He knew it would hold an answer for him, and if only he could get to it, there was still a chance for him.

It was no use, this nameless life. He had spent enough time as a rootless being, without home or heritage. He had come to accept Valerian's abuse of him as normal, but Willow had shown him enough love to make him see that it was not. He had to find answers now. He needed to know who his parents were. Maybe he would never know who his mother was, but one look in the book would at least tell him the truth about Valerian.

Boy watched as all sorts of feelings passed through Bedrich's mind, as he contemplated what it would be like to be free after untold years.

'I need your help,' Boy said, trying to judge Bedrich's mood. Boy was pleased to see he seemed calm.

Bedrich nodded.

'When you get out, will you do something for me?'

Bedrich nodded again.

'Yes,' he said, gently. 'Of course. I'll try.'

'Thank you,' said Boy. 'Thank you. I need you to find someone for me and take her a message. Can you do that?'

'Oh, yes,' said Bedrich, 'Whatever you say!'

Encouraged, Boy went on.

'I need you to find a girl, a girl called Willow. She works at an orphanage called St Stephen's. It's run by a woman called Martha.'

'Martha, Martha. Yes,' said Bedrich.

'When you find Willow, tell her where I am. Tell her to steal the book and bring it here.'

Bedrich looked at Boy, staring straight into his eyes for almost the first time since they had met.

'What did you say?' he asked.

Something in his manner put Boy on his guard, instantly. He thought about what he had said.

'I said . . . tell Willow to—'

'Not that,' said Bedrich. 'What you said after that.'

'There's . . . a book,' Boy said, slowly. He had only dared talk of it to Bedrich believing it could mean nothing to him. 'It's very powerful and—'

'And it's dangerous,' said Bedrich. He held up his hand to stop Boy from speaking. 'Oh yes, I know about the book. Only I thought it had been dealt with. Long, long ago.'

13

'Maxim!' yelled Frederick. 'Dammit, Maxim! Where are you?'

'Coming, Sire. Coming!'

Frederick sat up in bed, propped up on dozens of small velvet cushions. His bed was a vast thing, far too big for such a little man. In his white nightgown and nightcap he looked like a sailor marooned in a sea of silken sheets.

'Blast this bed!' he cursed. 'Why can't I have something more comfortable?'

Maxim hurried from his own impressive rooms a little way down the corridor to Frederick's chambers, the most sumptuous part of the Palace.

He strode down the corridor, oblivious to the spectacular views across the rest of the Palace and down over the City.

'Max-im!' screeched the Emperor from his bed chamber.

Maxim rushed through the doorway and almost slipped on the ridiculously polished floor.

'Sire?' he said.

'Maxim. Why are you always so slow? Anyone would think you are trying to kill me. Don't you understand I have needs?'

'My apologies, Sire,' Maxim said, trying to keep any note of irritation from his voice. 'I was attending to some other matters.'

'Well, don't,' Frederick snapped. 'You attend to me and me alone.'

'Indeed, Sire. The matters I speak of were concerned with—'

'I'm not interested, Maxim. Understand me! Now listen. I want to see some progress. You're dragging your heels.'

'Sire?' Maxim said, with too much of a question in his voice.

'Don't question me, dammit! I want to see some results! Bring the Court seers to me. I want to see what they think about what you're doing. Or what you're not doing . . .'

Frederick stared straight at Maxim. The tall man looked at the floor, his eyes burning. He thought about the useless wretches Frederick insisted on maintaining at Court and fumed, but he said nothing.

'You've been dragging your heels and I want results. And soon. I'm getting older by the day and I don't feel at all well. This bed hurts me for a start. You've no conception of it. None at all.'

'I will have it—'

'Just listen to me. You know what I asked you to do, so do it. If not, I'll find someone else to do it. In the meantime, bring the seers to me. Let's see what they have to say. You've been dragging your heels. If you had only kept that boy perhaps you might have got somewhere by now.'

'The . . . boy, Sire? The boy from the magician's house?'

'Yes, yes, of course the boy from the magician's house.

'Who else do you think I mean? If you hadn't had him killed . . .'

Maxim cursed the whims of the Emperor, but restrained himself from saying what he really thought. He wasn't going to let this chance go by, however.

'Ah . . . but Your Highness is absolutely right. Fortunately, it was . . . not possible to dispatch the boy as you wished. He is still in our dungeons . . .'

Frederick looked up at him sharply.

'As I wished, Maxim? As I wished? I made no such decision. I told you to lock him up until we were ready to see him, and you know I never change my mind! You know that to disobey me would mean your death, do you not? Is that not right?'

'No! No, Sire,' said Maxim hurriedly. How was he supposed to win with this cantankerous old swine? 'Of course I do everything you require of me, yet maybe I am . . . misremembering your instructions. Fortunately, everything is as you wish. He is indeed incarcerated in our dungeons. If you wish to see the boy . . . ?'

'No, I do not,' Frederick said. 'Well, not yet. Have him cleaned and then bring him to Court. Let us see what he knows. And then, if he still proves useless, you can drown him.'

Maxim swore silently at the floor as he averted his face from Frederick's view once more.

'Very good, Sire,' he said. 'At once.'

He left, shutting the door behind him just a little too hard.

14

Willow hurried through the darkening City streets yet again, heading south, over the river, her companion at her side.

Kepler.

As they crossed the wide street known as The Parade, Willow pulled her shawl about her more closely as she was struck by a sharp and cold wind that sent the snowflakes into flurries.

An hour or so later they turned into a rancid little alley called The Bucket, named after a low-life drinking den halfway along it. At the far end the river lay before them.

They crossed at St Olaf's Bridge, a fantastic span of three powerful arches, wide and noble in its construction. At each of the two piers where stone thrust its way into the riverbed, the thoroughfare widened into a bay, where the ponderous or weary might consider the flow of water and time passing under the bridge's span. On both piers was a small cage, just big enough to permit a man's body to be forced inside. Willow shuddered as she passed them, but fortunately, it had been many years since they had been used.

At the far bank, the street plummeted rapidly back into

the chaos of the City's maze of streets, and any sense of architectural order given by the bridge vanished.

But after a turn or two, there was the Palace mound ahead of them, pressed against a bend in the river.

After she had bumped into Kepler by the North Gate the day before, they had returned to his house, arguing all the way. Yet each knew they needed the other.

They had made their way back across the City as fast as they could, for the night and the snow were deepening. Even without Kepler's company Willow would have known her way unerringly.

On reaching the house, Kepler had provided some bread and cheese for which Willow was truly grateful. Kepler was an intelligent man, a great intellect, but he had seemed clumsy and slow as he prepared the food for Willow, as if it was something he never did. It was no feast, but had been enough to sustain her.

As soon as dawn had come, Kepler collected things in a large shoulder bag, and they had set out once more for the Palace.

This morning the arguments had stopped, they had barely spoken.

'We must hurry,' Kepler said, as he got things together. 'He's in danger there.'

'I know,' Willow replied.

'Do you? You don't know anything of the Palace! The people inside. And there's one to be most feared.'

'Who?'

'A man called Maxim. He's the Emperor's right hand. He has a reputation.'

'What?' asked Willow.

386

'It would frighten you to know, child,' Kepler said.

Willow stopped and waited for Kepler to notice that she had. After a few paces he saw she was no longer with him, and turned.

'You think it will scare me?' Willow shouted. 'After all I've been through?'

Kepler shook his head.

'Maybe not,' he said. 'But there is little to tell. Maxim is a dangerous man, with great influence over the Emperor and life in Court. We must be most careful of him.'

'Why?' asked Willow.

'Listen, girl,' Kepler snapped, 'you ask too many questions. I've agreed you may be able to help me find Boy, and that's enough for now. So be silent!'

Kepler would say no more. He turned and walked on, and Willow had no choice but to follow.

Now they were deep in their own thoughts, which were more similar than they might have known. Both were thinking about Boy, though as they walked Willow glanced from time to time at Kepler's sack. They had agreed their plan the night before, but Willow couldn't help wondering exactly what it was that Kepler had brought with him.

15

Boy struggled to believe what Bedrich was saying.

'Yes, I know about the book,' he said. 'I thought it had been dealt with long ago.'

'How?' cried Boy. 'How can you know about it?'

'I know it!' Bedrich said, firmly. 'I know the book. I once looked into it myself . . .'

He stopped, took a deep breath.

'It did me no good. It has done others much worse.'

That was true. Boy thought of Valerian. The book hadn't saved him after all, though it might have done at the cost of Boy's life.

'But how?' asked Boy. 'When?'

Bedrich looked at Boy, held his eyes for a long time.

'What does a poor wretch like you know about it?' he asked. 'A street child like you.'

Boy shook his head.

'I don't live on the streets, not any more. I live with . . . lived with a man. A great man called Valerian.'

'The magician?' asked Bedrich, raising an eyebrow.

'You knew him?' Boy asked.

'No. Only by reputation. Fifteen, maybe twenty years ago. He was a scholar at the Academy, but was disgraced.'

Boy ignored this.

'Valerian wanted the book,' he said. 'We searched for it. In nasty places.'

'The book is power. That much I know. But why exactly did he want it?'

'He was in trouble. He . . .'

Boy stopped. It seemed impossible to explain everything that had happened in the last few weeks.

Bedrich didn't stop though.

'You speak of him as if he has gone. He is dead?'

Boy nodded.

'So he didn't get the book, to save him from this trouble?'

Boy shook his head.

'No, he did get it. He did, but . . .'

'But? What happened?'

'To save himself . . . to save himself would have meant killing me . . .'

'And he refused? What a noble gesture!'

Boy shrugged. It wasn't quite like that, but in the end Valerian *had* died instead of him. Bedrich sensed Boy's hesitation.

'But he must have been a great man to die instead of you. Why else would he have done it?'

'He was my father,' Boy said.

The words sounded strange on his lips. He knew he might be lying, that he didn't really know the truth. But it was easier to tell Bedrich that, than to have to explain it all to him.

'What a strange boy you are!' Bedrich declared.

Boy said nothing.

'So you know about the book, about its power. And its danger.'

'Willow always said it was dangerous, right from the start, but I don't see why. It's full of knowledge, and knowledge is good. Valerian always said so, and he was never wrong.'

'But the book is different. Maybe if it revealed the whole truth of a matter, it would be a good thing. But it does not. It is treacherous and malevolent. It reveals only some of the truth. It shows something different to each person. Sometimes it shows nothing at all, but when it does, you have to be very careful you understand that what it is telling you is only part of the picture.'

'But Willow looked into it. She looked over Valerian's shoulder, and saw he was about to try to . . .'

He stopped. He didn't want to tell Bedrich that Valerian had tried to kill him.

'What?' asked Bedrich. 'What is it? Are you beginning to understand? The doubtful nature of what the book reveals, the dangers?'

Boy nodded. He was happy to change the subject.

'That song you were singing. How do you know it? And how do you know about the book? I thought it was a secret.'

'It was. It should have been,' said Bedrich. 'But things change, obviously. I know about the book, for it was once here. In the Palace.'

'Here?' Boy cried, 'Here?'

'Shh!' Bedrich hissed. 'Not so loud. Yes, the book was here. It's all so long ago now, such a long time. It's hard to remember it all.'

'Try,' Boy urged, 'Please, try.'

Bedrich put his head in his hands briefly, then looked up at Boy, blinking.

'The book. It came here. It was brought here to please the Emperor. You won't have seen the Emperor . . .'

Boy shook his head.

'No. I have. Briefly,' he said. 'I was amazed. I thought Maxim had to be the one in charge. Frederick doesn't look like he could be in charge of anything.'

Bedrich shook his head.

'That's what you think? Then you are mistaken. He's a hard and powerful man, despite his age, despite his weaknesses.'

'Some people don't even believe he's still alive. No one's seen him in years, in the City.'

'They wouldn't have. He never goes outside the Palace. I used to tell him he should go out. Take the air, exercise. It might have stopped him brooding over his health all the time. He was obsessed by his health. His heart, his nerves, his stomach. It was hard being his doctor, especially when he set so much store by those alchemists and necromancers of his . . .'

Boy felt Bedrich was drifting away again.

'The book,' he said. 'What about the book?'

'Yes. The book. Well, in a way it's all part of the same thing. Frederick was old even then. He must be ancient by now. Even in those days he was possessed by one thought: the Imperial Line.'

'What?' asked Boy.

'The Line. He is the last of the Imperial Line. There is no one to succeed him when he dies. Desperate for children, but with no heir to the throne, he began to worry that he would die and leave the Empire without an Emperor. Empire! What nonsense! This pox-ridden city is all that's left of it. But nonetheless, all those Dukes and Lords are upstairs waiting to fight it out when he goes! You see?'

'Yes,' nodded Boy. 'Yes, but what about the book?'

'I'm getting to it,' said Bedrich. 'It's all part of the same thing. He was obsessed, as I told you, about having an heir. And everyone in Court was trying to placate him, and please him, all the while hoping for favours in return – money, a title, things like that. One day, a musician arrived in Court from the countryside. A handsome man, and of reasonable breeding. He came with a song and a present. First he sang the song, and the Emperor was even gracious enough to seem to enjoy it. He must have been in a rare good mood that day.'

Bedrich had closed his eyes, as if seeing the events all over again.

'And the song was a beautiful song. Beautiful but sad. He came from a musical family. Many members of his family were gifted musically, but although they were noble, they were not wealthy. But there was something else. The present. I do not know where he came upon it, but the musician had brought with him a terrible thing, though at the time it was held to be marvellous and wonderful. The book.

'And this was his present to the Emperor. He was rewarded immediately with his weight in gold. And there was more to follow. As the book foretold things and they came to pass, the man and his family were rewarded with land, titles, money and more.

'And more than this, the Emperor even took a daughter of the family as his mistress. Sophia. This was deemed a great honour to the family. She was so beautiful, and clever, too. It was she who had written that sad song.

'And on the day . . . the day when . . .'

Bedrich stopped. He seemed to have lost his way in the story.

'Go on,' Boy said gently.

'It's so long ago,' said Bedrich, but Boy could tell that this was not the reason he had stopped. 'On that day. The book foretold that the Emperor was indeed to father children! On that day, the man and his family were showered beyond all measure with things rich and golden. They were granted permission to build a church in their village, and the members of the family moved within Court as if they were themselves royalty.'

With a shock Boy realised that he was listening to something of which he knew a part.

'Tell me,' he said, 'what was the name of this family?'

When Bedrich opened his mouth to answer, Boy already had the same word on his lips.

'Beebe.'

Boy felt his heart begin to race light and fast in his chest. He felt sick.

'Beebe,' said Bedrich again. 'For a while, what a great and beautiful family they were. So beautiful.'

Suddenly footsteps sounded along the corridor outside the dungeon.

'They're coming to take you!' Boy whispered. 'To let you out! You won't forget about Willow, will you? And the book?'

'I will have nothing to do with that book. I refuse.'

'But it is my only chance . . .'

'If that is your only chance, you have no chance,' Bedrich said. 'But I will find the girl. Willow.'

The door began to rattle, and creak open.

'All right,' said Boy, 'All right. But quick! Tell me what happened to the Beebes. What happened to the book's prediction?'

The jailer approached. He was not alone this time. There were two flunkeys accompanying him.

'Tell me,' whispered Boy. 'What happened?'

Bedrich shook his head.

'It was not to be,' he said. 'The prediction was . . . awry. The Beebes were disgraced. The Emperor blamed them for what had happened. Stripped them of almost everything. The book ruined them. It will ruin you too, if you let it.'

The jailer was at the cells.

'Getting friendly, are we?' he said blankly. 'That's a shame. Time for you to go.'

Bedrich stood up. Boy could feel the tension, the anxiety in him. After so long, to be nearly free was almost too much.

But the jailer walked to Boy's cell and stuck his key in that lock instead.

'You,' he said. 'You're to go with these men. Any trouble and you'll be back down here before you can breathe.'

Boy didn't move.

'But what about me?' Bedrich said.

The two men moved into Boy's cell and started to walk him out of the dungeon.

'Maxim's coming to see to you,' the jailer said to Bedrich.

'To set me free?' Bedrich cried desperately. 'He's coming to set me free?'

As he was taken away, Boy looked back at Bedrich. He paused for a moment.

'Bedrich . . .' he began, but there was nothing to say, and he was roughly dragged forward again, to the doorway.

The door swung shut behind him and he heard Bedrich call out to the jailer.

'He's going to let me out! Isn't he?'

The echoes of his voice were cut short by the door clanging back into its iron frame.

'Right,' said one of the men to Boy. 'Upstairs with you. One stupid move and I'll break your neck.'

Bedrich sat down on the stone cold floor of the cell. His gilded cage had been taken from him, and the promise of release too. His head was so full of this misery that he didn't even notice a small spyhole swing shut in the ceiling just above his head.

The Palace

The Place of Treacherous Artifice

❧

Boy was hurried through the dark and twisting corridors of the dungeons once more, so cramped in places that even he, with his skinny frame, was forced to hunch up. One of the men walked in front, the other behind, prodding him in the back if he showed any signs of dawdling.

But Boy had no wish to dawdle. After another twist they came to a section of passage that Boy realised he knew. Just as in his dream, he was walking down the passage that went past the top of the steep and foul stairway down to nothingness. The smell rushed towards him like a beast itself, assaulting his senses. He hesitated, and felt another shove in his back. Boy forced one foot after the other, and the opening to the passageway drew closer until, holding his hand to his mouth and nose, he saw with relief that unlike his dream, the iron gate across the opening was shut.

His captors seemed to be hurrying too.

'Is that . . . ?' he began, but was shoved again.

This time he ignored it, and turned to face the man behind him.

'Is that where it lives?' he asked.

The man seemed taken aback.

'Is that where it lives?' Boy asked again.

'You shouldn't know anything about that,' the guard said. Boy failed to read the meaning in his voice. Was it fear? Or surprise? It certainly wasn't anger. Boy had expected to be hit for his question, but no blow came.

The other guard had now noticed that Boy had stopped and rushed back to see what was going on.

He grabbed Boy by the neck and dragged him into walking again. He turned to his friend.

'Of all places, you want to stop here?' he said.

They had moved out of the rough-hewn, damp stone underbelly of the Palace, and into the royal world proper.

Boy was shocked to find that it was night-time. Having been confined for days in darkness, longing for daylight, he had assumed that, when freed from the twilight world, the sun would automatically be shining. But it was the dead of night.

The Palace seemed to be asleep. There was very little noise from anywhere, and they saw no one as they moved through lavish panelled corridors into ever more marvellous chambers.

Boy stared about him.

Never in his life had he seen such wealth, such casual displays of incredible finery at every turn. Portraits in oil hung in gilded frames. Faces peered back from the paintings – haughty figures swathed in fur robes and dripping with jewels. The floor they were walking on was marble, marble pillars struck from floor to the high vaulted ceiling. The walls between were panelled wood painted a pale, pale green, the details picked out with gold. Above this panelling Boy stared open-mouthed at the carved wooden frieze that ran the length of the room. Whole forests were depicted in high relief – trees and bushes with animals peeping from behind, a bird pecking at a bunch of grapes, a swan gliding on a lake.

And this was just one of the galleries down which they had passed.

Boy faltered, unable to take in what he was seeing, but he was quickly moved on by yet another poke in his back.

'Come on, boy. I want to get to bed.'

'Where are we going?' asked Boy, but got no answer from either man.

'Up here,' one of them said as they turned into a spacious hallway, at the far end of which was a massive stone staircase that swept up and around out of sight above their heads.

Boy began to walk forward, but was stopped.

'Not there!' the guard snapped. 'Here.'

He pointed to where his friend had pulled a seemingly continuous section of the panelling away to expose a hidden staircase, tiny and twisting, that led up out of the hall.

'Move!

Boy did as he was told, and rushed into the tight stairwell before they could hit him again. Nonetheless, he felt a hand push him as the guards hurried up behind him. He sped up, growing dizzy as the spiral staircase twisted up and up into the Palace. It was getting darker with each turn, and Boy had to guess where his next footfall would be, when suddenly he stumbled out into a dazzlingly bright room.

He blinked, heard the door click shut behind him and a

key turn in a lock. When he looked around there was no sign of the stairway from where he had emerged, nor, for that matter, was there any sign of the guards.

He was alone.

2

Boy was in a smaller room this time, though still every bit as opulent as the rest of the Palace. He could see doors leading off at every side of the room, most shut, but on one side a set of double doors lay tantalisingly open.

Boy moved into the room beyond. In it he found a huge four-poster bed, with mattresses so deep their top was chest-height from the floor. Swags of midnight blue and yellow velvet hung from the bed's canopy. It looked incredibly inviting, and Boy wondered who was lucky enough to sleep in such a wonderful thing.

He stepped towards it, when suddenly he was aware of the sound of water splashing. Turning, he saw a small door leading out of the bedroom. Cautiously he pushed it open with his fingertips.

The door swung lightly away from him.

'Hello?' he ventured, but quietly.

He took a step inside.

A woman turned to face him.

Boy was shocked to see that, like his jailer, she was blind. She was an old woman, and yet Boy could see her blindness was from some awful accident, not due to her age. With disgust he wondered if many servants close to Frederick's secrets were made blind, deliberately.

'Oh!' she said. 'You're here sooner than they told me. Your bath isn't quite ready yet.'

She carried on with her work. Boy took a step further into the room. It was every bit as large as the bedroom, but in the centre of it stood not a bed but a large marble bath, carved to look like a porpoise breaking the surface of the sea. The bath itself was hollowed into its back.

The woman was busy pouring buckets of water into the tub. She had two, one with cold and one with steaming hot water. When they were empty she took them to the side of the room, lifted a hatch and placed them on a shelf inside. She pulled a bell-rope beside the hatch, and immediately the shelf dropped from view. A minute or so later, the shelf raised back into view, jerking slowly to its former position. She hoisted the buckets off deftly, and Boy saw that once again they were full of water, one hot, one cold.

He had never seen such sophistication. Bathing was something he did only very rarely. When he had lived on the streets he had only washed in summer, just to cool down, by running through one of the City's cleaner fountains. At The Yellow House, Valerian had made him wash once a week, 'whether he needed to or not'. But this had meant a cold slosh of water in a basin, a thing as far removed from the elaborate display before him as was possible.

'You must have the wrong idea . . .' Boy stammered. 'You can't mean me.'

'This is your bath, these are your rooms,' said the woman. 'Couple more buckets should do you.'

'I don't understand,' Boy said. 'I've been in the dungeon. They had me locked up in the dungeon. This can't be for me.'

'The Emperor wants to see you. You can't appear before an Emperor smelling like that.'

She didn't smile, or indeed betray any emotion, merely poured the last of her buckets into the vast bathtub.

'The Emperor?' asked Boy. 'What does he want to see me for?'

The woman didn't answer.

'Well, anyway, I don't want to see him. If you'll excuse me. I don't mean to be rude . . .'

Boy turned to leave. The woman made no effort to stop him as he ran from the bathroom back through the bedroom. Choosing a door at random, he burst from the room, and ran straight into a guard who was almost larger than the doorway. He bounced off and landed on his backside.

The guard, who barely seemed to have noticed, turned and looked down at Boy menacingly.

'Sorry,' said Boy. 'Wrong door.'

He got up, and shut himself back into his magnificent prison.

The old servant was waiting for him.

'The other doors are exactly the same,' she said. 'Have a bath. Go to bed. In the morning you're to go before the Emperor.'

'And food?' asked Boy. 'Can I have something to eat? I've only had—'

'It's on its way. But bath first. You could smell better, that's for sure. Take your clothes off.'

Boy gave up. He started to pull his shirt off, and the

woman left the room. He shook his head. She was kinder than the old blind man but nonetheless she was just as much his jailer.

As soon as Boy was naked he stepped into the water. It was very hot, and he had to lower himself slowly into the tub, bit by bit. He thought he had never felt water so hot. He got as far as putting his legs in, and noticed they were turning pink from the heat. Eventually he got all of himself into the bath, and lay back. He watched the steam rising all around him, and felt his eyelids begin to droop.

In another few seconds, he was asleep.

When he woke, he felt terrible. He had no idea how long he had been asleep, but the water was still warm, so it couldn't have been too long.

'Your food's here,' said a voice.

He jerked upright to see the old serving woman sitting on a chair at the far side of the room.

'You'd better eat it and get to bed,' she said. 'What's this, by the way?'

Boy saw what she was holding in her hands, had been fiddling with. It was his lock-pick – the old metal tendon.

'I found it in your clothes,' she said needlessly. 'I was going to throw it away, but then I thought maybe it's something valuable or important. Is it important?'

Boy struggled for an answer.

'Yes,' he said. 'Well, no. It's only important to me. It's . . . a lucky charm. Had it for years.'

The woman considered this. A frown crossed her face.

'I'm not supposed to . . .' she began. 'But I don't see it can do any charm. You can keep it.'

And with that she left the room. A moment later she came back, carrying a large towel and a nightshirt.

He grabbed the towel and pulled it around him.

They moved through into the bedroom, where a table had been laid so that it was overflowing with delightful, delicate things to eat. Once again Boy was amazed, having never seen such things in all his life.

'Don't eat too quickly,' the woman said, but Boy ignored her. He sat down and began to devour everything he could, not even stopping to ask what some of it was.

The serving woman sat quietly on a chair, half a smile flickering across her face all the time, listening to Boy eat.

'My!' she said, when he began to slow down, 'You were hungry, weren't you?'

For a moment, Boy felt like shouting at her. How stupid was she not to know the kind of slop he'd been given to eat for days! Of course he was hungry.

'Are you going to hang around while I do everything?' he asked instead.

'Sorry,' she said. 'Only it's been a while since we've had anyone up here in the Winter Rooms.'

Boy wondered who 'we' was.

'And your guests?' Boy asked. 'Are they always prisoners like me?'

'Don't say that. We try to make things as good as we can for our guests while they're here . . .'

She trailed off, then stood up to go.

'Eat up and go to sleep,' she said.

Boy looked at the bed. It was so tall there was a little ladder to take him up on to it.

He slipped under the sheets, but something was not

407

right. As he had had trouble adjusting to the comfortable yet small bed in Kepler's house after the rotten cot he'd had at Valerian's, he could not feel comfortable in this enormous bed.

He got up and, standing on the bed, pulled at the swags of velvet, and drew them together like curtains, so he was enclosed on all sides. It was immediately a dark and much smaller space, and feeling more at home, Boy shut his eyes, thoughts of Valerian drifting through his mind as he made his way down to sleep.

Despite the late hour, not everyone in the Palace was asleep. The old serving woman made her way wearily to her own modest room on the floor above the one where Boy was dozing. In the kitchens in the North Wing, servants were still scrubbing and scraping at pots, and further down into the Palace's guts, a tall figure robed in red made his way back from the dungeons. Once again there had been difficult work to be done down there, and there was more ahead.

3

Boy was pulled from his bed by a hand at his throat, before he was even awake. He fell to the ground and lay spluttering on the thick, soft carpet that surrounded the massive four-poster.

'No more lying!' Maxim shouted down at him.

Boy didn't even have time to think, let alone answer, before the powerful man snatched him up from the floor and flung him across the room. Fortunately almost all of the bedroom floor was covered by one plush rug or another, and he was not hurt.

Now at some distance from Maxim, he had time to think before another blow came.

'Wait!' Boy cried. 'What are you talking about? I don't even know what you're talking about!'

Maxim stopped halfway across the room.

'Then let me remind you,' he said. He ran one hand over the top of his smooth head. 'You recall our last conversation?'

Boy frowned.

'You were asking me—'

'About a book,' Maxim spat. 'About *the* book. Yes?'

Now Boy panicked. He couldn't remember exactly what

he'd said. He needed to lie consistently if he was going to bluff his way out of this.

'Oh. Yes,' said Boy. 'Yes, you were asking about Valerian's books. Have you found what you needed?'

Boy realised as soon as he said it that it was a mistake. Maxim closed the distance between them, and though Boy flinched, he still took most of a blow to the side of his head.

He fell to the ground, holding his head, feeling for blood, though there was none. Maxim yanked Boy to his feet and pushed his face close to Boy's.

'Listen, Boy. Listen!' he snarled. 'I know you are lying. I know you have the book somewhere. So make an end to your foolishness.'

'No . . .' stuttered Boy, 'No, I don't—'

'Yes, you do. You have the book. Or maybe it is your friend Willow who has it now?'

Boy's face betrayed him immediately.

'Willow!' he cried, and then he knew that Maxim somehow knew the truth.

'Yes, your friend Willow,' said Maxim smoothly. He dropped Boy back to the floor, went to fetch a chair and brought it back for himself to sit on. 'Let's have a little talk, shall we? Now that we understand each other. And now that you see it is pointless to lie any more.'

'Willow's got nothing to do with all this. You don't—'

'I decide what is important here. Understand me! Your conversations with your friend Bedrich were very helpful, much more forthcoming than you have been so far.'

Boy's thoughts whirled as he struggled to understand,

but it was obvious that Maxim had somehow been listening to them. He tried to remember what he and Bedrich had talked about, but he knew it was not good.

Everything. They had talked about everything.

'Yes, it was good of you two to become such friends after I had you put next to each other. And when you saw the chance to get a message out, you kindly took it . . .'

Maxim laughed, and Boy saw that the whole of his imprisonment had been a trick to get him to talk to Bedrich. It had seemed strange to Boy at the time that the old doctor had been moved in next to him.

Sickeningly, Boy realised that in talking to Bedrich he had exposed Willow to danger too. He cursed himself.

'What have you done to Bedrich?' Boy asked.

'He is well enough, for the time being.'

They needed him alive, Boy realised, to look after The Phantom. That was something else about Bedrich's release that hadn't made sense, but they had been too preoccupied with their own thoughts to see it at the time.

'What's going to happen to me?' Boy asked miserably.

'Silence!' Maxim shouted. 'Just tell me this: where is the book? Does your friend Willow have it?'

'No!' cried Boy.

'You're lying again! You will die if you persist. Are you that stupid? The girl has the book! Where is she?'

'No, no, she doesn't,' cried Boy. 'Really. Please believe me.'

Maxim said nothing, obviously trying to weigh up the truth or otherwise of Boy's words.

'Why should I believe you?'

'It's the truth. I swear it's the truth,' Boy said hurriedly. 'I don't know where the book is. I don't know where Willow is . . .'

'Come now,' said Maxim. 'You know your friend Willow is at the orphanage.'

Boy felt sick again.

'Yes,' said Maxim, 'you are right. I do have my men going there right now. So maybe we'll find the book sooner than I had hoped.'

'No!' cried Boy. 'She doesn't have the book!'

'Then who does? If your girl doesn't have it then who does? Tell me that!'

'I don't know,' said Boy. He dared not mention Kepler. That would show he knew more than he was pretending he did.

'Then maybe Willow will be more helpful than you have been,' Maxim said. 'And believe me, I am in no mood to reward unhelpful people, so think carefully about what you choose to say from now on. In ten minutes we are due in Court, where you will confirm everything I say to the Emperor. About the book, about the magician, about your friend. If you make the slightest mistake, I will have you back in the dungeon, but not for long. Perhaps you have seen a certain dark stairway, a flight down to the very depths of Hell? That is where you will be headed, my lying little Boy, if you make one more mistake. And your stay there will be a short one, believe me. Believe me.'

He pointed at another chair, on which some clean, new clothes lay.

'Get dressed,' he said. 'I will come back for you in five minutes. And remember, one mistake in Court will be your last.'

4

Once more Boy was simply awestruck by what he saw around him.

He had never seen anything like the Court before, never even imagined that anything so beautiful, so majestic, so elaborate could exist. How could he? He whose life had been spent on the streets, whose only contact with wealth was when he relieved some careless rich person of their purse.

It was not only the setting, but the people, dressed in magnificent clothes, with sculpted hair, or in some cases flamboyant wigs, and more jewellery than Boy had seen in his whole life.

Boy itched in his own new clothes as Maxim had walked him down to Court. They were stiff, heavy, formal clothes for a young man of the Palace, and Boy did not like them, but as he stood in Court for the first time he forgot all about them. His jaw dropped as he stared at everything, from the shining stone floor covered in thick rugs to the arched ceiling way above his head, painted with heavenly scenes, rich in blue and gold. Boy was so busy staring at everything that he didn't even notice that everyone else was staring at him. Hushed conversations flurried around the room.

'Shut your mouth, Boy,' Maxim hissed as Frederick arrived.

Frederick was brought into the Court on a low chair carried by four men. They placed him at the foot of the dais on which his throne stood, and they and everyone else in the room bowed as the small, old, thin man climbed up into his seat of power like a toddler climbing on to his father's lap.

The proceedings began.

'Where is the boy?' Frederick drawled.

Maxim grabbed Boy by his elbow, holding it so tightly it hurt, then marched him forward. Boy felt the eyes of everyone in the room fixed on him alone as he approached the throne. Everyone except the Emperor, whose face was turned to the ceiling.

'Why do we have to do everything so early?' he whined.

'Sire, it is nearly midday . . .' Maxim said, in as gentle a tone as he could muster.

'When will you learn that this Palace exists to operate around the hours I wish to keep and not any other way?'

Boy was almost embarrassed by the old man's bickering in front of all the nobles, but the Emperor was oblivious. Maxim was so used to these debates that he paid little attention, yet Boy found it utterly strange.

'This is the brat?' Frederick asked, still not actually looking at Boy.

Maxim nodded.

'Indeed, Sire. He goes by a rather strange name. His name is Boy.'

There was a titter around the Court and Boy felt himself flush with shame, and anger too.

Finally Frederick seemed to be interested in something.

'His name is Boy? How peculiar. Did the magician not give him a proper name?'

'Apparently he did not see fit to do so,' Maxim intoned slowly.

There was another giggle around the room, and Boy could stand it no more.

'That's not—' he began, but Maxim grasped his neck before he had really begun. The wind was plucked from his throat, and though Maxim let him go almost as fast as he had grabbed him, for a moment Boy was unable to breathe.

'Very well,' Frederick muttered. 'It matters not. What news is there? Does he have the secret?'

'Things are proceeding very well,' Maxim declared, 'as Boy will testify. The book will shortly be in our possession, and when it is, we will soon be able to attend to your immediate situation, just as you desire.'

Frederick did not seem impressed.

'Even now,' Maxim went on, 'my men are closing in on the book. The Boy has informed me of its whereabouts. It will be here before the day is out!'

Boy wondered how Maxim dared take such a risk. Did he really believe it? Maybe he was playing for time. Boy wondered where Willow was and hoped to God it was nowhere near the orphanage. One thing was for sure – the men of the Imperial Guard would not find the book there. At least it was safe with Kepler who, it seemed, Maxim knew nothing about. If Maxim got hold of the book, not only would he wield terrible power in the Palace, putting all their lives at risk, but Boy's chance of using it would be gone too.

Boy snapped out of his musings. He realised the whole Court was staring at him again. He looked at Maxim, who was glaring down at him.

'Is that not so?' Maxim asked, meaningfully.

Boy understood this was his moment, when he had to confirm everything Maxim had claimed.

'Yes,' he blurted out, almost shouting. 'Yes. The book. Yes.'

Frederick nodded, and smiled mirthlessly.

'Very well,' he said. 'For both your sakes I hope you're right. Now let us get on with the day's business . . .'

Maxim moved round to the side of the dais and motioned for Boy to follow.

There was a small commotion and a short fanfare, and then someone called out: 'Applicants for positions in the royal Palace!'

Maxim hissed to Boy where he stood at his side.

'Be quiet. Watch and say nothing. You have done enough for one day.'

Boy did as he was told. He had obviously slept late into the day, as Maxim had told Frederick it was midday. He had eaten far too much too quickly and his dreams had been strange affairs once more. Bits of them came back to him now as he vaguely watched what was going on in Court. He had been crawling down a tunnel, too low to stand upright in, and there had been something he had been trying to get to. He struggled to remember. Then it came back to him – not something, but someone. Willow. She had been at the end of the tunnel, but no matter how far he crawled, she remained as far away as ever.

In the Court, a man in black stepped forward. Several

other applicants had been curtly dismissed already, and Maxim was glad that the Emperor was not in a murderously vindictive frame of mind on this particular day. The man in black announced himself to be an alchemist.

Frederick stared at the ceiling.

'Really?' he said. 'Prove it! And quickly. My legs are beginning to ache sitting here all the time . . .'

The man bowed.

'Of course!' he said. 'My things!'

He called to the back of the room, where some flunkeys had been holding his equipment. In a few minutes he had set up a small burner over which sat a tripod.

He began to rummage in a bag, and pulled out a small stone crucible.

'I will now turn a small quantity of lead into gold, in this alchemical wonder, the secret system, the torment of the metals, the genesis through the twenty-seven transformations . . .'

Boy, who had become interested in the goings-on, muttered to himself.

'It's a trick.'

But he had been heard.

'Be quiet,' Maxim said, but Frederick leaned round in his throne.

'What did he say?'

'Nothing,' Maxim replied.

'I want to hear what the boy said,' Frederick said to Maxim acidly. 'What did you say, Boy?'

Boy hesitated.

'What did you say? Tell me!'

'I said it's a trick.'

'How do you know?' Frederick asked carefully.

The man in black seemed to hesitate. He opened his mouth to speak, and Frederick, not even looking in his direction, held up his hand.

'One more word from you and I'll have you killed right now.'

So, thought Boy, the old Emperor was sharp when he wanted to be.

'Now, Boy. Tell me how you know it's a trick,' Frederick said.

'It's a stage trick. The crucible has a false bottom made of wax. When it heats up, the wax melts and there's gold underneath already.'

There was a gasp around Court and everyone began to speak at once.

'The brat lies!' cried the alchemist, but before he could defend himself, Maxim snatched the crucible from the man's hand. He scratched inside it rapidly with his finger-nail, and then, just as quickly, stopped.

He held the crucible in the air, turning it over, showing the insides first to the assembly in Court, and then to Frederick. Flakes of wax fell to the floor.

From the base of the small crucible came the unmistakable glint of gold.

The room fell silent.

'Kill him,' said Frederick.

'No!' cried Boy. 'You can't kill him just for that! You can't!'

But no one paid Boy any attention, except Maxim, who walked over and clapped his hand across his mouth.

Boy turned away as the man was led struggling from the

room. He wrestled with Maxim, pulling his hand away from his mouth.

'I didn't mean for that to happen. I – you can't kill him.'

Maxim grasped Boy again and squeezed his throat.

'One mistake, Boy. Remember, one mistake.'

Boy fell silent.

The man had been an impostor, a trickster, but that was surely not reason enough to kill him? Boy had done much worse in his time. Much worse.

Frederick turned to Boy.

'Excellent Boy!' he cried. 'Well done! You have proved yourself a worthy young man already! Don't you think so, Maxim? Eh, Maxim? Clever Boy. We shall have to look after him. Eh, Maxim?'

Maxim forced a smile.

'Indeed,' he said.

'Worth keeping him after all, eh? You should take more notice of what I say, Maxim, then we might be closer to our goal!'

Maxim forced another thin smile, but in his eyes there was only anger, thinly veiled.

Boy said nothing, but watched the Emperor grinning at him stupidly, nodding in appreciation. He felt wretched for the man, responsible for his death. He could barely take in what was happening in Court, but he could not fail to notice what happened next.

'Next!' called a footman, and the crowd parted as the last applicants of the day took the risk of applying for favours within the royal Palace.

A man and a boy, both wearing hooded capes, made their way forward to the front of the Court.

They removed their hoods and Boy saw that the smaller figure was not a boy but a girl. A man and a girl.

Kepler and Willow.

5

'They had better be good,' Maxim muttered to Boy. 'Whoever they are, they had better be good. Once he's in the
mood for blood . . .'

Boy looked at Willow.

Yes, she had seen him, he could tell, from the way she
was looking anywhere but at him. It was the same with
Kepler. Both of them were studiously avoiding eye contact
with him. He understood what it meant. Say nothing, do
nothing to give us away. But Boy desperately needed to
warn them of the danger they were in.

They didn't know how their lives hung by a thread, and
that if they failed to impress the Emperor, their end would
have come.

Boy tried to catch Willow's eye, but she was having
none of it. She gazed straight ahead, paying attention only
to Kepler when necessary. Boy tried to twitch his head to
get her attention, but Maxim saw him.

'What are you doing, idiot? Be still. They're the last for
today, then you can go to your rooms until we have the
book.'

Boy stood still, shut his eyes, and prayed.

'What do you have to show us?' Maxim asked Kepler.

Kepler stepped forward.

'I am Arbronsius!' he declared. 'This is my assistant, Mina.'

He indicated Willow with a flourish of his hand.

'We have come far to your great city to demonstrate our mystical powers to Your Highness.'

'Get on with it, man,' Frederick barked.

Wordlessly Boy urged Kepler to hurry up. The old lunatic might have them killed for taking too long.

'Indeed,' Kepler said, searching in a bag at his feet. 'I just need some equipment . . .'

'Equipment? Equipment?' snapped Frederick. 'You're not some confounded telescopist, are you? Can't stand those upstarts!'

'No, indeed no,' Kepler said hurriedly. 'I have no truck with those modern natural philosophers, those scientists, treacherous telescopists!'

He sounded unconvincing to Boy, but then only Boy and possibly Willow knew that that was precisely what he was – a scientist, albeit one whose mind had definitely been influenced by the finding of the book. But Frederick and the rest of the Court seemed to have believed him, as he bent down once more and pulled some things from his bag.

'No, Sire, this is a truly magical appurtenance which I hold before you.'

With a flourish worthy of Valerian, Kepler pulled a short brass cylinder from his sack. Immediately Boy recognised it as the lens from the camera obscura, upon the end of which was mounted a frosted glass tube.

'Behold,' Kepler said dramatically, 'the Spirit Tube!'

Frederick said nothing, merely stifling a yawn with the back of his hand.

'The Spirit Tube is a conduit through which we can see the spirit world. Sometimes we are lucky enough to capture visions of this other world inside. Allow me to attempt a summoning!'

Kepler passed the device over for Willow to hold, while he moved his hands around it. He began to mutter under his breath, not loudly enough for anyone to hear. Boy was surprised. He had never imagined Kepler would have Valerian's ability to perform, yet that was precisely what he was doing. Boy knew Kepler had no magical powers, was a scientist pure and simple, yet as he watched, Kepler made a very fair show of playing the magician.

For a while nothing happened, then the tube began to glow with a yellowish green light, soft and sickly. Kepler held the tube high above his head for everyone to see, and then there was a gasp as people saw a face appear through the glow inside the tube.

Now Boy knew what he was seeing – it was basically the same trick Valerian had used to summon the fairy in his hands for the first part of the Fairyland Vanishing Illusion, his most famous trick. Perhaps this was something Kepler had shown him too. A question arose in Boy's mind. Was this why had Kepler sent him to The Yellow House to fetch the lens? Had he had this in mind even then?

'The Spirit Tube!' Kepler cried. Then he dropped it to the floor, the light disappeared, and he bowed at Frederick, praying he had done enough.

'Sometimes,' he added, rising again, 'we even hear voices from the other realm!'

Boy held his breath, hardly daring to look at Frederick. Willow stood a little behind Kepler, stone still.

Frederick stood and pointed at Kepler.

'Excellent!' he declared, looking like a spoilt little boy. 'Don't you think so, Maxim?'

'Very impressive,' said Maxim coolly.

'Yes, very,' said Frederick, turning back to Kepler. 'What was your name again?'

'Arbronsius,' Kepler said. 'And this is Mina.'

'Very good, very good. You may take rooms in the Palace, and you can show us more of your learning by and by.'

'Thank you, Sire,' Kepler said, bowing low. As he stood up he shot a glance at Boy, who nodded, ever so slightly.

Boy looked from Kepler to Willow, and saw the faintest trace of a smile cross her lips.

6

Boy was back in his chambers in the Winter Rooms. A different servant from last time was coming and going, doing this and that, tidying and clearing away the meal Boy had just eaten. She was young, and Boy had been relieved to see that she at least was not blind. He stood at the window, ignoring her, trying to get some bearings of the Palace, trying to work out where his room was in relation to the rest of it, but it proved difficult.

After a while he stopped thinking about the geography of the Palace, and watched the snowfall once more. His nerves were ragged, he felt edgy and scared. Seeing Willow again, here in the heart of danger, unnerved him. He not only had to worry about getting himself out, now he had to worry about her as well. He knew she was safe from Maxim's men, but what would happen when they returned empty-handed?

At least the Emperor liked him, but there was small consolation in that. Boy had seen how fickle he could be, how his mood might change on a whim.

Boy watched another flake of snow drift past the window, and automatically began to count, feeling a little calmer with every flake that fell.

He had no idea where Kepler and Willow were now. They had been led away in quite a different direction to the one he had taken to the Winter Rooms.

'Where do real guests go?' he asked the girl. 'Not prisoners like me.'

The girl stopped her work and looked puzzled.

'If I was a proper visitor,' Boy explained, 'where would I stay?'

The girl thought for a moment. She showed no sign of suspicion at Boy's questions.

'It depends on who they are. Lords are put in Fountain Court, Dukes in the Western State rooms.'

'What about people like the alchemists? That kind of person.'

'Oh,' said the servant. 'That's different. They all go to the Old South Tower.'

'And where's that?'

'Long way from here,' she said, turning to leave. 'Across the Great Court. It's the tallest tower in the whole Palace.'

Boy smiled. He could do something with the information the girl had given him.

There were guards outside each of the doors, but there was the secret stairwell by which he had first arrived in his rooms. That was locked, but then the older servant had also made a mistake by letting Boy keep his lock-pick.

Boy lay on the bed and waited for it to get dark.

It took Boy longer to get started than he had thought it would. Despite having first entered his chambers through the secret door, it took him half an hour of slowly searching round the walls to find it. Even when he did he could not actually be sure he had, so cleverly was it concealed.

It was not a hard lock to pick, once he managed to find the keyhole itself, which was hidden on the carved rail that ran right round the room. A flick with his lock-pick and the door popped open, hinged so cunningly that all the carved sections floated neatly away from their origin.

Boy made his way to his bed, and pulled some pillows together, arranging them to look like a sleeping figure. He pulled the sheets over the top, and stuck the corner of his nightshirt out of one side of the bed.

It was dark outside. It was even darker in the hidden stairwell, but Boy carefully took a small oil-lamp from his bedroom and set off down the stairs. He didn't exactly have a plan. He thought it would be best to get outside, assuming that it would be easier to find the Old South Tower from outside than by wandering aimlessly through endless corridors inside.

At the foot of the hidden stairwell he hesitated, pressing

his ear against the door, waiting to hear any kind of sound. None came, but he made himself wait for several minutes to be sure. Still nothing. He lowered the small handle and swung the door open, then putting the lamp on the bottom step he shut the door behind him, noting its position in the wall carefully before he did so. When the door was shut it was once again almost impossible to see.

The corridor was just as he remembered, only half-lit as most of the Palace seemed to be at night. There was the grand marble staircase leading away upstairs, and guessing that a hall of such importance had to be near an entrance to the Palace he set off for a set of doors opposite. He was right – he found himself in a slightly smaller hall beyond which he smelt the night air. There was a row of large doors right across the wall, all of them presumably leading outside, but Boy saw a much smaller door for informal use at each end, and made for the nearest of these. He was halfway through when he saw the guard, dozing on a narrow wooden perch by the other small door. Boy hurried through and gently shut the door behind him.

He was outside. For the first time in days he breathed fresh air and enjoyed the gentle wind that brushed his face, despite its coldness.

It was a moonless night, and Boy waited till he could see a little better before moving, but as his eyes adjusted to the dark, he saw a grey lawn in front of him.

Snow.

Snow covered everything, and was falling still. Immediately he saw a problem: footprints. He would leave footprints wherever he went, and even in the half-light he could see that the snow was untouched.

429

He stood on the steps of the Palace for a long time, getting more agitated. He couldn't go back, and in the end decided to hope for the best. If it snowed heavily enough through the night, it might cover up any tracks he left.

Nonetheless, he kept to the sides of the buildings, it being his natural preference to cling to the shadows and expose himself as little as possible.

He could not see the South Tower – in fact he couldn't see anything resembling a tower at all – but he had already learnt that the Palace was a highly convoluted assortment of buildings, and his view was obscured by the height of the square he was in.

Half an hour later he had worked his way past buildings great and small, along cloisters and down spiral stone staircases, over low walls and some high ones, all the while cursing the snow he had grown to love. His hands and feet were numb, and whenever he looked behind him he saw an awful trail of footprints, clear to him even in the darkness.

But now, as he looked across one more quadrangle, there was a huge tower, narrow and round. Boy could see the southern wall of the Palace not far beyond, and decided this had to be the South Tower. Suddenly he realised the futility of his situation.

He assumed the doors were locked, but that he would be able to open them. Given that he could get inside, he saw he had little chance of finding where Willow was. The Old South Tower stretched away above him into the snowy night sky. He counted eight floors at least before he could make out no more. As he approached the tower, he saw that while it had looked narrow from a distance it was actually enormous. He stopped, and tried to decide what to do. In a situation like this, Valerian would have stopped and turned to Boy. Boy could practically hear his voice.

'What do we need to do, Boy?' he would have asked. Even during those last few days, Valerian had always addressed Boy with the problem in hand logically, trying to get him to think logically too about the solution. The force of habit had been instilled in him well.

But what could he do? He skirted round the tower as far as he was able. He estimated there could be at least six rooms on each floor. He tried hard to calculate how many rooms that made if there were even only eight floors, but gave up before he had the answer. He understood it was useless.

He felt like screaming, shouting Willow's name and just running before anyone could catch them, but he knew that was stupid. They'd be caught long before they found their way to the outside world. Something in him would not give up, however.

He was moving back around the base of the building towards a doorway he had seen, when he noticed something strange at his feet. The snow was darker here, and slushy underfoot. Glancing up, he saw a low archway to his right that led down beneath a building at the foot of the tower. The trail of tainted snow led into the archway. Without thinking what he was doing, Boy walked towards the low archway, and then he heard a noise. It sounded like whimpering, like a hurt animal, but there was something else, too. A wet noise that Boy couldn't quite place.

Wishing he had brought the lamp with him, he stuck his head into the archway. The noise was more distinct.

He wondered if he should call out – if there was some-one hurt they might need help. But he couldn't risk giving himself away and it was not his problem. Even as he decided this, he thought of Willow and felt bad. She would have helped, even if it meant risking her own safety.

He moved a little way into the tunnel and was about to call out when he sensed something else – a smell which immediately made him understand what was happening. The darkened, wet snow, the gurgling noise, the whimper-ing. The smell was blood.

Without being able to help himself, he let out a cry of fear. The noise stopped and a dark shape moved before him. It was a hulking figure, crouched over something twitching on the ground. As it turned, Boy looked straight into its face.

For a moment there was nothing. Boy took in too many horrors in an instant. The poor thing dead on the tunnel floor. The Phantom sitting on its prey, blood dripping from its mouth. And its eyes – worst of all, its eyes.

The thing looked at him, failing to react, staring at him. Then Boy screamed and ran from the tunnel, heedless that anyone might hear him or see him as he flailed his way back across the Palace grounds.

It took him a long while to realise he was not being followed, but still he did not feel safe.

He kept on running the way he had come, his legs burning, a stitch in his side, and did not stop till he was back at the door from which he had emerged an hour or so before. He slowed only briefly as he let himself back in, past the sleeping guard. He hurtled back up through his secret stairwell to his rooms, where he locked himself in and stood shaking, his legs wobbling and his shoulders rising and falling. He climbed into bed, fully clothed, and began to cry at the shock of what he had seen.

After a long time he grew tired of crying, and only dull aching pain remained. He tried to push the sight from his mind, but it was futile. He could not shift from his thoughts the image of the poor animal – or worse, person – who had died at The Phantom's hands. And The Phantom itself. Not that large in truth. A small figure, but powerfully built, especially around its shoulders and arms, it had crouched like one of the apes Boy had once seen in the travelling menageries that sometimes came to the City. And its face. Its face was too awful to tell, and its hair was thin and patchy, revealing large areas of scalp underneath. The eyes were the worst of it – there was something about the eyes that had scared Boy to within an inch of his life. They were almost totally blank, with maybe nothing more behind them but the thought of killing, and yet that was not quite all. There was something else in those eyes that had burnt its way into Boy's mind and remained there now, yet Boy could not understand what it was.

Other thoughts rushed into his mind, not least the fear that he had left a trail that anyone or anything would be able to follow right back to the Winter Rooms, or at least to the entrance downstairs. He shivered, and longed for the snow to fall more thickly than ever, to hide his footprints, and to hide the blood, and to take all his pain away.

'Please snow, please snow, please snow,' he repeated to himself again and again.

Despite being fully clothed, despite the warmth of his room and the thickness of his sheets, Boy trembled as he desperately longed for sleep to come and take him.

8

It was not only thoughts of The Phantom that kept Boy awake. There was Willow too. What if she was not safely locked up in the Tower, with that thing on the loose? But then, nowhere in the city was really safe. He spent a wretched night anticipating the commotion that would start at daybreak when the bloody mess was discovered.

But when morning dawned, there was nothing. The old blind servant came and went, bringing him his breakfast, and said nothing of murder.

As she was leaving, Boy stopped her.

'What is it, Boy?'

'I just wondered if you'd heard anything happening in the Palace this morning. Anything strange.'

The woman shook her head.

'Same as ever,' she said.

After she left, Boy moved to the window. There had indeed been much more snow overnight, and Boy prayed it was enough to hide everything that had happened.

From his high vantage point he could see a man with a shovel clearing some of the footpaths around the small square beneath his window. The snow was coming down, and Boy began to feel calmer, but Willow was still on his mind.

His thoughts were broken as the door to the outer room of his chambers burst open.

Maxim strode in and Boy could see he was not in a good mood.

Had he learnt of Boy's nocturnal activities, or was he furious about the murderous Phantom? But it seemed no one knew that Boy had escaped, and no one knew, or cared, about who The Phantom killed either inside the Palace or out.

'The girl was not there!' Maxim marched right up to Boy, who kept his nerve and didn't flinch. That seemed to throw Maxim, who for once did not lash out. Boy had had enough of threats and beatings. He had seen something far worse last night, and somehow the shock of it had given him a weird strength. What was a physical blow compared to what he'd seen in the tunnel?

'I could have told you that,' Boy said, enjoying the irony of the situation. He knew exactly where 'the girl' was, right here in the Palace, while Maxim was scouring the City for her.

'How? Where is she?'

Under your very nose, Boy thought.

'I have no idea,' he lied, 'but I can tell you she's smarter than your guards. They won't find her.'

Maxim pushed Boy back against a wall.

'Are you going to hurt me again?' Boy asked flatly. He felt utterly calm.

Maxim was taken aback. The boy was in a strange mood, and he had no time for games.

'No,' he said. 'I'm not. But unless you tell me where the book is, I will send you somewhere where you will die. The dark flight? Remember that, Boy. Just remember that.'

Boy no longer felt so strong. He scratched his nose, looking away from Maxim.

'Ah,' said Maxim, 'So you know what I'm talking about? Good. Then tell me this: where is the book? If the girl has it, where is she? If not, who does have it? If you do not tell me now, I will have you taken straightaway . . .'

Boy edged away from the wall, and crossed to a window to look at the snow. What could he say? Even if he told Maxim about Kepler, that they were in the Palace, it still might not bring the book into his hands. Boy had no idea whether Kepler had it with him. It would have been a risk to bring it, it would have been a risk to leave it behind. And if he told Maxim all that, the one certain thing was that Willow would be in danger too. There was nothing he could say.

'I don't know,' he said, so calmly and clearly that Maxim could do nothing other than believe him. Boy felt he had been living on borrowed time ever since New Year's Eve. Valerian had nearly killed him then. He had changed his mind at the last moment, or had it changed for him, by Kepler telling him Boy was his son. Either Boy would have died, or his father. Now all he wanted was for Willow to be safe.

'Throw me to The Phantom, then, if you must. I can't tell you where the book is because I don't know.'

Boy expected Maxim to shout at him, to curse him, to beat him and to have him taken that very moment, but he did none of these things. He sat on a chair and shook his head.

Boy moved away from the window.

'Why?' he asked.

Maxim looked up.

'Why do you need the book? Why does the Emperor need it? It was here once before, and nothing good came of it.'

'The Doctor told you that, didn't he? He had his uses, but you know, I thought he might have lost his mind . . .'

'I think he very nearly did. What did he do to deserve that? What was it, to put him in prison for what . . . ? Ten years?'

'Fifteen,' Maxim corrected. 'Fifteen. He knew too much, things that he should not have done. I couldn't allow that. I was the only other person left alive who knew what he knew.'

'So why didn't you kill him?' Boy said bitterly. 'You kill people so easily here.'

Maxim looked at him wryly.

'Maybe not so easily in those days. But there was another reason. We needed his skills . . . as a doctor.'

'Why?' asked Boy, interested to see if Maxim would tell him about The Phantom, admit they knew of its existence, that they even cared for it and needed Bedrich to try to control its violent outbursts. He was to be disappointed.

'You think I'm going to tell you all the secrets in this place, Boy? Don't be so stupid. I am only interested in you for one reason: the book. You were with Valerian at the end; you must know what happened to it.'

Boy shook his head.

'The book was the last thing on our minds. Valerian was taken. Willow and I left The Yellow House. The Tower was a ruin. If your men didn't find it when they captured me then it must have been looted before I went back that day.'

Maxim studied Boy's face, as if trying to ascertain the truth of his words.

'But why do you need it anyway?' Boy asked. 'Why does the Emperor need it?'

'Because he's mad!' Maxim spat, then paused. He sighed. 'I need it to give the Emperor the one thing he hasn't got: life.'

'What do you mean?' asked Boy. 'He's alive now . . .'

'You noticed? Hmm. But for how much longer? He's seventy-eight now and, as you see, as frail as a man twenty years older. He's a puny, feeble, fake old man, and he wants to live for ever.'

'He wants to what?' spluttered Boy.

'He wants to live for ever,' Maxim said, as if it were the most reasonable thing in the world. 'There is no one to succeed him. He is the last of a direct family line that stretches back for seven centuries at least. When he dies . . .'

'And so he wants to live for ever, instead? He's mad!'

Maxim glanced at Boy, not very interested.

'I should have you killed for that. But yes, you're right. Unfortunately for me, I have to find a way of making him immortal, before he gets tired of me failing to do so.'

'I see,' said Boy. 'Or rather, I don't see. He wants to be made immortal. Say you find the book – say you find the book and find an answer. What then?'

Now Maxim did seem interested in what Boy was saying.

'What do you mean?'

'Well, suppose the book tells you a magical thing to do to him, to make him live for ever. A spell or whatever. You do this thing to the Emperor, and he thinks he's immortal.'

'What of it?'

'Well, how's he going to know any different unless he dies?'

There was a long silence, during which Maxim stared hard at Boy. The moment was broken by a knock at the door. The younger serving girl came in, without waiting to be invited.

'Maxim, Sir,' she began. 'Sir, you—'

'Not now!' Maxim shouted.

'But Sir, the Emperor wants you. Right now, Sir.'

'Dammit!' Maxim said, rising from his chair. 'Very well, I'm coming.'

He turned to Boy.

'Don't go anywhere, will you?' he said, smiling. 'You've reached the end of your usefulness. You will stay here until I think what to do with you.'

Boy stood up.

'But, Sir,' the girl said to Maxim, 'His Highness wants to see Boy too. He says he's to attend Court from now on.'

Maxim swore and grabbed the girl by the arm.

'Are you sure?' he barked, but there was no reason to suppose otherwise. He let her go, kicked a chair over, and stormed from the room.

'Get here!' he yelled over his shoulder.

440

Boy skittered out of the door after Maxim, marvelling at how his life might just have been saved by the City's legendary, lunatic, decrepit Emperor.

9

Willow. The first thing Boy saw on entering Court, through the crowds of people, was Willow. She had spotted him immediately too, and smiled. Boy risked a smile back, while Maxim's attention was taken with hurrying over to the Emperor, who was already sitting in his throne, awaiting their arrival.

Maxim had guessed that Frederick was in a bad mood, and he was right.

'So, Maxim, you have failed again!'

The Emperor's high, weedy voice sailed over the hushed court room, and the silence that followed was absolute.

Boy could sense the tension in the room. Even during his short time there he had learnt what a perilous existence they all led, living on the Emperor's whims. Maxim was no exception, and Boy's own safety hung precariously between the Emperor and his right-hand man.

'Well, Maxim, what do you have to say?'

Boy took his chance.

He had lagged behind Maxim, on whom the whole attention of the Court was now focussed. Ever so slowly, trying to think himself as small and unnoticeable as possible, Boy side-stepped towards Willow and Kepler. No one seemed to notice; all eyes in the room were fixed on the scene playing out between Frederick and Maxim.

'Well! You have failed to find the book! What exactly do you intend to do now?'

Maxim took a step forward and seemed to be about to speak, but Frederick was working himself up into a rage.

'I charge you with one simple duty, and you consistently fail to deliver your promises! I swear you are doing it deliberately! You want me to die, do you? Do you? Well, you'll be gone long before me, Maxim. I've had enough! I've had enough of your pathetic excuses and it won't be allowed to continue!'

Boy had made it to Willow's side.

He brushed the back of her hand with his, but could think of nothing to say.

'Boy,' Willow said.

Kepler turned and saw who it was.

He smiled, then frowned. He glared at Boy.

'You mustn't be seen with us,' he hissed. 'It's dangerous.'

'You don't understand,' Boy whispered back. 'It's more dangerous here than you know.'

'What do you mean?' Willow asked.

Boy was about to answer, but noticed that one of the ladies standing nearby was looking at them. Boy turned away from Willow and pretended to watch the scene unfolding in front of them. After a while he spoke to Willow without looking at her, keeping his eyes on Frederick and Maxim.

'It's dangerous. Those two for a start,' he whispered, and nodded slightly towards the dais. 'But there's something else. The Phantom. The Phantom lives here, under the Palace.'

Boy risked looking round at Willow. Her face was a picture of confusion. Boy looked forwards again.

'Later,' he whispered, so quietly that only she could hear. 'Meet me here tonight.'

Frederick, meanwhile, was working himself into an even greater rage. Finally Maxim managed to speak.

'Sire, I wonder how you came across the news that I do not have the book?'

'From the Captain of the Imperial Guard.'

'But my men—'

'*Your* men, Maxim? *Your* men? The Imperial Guard are mine. They do not serve you! They serve me! You forget your place. The Imperial Guard exist to serve me and I spoke to their Captain earlier today, who tells me that the book was not found on their expedition across the City!'

Frederick was purple with rage now, so angry that he might do anything.

'But Sire,' Maxim said calmly, 'we do have the book.'

He stopped for effect, to emphasise his words.

'*What?*' said Frederick crisply.

Boy and Willow were transfixed.

'We *do* have the book,' Maxim continued. 'It *was* found on the mission to the City. Even now it is in my chambers. I was on my way here to bring you this great news. I will begin consultation immediately, after I have . . . spoken to the Captain of the Guard.'

Boy turned to Willow, who shook her head ever so slightly. Of course he didn't have the book, so what game was he playing at? Whatever it was, Boy knew the stakes were being raised ever higher with each passing moment.

'When can I see it?' Frederick asked deliberately.

'But Sire, I thought it best if it remained safe with me,' Maxim said cautiously. He approached the dais, and whispered.

'After what happened . . . before, it might be best to keep it hidden . . .'

Frederick's face was a horrible picture. Memories swept through the old Emperor's mind, contorting his features into anguish. The look froze on his face briefly, then he shook himself.

'Yes,' he said, feebly, 'Yes. You're right, Maxim.'

Maxim stood upright again and spoke brightly.

'Is it not wonderful news? At last our goal is in sight.'

Frederick nodded, looking like a child in his huge throne.

'Yes,' was all he said.

'I shall ensconce myself in my rooms. I will devote all hours of day and night to this endeavour. I will consult and scry, and when I have an answer from the book we will prepare to make you . . . immortal!'

He finished with a flourish so extravagant that the whole Court burst into applause without even really wanting to.

Frederick sat on his throne, his mouth twitching slightly as he tried and failed to regain his composure, though no one noticed.

While people were talking and clapping, Boy leant in to Willow so that only she could hear him.

'Are you locked in?'

Willow shook her head.

'Good, then tonight. After midnight.'

Kepler grabbed Willow's arm and began to pull her away. She was about to protest when she saw why. Maxim was striding over towards Boy. The Court was over and people were starting to leave. Maxim came up to Boy and for a moment glanced at Willow and Kepler. He seemed to be about to say something.

'Are we going now?' Boy said quickly to Maxim, trying to show no interest in Willow or Kepler. 'Can I help you?'

Maxim was still looking at Willow, a question on his lips, but now he turned to Boy.

'Help me? Help me!' he snorted. He grabbed Boy and began to walk him out of the Court. Boy dared not risk a look back at Willow.

'Of course you can't help me. But unfortunately, Emperor Frederick thinks you are useful, so you will come with me for the time being. When I have made him immortal, however, it will be a different story.'

They had left the room now and were heading back upstairs.

'What?' Boy asked. 'What will happen to me then?'

Maxim didn't break step.

'You will have outlived your usefulness. You and all those tricksters and charlatans who hang around him like flies on a carcass.'

'But you don't even have the book!' Boy cried.

That did make Maxim stop. He slapped his hand over Boy's mouth and pushed him against a wall.

'Do you want everyone in the Palace to hear?' he

snapped. 'Keep that to yourself, or I'll finish you off now and tell Frederick you had an accident.'

He held his hand on Boy's mouth for a long time, until a serving girl appeared at one end of the corridor they were in. Maxim let Boy go and pulled him into a walk again.

'So be careful,' he said. 'Be careful what you say. Anyway, you won't have a chance to speak to anyone else. You can stay in your room until I'm ready for you.'

'But how are you going to make him immortal? You don't have the book.'

They were at the doors to Boy's chamber.

Maxim pushed him inside and closed the door behind them, so the guard outside could not hear.

'No!' he said. 'I don't have the book. And I don't need it either.'

He turned to leave, and opened the door again.

'I don't understand,' Boy said.

'Really? You should do. It was you who provided the solution. I can't believe I didn't think of it myself. I have been too absorbed by it all, maybe. It doesn't matter now. You will excuse me. I have to visit the Captain of the Guard. I think it's time he was replaced.'

10

Night in the Palace.

Different worlds enacted themselves in different parts of the Palace, but it would have been a mistake to suppose these worlds were entirely isolated from each other, for they were all part of a single, if intricate, dance.

In the Royal Bedchambers, Frederick snored gently, muttering in his sleep, through which pleasant dreams of his coming immortality wrestled with nightmares of less pleasant things, things from the past that he had thought were forgotten. He wore a red nightcap, whose long red tassel dangled across his face, looking in the half-light like a trail of dried blood.

He turned in his sleep, calling out from time to time but not waking. The guards at his door ignored it all, being well used to the Emperor's ways.

Nearby, away in the adjacent wing of the Palace, the Emperor's right hand, confidant, doctor, servant, adviser and counsellor, Maxim, paced around his study. Finally he sat down in a velvet armchair by the fire, and scratched his bald head. He was weighing up certain matters. He had an answer for Frederick now. He had a solution. If it worked, then all would be well, and Maxim would be safe. If it failed, then the irritable old fool might have him sent down that dreadful stairway himself. But he had decided one thing, and that was that to fail to act at all would probably be fatal anyway. Frederick was getting more erratic with each day that passed. Maxim knew he was living on borrowed time, and that he had probably stalled as much as he was able to. He had to do something now, that was for sure.

Idly he threw more coals on to the fire, and as he did so, thoughts flowed into his head. What a strange life it had been! He didn't want it to end now, but there had been so much death, so much killing, and now that he was older and maybe a little wiser, he saw it as a disease. Death had been all around him for so long, and he felt in very real danger of catching the dying disease himself.

When he'd been in the dungeons he'd heard Bedrich singing that song, the song from so long ago, written by Sophia Beebe in the days when her family was in favour in the Palace. Since he'd heard it again he hadn't been able to shift it from his mind for very long. It seemed so apt at the moment – maybe that was why all these thoughts of the past were coming back to him now, all these thoughts of death.

Had she even used the book herself? Foreseen her own future, and that of everyone else tied up in its demonic designs? It was an appalling thought, one which made him feel powerless. Still the tune ran through his head, and he hummed to himself.

> *Surely you won't run?*
> *When your boat is ready to sail.*

Surely you will stand
And face the gentle rain?
In the morning you should think
You might not last unto the night,
In the evening you should think
You might not last unto the morn.
So dance, my dears, dance,
Before you take the dark flight down.

Maxim stopped singing and spat bitterly into the fire. He was far from ready to take the journey, the long dark journey to oblivion. He would beat the Emperor at his own game yet, and do away with all the hangers-on who made his life so much more complicated than it need be. If it was just him and the Emperor, he could have controlled things the way he wanted them, but the old fool took too much notice of the alchemical quacks, and Maxim suffered as a result, having to be at his beck and call, and all the while keeping one eye out for threats and challenges to his position. But not for much longer. One way or the other, it would be over soon.

And then there was Boy, who once again sat by the darkening window watching the snow unbelievably still falling from the clouded heavens, hiding all trace of dirt and grime from view. He waited until it was dark and then waited some more. Someone brought him his supper, and he ate it gratefully enough. He reflected grimly that he was eating better than he ever had in his whole life, and yet he wanted nothing more than to escape.

Escape.

It was the only thing to do. Find Willow and escape.

Kepler could look after himself as far as Boy was concerned.

Boy waited all through the dark evening, after his tray had been taken away, waited and waited for each tolling of the City and Palace bells, until midnight came. As he waited he inevitably started to think about Valerian. Valerian, his father. No, he didn't know that for sure, but he felt it. At least, he felt there was something in the way Kepler had tried to conceal what he had spoken, that told him it was the truth. And what then? If he had lived with his father all those years, being bullied and tormented, and not even realised it, did that bring him peace? It might not tell him everything, and he might never know who his mother was, but it would be a start. At least then he would know something about himself, in the way other people did.

The midnight bells struck softly through the snow-laden night. Once again Boy made his way with his lock-pick down the secret stairwell, but this time headed for the Court itself. He knew his way around a few parts of the Palace quite well now, from his rooms to the Court, but nonetheless he felt on unknown ground as he approached the huge chamber. By night, and with no one else around, it was a very different place. During the day it was full of colour and life and people and wealth. By night, it was a different thing. The place seemed even bigger when empty, and the colours muted. It was a deserted, forgotten place. Haunted.

Boy stole across the marble ocean of the floor, and was happier when his footfalls fell on thick carpets instead. He tried to decide where to wait for Willow, and spotted a corner by the side of the fireplace that would be perfect. He was making for it when Willow stepped from the shadows.

'Boy!' she cried, and rushed to him.

They held each other for a long time before either one of them spoke again.

Finally they pulled apart, and looked at each other. There were too many questions. Too many words that needed to be spoken.

'How are you?'

'What happened? You didn't come—'

'I know. I'm sorry. I was captured. There was no way to tell you . . .'

Willow held Boy's hands. They moved and sat down next to each other on the dais, just in front of the throne. Two small figures dwarfed by the vastness of the darkened Courtroom.

'What did you mean about The Phantom?' Willow asked.

'Just what I said!' Boy said. 'It lives in the Palace – under it, really. I was kept in the dungeons, and there's a flight of stairs that leads down to somewhere even deeper. That's where it lives, then comes out to . . .'

Boy stopped. He didn't want to think about it.

'And they don't know about it?'

'Oh yes, they do. Well, Maxim does, at least. They seem to tolerate it as long as it doesn't murder in the Palace itself . . .'

'Don't worry,' Willow said, seeing Boy was upset by it. 'We're together again now.'

'But what did you think when I didn't meet you by the fountain?'

'I knew. I knew you wouldn't just leave me. But I was so worried.'

'How did you know I was here?'

'A feather. They left a white feather behind in the house. Kepler said it was the Imperial Guard.'

'He was right. I should thank him for that, at least.'

Willow shrugged.

'I don't like him. I suppose he's trying to help, but I really don't like him.'

'He's come here to get me back, I suppose?'

Willow nodded.

'I don't understand,' Boy said. 'I know he thinks I belong to him now that Valerian's gone, but you wouldn't think he'd risk his life to do it, would you?'

'Never mind,' Willow said. 'We can forget him. Boy, let's just get out of here right now and start again, as we meant to.'

'Yes,' said Boy. 'Yes.'

'There is one thing though. I don't know that there's a good time to tell you, so I think I should tell you now.'

'What?' Boy asked, wondering why he suddenly felt scared.

Willow hesitated.

'What?' Boy asked. 'Tell me!'

'Boy. It's about Valerian. He's not your father.'

Boy said nothing, but flinched as if he had been struck.

'No,' he said. 'That's not true. No. You can't know that.'

'Boy,' said Willow gently, 'it's true. I found out from Kepler.'

453

'He told you?'

'Not exactly. We were talking about you. Well, arguing really. I told him he'd been terrible to you, to split us up, to send you back to The Yellow House, and only a few days after you'd seen your father die.'

'What did he say?'

'He shouted at me that your father wasn't dead. He said he only told Valerian that to make you live.'

Boy said nothing now, but just sat, slowly shaking his head.

'He gambled that Valerian would believe him, that there was one small bit of Valerian that wanted to believe he had a son, and could not kill that son for his own sake.

'Valerian told us he made the pact to spend one night with the woman he desired. And he did, but in the morning she still rejected him.

'Kepler told me something, something I'd already suspected. He loved that woman too. She was called Helene. That was why he and Valerian fell out, became enemies when they had been friends before. Neither of them saw Helene again, but Kepler knew he could use that story to make Valerian believe you were his son, even just for a short while. Long enough, in fact, for him to go to his death instead of you to yours. But he's not your father. He's not.'

'Then who is?' Boy cried. 'Who is?'

'I don't know,' Willow said. 'Kepler wouldn't say, and when I pushed him for an answer, he got angry and sent me to bed.'

She stopped, trying to think of what she could say to Boy, who sat with his head hanging in his hands, but found no words that could help.

'I'm sorry,' was all she said in the end. 'Let's get away from here at least, shall we? There'll be time later to think.'

Boy looked up at her.

'No,' he said.

'What do you mean?' Willow asked.

'I mean, no. I'm not going anywhere. Not until I have some answers. I don't want to think about things later. I want some answers now.'

Willow put her hand on Boy's arm, but he did not take it. He stood and looked down at her. She had never seen him like this before.

'I've had enough, Willow,' he said. 'I've had enough of not knowing who I am, who my parents were, where I was born. I don't even have a name!'

'Yes, you do. You're Boy. You told me that . . .'

'I don't care what I told you! I want a proper name. I want to know who I am! I'm not going anywhere until I get some answers.'

'Please, Boy, let's go. Let's get out of this bad place first and then think about it later. Please?'

'No,' said Boy. 'No. I'm staying here.'

'But what good will that do?'

'The book,' said Boy. 'The book is here, isn't it? Maxim may think he's just pretending it is, but it is here. Kepler has it, doesn't he?'

Willow looked at the floor.

'Yes, I think he does,' she said quietly.

'Then I'm going to look in it.'

'No!' Willow said, gripping his arm tightly. 'You know how dangerous it can be! You mustn't.'

'I don't care how dangerous it is. Haven't you been listening to me at all? I want to know the truth about myself now, no matter what the risk. I have to know!'

Willow shook her head.

'But we can't even get to it. I think it's in the bag he brought with him. It's very heavy and I've seen precious little else come out of there. But he never leaves me alone. We'd never get the chance to see.'

'Then we'll make a chance,' said Boy. 'That's all there is to it.'

Willow stared at Boy. There was something new about him, something stronger than she had ever seen before.

'The only question,' Boy said, 'is will you help me?'

Willow stood and held Boy's hands for a long time. She smiled, gazing into his eyes.

'Of course I'll help you. We're together now, see?'

Boy smiled, and leant towards Willow. He kissed her and smiled, then looked more serious again, the air of strength returning to him.

'Listen to me then,' he said. 'We don't have much time. Maxim's about to make his move, and when he does, he'll kill us all. You, me, Kepler. All the alchemists and astrologers. No one will be safe once Frederick's immortal. Tomorrow we will be in Court. Kepler will be called too. And we'll make a chance to look at the book. I'm fighting now, Willow. I've been pushed around enough and I'm going to put an end to it.'

Willow smiled and nodded. She only wished she felt as sure as Boy seemed to be.

11

Boy was right. Maxim was ready to make his move. When Boy woke next morning he found the young serving girl already in his room.

'What is it? What's going on?'

Boy got down out of bed and scratched his nose.

'Today's the day!' the girl declared.

'What are you talking about?'

'The Emperor. Maxim's going to make him immortal today. This evening, in Court.'

Boy almost felt like laughing.

'Don't you understand?' he asked as he got dressed. 'Don't you understand anything about this place? What do you think will happen once Frederick's immortal?'

'What?' asked the girl, surprised.

'No one will be safe. Maxim will see to that. And Frederick will just go on getting madder and madder with no end to it all.'

The girl ignored him, and began to tidy things in the room. Boy gave up.

'There's one person who's not invited,' she said, not smiling. 'You.'

Boy raised an eyebrow.

'Maxim says you're to remain here.'

Boy smiled. It might work in his favour. Maybe he could get to the book while everyone else was occupied in Court.

He crossed to the window and scowled at the falling snow. He had had enough of it. He had believed it was going to help him, he had trusted it to hide all the horror away, but it had failed. He cursed it, and himself for being so stupid as to think it could save him. He was going to have to save himself.

12

The whole Palace was astir. The news had spread from the highest bell tower to the lowest cellar. Everyone was talking about the Emperor's immortality.

There was a huge uproar in the Old South Tower, where Frederick's astrologers and other advisers were shocked. Willow and Kepler listened to the debates over the communal breakfast they took in the Tower refectory. There was disagreement over what it would mean, and over exactly what Maxim was going to do, and much, much argument about the book, and about whether it even existed, never mind whether Maxim had it or not.

Kepler stared silently at the plate in front of him. He and Willow were the only people in the room not discussing the forthcoming events.

'Don't be so obvious,' she hissed.

Kepler looked up and saw what she meant.

'Let's go back to our rooms,' he said.

'What do you think Maxim's going to do?' Willow asked, as they walked up the spiral staircase that led to their chambers.

'I don't know. Just what he says, probably.'

'But he doesn't have the book,' Willow said. 'You have it, don't you?'

'Be quiet!' They had reached their rooms at the very top of the Tower, and Kepler flung the door shut behind them.

'Yes, I do have the book, and if anyone finds that out we're as good as dead. Just to own it means death! People will kill to own it. So keep quiet.'

He stormed off across the room.

'But why did you bring it?'

'I couldn't take the risk of leaving it anywhere. Nowhere is safe. They'd ransacked The Yellow House looking for it. If they made a connection from Valerian to me, as they undoubtedly will sooner or later, they'd have gone looking for it at my house too. The only safe place is where I can keep an eye on it.'

'But what are we going to do?' Willow asked. She knew full well what her plans with Boy were, but if Kepler's own plans got in the way, the situation could get very complicated.

'I don't know. It's turned out differently from what I planned. And once Maxim does his performance today . . .'

'You mean you got us in here with no idea about getting us out again?'

'Getting in was the hard part, but that's not what I mean. And if I can get things back to what I had planned, we won't need to worry about getting out again.'

'What do you mean?' Willow asked.

'Enough. You'll see later. Now tell me what you and Boy spoke about yesterday.'

'No!' said Willow. 'I want to know what you mean. Why won't we need to worry about getting out?'

'I said enough! Tell me what you and Boy spoke about at Court.'

'You expect me to tell you, since you won't trust me with your plans? You can think again!'

Kepler grunted and strode to the window, where he gazed out at the City far below.

Willow watched him, then her eyes were drawn to the large leather bag lying under Kepler's bed. Its mouth lay slightly open, and though she couldn't be sure, Willow thought she could see the corner of a book poking out. Not just any book, but a huge, weighty tome: the book. The book from the Dead Days when Valerian had died.

And now Boy wanted to look inside it. Her heart began to race.

13

Boy had spent the day idly, locked up in his luxurious prison, and dusk had fallen. The ceremony was due to start in Court soon, and he had been prepared to wait for a good moment to sneak out and down to the Tower.

To the Tower to find the book, and then . . .

Then to know who and what he really was. If Valerian was not his father, then who? Kepler must know – he'd looked in the book enough by now to know all about Boy, surely, assuming that that was what he was looking for. Kepler seemed to have become obsessed by Boy, by possessing him as Valerian had. Boy couldn't believe Kepler didn't have all the answers.

And Valerian? Boy thought deeply about his former master, and despite all the hurt and pain he'd inflicted, Boy could find nothing in his heart now for Valerian, nothing but sorrow. Sorrow that he had died, that they had failed to make things better between them, but more than these regrets was a greater sorrow.

That Valerian wasn't his father after all.

Maxim might not have wanted Boy to be present during the ceremony but Frederick had other ideas, and once again had ordered that his new plaything be brought to Court. Boy cursed his luck.

A guard walked him down through the Palace to find Maxim himself waiting outside the door to the Court. He dismissed the guard and watched him go.

'You will say nothing unless I tell you to,' Maxim threatened. Boy acted suitably cowed. It wouldn't hurt for Maxim to think he was too scared to act.

'The old fool wants you here. You're his favourite new pet, and there's nothing I can do about that. Not yet. So behave yourself.'

Boy nodded.

Maxim opened the door and they entered.

Yet again the Palace outshone its own magnificence. The room had been decorated with flags and banners; strips of red and gold silk hung all around, encrusted with jewels that sparkled in the light from four massive chandeliers that hung from the painted ceiling. The room was packed, far more than usual. Boy looked around for Willow, but could not see her or Kepler.

There was standing room only, and precious little of that. Boy marvelled at the accumulation of wealth upon each person present. Even the lowliest members of the Palace were dressed in fine clothes, maybe only brought out on occasions of the greatest importance. And there could be no occasion more important than this: the Bestowing of Immortality on Emperor Frederick.

A fanfare rang out across the room, and the Emperor was carried in on a large chair slung between two poles, festooned with more ribbons of red and gold, supported by four men. The people struggled to allow him by, and it took some time for the small cortege to make its way through the overcrowded Court to the dais.

Once there, Frederick climbed up on to his throne as usual, and turned to face the assembly. He smiled, and Boy almost felt sorry for him, but was then horrified to see the Emperor looking straight at him.

'Boy! There you are. Come here! You must be here.'

Boy hesitated, and looked at Maxim, who inclined his head slowly.

'Yes, you must be here,' Frederick drawled. 'You are a good and faithful servant to the Empire. If more of these idiots acted with your quick thinking maybe it wouldn't have taken so long to get to where we are today . . .'

Maxim and Boy stood at the foot of the dais. Frederick looked around once more, and coughed.

'People,' he said, in his wavering voice, 'today is a great day. Thanks to my hard work and struggles, I will today achieve a wonderful thing. I am an old man; there is no heir to the throne. But this problem will be a problem no longer. I have created a superb solution. It will make everything well. You will not be deprived of your beloved Emperor after my death, for I am not going to die. In a few moments I will have Maxim do . . . whatever it is he must do . . . and I will become immortal!'

There was a gasp and then a murmur around the Court room. Even though everyone knew already that this was what the old Emperor had been seeking, it was still a shock to actually hear him say it.

Frederick frowned at Maxim.

'Why don't they cheer?' he asked.

'They're just too happy to express what they really feel, Sire,' Maxim said, and he nodded to a guard. Boy watched as the guard pulled his sword an inch or two from its scabbard and glared at some people near to him. They immediately started to clap, and as others began to applaud and cheer, the Emperor sat back on his throne, apparently satisfied.

Maxim chewed his lip and ran one hand across the top of his bald head. He let the cheering continue for a full minute or two. It would be a good idea, he thought, to put the Emperor in as good a mood as possible. Finally he raised his hand.

'Loyal servants of the Imperial Throne, Lords, Ladies, Dukes, Duchesses, Marquises. Behold! For today is the first day of a new chapter in the history of the Empire, and you are its witnesses.

'I have obtained knowledge that was occult but is now no longer hidden, for it has fallen into my hands – knowledge that will free our Emperor from the constraints of mortality. Having made certain careful preparations, I am about to perform the ritual that will bestow everlasting life on Emperor Frederick, the Magnificent!'

He paused, and after a moment, a subdued cheer came from the assembled crowd.

'Of course,' Maxim continued, 'this ritual is delicate and powerful in equal measure. It cannot be witnessed directly. We will begin at once.'

He nodded once more to two of the guards standing near the throne.

'The screen!' he cried.

A large screen made of a wooden frame over which red silk had been stretched was placed round the three forward sides of the dais, so that Frederick was hidden from view.

As he disappeared from sight, the Emperor still wore a silly smile. He lifted a hand to his people, and then was gone. Boy stood by the dais, staring at Maxim, who clapped his hands. From the back of the hall, another servant brought forward a tray, on which were certain objects – magical devices, no doubt, but nothing that Boy thought could bestow immortality. A wand, a cup, a potion and some herbs was all Boy could see as the things were taken up the steps of the dais and behind the screen. Suddenly, as Boy watched Maxim, he was reminded of something. He had a feeling that he had seen all this before. He'd described it to Valerian once, who had told him it had a French name – *déjà vu*. Already seen, Valerian had said. That was just what Boy felt as he watched Maxim, but this *déjà vu* had a mundane explanation. Boy had seen this countless times before, on stage with Valerian. A flowery speech, a few props, a screen. It was all exactly as Valerian had done it on stage, pulling some illusion or other and fooling a whole crowd into believing something impossible.

What was Maxim up to?

He stepped to the front of the dais once more, exactly like Valerian stepping to the front of the stage to make sure he had the audience's attention before performing the trick.

'Behold!' he cried. 'In a few moments, your Emperor will be immortal!'

And he whipped behind the screen.

A murmur spread round the room, so that he could not hear anything that was going on behind the screen, but from where he stood, Boy realised he could see vague shapes moving behind it. Maybe Maxim had intended it, maybe not, but the light from lamps on the wall behind the dais was casting the shadows of Maxim and Frederick on to the silk of the screen.

Boy watched, and realised others had noticed this too. It was hard to tell exactly what was going on, but Boy saw Maxim pick up the cup. He handed it to Frederick, who put it to his lips.

Boy's heart jumped. That was it! Maxim was simply going to poison Frederick. Right there, in front of everyone, he was going to poison him, and then claim he had died in the arduous process of achieving immortality.

Boy moved, but a guard saw him and barred his way. Boy saw Frederick drink from the cup. He waited for a scream of pain, or for Frederick to collapse to the floor, but nothing happened. The Emperor gave the cup back to Maxim, who set it down.

Shapes continued to move, but Boy could see nothing of Frederick now. Maxim came and went around the throne, waving his hands in front of it, picking other things up from the tray, putting them down again. Finally, even Maxim's movements ceased. There was nothing, nothing at all, and the muttering in Court grew louder and louder.

The guard holding Boy was now so fascinated himself by what was going on that he let go of him, and moved closer to the screen. He took another step. He was just about to put his head around the back of it, when it flew forwards and clattered down the steps. Maxim stood with arms upraised.

'Behold!' he cried again. 'Emperor Frederick is now immortal!'

There was a stunned silence, and then the cheering and

shouting and clapping began. The Emperor sat on his throne, as he had before. He was alive, Boy could see that, but there was something not quite right about him. He still had a foolish grin on his face, but his eyes seemed to be drifting all around the room, roaming unfocused from floor to ceiling.

Boy looked at the cup, now on its side and empty of whatever it had contained, and then looked at the Emperor again. What had Maxim given him?

People began to press forwards, watching as the Emperor moved not a muscle. The astrologers and alchemists peered at him closely. Maxim stepped in front of one of them who was getting a little closer than the others.

'What's wrong with him?' someone said.

'Nothing!' Maxim said. 'Nothing. The process is an exhausting one. It will take a short while for the effects to wear off, and then . . . yes! See! Already His Highness is restored to himself! But no, it is more than that. For he is now immortal!'

It was true. That the Emperor was becoming normal again was true.

He stood. A perfectly normal action, but it produced a gasp from the crowed, who all drew back.

'Is it done?' he said to Maxim. 'Am I immortal now?'

His voice was not quite right, though. There was something wrong with it, something Boy couldn't place, as if he was talking in a dream.

'Oh, yes!' Maxim said confidently. 'You are now immortal. And since that is the case, I trust Your Highness will no longer see the need for the presence of certain people in Court.'

Boy looked around. He could see guards moving around the walls of the Court, making for where he and the astrologers stood. Finally he saw Willow and Kepler, standing with the other advisers.

Frederick nodded.

'I am immortal,' he said, as much to himself as anyone else. He spoke more normally.

'Immortal,' Maxim repeated. 'So there is no need for these useless diviners any more.'

Boy understood now. He saw the whole thing, and understood what Maxim had meant when he said that it was *he* who had provided the solution. A very final one for some.

'No!' he cried, jumping forward. 'No! It's a trick!'

A guard grabbed him and threw him to the floor.

He wrestled free and ran to the dais, where he jumped on to the steps.

'It's a trick! It's a trick!'

Maxim made for him, as did two more guards, but Frederick stepped between them and Boy.

'Stay!' he cried. The guards hesitated, Maxim did not.

He caught Boy and put out his hand to one of the guards.

'Quick! Give me your sword.'

'Do nothing!' Frederick shrieked at the guard, who remained where he was. 'And you, Maxim, will wait too until we hear what Boy has to say. He was faithful to us once and we will hear what he has to say. If it is false he will die, but I shall be the judge! I am the immortal Emperor, and I shall be heard!'

Maxim stopped.

'You cannot take the words of this Boy above me! I have given you the greatest—'

'Silence!' Frederick screamed so loud that Maxim jumped. 'Now, Boy, what do you have to say? And be very careful what you say.'

Boy got up from the floor and edged away from Maxim. He looked around the Court, saw Willow and the fear on her face, and felt himself grow stronger.

He pointed at Maxim.

'It's a trick! He hasn't made you immortal. He hasn't done anything to you, except maybe drugged you for ten minutes! He's bluffing.'

'What do you mean?'

Maxim took a step towards Boy, his face full of menace. Boy stepped back, but kept talking.

'I gave the idea to him.'

'What idea?'

'About being immortal. I said to him, how do you know you're immortal until you die?'

There was total silence.

'I . . . what?' asked Frederick. 'I . . .'

'It's very simple,' Boy said, 'How do you know you're immortal now unless you die? Are you willing to try to find out? He's trying to trick you, because there's no other way to know.'

Now people understood and the Emperor too.

He turned to Maxim.

'Is this true?'

Maxim fought to stay calm. Boy knew he would give himself away if he lost his cool now.

'Of course not! The brat lies! Have him taken away and slaughtered at once.'

He made a signal to a guard, but again Frederick stopped him.

'The next man who obeys anyone else's orders will die. You all listen to me, not Maxim! Now, Maxim, why do you say the Boy is lying?'

'Because he's a lying urchin. You can't—'

'He doesn't even have the book!' Boy cried. 'Ask him to show you the book!'

Maxim's face was disfigured with rage, but still he managed to speak calmly.

'There's no need to have the book. It's too powerful to bring down here . . .'

Frederick stopped him.

'Bring me the book, Maxim.'

Maxim said nothing; he was utterly motionless.

'Bring me the book now, Maxim, or you will die.'

It was too much. Maxim was trapped. There was no way to escape.

'No!' he screamed. 'I don't have the cursed book! And you aren't immortal! How could you be? It's impossible!'

Frederick recoiled as if he had been struck.

'Traitor!' he screamed.

'You stupid fool! Did you really think I could make you immortal?'

Maxim laughed bitterly, flung his hand out at the crowd.

'Look at them! They've all been waiting for you to die for years! And why? Because you don't have an heir! So you wanted to be immortal instead. Well, you're a bigger fool than I ever thought! And a liar, too. You do have an heir, don't you, Frederick? Why don't you tell everyone all about it?'

'Guards! Kill him!' Frederick yelled hurriedly. 'Kill him!'

Maxim laughed, and backed away around the side of the throne. Then he darted behind the massive chair. He flicked something in the wall and a secret door opened. He disappeared and the door shut behind him.

A guard ran over and tried to find the catch Maxim had used.

'It's locked from the inside,' he said.

Frederick was mad with rage. He practically jumped on to his throne, and stood there, quivering.

'Find him! Search the Palace. Close all exits! Bring him to me!

The Tower

The Place of Revelation

The whole Court was in turmoil.

Guards were running here and there, as Frederick shouted orders from atop his throne.

Willow saw her chance and ran to Boy. Kepler hurried after her, pushing his way through the crowds, but Willow was faster and more nimble.

'Quick!' she said to Boy. 'Now's our chance.'

'Kepler's after us!'

'He can't follow both of us. Split up. I'll meet you in the South Tower. You know the way?'

Boy nodded.

'Go!' he cried, and pushed Willow away from him. She skittered towards the nearest door, just as Kepler got to Boy.

'Got you!' he said. 'You're coming with me. I need you.'

Boy wriggled free. Amongst all the chaos around them, no one was paying them any attention.

'No!' Boy cried. 'I don't want to.'

'But it's not safe for you here!' Kepler shouted.

'I know that!' Boy laughed. 'It's not safe for anyone here.'

'You don't understand,' Kepler said. 'You're mine. You're all I need.'

'Get away from me!' Boy cried.

He turned and began to push his way through the crowd. Kepler pursued him, trying to get past people, but he could not keep up with Boy, who was used to moving his small frame through tight places. Boy was about half-way across the room, making for another door, when the noise in the room suddenly increased tenfold.

There were screams from the door, and a huge swell of people pushed back from the main entrance to the Court. Boy could see ladies being crushed in the panic, men screaming to get away, as a circle opened in the crowds.

There was Maxim, advancing on Frederick who was still dancing about madly on the throne. But Maxim was not alone – he had brought someone, or rather something, with him. He held a chain of iron links in his hand, at the far end of which was a struggling, snarling, spitting creature.

The Phantom.

It could be nothing else but the creature Boy had met in the tunnel, squatting over its victim in the trampled snow.

Screams flew to the heaven-painted ceiling, some of the courtiers fainted on the spot as The Phantom was led against its will through the shiny bright Courtroom. It scrabbled on the polished floor, fighting to keep on its feet, which were callused and strong. It loped on its hands, moving like an ape, though Boy could see it really was human in an appalling, twisted way. It pulled against its chain, trying to get away from the bright world into which it had been dragged, but Maxim was a powerful man and headed unerringly for Frederick.

No one else in the room moved. Boy looked at the

Emperor. There was horror, anger, fear, disgust and repulsion but, strangely, no surprise on his face.

'So!' Maxim shouted.

He reached the foot of the dais, and turned and yanked so hard on The Phantom's chain that it lost its footing entirely and went skidding on to the floor, where it tried and failed at first to find its feet.

'So! Beautiful people!'

The room fell silent, everyone staring open-mouthed at the creature struggling at Maxim's feet.

'So! There is your Emperor, Frederick the magnificent! Frederick, who wished to be made immortal because he had no heir, no son to succeed him! But he lies!

'He lies! For there is a story to tell. Fifteen years ago, he took a consort. Sophia Beebe! And the book prophesied that there would be an heir. That much some of you know. You may remember that the Beebes were disgraced, and you may believe that the offspring died! But you were lied to!

'You want a son, Frederick? Well, here's your son! This killing thing, kept hidden from everyone for fifteen years. Your son, Frederick! Your son, this beast!'

Frederick stood on his throne, stricken with horror. He glanced from The Phantom to his people, who began to call out in fear and shame at what they were witnessing.

The Phantom had got to its feet, and squatted, crouching, spitting and struggling on its short chain. Boy could not take his eyes off it. There was something offensive, yet fascinating, about it. It was only a child really, but malformed and powerful beyond its years.

'No,' Frederick said, quietly, weakly, 'No, it—'

479

'Don't lie!' Maxim shouted. 'You know it as well as I do, as well as Bedrich did! The only other witness from those days! You wanted an heir? Well, this is the rightful heir to the throne.'

'Guards!' Frederick screamed. 'Arrest him! Arrest him! And take that . . . thing . . . away!'

Maxim snarled as three guards closed in on him. Swiftly he moved close to the beast and loosed the chain from its neck. Maxim began to back off and one of the guards made for him.

Faster than Boy imagined possible, The Phantom, who thought it was being attacked, leapt at the guard, and clawed him away in a second. Blood welled across the polished floor, and people screamed. The chaos that had been stilled while Maxim made his speech returned in a moment. There was pushing and shouting, another guard tried to swing his sword at The Phantom, who jumped right over the blade, dispatching his assailant with ease as he landed on his feet again.

Maxim ran. The Phantom, maddened by fury and fear, lashed out at anyone who came near.

Boy joined others running from the room, but stumbled, and went sprawling over several other people. Kepler was nowhere to be seen, but the panic was universal. The furore continued behind them as the beast became frenzied, lunging at people indiscriminately. Boy got to his feet, and saw that he was bleeding. He had fallen on the sword of one of the guards, which was so sharp he hadn't felt anything at first. He now bled from a gash in his forearm. He grabbed it with his other hand and ran for his life. He had to get to the South Tower and find Willow.

He made it through the door, and tried to work out which way to go.

The screaming continued in the Court. Frederick was jumping up and down on his throne, ranting, but could no longer be heard. He was raving nonsensically now, having come face to face with the hideous creature he had tried to hide for fifteen years.

The Phantom, still on the loose, saw a gap in the crowd and loped towards the door. No one tried to get near it to stop it. A dozen guards who had attempted to lay on the floor, badly injured.

As it emerged from the Court, it saw something it liked. Blood. A trail of blood leading out across the marble floor of the hall.

It followed.

2

Boy ran as fast as he could, leaving the screams behind him. He hurried through the Palace, through bits he knew then bits he didn't, trying frantically to remember Willow's description of the interior route to the Old South Tower.

He passed no one. It seemed that the entire Palace had been present for Frederick's immortality ceremony, and everyone had seen the farce it had become. Likewise, everyone had witnessed the horror of The Phantom – everyone except Willow. Boy quickened his pace, but he had to remember what she had said, and it would be worse to get lost altogether.

He came to a junction and couldn't remember Willow's instructions. For a moment he hesitated, then guessed left. Years of navigating the City's maze-like streets had given him a good sense of direction, and he decided to trust it now.

He was right. As he ran down a long corridor with tall windows, he could see the South Tower to his left through the snowfall. The corridor turned and he came to the foot of the Tower, in a small hall with a spiral staircase.

Noting the position of the door to the outside, he began

to leap the stairs, two at a time. He didn't notice the spattered blood he was leaving behind as he went.

Willow and Kepler's rooms were at the very top of the Tower. Boy cursed. The stairs were very steep and dark and he couldn't make his legs go fast any more. But at least Willow should be easy to find – he just had to make it to the top of the staircase.

Suddenly he could go no higher. He put his foot up for the next step and there was none. He stumbled forward and looked about him.

'Willow?' he called, but quietly.

There was no answer. He could see doors in front of him and to the side, three in all.

He looked around. Everyone was in Court, or running screaming from The Phantom. He decided he could risk shouting.

'Willow! Are you there?'

Still no answer. There was nothing else for it.

Boy made for the door nearest to him and opened it.

Immediately he saw Willow. She was sitting cross-legged on the floor, facing him. As he walked in, she looked up. There was an odd expression on her face, which stopped Boy where he was. Not a look of surprise, or joy, or relief – it was something else, something like fear.

On the floor in front of Willow lay the book, wide open.

Boy pointed dumbly at the book.

'Did you . . . ?' he began, but stopped. He didn't know what he was asking.

'Boy . . .' Willow said, slowly. Then she noticed his arm. 'You're hurt!'

'It's all right,' said Boy. 'It's not too bad . . .'

'Let me look at it,' said Willow, getting to her feet.

Boy shook his head. They were wasting time.

'No!' he cried. 'The book. You've read the book!'

Willow stood like a guilty child, the book at her feet. She looked down at it.

'You've read the book, Willow! Tell me! What does it say?'

'Boy . . . I—'

'What did it tell you? Tell me! Or I'll read it myself.'

'No!' Willow cried.

Boy strode to where the book lay on the floor. Willow grabbed his arm to stop him and Boy howled with pain. He shoved her away with his good arm and sat down in front of the book.

'No!' cried Willow, and tried to pull the book from Boy.

'Leave me alone!' Boy screamed at her. He pushed at her hands.

'No, Boy! Don't read it! Don't read it! Please!'

Something desperate in Willow's voice struck Boy. He hesitated.

'Why not?' he said, his voice faltering. 'Why not? I have to know.'

Willow shook her head.

'Maybe it's best you don't. Maybe it's not what you want to hear. Maybe—'

'Just tell me, Willow.'

'All right. But I want to tell you something first.'

Boy waited for her to go on.

'I want you to know I love you.'

Boy showed no emotion, nothing.

'Tell me,' he said quietly.

484

'Valerian's not your father,' Willow said. 'That's true.'

'Then who?' asked Boy.

'I don't—'

'Don't tell me you don't know,' Boy said.

'No, it's not that. It's just that I don't think you'll want to know. Boy, your father – your father is the Emperor. Frederick.'

Boy stood speechless, stunned into silence. A strange look came into his eyes. He smiled, then began to laugh, but stopped just as quickly.

'Don't talk rubbish,' he said. 'That's ridiculous . . .'

'I've seen it all, Boy. I've seen it all. Fifteen years ago, the Emperor had a son by one of the Beebe women. Sophia.'

'Yes, I know. There was something wrong with it. Willow! You weren't there! It's The Phantom, Willow. It's grown into some kind of monster. Maxim let it loose in the Court. It's gone crazy, hurting people . . .'

Willow did not seem surprised.

'I know. I saw it in the book. About the strange baby. Frederick had it taken away from Sophia, put it in the dungeons, imagining it would die. But it didn't, and even Frederick couldn't bring himself to have his own flesh and blood killed. And he believed he couldn't kill the son the book had foretold. That he would risk Fortune's retribution if he tried to alter the path of Fate by killing the child. But that's not the son I'm talking about, Boy.

'There were twins. One hideous, the other normal. Sophia was horrified by what Frederick had done to her baby, and furious. In revenge, she escaped one night with the healthy child.

485

'Frederick began to persecute the Beebes. They fell from favour overnight. He confiscated lands and money and removed titles he had bestowed only a little while before. He searched high and low for Sophia.

'Knowing she would be pursued, Sophia tried to hide her tracks. She faked the death of the child. I don't know what happened exactly. I saw in the book . . . I saw the mill race at Linden, and people dragging a woman's body from the water. All I know is that the baby did not die. Somehow, someone must have saved it, and it grew into a boy. A boy who lived on the streets for years, by himself.

'You, Boy. You. You're Frederick's son.'

She stopped.

Boy stared through her as if she was a ghost, but if anything it was he who felt like a ghost.

'This can't be true . . .' he said.

'It's the truth. It may not be the truth you want, but it's the truth all the same.'

She put her hand out to him. He didn't push it away but he didn't take it either.

'What did you want to find, Boy? What did you think would make you happy?'

Boy shook his head.

'I don't . . . I don't think . . .' he trailed off, lost for words. 'I don't know if I wanted to be happy, I just wanted to know.'

'And now that you do . . .'

'I can't believe it. Frederick . . . my father.'

'It's funny. He's so tiny, like you . . .'

'Funny?' cried Boy, 'Funny? That's not what—'

'I'm sorry!' Willow said. 'I only mean—'

'Never mind,' Boy said. 'It's just – that means that The Phantom . . . is my *brother*.'

Willow nodded.

'And Boy, do you know what else it means?'

Boy looked up at her.

'What?'

'When Frederick dies . . . you'll be Emperor.'

Boy walked over to the window, beyond which was a small balcony. He put his hand to the catch and pushed the narrow glass door open.

'Boy . . .' said Willow.

He stepped out on to the balcony, and watched the snow. He stood there, staring at the thousands of snow-flakes plummeting to the end of their journey, the end of their dark flight down.

He wanted so much to join them.

But only for a moment. He turned back to Willow.

'Willow,' he said.

'Boy?'

'I want to tell you some things, too. I love you too. But listen to me. I know who my parents are now. I've got my answers. They're not answers I like very much. Sophia Beebe, who died fifteen years ago. The Emperor.'

'But he's your father!' Willow cried.

'Yes,' said Boy. 'But . . . no. No. I've been stupid. I've been so desperate to find out, to find the truth, and now that I have, it's all meaningless. It doesn't alter who I am.'

Willow smiled. She nodded.

'It doesn't change me,' Boy went on. 'I was wrong to think it would. I'm just me, Willow. I'm Boy, who lived on the streets, who lived with Valerian, and now who's in love with you. That's who I am.'

Willow rushed over to him and they held each other tight.

'And now I know,' Boy said, 'I don't want anything to do with him. I'm not going to be anyone's Emperor. Only you and I know about this . . .'

'No, Kepler knows.'

Boy swore.

'Of course!'

'Kepler knows. That's why he's been trying to get to you.'

'What? To get me out of here?'

'No, he wanted to bring you here.'

Boy shook his head.

'I don't understand.'

'Kepler knows who you are. He's known it ever since he got the book. Ever since he cast your horoscope. And he knew immediately he could use you. He wanted to bring you here and present you to the Emperor – you, his long-lost son. He wasn't quite the unassuming scientist Valerian thought he was. He craved power, having spent years in the wilderness after leaving the Academy. He thought that if he brought you here, and the book too, he'd be showered with money, power. He intended to take Maxim's place.'

'I can't believe it. That's why he's been so desperate to hang on to me?'

'Yes. It makes sense. Only it happened too soon. You coming here, I mean. He wanted to do things in his own time. He knew about Maxim, he told me how dangerous

488

he is. He was wary of him, and wanted to take things carefully.'

'So why did he tell Valerian I was his son?'

'It was all he could think of to save you. He knew you were the right age, so he told Valerian the one thing that could save you, and it worked. But all the time he had other plans for you. To bring you here, use you, to get the position of power he wanted.'

Boy said nothing, taking time to think it all through. He roused himself, turned to Willow.

'It doesn't matter,' he said firmly. 'All that matters is that I'm not going to be anyone's Emperor. We—'

He stopped.

'What?' Willow cried. He was staring past her, over her shoulder.

'Willow!' he choked. He didn't move.

Sensing the fear in Boy's body, Willow turned slowly in his arms, until she saw.

The Phantom.

The Phantom was standing in the doorway of the room. It stared hard at both of them, and lifted one finger to its mouth, licking it. Boy could see blood on the finger – *his* blood.

The beast took a step forward, and in the lamplight of the room, Boy could see its face clearly for the first time. Now at last he knew what it was that had horrified him the night he had run into The Phantom in the Palace tunnels. What it was about the thing's eyes. It was that they were his own.

His brother. His mutated monster of a brother.

Boy and Willow waited for the attack, yet still it paused.

It seemed not to have noticed Willow at all, but kept its eyes fixed on Boy alone.

Eye to eye, their gaze met, Boy and beast. Boy looked deep into those eyes. Beyond the tragic face, beyond the watery grey film across the eyes themselves, and further, he looked into The Phantom's mind.

Were there thoughts there? Real thoughts? Or just impulses: to kill, to eat, to run?

There had to be more to his brother than that. Boy took a deep breath, and smiled.

Boy stepped forward, and put his hand out.

The Phantom looked at Boy, put his head on one side, like a dog considering something. It licked the blood on its fingers once more, and moved slowly forward.

There was a clattering of feet on the steps, and Kepler burst into the room.

'No!' he shrieked, and flung himself at The Phantom from behind.

The Phantom, taken by surprise, was thrown to the floor, but pulled Kepler down with him, knocking over the table with the lamp. The lamp shattered and oil spread across the floor, a moment later catching fire and exploding. The room was lit only by the flames flickering up the side of the overturned table.

Willow screamed.

Boy screamed too.

'No!'

But it was too late. The Phantom rose and attacked Kepler, who had at least come armed with a knife.

Boy watched horrified as the two figures struggled to their feet. They stumbled as one body, and backed into the burning table, which caught on The Phantom's rag clothing instantly. It shrieked with pain and lashed out at Kepler, dashing him backwards on to the balcony.

'No! Stop it! Stop it!' Boy cried, but it was no use.

The Phantom lurched after Kepler, who was getting to his feet. The Phantom hit him hard in a crazed attack that sent them both hurtling towards the balustrade. Boy and Willow watched horrified as both figures plunged over the balcony.

Boy rushed out and was in time to see the burning figures plunge like a comet through the snowy night to the flags of the courtyard below. They were still.

'No!' he cried, heedless that the whole Palace could hear him. 'No!'

Willow hurried to his side and looked down. She buried her face in Boy's neck.

Boy put his arm around her.

'Come on,' he said. His voice sounded calm and strong.

Willow looked up at him.

'It's time we left,' he said, 'but there's one more thing we have to do first.'

Willow nodded.

The book.

They both turned to where it lay on the floor, a few feet from the burning table. The book which had caused so much pain and death.

Together, they made their way over to the book, and knelt by it. What they did next was not easy. It seemed to be radiating hostility towards them, as if it knew. They began to shake as they lifted the thing between them, the book itself suddenly feeling much heavier than before.

'Maybe . . .' began Willow, but Boy shook his head.

'No,' he said, powerfully. 'It's the end.'

They opened it up and fanned its pages into the flames of the burning table.

'Die,' said Boy under his breath. 'Die.'

But the book would not burn. The flames seemed to lick around its pages and cover, but they would not take. It was as if it was impervious to fire.

'It won't burn!' cried Willow. 'It won't!'

They watched, terrified, as if they'd been caught trying to kill someone. The book sat in the flames, and they grew more afraid.

'It won't burn . . .' cried Willow again.

'No!' Boy said, 'Look! I think it's . . .'

He was right.

The book hissed, like green birch logs. It crackled, and seethed, and spat spots of flame at them, but it was catching.

'Burn!' Boy shouted. 'Burn!'

The book burned.

The spitting got worse and Boy and Willow backed away as finally the ancient, stained, grimy, ink-littered pages began to burn properly. Page by page caught, a lovely orange flame spreading across it, running the paper into blackness, before vaporising as hot carbon dust.

With each page that went, Boy and Willow felt their hearts grow lighter, and their fears recede.

The cover had caught now, and the leather was giving

off noxious curls of stinking smoke that made their eyes water.

'Die,' Boy whispered. 'Go.'

Willow held Boy's hand.

'It's time we went too,' she said.

So they did.

3

Boy and Willow walked through the City streets. It felt to them both as if they had been away for years, although it was only a matter of days. So much had happened.

The snow was falling still, but it seemed possible that it was easing. Rumours of food shortages were spreading, though, and people wore grim expressions as they went about their business in the bitter January morning.

They'd risked spending the night at Kepler's house, having fled the Palace. It had been easier to escape than they might have imagined with chaos still spreading from the Court, people dead or wounded by The Phantom, guards searching for Maxim and Frederick barking away atop his throne. In all this madness, they had been able to leave the South Tower unobserved. They'd run along through the various Palace courtyards until they found themselves by one of the outer walls.

They still had to get out somehow, and it was the snow that had saved them after all, the irony of which was not lost on Boy. He had yearned for forgetting all through the snowfall, and in the end it *was* the snow that had saved them, though in a much more mundane way. From the top of the Palace wall, they saw that a huge drift of snow had formed between the wall and the bank from which it rose. Holding hands, they had dared to jump, and tumbled down the thick, sloping snowdrift as gently as if they had landed on a goose-feather quilt.

As they left the Palace behind and crossed the river, they saw that the Old South Tower was alight, flames shooting up into the snow-speckled night sky around them, sparks dancing upwards as the snowflakes fluttered down.

'That's the end of the book,' Willow said.

'Yes,' Boy replied. 'It will cause no more suffering.'

Willow smiled and held Boy's hand.

'What is it?' she asked.

'People were wrong about him,' Boy said, 'Maybe he wasn't just a monster. Maybe if someone had looked after him . . .'

'Your brother?'

Boy nodded.

Willow thought of something else.

'He tried to save you, you know. Perhaps he did genuinely care for you.'

She meant Kepler.

'No,' said Boy, shaking his head. 'He only wanted me, needed me alive, to get what he wanted.'

'Oh!' cried Willow, and turned, grabbing Boy's hands.

'What?' asked Boy, 'What is it?'

'The book!' said Willow. There was something else I saw in the book.'

Willow saw a look of alarm on Boy's face.

'What?' he asked. 'What did you see?'

'Your name!'

'No!' cried Boy. 'No! Don't tell me! I don't want to know.'

'But Boy . . .' Willow said.

'No! I don't want to know. I am Boy, that's all. That's all I want to be.'

'But Boy, you don't understand. What I saw. In the book I saw Sophia, your mother, escaping with you. It was all so quick. She knew she had to escape with you, so she fled the castle, and headed out to the countryside. But she hadn't even had time to give you a name.'

'So I never had a name at all?' said Boy. He seemed calm; there was no anger, no pain in him now.

'No,' said Willow. 'No. Except, in the book, I heard your mother talking to you all the time, as she hurried along with you in her arms. Talking to you, talking, talking, hushing your cries, blessing you with love, and all she called you was Boy, my lovely Boy, my darling little Boy. Boy.'

Boy moved closer to Willow. She pulled him towards her, looked deep into his eyes.

'Boy. That's what she called you,' she said. 'That's your real name, after all. Boy.'

She put her arms round him, and held him fast until his tears were gone.

Now, in the dim light of the following morning, they were leaving. They'd found a decent stash of money in the study, and had packed clothes and blankets and Kepler's valuables into two large bags. It was all they had, but it was more than either of them had ever owned before, and they knew it would be enough.

'They will probably never come looking for you,' Willow said. 'There's too much confusion there.'

'I know,' said Boy, 'but that's not the only reason we're leaving.'

'To think Frederick was so desperate for an heir, and there you were, right under his nose. Now there's only you and me that know.'

She laughed.

'What?' asked Boy.

'Just think. You're the heir to the Empire. And if we ever tried to tell anyone, no one would believe us!'

She stopped.

'Are you sure, Boy? Are you sure? You'd be very rich. Powerful!'

Boy looked at her.

'In that madhouse? With those lunatics? No, Willow, we don't need money or power. We just need enough to get by, and each other. And I think we'll do that best somewhere else.'

They walked on, heading for the City gates.

Their route took them past St Valentine's Fountain. They both smiled, but remained silent until it was far behind them.

'But where are we going to go?' Willow asked, not for the first time, as they reached the Northern Gate.

They stood on the threshold.

Behind them lay the huge, rambling, decrepit, awful, wonderful City, more or less all they had ever known. Their whole past lay in its maw. Ahead of them lay nothing they could see, but the emptiness and whiteness of a snow-laden, unknown future.

'I don't know,' said Boy.

'We could go to Linden. After all, you're a Beebe, sort of.'

'After what we did to their church? I don't think so. Anyway, I think I've got it wrong all these years. Wanting to have a past. To go back to Linden would be to make the same mistake. So let's go and find a future, shall we?'

They pulled their coats around them, and walked out into the pure white countryside, and as they did so, the snow began to ease. A small break opened in the clouds above them, and a weak but warming winter sun shone down on their path.

Epilogue

Midnight in the Imperial Court of Emperor Frederick III. The Court is empty.

The Emperor sits on his throne, brooding.

'Maxim!' he calls, in his high, pathetic voice. 'Dammit, Maxim, where are you?'

He waves a hand in the darkness, and flakes of his ancient skin drift up into the gloom.

'Maxim, I need your help! I don't think you understand. Sometimes I really think you're trying to kill me! Do you hear me? You have no idea how difficult it is for me. You should help me more, Maxim. You really should understand. I need a solution, Maxim. Yes! And you're going to find it for me.

'Maxim, are you listening? Maxim! Maxim!'

The Emperor calls out in the darkness, in his madness, forgetting, forgetting.

Forgetting that things have changed, forgetting what has happened, forgetting what he's decreed.

And far beneath the Emperor, chained to a rough stone wall at the bottom of the dark flight of stairs where the

Emperor's sad son used to lurk, lies Maxim, blinking in the darkness.

> *So dance, my dears, dance,*
> *Before you take the dark flight down*

Also by Marcus Sedgwick

The Foreshadowing

It was then that I saw the raven. It was a huge bird, and at first I could only marvel at its beauty. The blackness of its feathers was perfect. It fixed an eye on me and put its head on one side, and only then did I see what it was standing on. It spoke in the voice of the dead upon which it was feeding.

'You!' it said. 'You alone saw the horror of war, and wept when we did not believe you.'

It is 1915. Seventeen-year-old Sasha Fox lives a privileged life, but her brothers, Edgar and Tom, cannot avoid the war, and Sasha has a terrible gift. She can see the future.

Her premonitions show her brutal horrors on the battlefields of the Somme, corpse worms crawling over the faces of soldiers soon to die. And worse, they show her what will happen to Edgar and Tom.

Like the prophetess Cassandra, who witnessed a different war on the plains of Troy, Sasha is trapped by her tragic power. Cursed by a fate too awful to bear – for who wants to see the end of their own story . . . ?

'The sixth novel by the incomparable Marcus Sedgwick, and undoubtedly his finest yet . . . A powerful and mesmerizing story . . . Devastatingly good.'
Publishing News

My Swordhand is Singing

'He came to the gate of the graveyard. There could be no doubt. The wool ran over the fence next to the gate, as if his quarry had sailed clean over it. Dumbly, he gripped it, as if it were a lifeline, when in reality it was leading him towards death itself . . .'

In the bitter cold of an unrelenting winter Tomas and his son, Peter, arrive in Chust and settle there as woodcutters. Tomas digs a channel of fast flowing waters around their hut, so they have their own little island kingdom.

Peter doesn't understand why his father has done this nor why his father carries a long, battered box, whose mysterious contents he is forbidden to know.

But Tomas is a man with a past; a past that is tracking him with deadly intent. As surely as the snow falls softly in the forest of one hundred thousand silver birch trees, Father and son must face a soul-less enemy and a terrifying destiny.

Set in the remote and forbidding landscapes of the seventeenth century this is a heart-rending story of loss and redemption, and inspired by the original vampire folklore of Eastern Europe it represents a unique regeneration of a timeless myth.